Re-Creations

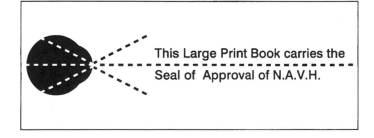

This Large Print Book carries the
Seal of Approval of N.A.V.H.

Re-Creations

Grace Livingston Hill

Thorndike Press • Thorndike, Maine

Published in 1998 by arrangement with Munce Publishing.

Thorndike Large Print ® Romance Series.

The tree indicium is a trademark of Thorndike Press.

The text of this Large Print edition is unabridged.
Other aspects of the book may vary from the original edition.

Set in 16 pt. Plantin by Minnie B. Raven.

Printed in the United States on permanent paper.

Library of Congress Cataloging in Publication Data

Hill, Grace Livingston, 1865–1947.
    Re-creations / Grace Livingston Hill.
      p.   cm.
    ISBN 0-7862-1378-7 (lg. print : hc : alk. paper)
    1. Large type books.   I. Title.
    [PS3515.I486R4   1998]
    813'.52—dc21   97-51960

Re-Creations

**1** Cornelia Copley pressed her face against the window-pane of the car and smiled with brave showing of courage as the train moved away from the platform where her college mates huddled eagerly for the last glimpse of her.

"Don't forget to write, Cornie!" shouted a girl with black eyes and a frantic green sweater over a green and yellow striped sport-skirt.

"Remember you're to decorate my house when I'm married!" screamed a pink-cheeked damsel with blue eyes and bewitching dimples.

"Be sure to come back for commencement!" chorused three others as the train got fairly under way.

Cornelia watched the staid old gray buildings pencilled over with the fine lines of vines that would burst into green tenderness as soon as the spring should appear, and thought how many good times she had had within those walls, and how terrible, how simply unthinkable it was that they were over forever, and she would never be able to graduate! With gathering tears in her throat and blurring into her vision she watched till the last flutter of the flag on the top of Dwight Hall vanished, the big old cherry-tree gnarled and black against the November sky faded into the end of the library, and even the college hedge was too far back to discern; then she settled slowly back into her seat, much as a bit of wax candle might melt and droop before the outpouring of sudden heat. She dropped into her seat so sadly and so crushingly that the sweet-faced lady in the long seal-skin coat across the aisle turned and looked commiseratingly at her. Poor child! Now what was she having to endure she wondered, as she watched the sweet lips drop at the corners, the dimples around the eyes disappear, and the long lashes sweep down too late to catch the great tear that suddenly rolled out and down the round, fair cheek.

Cornelia sat with her face turned toward the window, and watched the familiar way for a long time through unseeing eyes. She was really looking into a hard and cruel future that had suddenly swooped down upon her and torn her from her mates, her career in life, all that she thought she held dear, and was sending her to an undesirable home among a family who did not understand her and her aspirations nor appreciate her ability. Her mouth took on hard little alien lines, and her deep, dreamy eyes looked almost steely in their distress. It all seemed so unnecessary. Why couldn't father understand that her career meant so much, and another year or two in college would put her where she could be her own mistress and not be dependent upon him? Of course she couldn't argue with him about it just now after that rather touching letter he had written; but if he had only understood how important it was that she should go on and finish her course, if only *any* of them had ever understood, she was sure he would have managed someway to get along without recalling her. She took out the letter and read it over again. After all, she had scarcely had time to read it carefully in all its details, for a telegram had followed close upon it bidding her come at once, as she was badly needed, and of course she had packed up and started. This was the letter, written in a cramped, clerkly hand:

Dear Daughter,

I am very sorry to have to tell you that your mother, who has been keeping up for the last six months by sheer force of will, has given out, and seems to be in quite a serious condition. The doctor has told us that nothing but absolute rest and an entire change will save her to us, and of course you will understand that we are so rejoiced over the hope he holds out that we are trying to forget the sorrow and anxiety of the present, and to get along as best we can without her. I have just returned from taking her, with the assistance of a trained nurse, to the Rest Cure Sanitarium at Quiet Valley over at the other end of the State, where the doctor tells me she will have just the conditions and treatment that her case requires. You will be glad to know that she was quite satisfied to go, feeling that it was the only possible thing left to do, and her main distress was that you would have to leave college and come home to take her place. My dear Nellie, it grieves me to the heart to have to write this and ask you to leave your beloved work and come home to help us live, but I see no other way out. Your Aunt Pennell has broken her leg, and will not be able to be about all winter; and, even if she were well enough, she never seems to understand how to get along with Harry and Louise.

And then, even if there were any one else, I must tell you that there is another reason why coming home is necessary. It is that I cannot afford to let you stay at college. I cannot tell you how hard it looks to me written out on paper, and how my spirit sinks beneath the thought that I have come to this, that I cannot afford to let my daughter finish her education as she had planned, because I have not been able to make money enough to do all the other things that have to be done also. I have tried to keep the knowledge of my heavy losses from you until you should be through with your work at college. Mother and I thought we could get along and not let you know about it, because we knew you would insist on coming right home and helping; but now since mother has broken down you will have to be told the truth. Indeed, I strongly suspect that your mother in her great love for you and the others has brought on this weak state of health by overdoing, although we tried all we could to keep her from working too hard. You will, I know, want to help in every way you can, so that we shall be able to surround your dear mother with every necessity and even luxury that she should have, and so make her recovery more sure and speedy. It costs a good deal at Quiet Valley. It is an expensive place; but nothing is too good for your dear patient mother, who has quietly been giving her very life for us all without letting us know how ill she was.

There is another painful thing I must tell you, and that is that we have had to move from our old home, also on account of the expense, and you will not find it nearly so pleasant or convenient here as at the old house; but I know my brave daughter will bear it like a soldier, and be as helpful and resourceful as her mother has always been. It gives me great comfort to think of your immediate coming, for Louise is working too hard for so young a girl. Harry helps her as much as he can. Moreover, I feel troubled about Carey. He is getting into the habit of staying out late with the boys, and — but you will know how to help him when you get here. You and he were always good comrades. I cannot tell you what a tower of strength you seem to me to be just now in this culmination of trials. Be sure to telegraph me on what train you will arrive, and we will meet you.

With deep regret at the necessity of this recall, which I know will be a great trial to you,

Your loving father

Cornelia looked like anything but a tower

of strength as she folded the letter and slipped it back into her handbag with a deep-drawn sigh. It had given her the same feeling of finality that had come when she first read it. She had hoped there might be a glimmer, a ray, somewhere in this second reading that would help her to hope she might go back to college pretty soon when she had put the family on its feet again and found the right person to look after them. But this money affair that father laid so much emphasis upon was something that she could not quite understand. If father only understood how much money she could make once she was an interior decorator in some large established firm he would see that a little money spent now would bring large returns. Why, even if he had to borrow some to keep her in college till her course was finished, he would lose nothing in the end.

Cornelia put her head back against the cushion and closed her eyes wearily. She hadn't slept much the night before, and her nerves were taut and strained. This was the first minute in which she had done anything like relax since the letter came — right into the midst of a junior show in which she had had charge of all the stage settings! It really had been dreadful to leave when she was the only one who knew where everything should be. She had spent half the night before making drawings and coloring them, and explaining to two half-comprehending classmates; but she was sure they would make some terrible mistake somewhere, and she would be blamed with the inharmony of the thing. It was too bad when she had acquired the reputation of being the only girl in college who could make such effects on the stage. Well, it couldn't be helped!

Of course she was sorry her mother was sick, but father spoke hopefully, confidently about her, and the rest would probably do her good. It wasn't as if mother were hopelessly ill. She was thankful as any of them that that had not come. But mother had always understood her aspirations, and if she were only at home would show father how unreasonable it was for her to have to give up now when only a year and a half more and the goal would be reached, and she could become a contributing member of the family, rather than just a housekeeper!

Over and over the sorrowful round Cornelia's thoughts went as mile after mile rushed away under the wheels and home drew nearer. Now and then she thought a little of how it would be when she got home; but when one had to visualize an entirely new home about which one had not heard a thing, not even in what part of the city it was located, how could one anticipate a home-coming? They must have just moved, she supposed, and probably mother had worked too hard settling. Mother always did that. Indeed, Cornelia had been so entirely away from home during her college life that she was almost out of harmony with it, and her sole connection had been gay little letters mostly filled with what she was going to do when she finished her course and became an interior decorator.

It was almost two years since she had been at home, for last summer and the summer before she had spent in taking special courses in a summer school not far from her college, and the intervening Christmas she had been invited to a wonderful house party in New York at the home of one of her classmates who had unlimited money and knew just how to give her friends a good time. Mother had thought these opportunities too good to be wasted, and to her surprise father also had been quite willing for her to spend the extra time and money, and so she had grown quite away from the home and its habits. She began to feel, as she drew nearer and nearer to the home city, almost as if she were going among strangers.

It was growing quite dusky, and lights were glinting out in stray farmhouses along the way. The train was due in the city at seven o'clock. It was almost six, and the box of fudge that the girls had supplied her with had palled upon her. Somehow she did not feel hungry, only sick at heart and woefully homesick for the college, and the ripple of laughter and chatter down the corridors; the jokes about college fish, and rice pudding; the dear, funny interchange of confidences; even the themes that had to be written! How gladly would she go back now and never grumble about anything if she only knew she could finish without an interruption, and then to the city to take bachelor apartments with Mable and Alice as they had planned, and get into big work! O the dreams, the bubbles that were being broken with all their pretty glitter of rainbow hues gone into nothingness! O the drab monotony of simple home life!

So her thoughts beat restlessly through her brain, and drove the tears into her smarting eyes.

Presently the train halted at a station, and a small multitude rushed in, breezy, rough, and dirty, with loud voices and garments covered with grease and soil; toilers of the road, they were going back to the city, tossing their clamor across the car, settling their implements out of the way under their big muddy shoes. One paused before Cornelia's empty half seat, and suddenly before he could sit down a lady slipped into it, with a smile and a motion toward a whole empty seat across the aisle. The man accepted the offer good-naturedly, summoning a fellow laborer to share it with him, and Cornelia looked up relieved to meet the smile of her seal-clad former neighbor across the aisle.

"I thought it would be pleasanter for us both dear, if I came over here," she murmured with a smile. "They were pretty strong of garlic."

"Oh, thank you!" said Cornelia, and then grew shy as she noticed the jewels on the delicate hand that rested on the soft fur. What part had she in life with a woman like this, she who had to leave college because there wasn't money enough to let her stay till she had finished? Perhaps she was the least bit ungracious to the kindly woman who had made the move obviously for her protection, but the kindly stranger would not be rebuffed.

"I've been watching you all the after-

17

noon," she said. "And I'm glad of this opportunity of getting acquainted with you if you don't mind. I love young people."

Cornelia wished her seatmate would keep still or go away but she tried to smile gratefully.

"I was so interested in all those young people who came down to see you off. It reminded me of younger days. Was that a college up on the hill above the station?"

Now indeed was Cornelia's tongue loosed. Her beloved college! Ah, she could talk about that even to ladies clad in furs and jewels, and she was presently launched in a detailed description of the junior play, her face kindling vividly under the open admiration of the white-haired, beautiful woman, who knew just how to ask the right questions to bring out the girl's eager tale, and who responded so readily to every point she brought out.

"And how is it that you are going away?" she asked at last. "I should think you could not be spared. You seem to have been the moving spirit in it all. But I suppose you are returning in time to do your part."

Cornelia's face clouded over suddenly, and she drew a deep sigh. For the moment she had forgotten. It was almost as if the pretty lady had struck her in the face with her soft, jewelled hand. She seemed to shrink into herself.

"No," she said at last sadly, "I'm not going back — *ever*, I'm afraid." The words came out with a sound almost like a sob, and were wholly unintentional with Cornelia. She was not one to air her sorrows before strangers, or even friends, but somehow the whole tragedy had come over her like a great wave that threatened to engulf her. She was immediately sorry that she had spoken, however, and tried to explain in a tone less tragic. "You see, my mother is not well and had to go away, and — they — needed me at home."

She lifted her clouded eyes to meet a wealth of admiration in the older woman's gaze.

"How beautiful! To be needed, I mean," the lady said with a smile. "I can think just what a tower of strength you will be to your father. Your father is living?"

"Yes," gasped Cornelia with a sudden thought of how terrible it would be if he were gone. "Oh, yes; and it's strange — he used these very words when he wrote me to come home." Then she grew rosy with the realization of how she was thinking out loud to this elegant stranger.

"Of course he would," asserted the lady.

"I can see that you are! I was thinking that as I watched you all the afternoon. You seem so capable and so — *sweet!*"

"Oh, but I'm *not!*" burst out the girl honestly. "I've been real cross about it ever since the letter came. You see," — and she drew her brows earnestly trying to justify herself, — "you see I can't help thinking it's all a mistake. I'm glad to go home and help, but some one else could have done that, and I think I could have helped to better purpose if I had been allowed to stay and finish my course, and then been able to help out financially. Father has lost some money lately, which has made things hard, and I was planning to be an interior decorator. I should soon have been able to do a good deal for them."

"Oh, but my dear! No one can take a daughter's place in a home when there is trouble, not such a daughter's place as you occupy, I'm sure. And as for the other thing, if you have it in you it will come out, you may be sure. You'll begin by decorating the home interior, and you won't lose anything in the end. Such things are never lost nor time wasted. God sees to that, if you are doing your best right where He put you. I can just see what an exquisite spot you'll make of that home, and how it will rest your mother to know you are taking her place."

Cornelia sadly shook her head.

"There won't be any chance for decorating," she said slowly. "They've had to move away from the home we owned, and father said it wasn't very pleasant there."

"All the more chance for your talents!" said the lady with determined cheerfulness. "I know you have a sense of the beautiful, for I've been studying that lovely little hat you wear, and how well it suits your face and tones with your coat and dress and gloves. How ever unpleasant and gloomy that new house may be, it will begin to glow and blossom and give out welcome within a short time after you get there. I should like to look in and prove the truth of my words. Perhaps I shall sometime, who knows? You just can't help making things fit and beautiful. There's a look in your face that makes me sure. Count the little house your opportunity, as every trial and test in this world really is, you know, and you'll see what will come. I know, for I've seen it tried again and again."

"But one can't do much without money," sighed Cornelia, "and money is what I had hoped to earn."

"You'll earn it yet, very likely; but, even if you don't, you'll do the things. Why, the prettiest studio I ever saw was furnished with old boxes covered with bark and lichens, and cushioned with burlap. The woodwork was cheap pine stained dark, the walls were rough, and there was a fireplace built from common cobblestones. When the tea-kettle began to sing on the hearth, and my friend got out her little cheap teacups from the ten-cent store, I thought it was the prettiest place I ever saw, and all because she had put herself into it and not money, and made everything harmonize. You'll do it yet. I can see it in your eyes. But here we are at last in the city, and aren't you going to give me your address? Here's mine on this card, and I don't want to lose you now I've found you. I want you to come and see me sometime if possible, and if I get back to this city again sometime, — I'm only passing through now, and meeting my son to go on to Washington with him in the morning, — but if I get back this way sometime soon I want to look you up if I may, and see if I didn't prophesy truly, my dear little Interior Decorator."

This was the kind of admiration Cornelia was used to, and she glowed with pleasure under it, her cheeks looking very pretty against the edge of brown fur on her coat-collar. She hastily scribbled the new address on one of her cards and handed it out with a dubious look, almost as if she would like to recall it.

"I haven't an idea what kind of a place it will be," she said apologetically. "Father seemed to think I wouldn't like it at all. Perhaps it won't be a place I would be proud to have you see me in."

"I'm sure you'll grace the place, however humble it is," said the lady with a soft touch of her jewelled hand on Cornelia's. And just then the train slid into the station and came to a halt. Almost immediately a tall young man strode down the aisle and stood beside the seat. It seemed a miracle how he could have arrived so soon, before the passengers had gathered their bundles ready to get out.

"Mother!" he said eagerly, lifting his hat with the grace and ease of a young man well versed in the usages of the best society. And then he stooped and kissed her. Cornelia forgot herself in her admiration of the little scene. It was so beautiful to see a mother and son like this. She sighed wistfully. If only Carey could be like that with mother! What an unusual young man this one seemed to be! He didn't look like a molly-coddle, either. He treated his mother like a beloved comrade. Cornelia sat still watching, and then the mother turned and introduced her.

"Arthur, I want you to meet Miss Copley. She has made part of the way quite pleasant and interesting for me."

Then Cornelia was favored with a quick, searching glance accompanied by a smile which was first cordial for his mother's sake, and then grew more so with his own approval as he studied her. The girls his mother picked were apt to be satisfactory. She could see he was accepting her at the place where his mother left off. A moment more, and he was carrying her suitcase in one hand and his mother's in the other, while she, walking with the lady, wondered at herself, and wished that fate were not just about to whirl her away from these most interesting people.

Then she caught a glimpse of her father at the train gate, with his old derby pulled down far over his forehead as if it were getting too big, and his shabby coat-collar turned up about his sunken cheeks. How worn and tired he looked! yes, and old and thin. She hadn't remembered that his shoulders stooped so, or that his hair was so gray. Had all that happened in two years? And that must be Louise waving her handkerchief so violently just in front of him. Was that Harry in that old red baseball sweater with a smudged white letter on his breast, and ragged wrists? He was chewing gum, too! Oh, if these new acquaintances would only get out of the way! It would be so dreadful to have to meet and explain and introduce! She forgot that she had a most speaking face, and that her feelings were quite open to the eyes of her new friends, until she suddenly looked up and found the young man's eyes upon her interestedly, and then the pink color flew over her whole face in confusion.

"Please excuse me," she said, reaching out for her suitcase. "I see my father," and without further formalities she fairly flew down the remainder of the platform and smothered herself in the bosom of her family, anxious only to get them off to one side and away from observation.

"She's a lovely girl," said the lady wistfully. "She wants to be an interior decorator, and make a name and fame for herself, but instead she's got to go home from college and keep house for that rabble. Still, I think she'll make good. She has a good face and sweet, true eyes. Sometime we'll go and see her and find out."

"M'm!" said the son, watching Cornelia escape from a choking embrace from her younger brother and sister. "I should think that might be interesting," and he walked quite around a group of chattering people greeting some friends in order that he might watch her the longer. But when Cornelia at last straightened her hat, and looked furtively about her, the mother and son had passed out of sight, and she drew a deep sigh of thanksgiving and followed her father and the children downstairs to the trolley. They seemed delightful people, and under other circumstances she might have heartily enjoyed their company; but if she had hard things to face she didn't want an audience while she faced them. Her father might be shabby and old; but he was her father, and she wasn't going to have him laughed at by anybody, even if he didn't always see things as she thought he ought to see them.

 **2** It was a long ride, and the trolley was chilly. Cornelia tried to keep from shivering and smile at everything Louise and Harry told her, but somehow things had got on her nerves. She had broken out into a perspiration with all the excitement at the station, and now felt cold and miserable. Her eyeballs ached with the frequent tears that had slipped their salt way that afternoon; and her head was heavy, and heavier her heart.

Across the way sat her father, looking grayer and more worn in the garish light of the trolley. His hair straggled and needed cutting, and his cheeks were quite hollow. He gave a hollow cough now and then, and his eyes looked like haunted spirits; but he smiled contentedly across to her whenever he caught her glance. She knew he meant that she should feel how glad he was to get her back. She began to feel very mean in her heart that she could not echo his gladness. She knew she ought to, but somehow visions of what she had left behind, probably forever, got between her and her duty, and pulled down the corners of her mouth in a disheartening droop that made her smiles a formal thing, though she tried, she really did try, to be what this worn old father evidently expected her to be, a model daughter, glad to get home and sacrifice everything in life for them all.

These thoughts made her responses to the children only half-hearted. Harry was trying to tell her how the old dog had died and they had only the little pup left, but it was so game it could beat any cat on the street in a fight already, and almost any dog.

Louise chimed in with a tale about a play in school that she had to be in if Nellie would only help her get up a costume out of old things. But gradually the talk died down, and Louise sat looking thoughtfully across at her father's tired face, while Harry frowned and puckered his lips in a contemplative attitude, shifting his gum only now and then enough to keep it going and fixing his eyes very wide and blue in deep melancholy upon the toe of his father's worn shoe. Something was fast going wrong with the spirits of the children, and Cornelia was so engrossed in herself and her own bitter disappointment that she hadn't even noticed it.

In the midst of the blueness the car stopped, and Mr. Copley rose stiffly with an apologetic smile toward his elder daughter.

"Well, this is about where we get off, Nellie," he said half wistfully, as if he had done his brave best and it was now up to her.

Something in his tone brought Cornelia keenly to her senses. She stumbled off the car, and looked around her breathlessly, while the car rumbled on up a strange street with scattering houses, wide open spaces reminding one of community baseball diamonds, and furtive heaps of tin cans and ashes. The sky was wide and open, with brilliant stars gleaming gaudily against the night, and a brazen moon that didn't seem to understand how glaringly every defect in the locality stood out; but that only made the place seem more strange and barren to the girl. She had not known what she expected, but certainly not this. The houses about her were low and small, some of them of red brick made all alike, with faded greenish-blue shutters, and a front door at one side opening on a front yard of a few feet in dimensions, with a picket fence about it, or sometimes none at all. The house her father was leading her to was a bit taller than the rest, covered with clapboards weather-beaten and stained, guiltless of paint, as could be seen even at night, high and narrow, with gingerbread-work in the gable and not a porch to grace its poor bare face, only two steps and a plain wooden door.

Cornelia gasped, and hurried in to shut herself and her misery away from the world. Was this what they had come to? No wonder her mother had given out! No wonder her father — But then her father — how could he have let them come to a place like this? It was terrible!

Inside, at the end of the long, narrow hall the light from the dining-room shone cheerfully from a clean kerosene-lamp guiltless of shade, flaring across a red and white table-cloth.

"We haven't done a thing to the parlor yet," said the father sadly, throwing open a door at his right as Cornelia followed him. "Your mother hadn't the strength!" he sighed deeply. "But then," he added more cheerfully, "what are parlors when we are all alive and getting well?"

Cornelia cast a wondering look at him. She had not known her father thought so much of her mother. There was a half-glorified look on his face that made her think of a boy in love. It was queer to think it, but of course her mother and father had been young lovers once. Cornelia, her thoughts temporarily turned from her own brooding, followed into the desolate dining-

30

room, and her heart sank. This was home! This was what she had come back to after all her dreams of a career and all her pride over an artistic temperament!

There was a place set for her at one end of the red-clothed table, and a plaintive little supper drying up on the stove in the kitchen; but Cornelia was not hungry. She made pretence of nibbling at the single little burned lamb-chop and a heavy soda-biscuit. If she had known how the children had gone without meat to buy that lamb-chop, and how hard Louise had worked to make these biscuits and the applesauce that accompanied them, she might have been more appreciative; but as it was she was feeling very miserable indeed, and had no time from her own self-pitying thoughts to notice them at all.

The dining-room was a dreary place. An old sofa that had done noble duty in the family when Cornelia was a baby lounged comfortably at one side, a catch-all for overcoats, caps, newspapers, bundles, mending, anything that happened along. Three of the dining-room chairs were more or less gone or emaciated in their seats. The cat was curled up comfortably in the old wooden rocker that had always gone by the name of "Father's rocker," and wore an ancient

31

patchwork cushion. The floor was partly covered by a soiled and worn Axminster rug whose roses blushed redly still behind wood-colored scrolls on an indiscriminate background that no one would ever suspect of having been pearl-gray once upon a time. The wall-paper was an ugly dirty dark-red, with tarnished gold designs, torn in places and hanging down, greasy and marred where chairs had rubbed against it and heads had apparently leaned. It certainly was not a charming interior. She curled her lip slightly as she took it all in. This her home! And she a born artist and interior decorator!

Her silence and lack of enthusiasm dampened the spirits of the children, who had looked to her coming to brighten the dreary aspect of things. They began to sit around silently and watch her, their keen young eyes presently searching out her thoughts, following her gaze from wall-paper to curtainless window, from broken chair to sagging couch.

"We haven't been able to get very much to rights," sighed Louise in a suddenly grown-up, responsible tone, wrinkling her pink young brow into lines of care. "I wanted to put up some curtains before you got here, but I couldn't find them. Father

wouldn't let me open
came home to hel
enough around fr
now."

"Of course,
briefly and not a.
heart she was t.
wouldn't make any di.
use of trying to do anyt
pose the beautiful strange
so sure she would make h.
could see her now. What wou.
She drew a deep sigh.

"I guess maybe I better go to be
Louise suddenly, blinking to hide .
dency to tears. It was somehow all so
ferent from what she had expected. She ha
thought it would be almost like having
mother back, and it wasn't at all. Cornelia
seemed strange and difficult.

"Yes," said the father, coming up from
the cellar, where he had been putting the
erratic furnace to bed for the night; "you
and Harry better get right up to bed. You
have to get up so early in the morning."

"Perhaps you'd like to come, too," said
Louise, turning to Cornelia with one more
attempt at hospitality. "You know you have
to sleep with me; that is I sleep with you."
She smiled apologetically. "There isn't any

33

you know," she explained as
look of dismay on Cornelia's
ted to fix up the linen-closet for
her couldn't find another cot yet.
eps on one cot up in a little sky-
ce in the third story that was only
for a ladder to go up to the roof.
has the only real room on the third
and there aren't but two on the sec-
besides the little speck of a bathroom
the linen-closet."

A sudden realization of the trouble in the
tle sister's eyes and voice brought Cornelia somewhat to her senses.

"That's all right, chicken," she said,
pinching the little girl's cheek playfully. "We
won't fight, I guess. I'm quite used to a
roommate, you know."

Louise's face bloomed into smiles of
hopefulness.

"Oh, that will be nice," she sighed. "Are
you coming to bed now?"

"You run along, Louise," put in her father. "I guess Nellie and I will have a bit
of a talk before she comes up. She'll want
to know all about mother, you know."

The two children withdrew, and Cornelia
tried to forget herself once more and bring
her reluctant thoughts to her immediate future and the task that was before her.

"What is the matter with mother?" she asked suddenly, her thoughts still half impatient over the interruption to her career. It was time she understood more definitely just what had come in to stop her at this important time of her life. She wished that mother herself had written; mother never made so much of things, although of course she didn't want to hurt her father by saying so.

"Why, she was all run down," said Mr. Copley, a shade of deep sadness coming over his gray face. "You see she had been scrimping herself for a long time, saving, that the rest of us might have more. We didn't know it, of course, or we would have stopped it." His voice was shamed and sorrowful. "We found she hadn't been eating any meat," — his voice shook like an old man's, — "just to — save — more for the rest of us."

Cornelia looked up with a curl on her lip and a flash in her eyes; but there was something in her father's broken look that held back the words of blame that had almost sprung to her lips, and he went on with his tale in a tone like a confession, as if the burden of it were all on him, and were a cloak of shame that he must wear. It was as if he wanted to tell it all at its worst.

"She didn't tell us, either, when she began to feel bad. She must have been running down for the last three years; in fact, ever since you went away. Though she never let on. When Molly had to go home to her folks, your mother decided not to try to keep a servant. She said she could get along better with sending out the washing, and servants were a scarce article, and cost a lot. I didn't want her to; but you know how your mother always was, and I had kind of got used to letting her have her own way, especially as about that time I had all I could do night and day at the office to try to prevent what I saw was coming for the business. She worked too hard. I shall never forgive myself!" He suddenly buried his face in his hands, and groaned.

It was awful to Cornelia. She wanted to run and fling her arms about his neck and comfort him;. yet she couldn't help blaming him. Was he so weak? Why hadn't he been more careful of the business, and not let things get into such a mess? A man oughtn't to be weak. But the sight of his trouble touched her strangely. How thin and gray his hair looked! It struck her again that he looked aged since she had seen him last. It gave her the effect of a cold douche in her face.

"Don't father!" she said, her voice full of suppressed pain, and a glint of tenderness.

"Well, I know I oughtn't to trouble you this way, daughter," he said, looking up with a deprecatory smile; "but somehow it comes over me how much she suffered in silence before we found it out, and then I can't stand it, especially when I think what she was when I married her, so fresh-faced and pretty with brown hair and eyes just like yours. You make me think a lot of her, daughter. Well, it's all over, thank the Lord," he went on with a sigh, "and she's on the mend again. You don't know what it was to me the day of the operation."

"Operation!" The word caught in Cornelia's throat, and a chill of horror crept over her. "Why, you never told me there was an operation!"

"I know," her father said apologetically. "That was mother, too! she wouldn't have you troubled. She said it was just your examination time, and it would mean a great deal to you to get your marks; and it would only be a time of anxiety to you, and she was so sure she would come out all right. She was wonderfully brave, your mother was. And she hoped so much she'd be able to get up and around, and not have to bring you home till your course was over. We meant to manage it somehow; but you see we didn't know how serious it was, and how she would have to go away and stay a long time till she was strong."

Cornelia's eyes were filled with tears now. She had forgotten her own disappointments and the way she had been blaming her father, and was filled with remorse for the little mother who had suffered and thought of her to the last. She got up quickly, and went over to gather the bowed head of her father into her unaccustomed arms and try somehow to be daughterly. It was strange because she had been away so long and had got out of the way of little endearments, but she managed it so that the big man was comforted and smiled at her, and told her again and again how good it was to have her back, almost as good as having her mother. Then he stroked her hair, looked into her wise young eyes, and called her his little Nellie-girl, the way she could remember his doing before she went away to school.

When Cornelia went upstairs at last with the kerosene-lamp held high above her head so that she would not stumble up the steep, winding staircase, she had almost forgotten herself and her ambitions, and was filled with a desire to comfort her father.

She dropped into her place beside the sleeping sister with a martyr-like quiet, and failed to notice the discouraged droop of the little huddled figure, and the tear-strained cheek that was turned toward the dingy wall. The dreariness of the room and the close quarters had brought depression upon her spirits once more, and she lay a long time filled with self-pity, and wondering how in the world she was ever to endure it all.

3

In the dimness of the early morning Louise Copley awoke with a sigh to consciousness, and softly slid her hand down to the floor under the bed, where she had hidden the old alarm-clock. With a sense that her elder sister was still company she had not turned on the alarm as usual, and now with the clock-like regularity and a sense of responsibility far beyond her years she had wakened at a quarter to six as promptly as if the whir of the alarm had sounded underneath her pillow.

She rubbed her eyes open, and through the half-lifted fringes took a glance. Yes it was time to get up. With one more lingering rub at her sleepy young eyes she put the clock back under the bed out of the way, and stole quietly over the footboard, watching furtively her sleeping sister. How pretty Nellie was even in the early gray light of morning, with all that wavy mane of hair sweeping over the pillow, and her long lashes lying on the pink curve of her cheek! Louise wondered incredulously whether she would be half as pretty as that when she was as old as her sister.

It was nice to have a big sister at home,

but now she was here Louise wondered in a mature little housewifely way what in the world they were going to do with her. She didn't look at all fit for cooking and things like that, and Louise sighed wearily as she struggled with the buttons, and thought of the day before her, and the endless weeks that must go by before they could hope for the return of the dear mother who had made even poverty sweet and cheerful. And there was that matter of a spring hat, and a costume to wear at the school entertainment. She stole another glance at the lovely sleeping sister, and decided it would not do to bother her with little trifles like that. She would have to manage them somehow herself. Then, with the last button conquered, and a hasty tying back of her yellow curls with a much-worn ribbon, she tiptoed responsibly from the room, taking care to shut the latch securely and silently behind her.

She sped downstairs, and went capably at the kitchen stove, coaxing it into brightness and glancing fearfully at the kitchen clock. It was six o'clock, and she could hear her father stirring about in his room. He would be down soon to look after the furnace, and then she must have breakfast on the table at once, for he must catch the six-fifty-five car. The usual morning frenzy of rush seized her, and she flew from dining-room to pantry, to the refrigerator for butter, out to the front door for the bottle of milk that would be there, back to the pantry cutting bread, and back to the stove to turn the bacon and be sure it did not burn. It was a mad race, and sometimes she felt like crying by the time she sat down to the table to pour her father's coffee, which somehow, try as she would, just would not look nor taste like mother's. She was almost relieved that her sister had given no sign of awakening yet; for she had not had time to make the breakfast table look nice, and it was so kind of exciting to try to eat in a hurry and have "sort of company" to think about at the same time.

The father came downstairs peering into the dining-room anxiously, with an apology on his lips for his eldest child.

"That's right, Louie; I'm glad you let her sleep. She looked all wearied out last night with her long journey, and then I guess it's been a kind of a shock to her, too."

"I guess it has," said the little girl comfortably, and passed him his cup of coffee and the bread-plate. They both had a sense of relief that Cornelia was not there and that there was a legitimate reason for not blaming her for her absence. Neither had yet been willing to admit to their loyal selves that Cornelia's attitude of apathy to the family strait had been disappointing. They kept hoping against hope.

Mr. Copley finished his coffee hurriedly, and looked at his watch.

"Better let her sleep as long as she will," he said. "She'll likely be awake before you need to go to school; and, if she isn't, you can leave a note telling her where to find things. Where's Harry? Isn't he up?"

"Oh, yes, he went to the grocery for the soup-bone he forgot to get last night. I was going to put it on cooking before I left. I thought maybe she wouldn't know to —"

"That's right! That's right! You're a good little girl, Louie. Your sister'll appreciate that. Make Harry eat a good breakfast when he gets back. It isn't good to go out on an empty stomach; and we must all keep well, and not worry mother, you know."

"Yes, I know," sighed the little girl with a responsible look; "I made him take a piece with him, and I'm saving something hot for him when he comes back. He'll help me with the dishes, he said. We'll make out all right. Don't you worry, father, dear."

The father with a tender father-and-mother-both smile came around, and kissed her white forehead where the soft baby-gold hair parted, and then hurried away to his car, thankful for the mother's look in his youngest girl's face; wondering whether they had chased it forever away from the eldest girl's face by sending her too young to college.

It was to the soft clatter of pots and pans somewhere in the near distance that Cornelia finally awakened with a sense of terrible depression and a belated idea that she ought to be doing something for the family comfort. She arose hastily, and dressed, with a growing distaste for the new day and what was before her. Even the view from the grimy little bedroom window was discouraging. It was a gray day, and one could see there were intentions of rain in the mussy clouds that hurled themselves across the distant roof-tops. The window looked out into the back yard, a small enclosure with a fence needing paint, and dishearteningly full of rusty tin cans and old, weather-stained newspapers and rubbish. Beyond the narrow dirty alley were rows of other similar back yards, with now and then a fluttering dishcloth hanging on a string on a back porch, and plenty of heaped-up ash cans everywhere you looked. They were the back doors of houses of the poorer class, most of them two-story and old. Farther on there was an excellent view of a large and prosperous dump-heap in a wide, cavernous lot that looked as if it had suffered from earthquake sometime in the dim past and lost its bottom, so capacious it seemed as its precipitous sides sloped down, liberally coated with "dump." Cornelia gave a slight shiver of horror, and turned from the window. To think of having to look at a view like that all summer. A vision of the cool, leafy camp where she had spent two weeks the summer before floated tantalizingly before her sad eyes as she slowly went downstairs.

It was a plaintive little voice that arrested her attention and her progress half-way down, a sweet, tired young voice that went to her heart, coming from the open kitchen door and carrying straight through the open dining-room and through the hall up to her.

"I guess she doesn't realize how much we needed her," it said sadly; "and I guess she's pretty disappointed at the house and everything. It's pretty much of a change from college, of course."

Then a young, indignant high tenor growl:

"H'm! What does she think she is, anyway? Some queen? I guess the house has been good enough for us. How does she think we've stood being poor all these years just to keep her in college? I'd like to know. This house isn't so much worse'n the last one we were in. It's a peach beside some we might have had to take if these folks hadn't been just moving out now. What does she want to do anyhow? Isn't her family good enough for her, or what? If I ever have any children, I shan't send 'em to college, I know that. It spoils 'em. And I don't guess I'll ever go myself. What's her little old idea, anyway? Who crowned her?"

"Why, she wants to be an interior decorator," said the little sister, slowly hanging up the dishcloth. "I guess it's all right, and she'd make money and all; only we just couldn't help her out till she got through her course."

"Interior decorator!" scornfully said the boy. "I'd be satisfied if she'd decorate my interior a little. I'd like some of mother's waffles, wouldn't you? And some hash and johnnycake. Gee! Well, I guess we better get a hustle on, or we'll be called down for tardiness. You gotta wake her up before you go?"

"Father said not to; I'm just going to leave a note. It's all written there on the dining-room table. You put some coal on the range, and I'll get my hat and coat";

and the little sister moved quickly toward the hall.

Cornelia in sudden panic turned silently, and sped back to her room, closing the door and listening with wildly beating heart till her young brother and sister went out the door and closed it behind them. Then, obeying an impulse that she did not understand, she suddenly flung her door open, and flew to her father's front bedroom window for a sight of them as they trudged off with piles of books under their arms, two valiant young comrades, just as she and Carey used to be in years so long ago and far away that she had almost forgotten them. And how they had stabbed her, her own brother and sister, talking about her as if she were a selfish alien, who had been living on their sacrifices for a long time! What could it possibly mean? Surely they were mistaken. Children always exaggerated things, and of course the few days or perhaps weeks since their father had lost his money had seemed a long time to them, poor little souls. Of course it had been hard for them to get along even a few days without mother, and in this awful house. But — how could they have talked that way? How terrible of them! There were tears in her eyes and a pain in her heart from the words, for, after all, in spite of her self-centered abstraction she did love them all, they were hers, and of course dearer than anything else on earth. Yes, even than interior decorating, and of course it was right that she should come home and make them comfortable, only — if only!

But the old unrest was swept back by the memory of those cutting words in the young high voices. She sank down in an old armchair that stood by the window, and let the tears have their way for a minute. Somehow she felt abused by the words of the children. They had misjudged her, and it wasn't fair! It was bad enough to have to give up everything and come home, without being misjudged and called selfish.

But presently the tears had spent themselves, and she began to wipe her eyes and look around. Her father's room was as desolate as any other. There was no evidence of an attempt to put comfort into it. The upper part of the heavy walnut bureau, with its massive mirror that Cornelia remembered as a part of the furniture of her mother's room since she was a baby, had not been screwed to the bureau, but was standing on the floor as if it had just moved in. The bureau-top was covered with dust, worn, mussed neckties, soiled collars, and a few old letters. Her father's few garments were strewn about the room and the open closet door revealed some of her mother's garments, old ones that Cornelia remembered she had had before she herself went to college.

On the unmade bed, close beside the pillow, as if it had been cherished for comfort, was one of mother's old calico wrappers. It was lying where a cheek might conveniently rest against it. Somehow Cornelia didn't think of that explanation of its presence there at first; but later it grew into her consciousness, and the pathetic side of it filled her with dismay. Was life like this always, or was this a special preparation for her benefit?

Somehow, as she sat there, her position as a selfish, unloving daughter became intolerable. Could it be possible that the children had spoken truly and that the family had been in straitened circumstances for a longer time than just a few weeks, on account of keeping her in college? The color burned in her cheeks, and her eyes grew heavy with shame. How shabby everything looked! She didn't remember it that way. Her home had always seemed a comfortable one as she looked back upon it. Somehow she could not understand. But the one thought that burned into her soul was that they had somehow felt her lacking, ungrateful.

Suddenly she was stung into action. They should see that she was no selfish, idle member of the family group. At least, she could be as brave as they were. She would go to work and make a difference in things before they came home. She would show them!

She flew to the tumbled bed, and began to straighten the rumpled sheets and plump up the pillows. In a trice she had it smoothly made. But there was no white spread to put over it, and there were rolls of dust under the bed and in the corners. The floor had not even a rug to cover its bareness. Worn shoes and soiled socks trailed about here and there, and several old garments hung on bedposts, drifted from chairs, and even lay on the floor. Cornelia went hastily about, gathering them up, sorting out the laundry, setting the shoes in an even row in the closet, straightening the bureau, and stuffing things into the already overflowing drawers, promising them an early clearing out as soon as she had the rest of the work in hand. Poor father! of course he was not used to keeping things in order. How a woman was missed in a house! She hadn't realized it before. The whole house looked as if the furniture had just been dumped in with no attempt to set things right, as her father had said. She must get the broom, and begin.

She hurried out into the hall, and a glimpse of the narrow stairway winding above her drew her to investigate. And then a sudden thought. Carey. Where was Carey? Hadn't he come home at all last night? She had no recollection of hearing him, and yet she might have fallen asleep earlier than she thought. She mounted the stairs, and stood aghast before the desolation there.

The little closet Louise had spoken of with its skylight, and its meagre cot of twisted bedclothes, its chair with a medley of Harry's clothes, and its floor strewn with a varied collection, was dreary enough; but there was yet some semblance of attempt at order. The muddy shoes stood in a row; some garments were in piles, and some hung on nails and there had been an attempt at good housekeeping by the young owner. There was even a colored picture of a baseball favorite, and a diagram of a famous game. One could feel that the young occupant had taken possession with some sense of ownership in the place. But the front room was like a desert of destruction

51

whereon lay bleaching the bones of a former life as if swept there by a whirlwind.

The headboard and footboard of the iron bedstead stood against the wall together like a corpse cast aside and unburied. On the floor in the very middle of the room lay the springs, and upon it the worn and soiled mattress, hardly recognizable by that name now because of the marks of heavy, muddy shoes, as if it had been not only slept upon but walked over with shoes straight from the contact of the street in bad weather. Sheets there were none, and the pillow soiled and with a hole burnt in one corner of its ticking lay guiltless of a pillow-case, with a beaten, sodden impression of a head in its centre. There was a snarl of soiled blanket and torn patchwork quilt across the foot, tossed to one side; and all about this excuse for a bed was strewn the most heterogeneous mass of objects that Cornelia had ever seen collected. Clothes soiled and just from the laundry, all in one mass, neckties tangled among books and letters, cheap magazines and parts of automobiles, a silk hat and a white evening vest keeping company with a pair of greasy overalls and two big iron wrenches; and over everything cigarette-stumps.

The desolation was complete. The bureau

had turned its back to the scene in despair, and was face to the wall, as it had been placed by the movers. It was then and not till then that Cornelia understood how recent had been the moving, and how utter the rout of the poor, patient mother, whose wonderful housekeeping had always been the boast of the neighborhood where they had lived, and whose fastidiousness had been almost an obsession.

Cornelia stood in the door, and gasped in horror as her eyes travelled from one corner of the room to another and back again, and her quick mind read the story of her brother's life and one deep cause of her dear mother's breakdown. She remembered her father's words about Carey, and how he hoped she would be able to help him; and then her memory went back to the days when she and Carey were inseparable. She saw the bright, eager face of her brother only two years younger than herself, always merry, with a jest on his lips and a twinkle in his eyes, but a kind heart and a willingness always to serve. Had Carey in three short years fallen to this? Because there was no excuse for an able-bodied young man to live in a mess like this. No young man with a mite of self-respect would do it. And Carey knew better. Carey had been brought up to take care of himself and his things. Nobody could mend a bit of furniture, or fix the plumbing, or sweep a room, or even wash out a blanket for mother, better than Carey when he was only fifteen. And for Carey as she knew him to be willing to lie down for at least more than one night in a room like this and go off in the morning leaving it this way, was simply unthinkable. How Carey must have changed to have come to this! As her eyes roved about the room, she began to have an insight into what must be the trouble. Self-indulgence of a violent type must have got hold of him. Look at the hundreds of cigarette-stumps, ashes everywhere. The only saving thing was the touch of machinery in the otherwise hopeless mass; and that, too, meant only that he was crazy about automobiles, and likely fussed with them now and then to re-pair them so that he would have opportu-nity to ride as much as he liked. And Carey — where was Carey now?

She turned sadly away from the room, and shut the door. It was a work of time to think of getting that mess straightened out into any sort of order, and it made her heart-sick and hopeless. She must look far-ther and learn the whole story before she began to do anything.

She stumbled blindly downstairs, only half glancing into the messy bathroom where soap and toothbrushes got standing room indiscriminately where they could; took a quick look into the small enclosure that Louise had described as a "linen-closet," probably on account of a row of dirty-looking shelves at one end of the apartment; looked hesitatingly toward the door of her own room, wondering whether to stop there long enough to make the bed and tidy up, but shook her head and went on downstairs. She must know the whole thing before she attempted to do anything.

The stairs ascended at the back of the hall, with a cloak-closet under them now stuffed with old coats and hats belonging to the whole family. Opposite this closet the dining-room door opened. All the space in front was devoted to the large front room known as the "parlor." Cornelia flung the door open wide, and stepped in. The blinds were closed, letting in only a slant ray of light from a broken slat over the desolation of half-unpacked boxes and barrels that prevailed. Evidently the children had mauled everything over in search of certain articles they needed, and had not put back or put away anything. Pictures and dishes and clothing lay about miscellaneously in a confused heap, and a single step into the room was liable to do damage, for one might step into a china meat-platter under an eider-down quilt, or knock over a cut-glass pitcher in the dark. Cornelia stopped, and rescued several of her mother's best dishes from a row about the first barrel by the door, transferring them to the hall-rack before she dared go in to look around.

The piano was still encased in burlap, standing with its keyboard to the wall, an emblem of the family's desolation. As her eyes grew accustomed to the dim light, Cornelia gradually began to identify various familiar objects. There were the old sofa and upholstered chairs that used to be in the nursery when Louise and Harry were mere babies. The springs were sagging and the tapestry faded.

She searched in vain for the better suite of furniture that had been bought for the living room before she went to college. Where was it? It hadn't been in the dining-room the night before, she was sure; and of course it couldn't be in the kitchen. Could there be a shed at the back somewhere, with more things that were not as yet unpacked? With a growing fear she slipped behind some barrels, and tried to find the big bookcase with the glass doors, and the mahogany tables that mother had been so proud of because they had belonged to her great-grandmother, and the claw-legged desk with the cabinet on the top. Not one of them was to be found.

A horrible suspicion was dawning in her mind. She waited only to turn back the corners of several rolls of carpet and rugs, and make sure the Oriental rugs were missing, before she fled in a panic to the back of the house.

Through the bare little kitchen she passed without even noticing how hard the children had worked to clear it up. Perhaps she would not have called it cleared up, her standard being on an entirely different scale from theirs. Yes, there was a door at the farther side. She flung it open, and found the hoped-for shed, but no furniture. Its meagre space was choked with tubs and an old washing-machine, broken boxes and barrel-staves, a marble table-top broken in two, and a rusty wash-boiler. With a shiver of conviction she stood and stared at them, and then slammed the door shut, and, flinging herself into a kitchen chair, burst into tears.

She had not wept like that since she was a capable, controlled little girl; but the tears somehow cleared the cobwebs from her eyes and heart. She knew now that those beautiful things of her mother's were gone, and her strong suspicions were that she was the cause of it all. Some one else was enjoying them so that the money they brought could be used to keep her in college! And she had been blaming her father for not having managed somehow to let her stay longer! All these months, or perhaps years for aught she knew, he had been straining and striving to keep her from knowing how hard he and her dear mother were saving and scrimping to make her happy and give her the education she wanted; and she selfish, unloving girl that she was, had been painting, drawing, studying, directing class plays, making fudge, playing hockey, reading delightful books, attending wonderful lectures and concerts, studying beautiful pictures, and all the time growing farther and farther away from the dear people who were giving their lives — yes, literally giving their lives, for they couldn't have had much enjoyment in living at this rate — to make it all possible for her!

Oh! she saw it all clearly enough now, and she hated herself for it. She began to go back over last night and how she had met them. She visualized their faces as they stood at the gate eagerly awaiting her; and she, little college snob that she was, was ashamed to greet them eagerly because she was with a fine lady and her probably snobbish son. Her suddenly awakened instinct recalled the disappointed look on the tired father's face and the sudden dulling of the merry twinkles of gladness in the children's eyes. Oh! she could see it all now, and each new memory and conviction brought a stab of pain to her heart. Then, as if the old walls of the house took up the accusation against her, she began to hear over again the plaintive voices of Louise and Harry as they wiped the dishes and talked her over. It was all too plain that she had been weighed in the balances and found wanting. Something in the pitiful wistfulness of Harry's voice as he had made that quick turn about interior decoration roused her at last to the present and her immediate duty. It was no use whatever to sit here and cry about it when such a mountain of work awaited her. The lady on the train had been right when she told her there would be plenty of chance for her talents. She had not dreamed of any such desolation at this, of course; but it was true that the opportunity, if one could look on it as an opportunity, was great, and she would see what she could do. At least things could be clean and tidy. And there should be waffles! That was a settled thing, waffles for the first meal. And she arose and looked about her with the spirit of victory in her eyes and in the firm, sweet line of her quivering lips.

What time was it, and what ought she to do first? She stepped to the dining-room door to consult the clock which she could hear ticking noisily from the mantel, and her eye caught her sister's note written large across the corner of a paper bag.

Dear Nellie,

I had to go to school. I'll get back as soon after four as I can. You can heet the fride potatoes, and there are some eggs.

Louie

Suddenly the tears blurred into her eyes at thought of the little disappointed sister yet taking care for her in her absence. Dear little Louie! How hard it must have been for her! And she remembered the sigh she had heard from the kitchen a little while ago. Well, she was thankful she had been awakened right away and not allowed to go on in her selfish indifference. She glanced at the clock. It was a quarter to nine. She had lost a lot of time mooning over her own troubles. She had but seven hours in which to work wonders before any one returned. She must go to work at once.

 **4** A hasty survey of the larder showed a scant supply of materials. There were flour and sugar and half a basket of potatoes. Some cans of tomatoes and corn, a paper bag of dried beans, another of rice, two eggs in a basin, and a dish of discouraged-looking fried potatoes with burnt edges completed the count. A small bit of butter on a plate and the end of a baker's loaf of bread had evidently been left on the dining-room table for her. There were a good many things needed from the store, and she began to write them down on the other side of her sister's note. A further investigation revealed half a bottle of milk that had soured. Cornelia's face brightened. That would make a wonderful gingerbread, and she wrote down "Molasses, soda, brown sugar, baking-powder," on her list.

It wasn't as if Cornelia hadn't spent the first sixteen years of her life at home with her mother, for she knew how to cook and manage quite well before she went away to school; only of course she hadn't done a thing at it since she left home, and like most girls she thought she hated the very idea of kitchen work.

"Now, where do they buy things?" she wondered aloud to the clock as if it were alive. "I shall have to find out. I suppose if I take a basket and go far enough, I shall come to a store. If I don't I can ask somebody."

She ran upstairs, and got her hat and coat, and patted her pocketbook happily. At least she was not penniless, and did not have to wait until her father came home for what she wanted to get; for she had almost all of the last money her mother had sent before her illness. It had been sent for new spring clothes, and Cornelia had been so busy she had not had time to buy them. It sent a glad thrill through her heart now, strangely mingled with a pang at the things that she had planned and that now would not be hers. Yet, after all, the pang did not last; for already her mind was taken up with the new interests and needs of home, and she was genuinely glad that she had the money still unspent.

Down the dull little street she sped, thinking of all she had to do in the house before the family came home, trying not to feel the desolation of the night before as she passed the commonplace houses and saw what kind of a neighborhood she had come to live in, trying not to realize that almost every house showed neglect or poverty of some kind. Well, what of it? If she did live in a neighborhood that was utterly uncongenial, she could at least make their little home more comfortable. She knew she could. She could feel the ability for it tingling to her very finger-tips, and she smiled as she hurried on to the next corner, where the gleam of a trolley track gave hint of a possible business street. She paused at the corner and looked each way, a pretty picture of girlhood, balancing daintily on her neat little feet and looking quite out of place in that neighborhood. Some of her new neighbors eyed her from behind their Nottingham lace curtains and their blue paper shades, and wondered unsympathetically where she came from and how she had strayed there, and a young matron in a dirty silver lace boudoir-cap with fluttering pink and blue ribbons came out with her market basket, and gave a cool, calculating stare, so far in another world that she did not mind being caught at it.

The boudoir-cap was almost too much for Cornelia, bobbing about the fat, red face of the frowsy woman; but the market basket gave her a hint, and she gracefully fell in behind her fellow shopper, and presently arrived at a market.

About this time Mrs. Knowlton and her

son sat in the hotel dining-room downtown, eating their breakfast. A telegram had just been laid beside the son's plate, and he looked up from reading it with a troubled brow.

"I'm afraid I'm going to have to upset our plans again," he said. "I'm awfully sorry, mother; but Brown is coming on from Boston expecting to meet me at noon; and I guess there's nothing to do but wait until the two o'clock train. Shall you mind very much?"

"Not at all," said his mother, smiling. "Why should I mind? I came on to be with you. Does it matter whether I'm in Philadelphia or Washington?"

"Is there anything you would like to do this morning? Any shopping? Or would you like to drive about a bit?"

She shook her head.

"I can shop at home. I came here to be with you."

"Then let's drive," he decided with a loving smile. "Where would you like to go? Anything you want to see?"

"No — or wait. Yes, there is. I've a fancy I'd like to drive past the house where that little girl I met on the train lives. I'd like to see exactly what she's up against with her firm little chin and her clear, wise eyes and her artistic ways."

"At it again, aren't you, mother? Always falling in love and chasing after your object. You're worse than a young man in his teens"; and he smiled understandingly. "All right; we'll hunt her up, mother; only we shan't have much time to stop, for I have to be here sharp at twelve thirty. Do you know where she lives?"

"Yes, I have her address here," said his mother, searching in her silver bag for the card on which Cornelia had written it. "But I don't want to stop. It wouldn't do. She would think me intruding."

The young man took the address, and ordered a taxicab; and five minutes after Cornelia entered the door of her home with her arms full of bundles from market and grocery a taxicab crawled slowly by the house, and two pairs of eyes eagerly scanned the high, narrow, weather-stained building with its number over the front door the only really distinct thing about it.

"The poor child!" murmured the lady.

"Well, she sure is up against it!" growled the son, sitting back with an air of not looking, but taking it all in out of the tail end of his eye the way young men can do.

"And she wants to be an interior decorator!" said the mother, turning from her last look out the little window behind.

"She's got some task this time, I'll say!" answered the son. "It may show up more promisingly from the interior, but I doubt it. And you say she's been to college? Dwight Hall, didn't you say, where Dorothy Mayo graduated? Some come-down! It's a hard world. Well, mother, I guess we've got to get back or I'll miss my appointment;" and he gave the chauffeur directions to turn about.

More rapidly they passed this time, but the eyes of the woman took in all the details, the blank side wall where windows ought to have abounded, the shallow third story obviously with room for only one apartment, the lowly neighbors, the dirty, noisy children in the street. She thought of the girl's lovely refined face, and sighed.

"One might, of course, do a great deal of good in such a neighborhood. It is an opportunity," she murmured thoughtfully.

Her son looked amused.

"I imagine she'll confine her attention to the interior of her own home if she does anything at all. I'm afraid if I came home from college to a place like that, I'd beat it, mother mine."

His mother looked up with a trusting smile.

"You wouldn't, though!" she said sunnily, and added thoughtfully, "And she won't either. She had a true face. Sometime I'm coming back to see how it came out."

Meantime, Cornelia in the kitchen started the fire up brightly, put on the tea-kettle, and began to concoct a soft gingerbread with the aid of the nice thick sour milk. When it was in the oven, she hunted out her mother's old worn breadraiser, greased the squeaking handle with butter, and started some bread. She remembered how everybody in the family loved mother's home-made bread; and, if there was one thing above another in which she had ex-celled as a little girl in the kitchen, it was in making bread. Somehow it did not seem as though things were on a right basis until she had some bread on the way. As she crumbled the yeast cake into a sauce dish and put it a-soak, she began to hum a little tune; yet her mind was so preoccupied with what she had to do that she scarcely remem-bered it was the theme of the music that ran all through the college play. College life had somehow receded for the present, and in place of costumes and drapery she was considering what she ought to make and bake in order to have the pantry and refrig-erator well stocked, and how soon she might with a clear conscience go upstairs and start clearing up Carey's bedroom. She couldn't settle rightly to anything until that awful mess was straightened out. The consciousness of the disorder up there in the third story was like a bruise that had been given her, which made itself more and more felt as the minutes passed.

When the cover was put down tight on the breadraiser, Cornelia looked about her.

"I really ought to clean this kitchen first," she said thoughtfully, speaking aloud as if she and herself were having it out about the work. "There aren't enough dishes unpacked for the family to eat comfortably, but there's not room on those shelves for them if they were unpacked."

So, with a glance at the rapidly rising gingerbread that let out a whiff of delicious aroma, she mounted on a chair, and began to clear off the top shelves of the dresser. It seemed as if there had been no system whatever in placing things. Bottles of shoe-blacking, a hammer, a box of gingersnaps, a can of putty, and several old neckties were settled in between glass sauce-dishes and the electric iron. She kept coming on little necessities. With small ceremony she swept them all down to an orderly row on the floor on the least-used side of the room, and with soap, hot water, and a scrubbing-brush went at the shelves. It didn't take long, of course; but she put a great deal of energy into the work, and began to feel actually happy as she smelled the clean soap-suds, and beheld what a difference it made in the shabby, paintless shelves to get rid of the dirt.

"Now, we've at least got a spot to put things!" she announced as she took the gingerbread-tins out of the oven, and with great satisfaction noted that she had not forgotten how to make gingerbread in the interval of her college days.

The gingerbread reminded her that she had as yet had no breakfast, but she would not mar the velvet beauty of those fragrant loaves of gingerbread by cutting one now. She cut off a slice of the dry end of a loaf, and buttered it. She was surprised to find how good it tasted as she ate it going about her work, picking up what dishes on the floor belonged back on the shelves, washing and arranging them. Later, if there was time, she would unpack more dishes; but she must get up to Carey's room. It was like leaving something dead about uncovered, to know that that room looked so above her head.

It was twelve o'clock when she at last got

permission of herself to go upstairs; and she carried with her broom, mop, soap, scrubbing-brush, and plenty of hot water and old cloths. She paused at the door of the front room long enough to rummage in the bureau drawers and get out an old all-over gingham apron of her mother's, which she donned before ascending to the third floor.

In the doorway of her brother's room she stood appalled once more, scarcely knowing where to begin. Then, putting down her brushes and pails in the hall, she started in at the doorway, picking up the first things that came in her way. Clothes first. She sorted them out quickly, hanging the good things on the railing of the stairs, the worn and soiled ones in piles on the floor, ready for the laundry, the rag-man, and the mending-basket. When the garments were all out, she turned back; and the room seemed to be just as full and just as messy as it had been before. She began again, this time gleaning the newspapers and magazines. That made quite a hole in the floor space. Next she dragged the twisted bedclothes off the mattress, and threw them down the stairs. Somehow they must be washed or aired or duplicated before that bed would be fit to sleep in. After a thoughtful moment of looking over the banisters at them she descended, and carried them all to the little back yard, where she hung them on a short line that had been stretched from the fence to the house. They made a sorry sight, but she would have to leave them till later. The sun and air would help. There wasn't much sun, and there was still a sharp tang of rain in the air; it had been raining at intervals all the morning. Well, if it rained on them, they certainly needed it; and anyhow it was too late in the day for her to try to wash any of them. She must do the best she could this first day.

Thus she reasoned as she frowningly surveyed the grimy blankets, her eyes lingering on a scorched place near the top of one. Suddenly her expression changed: "You've just *got* to be washed!" she said firmly, and snatching the blankets from the line, rushed in to arrange for large quantities of hot water, cleared off the stationary tubs, and dumped in the blankets, shaved up the only bar of soap she could find, and then went rummaging in the front room while the water was heating. Of course all this took strength, but she was not realizing how weary she was growing. Her mettle was up, and she was working on her nerve. It was a mercy with all she had before her that she was well and strong, and fresh from gymnasium and basketball training. It would take all her strength before she was done.

She emerged from the parlor twenty minutes later triumphant, with a number of things that she was sure would be needed. She went to work at the blankets with vigor, rubbing and pulling away at the scorched place until it was almost obliterated. Did Carey smoke in his sleep she wondered, or did he have guests that did? How dreadful that Carey had come to this, and she away at college improving herself and complacently expecting to make her mark in the world!

The blankets were cleanly steaming on the line in half an hour more, and she glanced at the clock. A whole hour had gone, and she must hasten. She sped back upstairs, and went to work again, dragging out the furniture to the hall, picking up books and magazines from the floor, till the room was stark and empty save for cigarette-stumps. She surveyed them in disgust, and then assailed the room with brushes, brooms, and mop. She threw the windows wide open, and swept the wall down vigorously. Before her onslaught dust and ashes disappeared, and even the dismal wall-paper took on a brighter hue.

"It's got to come off and be repapered or

painted some pretty, soft, pastel shade," she threatened in an undertone to herself as she surveyed the room after soap and water had done their best on floor, wood-work, and windows. She was looking at the bleary wall-paper with a troubled frown.

Of course she couldn't do everything in a day, but Carey's room must be clean and inviting before she would be satisfied. No wonder he stayed out late nights, or didn't come home at all, perhaps, with such a room as that. There ought to be more windows, too. What a pity the builder had been so stingy with them! It was a dark, ugly hole; and there was no need for it, for the room occupied the whole end, and could have had openings on three sides and been delightful.

Suddenly she began to feel a great weariness stealing over her, and tears coming into her eyes. She was overwhelmed with all that was before her. She sat down on the upper stair, and looked about her discouragedly. All these things to be put somewhere! And time going so fast! Then she remembered her bread, and with an exclamation rushed down to put it into the pans.

It had risen almost to the top of the breadraiser, and with a mental apology for her forgetfulness she hastened to mold it out into loaves and put it into the greased tins. When it was neatly tucked up under a bit of old linen she had found in the sideboard drawer, she began to prepare the meat for dinner and put it on to cook, a beautiful big pot-roast. She deftly seared it with an onion in a hot frying-pan, and put it to simmer in boiling water with the rinsings of the browned pan, being careful to recall all her mother's early instruction on the subject. She could remember that pot-roast was always a favorite dish at home, and she herself had been longing for a taste of real home-cooked pot-roast ever since she had been away.

She fixed the fire carefully so that the meat would simmer just enough, and not boil too hard and make it tough, and gave a despairing glance at the clock. How fast the minutes flew! She ought to go back upstairs, but it was a quarter to three, and she wanted to get the table set for dinner before she left, so that the dining-room would have a pleasant look to the children when they came home. She was quite breathless and excited over their coming. She felt as if she would be almost embarrassed before them after the conversation she had overheard in the morning.

So she attacked the dining-room with

broom and duster, wiped off the window-panes, and straightened the shade, swept away a mass of miscellaneous articles from the clockshelf, cleared off the sideboard, hunted out a clean old linen cover, polished the mirror, and found a clean tablecloth. But the tablecloth had a great hole in it, and fifteen valuable minutes were wasted in finding a patch and setting it hastily in place with a needle and thread that also had to be hunted for. Then some of the dishes had to be washed before they were fit for use, as they were covered with dust from packing; and all together it was five minutes to four before Cornelia finally had that table set to her satisfaction, and could stand back for a brief minute and take it in with tired but shining eyes. Would they notice the difference and be a little glad that she had come? They had taken her for a lazy snob in the morning. Would they feel any better about it now?

And the table did look pretty. It was set as a table should be set, with dishes and glasses and silver in the correct places, and napkins neatly folded; and in the centre was a small pot of pink primroses in full bloom. For it would not have been Cornelia if there had not been a bit of decoration about somewhere, and it was like Cornelia when she went out to market, and thought of meat and bread and milk and butter and all the other necessities, to think also of that bit of brightness and refinement, and go into a small flower-shop she was passing to get this pretty primrose.

Then in panic the weary big sister brought out one loaf of gingerbread, cut several generous slices, left it on the sideboard in a welcome attitude, and fled upstairs to finish Carey's room.

Five minutes later, as she was struggling with the bedsprings trying to bring them into conjunction with the headboard, she heard their hurrying feet, and, leaning from the window, called:

"Children! Come up here a minute, and help me."

"I can't," shouted Harry with a frown; "I got a job afternoons, and I gotta hustle. I'm late a'ready, and I have to change my clo'es!" and he vanished inside the door.

"I have to go to the store for things for dinner!" reproved the young sister stiffly, and vanished also.

Cornelia felt suddenly in her weariness like sitting down on the floor in a fit of hysterical laughter or tears. Would they never forgive her? She dropped on the floor with her head wearily back against the window and closed her eyes. She had meant to tell them about the gingerbread, but they had been in such a hurry; and somehow the spirit seemed gone out of her surprise.

Downstairs it was very still. The children had been halted at the entrance by the appetizing odor of cooking.

"Sniff!"

"Oh, gee!" said Harry. "It smells like mother was home."

Louise stalked hurriedly to the dining-room door.

"Harry Copley, just look here! Now, what did I tell you about college girls?"

Harry came and stood entranced.

"Oh, gee!" he murmured. "Isn't that just great? Oh, say, Lou Copley, just gaze on that sideboard! I'll tell the world this is some day!" and he strode to the sideboard, and stopped all further speech by more than a mouthful of the fragrant ginger-cake.

The little housewife took swift steps to the kitchen door, and sniffed. She took in the row of plump bread-tins almost ready to go into the oven, the gently bubbling kettle with its fragrant steam, the shining dresser with its neat rows of dishes that she had never been able to find; and then she whirled on her astonished brother.

"Harry Copley! You answered her real

mean! You go upstairs and apologize quick! And then you beat it, and change your clothes, and get to work. I'll help her. We're going to work *together* after this, she and I"; and, seizing a large slice of gingerbread in her passing, she flew up the stairs to find her sister.

5

They appeared in the doorway suddenly after a sound like locomotives rushing up the stairs, and surrounded her where she sat after one astonished pause at the doorway, staring around the unfamiliar apartment. They smothered her with hugs and kisses, and demanded to know how she got so much done, and what she wanted of them anyway; and they smeared her with gingerbread, and made her glad; and then as suddenly Harry disappeared with the floating explanation trailing back after him:

"Oh, gee! I gotta beat it."

A few rustling movements in his own little closet of a room, and he was back attired in an old Boy Scout uniform, and cramming down the last bite of his gingerbread.

"Anything I can do before I go? Oh, here!" as he saw his sisters about to put the bed together. "That won't take a second! Say, you girls don't know how to do that. Lemme."

And, surprising to state, he pushed them aside, and whacked the bed together in no time, slatted on the mattress with his sturdy young arms and was gone down through the dining-room and out into the street with another huge slice of ginger-bread in his hands.

Cornelia straightened her tired shoulders, and looked at the subdued bed wonderingly. How handily he had done it! How strong he was! It was amazing.

Louise stood looking about with shining eyes.

"Say, Nellie, it looks lovely here, so clean and nice. I never thought it could be done, it looked so awful! I wanted to do something, and I know mother felt fierce about not fixing his room before she left; but I just couldn't get time."

"Of course you couldn't, dear!" said Cornelia, suddenly realizing how wise and brave this little sister had been. "You've been wonderful to do anything. Why didn't they send for me before, Louie? Tell me, how long had you been in this house before mother was taken sick?"

"Why, only a day. She fainted, you know, trying to carry that marble bureau-top upstairs, and fell down."

"Oh! My dear!"

The two sisters stood with their arms about each other, mingling their tears for a moment; and somehow, as she stood there, Cornelia felt as if the years melted away, the college years while she had been absent, and brought her back heart and soul to her home and her loved ones again.

"But Louie, dear, what has become of the best furniture? Did they have to rent the old house furnished? I can't find mother's mahogany, or the parlor things, anything but the piano."

The color rolled up into the little girl's face, and she dropped her eyes. "Oh, no, Nellie; they went long ago," she said, "before we even moved to the State Street house."

"The State Street house?"

"Why, yes, father sold the Glenside house just after you went to college. You knew that, didn't you? And then we moved to an old yellow house farther toward the city. But it was pulled down to make room for a factory; and I was glad, for it was horrid, and a long walk to school. And then we went to a brick row down near the factory, and it was convenient for father, but —"

"Factory? Father? What do you mean, dear? Has father gone into business for himself? He was a bookkeeper at Dudley and Warner's when I left."

"Oh, but he lost that a long, long time ago, after he was sick so long."

"Father sick? Louie! And I not told?"

"Why, I didn't know they hadn't told you.

Maybe mother wouldn't like it —"

"Tell me everything, dear. How long was father sick?"

"About a year. He lost his position, and then wasn't able to do anything for ever so long; and, when he got out of the hospital, he hunted and hunted, and there wasn't anything for him. He got one good job; but they said he had to dress better, and he lost that."

Cornelia sank down on the floor again, and buried her face in her hands.

"O Louie! And I was wearing nice clothes, and doing nothing to help! Oh, why didn't mother let me know?"

"Oh, mother kept saying she thought she could manage and it was father's dream you should get your education," quoted the little girl with dreamy eyes and the memory of many sacrifices sweetly upon her.

"Go on, Louie; what next?"

"Oh, nothing much. Mother sold the furniture to an 'antique' woman that was hunting old things; and that paid for father's medicine, and they said they wouldn't touch the money they had put in the bank for your college; and then father got the place at the factory. It's kind of hard work, I guess; but it's good pay, and father thought he'd manage to let you finish; only mother gave out, and then everything went to pieces."

The small, red lips puckered bravely, and suddenly the child threw her arms around her sister's neck, and cried out, sobbing, "Oh, I'm so glad you've come!" and Cornelia wrapped her close to her heart.

Into the midst of this touching scene there stole a sweetly pungent odor of meat boiling dry, and suddenly Cornelia and Louise smelled it at the same instant, and flew for the stairs.

"I guess it's not really burned yet," said wise Louise. "It doesn't smell that way," comfortingly. "My, it makes me hungry!"

"And oh, my bread!" exclaimed Cornelia as she rounded the top of the next flight. "It ought to go into the oven. It will get too light." They rescued the meat not at all hurt but just lusciously browned and most appetizing; and then they put the bread into the oven and turned their attention to potatoes and waffles.

"I'm going to make some maple-syrup," said Cornelia; "it's better home-made. I bought a bottle of mapleine this morning. We used to make maple fudge with it, and it's good."

"Isn't this great?" exclaimed the little girl, watching the bubbling sugar and water. "Won't father be glad?"

"But, Louie, where is Carey?" asked Cornelia suddenly.

The little girl's face grew dark.

"He's off!" she said shortly. "I guess he didn't come home at all last night. Father worries a lot about him, and mother did too; but he's been worse since mother was sick. He hardly ever comes in till after midnight, and then he smokes and smokes. Oh, it makes me sick! I told Harry if he grew up that way I'd never speak to him. And Harry says, if he ever does, he gives me leave to turn him down. Oh, Carey acts like a nut! I don't see how he can, when he knows how father has to work, and everything. He just won't get a position anywhere. He wants to have a good time. He plays ball, and he rides around in a rich fellow's car, and he has a girl! Oh, he's the *limit*."

Cornelia felt her heart sinking.

"What kind of a girl, Louie?"

"Oh, a girl with flour on her face, and an awful tight skirt; and when she goes out evenings, she wears her back bare way down almost to her waist. I saw her in a concert at our church, and she was dressed that way there; and folks were all looking at her, and saying it wasn't nice. She dances, too, and kicks, with lots of skirts and ruffles and things, made of chiffon; and she makes eyes at boys; and I know a girl at school that says she saw her smoking cigarettes at a restaurant once. You see it isn't much use to fix up Carey's room when he does things like that. He doesn't deserve it."

Cornelia looked aghast.

"Oh, but we must, Louie! We must all the more then. And perhaps the girl isn't so bad if we knew her, and — and tried to help her. Some girls are awfully silly at a certain age, dear."

"Well, you oughtta see her. Harry knows, and he thinks she's the limit. He says the boys all talk about her. She paints her face, too, and wears big black earrings down on her shoulders sometimes, and she wears her hair just like the pictures of the devil!"

Cornelia had to laugh at the earnest, fierce little face; and the laugh broke the tension somewhat.

"Well, dearie, we'll have to find a way to coax Carey back to us," she said soothingly, even while her heart was sinking. "He's our brother, you know; and we love him, and it would break mother's heart."

"Oh, I know," sighed the little girl. "I've tried to think of something; but we're so poor, and this house is dreadful. Of course, it's a lot better than State Street, though," she said, brightening.

"It is?" Cornelia's voice conveyed dismay.

"Oh yes," said Louise, not noticing her sister's face. "We hadn't any side windows at all there; the houses were close up, and there were very unpleasant people all around. It wasn't at all a good neighborhood. Carey hated it. He wouldn't come home for days and days. He said it wasn't fit for pigs."

"Where did he go? Where has he gone now, do you suppose?"

"Oh, off with the boys somewhere. Sometimes to their houses. Sometimes they take trips around. One of them has a car. His father's rich. But I don't like him. His name's Brand Barlock. He drives wherever he likes. They went to Washington once, and were gone a week. Mother never slept a wink those nights, just sat at the front window and watched after we went to bed. I know, for I woke up and found her so several times. He might've gone to Baltimore now. There's a game down that way sometime soon. I guess it was last night. Harry heard 'em talking about it. They go with the gang of fellows that used to play on our high school team when Carey was in school."

"School?" Cornelia caught at the word

hopefully. "Perhaps it's only fun, then, Louie. Maybe, it's nothing really bad."

"No. They're pretty tough," sighed the wise child. "Harry knows. He hears the boys talk."

"Well, dear, we'll have to forget it now, anyway, and get to work. We must fix Carey's room so he can sleep there tonight if he does come back, and we must have supper ready when father gets home."

The child brightened. "Won't they be surprised?" she said with a happy light in her eyes. "What do you want me to do? Shall I peel the potatoes?"

"Yes, do, and have plenty. We'll mash them, shall we? I found the potato-masher in the bottom of a barrel in the parlor; so I don't believe you've been using it lately."

"That's right. We had all we could do to bake them or boil them whole," said Louise. "You bake the bread, and I'll get the potatoes on. Then we'll have plenty of time to put those things away upstairs and make Carey's bed."

"Are there any clean sheets? I didn't know where to look."

"No, there's only one pair, and I kept them for you next week."

"We can't keep anything for me, duckie dear," said Cornelia, laughing. "Carey's got to have clean sheets this very night. I have a hunch he's coming home, and I want that room to be ready. That's the first step in getting him back to us, you know."

"Oh, well, all right," said the little sister. "They are in the lower drawer of our bureau. How good that bread smells! My, it was nice of you to make it! And how dear the dining-room table looks with that little flower in the middle. Some girls' sisters would have thought that was unnecessary. They would have made us wait for pretty things. But you didn't, did you? I guess that's what makes you an interior decorator, isn't it? Father and mother are awfully proud of you. They talked about it most every night before Carey got to going away, how you would be a great artist some day, and all that; and my! it most killed them to have to call you home."

Louise chattered on, revealing many a household tragedy, until Cornelia was cut to the heart and wanted to drop down and cry; only she had too much at stake to give up now.

They went upstairs presently with the clean sheets, and the blankets that had almost miraculously got themselves dry owing to a bright sun and a strong west wind that had arrived soon after they were put out;

and they had a beautiful time making that bed. Carey wouldn't know himself in such a bed. Then they hunted out a bureau-scarf, and they went through the tousled drawers of the chiffonier and bureau, and put things to rights, laying out a pile of things that needed mending or washing, and making the room look cheery and bright.

"It ought to have something pretty like a flower here, too," sighed Louise, taking a final glance around as Cornelia folded the old eider-down quilt in a self-respecting puff at the foot of the bed, and gave another pat to the clean white pillow. "I know!" said Louise suddenly flitting downstairs to her own room and hurrying back again with a small oval easel picture of her mother, dusting it carefully with her handkerchief as she came. "There! Won't that look better?"

"Indeed it will," said her sister, her eyes filling with tears as she looked into the loving eyes of the dear mother from whom she had been separated so long; "and perhaps it will do Carey good to look into his mother's eyes when he comes home; who knows?"

So they went down together to put the finishing touches to the supper and to talk of many things. Louise even got around to the play and the costume she was going to try to make; and Cornelia delighted her heart by saying she was sure she had just the very costume in her trunk, one that she wore in a college play herself, and she would help her make it over to fit.

Everything was ready for supper at last, and it was time within three minutes for father's car to arrive. Harry would likely meet him at the corner and come with him. Cornelia was taking up the pot-roast, and telling Louise about beating the mashed potatoes to make them lighter. The waffle-iron had been found under the piano-stool in the parlor, and was sizzling hot and well greased awaiting the fluffy batter. The hot maple syrup was on the table and everything exactly ready. Suddenly they heard a noisy automobile thunder up to the front of the house and pause, a clatter of voices, and the car thundered on again. Footsteps up the walk, and the front door banged open and shut; feet stamped up the stairs, while a faint breath of cigarette smoke trailed out and penetrated into the kitchen to mingle with the fragrance of the dinner. The two cooks stopped, and looked at each other understandingly.

"He's come," said the eyes of the little sister.

"We must make him very welcome," answered the eyes of the big sister, so tired she could hardly hold her young shoulders straight.

"Maybe he won't stay," whispered Louise softly a minute later. "Sometimes he doesn't; he might have a date."

"Here's hoping," said Cornelia gayly, as she dabbed the batter into the irons for the first waffle. "You'll have to contrive to catch him if he tries to go away, Lou."

"I wonder what he thinks of his room," giggled the little sister. "I guess maybe he thought he'd made a mistake and got into the wrong house."

It was all very still upstairs. There were not even any footsteps going around, not for what seemed like several minutes; then slowly the footsteps came down the stairs again, hesitating, paused at the second flight, and came on until they reached the open dining-room door.

Carey stood there gazing at the table as Louise came in bearing the dish of potatoes, and Cornelia followed her with the platter of meat, both earnestly intent and flushed with their work; and just at that moment, before the girls had looked up, the front door opened, and in came the father, with Harry whistling gayly behind him.

"Oh, gee!" he cried, stopping his whistling. "Don't that supper smell good? Here's hoping there's plenty of it."

It was at that instant that Cornelia looked up, and her eyes met the eyes of her handsome, reckless-looking brother, astonishment, bewilderment, shame, delight, and embarrassment struggling in his face.

6

"Nell!"

There was genuine delight in the boy's tone as he came forward to greet her, shyly, perhaps, and with a bit of shamed hesitancy because he could not but remember that the family had probably told her all about him, and she would of course disapprove of him as much as they did.

But Cornelia, with the steaming gravy-boat in one hand and a pile of hot plates in the other, turned a warm, rosy cheek up to him, her eyes still intent on putting down the dishes without spilling the treacherous gravy on the clean tablecloth.

"It's great to see you again, Carey," she said heartily, trying to make the situation as casual as possible. "Sorry to seem brief; but I have something luscious on the stove, and I'm afraid it'll burn. Sit down quick, won't you? — and be ready to eat it while it's hot. We'll talk afterward. I want to have a good look at you and see if you've grown more than I have."

Her voice trailed off into the kitchen cheerily, and not in the least as though she had been palpitating between hope and fear about him all the afternoon and working herself to a frazzle getting his room ready.

She returned almost immediately with the first plate of golden-brown waffles, and stole a furtive glance at him from the kitchen doorway. He had not yet seated himself, although the others were bustling joyously and noisily into their chairs. He was still standing thoughtfully, staring around the dining-room and at the table. As she approached, he gave her a furtive, sweeping look, then dropped his lashes and slid into his chair, a half-frown beginning to grow on his brow. He looked as if he were expecting the next question to be: "Why weren't you here last night? Where were you? Don't you know you were rude?" but none of those questions were voiced. His father did clear his throat and glance up at him gravely; but Louise with quick instinct began to chatter about the syrup that Cornelia had made. His attention was turned aside, and the tense expression of his face relaxed as he looked about the pleasant table and noticed the happy faces.

"It hasn't looked this way since your mother went away," said the father with a deep sigh. "How good that bread looks! Real home-made bread again! What a difference that makes!" and he reached out, and took a slice as if it were something merely to look at and feel.

"I'll say! That looks rare!" Carey volunteered, taking a slice himself and passing the plate. "Some smell, this dinner, what?" he added, drawing in a long, deep breath. "Seems like living again."

His father's tired eyes rested on him sadly, contemplatively. He opened his lips to speak; but Cornelia slid into her chair, and said, "Now, father, we're ready"; and he bowed his head and murmured a low, sad little grace. So Carey was saved again from a much-deserved reproof. Cornelia couldn't help being glad; and Louise looked at her with a knowing gleam in her eye as she raised her head, and broke into a brilliant smile. Louise had bitter knowledge of what it meant to have Carey reproved at a meal. There was always a scene, ending with no Carey.

"Yes, and," began Louise swiftly as soon as the "Amen" was concluded, "there's waffles *and* gingerbread! Think of that! And Nellie had time to fix up your bedroom, Kay. Did you go up there?"

"I should say I did! Nell, you're a peach! I never meant to have it looking that way when you came home. I sure am ashamed you had to dig that stuff all out. Some junk I had there. I meant to take a day off and clean house pretty soon."

"Well, now you can help me with some of the other rooms, instead," his sister replied, smiling, and hastened back to turn her waffles.

"I sure will!" said Carey heartily. "When do you want me? To-morrow morning? Nothing in the way of my working all day if you say the word. We used to make a pretty good team, Nell, you and I. Think we could accomplish a lot in a day."

"Yes, Carey hasn't any job to hinder him doing what he pleases," put in Harry with a bitter young sneer. "I'd uv had it all done by myself long ago if I hadn't had a job after school!"

"Yes, you young brag!" began Carey with a deep scowl. "You think you're it and *then* some!"

"It would seem as if you might have given a little time, Carey," began his father almost petulantly, with a look about his mouth of restraining less mild things that he might have said.

Louise looked apprehensively at her sister.

"Oh, well," put in Cornelia quickly, "you couldn't be expected to know what to do, any of you, till your big sister got home. You've all done wonderfully well, I think, to get as much done as you have; and I only blame you, everyone of you, especially father dear, for not sending for me sooner. It was really — well, criminal, you know, Daddy, to keep me in expensive luxury and ignorance that way. But I'm not going to scold you here before folks. We'll have that out after they've all gone to bed, won't we? We're going to have nothing but pleasant sayings at this supper table. It's a kind of reunion, you know, after so many years. Just think; we haven't all been together for — how long is it? — four years? Doesn't that seem really awful? When I think of it, I realize how terribly selfish I have been. I didn't realize it in college because I was having such a good time, but I have been selfish and lazy and absolutely thoughtless. I hope you'll all forgive me."

Carey lifted wondering eyes, and his scowl faded while he studied his pretty sister's guileless face thoughtfully. The attention was diverted from him, and his anger was cooling; but somehow he began to feel deep in his soul that it was really he that had been selfish. All their scolding and nagging hadn't made him in the least conscious of it; but this new, old, dear, pretty sister taking the blame on herself seemed to throw a new light on his own doings. Of course it was merely momentary, and made no very deep impression; but still the idea had come, and would never be quite driven away again.

The supper was a success from every point of view. The pot-roast was as tender as cheese; the mashed potatoes melted under the gravy like snow before the summer sun, and were enjoyed with audible praise; and the waffles sizzled and baked and disappeared, and more took their places, until at last the batter was all gone.

"Well, I couldn't hold another one," said Carcy, "but they certainly were jim-dandies. Say, you haven't forgotten how to cook, Nell!" and he cast a look of deep admiration toward his sister.

Cornelia, so tired she could hardly get up out of her chair after she dropped into it, lifted a bravely smiling face, and realized that she had scored a point. Carey had liked the supper and was over his grouch. The first night had been ushered in greatly. She was just wondering whether she dared suggest that he help wash the dishes when he suddenly jerked out his watch, glanced at it, and shoved his chair back noisily.

"Gee! I've gotta beat it," he said hurriedly as he strode to the hall door. "I've gotta date!" and before the family had drawn the one quick, startled, aghast breath of disappointment and tried to think of some way to detain him, or find out where he was going, or when he was coming back, he had slammed the front door behind him.

The father had an ashen-gray, helpless look; Louise's mouth drooped at the corners, and there were tears in her eyes as she held up her head bravely and carried a pile of plates out to the kitchen, while Harry with an ugly sneer on his young lips shoved his chair back, noisily murmuring: "Aw, gee! Gotta date! Always gotta date! When I grow up, I'll see if I always have to have a date!" Then he snatched an armful of dishes, and strode to the kitchen, grumbling in an undertone all the way.

Cornelia cast a quick, apprehensive look at her father, and said cheerily:

"Oh, never mind. Of course young men have dates; and when you've promised, you know it isn't easy to change. Come, let's get these dishes out of the way quickly; and then we can sit down and talk. It's great to all be together again, isn't it? Father, dear, how long do you suppose it will be before mother is well? Have you had a letter to-day?"

The father beamed at her again, and, putting his hand in his pocket, drew out an official-looking envelope.

"Yes," he said wistfully; "that is, a note from the nurse with the report. Of course she is not allowed to write. She just sends her love, that's all, and says she's getting well as fast as possible. She seems to be gaining a little. Here's the report."

They all gathered around it, studying the little white, mysterious paper that was to tell them how the dear mother was getting on, and then turned away little wiser. Suddenly Harry, noticing the sag of Cornelia's shoulder as she stood holding on to the back of her father's chair, turned with a swift motion, and gathered her into his strong young arms like a bear. Before she could protest he bore her over to the old, lumpy couch, where he deposited her with a gruff gentleness.

"There you are!" he puffed commandingly. "You lie there, and Lou and I will do the dishes. You're all in, and you don't know enough to know it."

"Nonsense!" said Cornelia, laughing and trying to rise. "I'm used to playing basketball and hockey, and doing all sorts of stunts. It won't hurt me to get a little tired. I'm going to wash those dishes, and you can wipe them."

"No, you're not. I say she's not, Lou, is

101

she?" and he held her down with his rough young force.

"Certainly not," said Louise grown-uply appearing with her hands full of knives and forks. "It's our turn now. She thinks we don't know how to wash dishes. Harry Copley, you just oughtta see all she's done by herself upstairs, cleaning Carey's room, and washing blankets, and all, besides making bread and gingerbread and everything. Come on upstairs and see. No, we won't go yet till the dishes are done. 'Cause Nellie would work while we were gone. Daddy, you just sit there and talk to her, and don't let her get up while we clean up. Then we'll take you upstairs."

So Cornelia lay still at last on the lumpy couch, and rested, realizing that she was "all in," and feeling well repaid for her hard work by the loving light in the children's eyes and her father's tender glance.

The thought of Carey hung in the back of her mind, and troubled her now and then; but she remembered that he had promised to help her in the morning, and somehow that comforted her. She succeeded in keeping the rest of the family so interested in her tales of college life that they did not remember their troubles.

When the dishes were done, Cornelia told

Louise how to set some buckwheat cakes for morning.

"I saw they were selling buckwheat cheap in the store," she explained; "and so I got some. It will soon be too warm to eat buckwheat cakes, and I'm just crazy to taste them again. I haven't had a decent one since I left home."

"Carey just loves 'em," said Louise thoughtfully.

"Aw, he won't get up in time to get any," sneered Harry.

"He might if he knew we were going to have 'em," said Louise.

"Let's write him a note, and leave it up on his bureau," said Cornelia brightly. "That'll be fun. Let's make it in poetry. Where's a pencil and a big piece of paper?"

"I've got some colored crayons," suggested Harry.

So Cornelia scribbled a minute, and produced the following, which Harry proudly copied in large illuminated letters on a piece of wrapping paper:

"The Copleys' breakfast's buckwheat cakes,
With maple syrup too;
They're light and tender, sweet and brown,
The kind you needn't chew.

So, Carey, rise at early dawn,
 And put your vesture on,
And come to breakfast in good time,
 Or they will all be gone!"

Louise danced up and down as she read it.

"O Nellie, Nellie, that's real poetry!" she declared, "and aren't we having a good time?"

"I should say we were!" declared Harry, beginning to make a large flourishing capital T with green and brown crayons. "Talk about dates!" contemptuously. "If a fella has got a good home, he oughtta stay in it!"

"O Nellie, it's so good to have you home!" sighed Louise suddenly snuggling down into her sister's tired arms. "I'm so glad your college is done!"

And all at once Cornelia realized that she too was glad. Here had she been nearly all this afternoon and evening, having a first-rate, beautiful time getting tired with hard work, but enjoying it just as much as if she had been working over the junior play. It came to her with a sudden start that just at this hour they were having one of the almost last rehearsals — without her! For a second it gave her a pang, and then she realized that she really and truly was just as much interested in getting Carey's room fixed up, and making a cheerful, beautiful living room some day for the family to gather in, and having good times to win back Carey, as ever she had been in making costumes for the girls and making the play a success by means of her delightful scenery. For was she not, after all, about to plan the scenery for the play of life in the Copley family? Who should say but there would be as much tragedy and comedy and romance in the Copley play as ever there had been at Dwight Hall? Well, time would tell, and somehow the last twenty-four hours had put her on a different plane, and enabled her to look down at her college life from a new angle. What had done it? Her knowledge of how her father and mother had struggled and sacrificed? The dearness of her young brother and sister in their sturdy, honest desire to be helpful and to love her and look up to her? Or was it her longing to hold and help the young brother who had been her chum and companion in the days before she had gone to college? At least, she could truly say in her heart that she was glad she was here tonight, and she was not nearly so dismayed at the dreary house and the sordid surroundings as she had been twenty-four hours before; for now she knew that it only spelled her opportunity, as that lovely lady on the train had suggested, and she was eager to be up and at it in the morning.

They all went up together to the third story presently, and stood in the swept and garnished front room, Mr. Copley going over to the bureau and touching with a tender movement of caress the picture of his wife that stood there and then looking toward the empty white bed with a wistful anxiety. Cornelia could almost read the words of his heart, and into her own there entered the burden of her brother, and she knew she would never rest in her own selfish ease again until she felt sure that Carey was all right.

She crept into bed beside Louise at last, almost too weary to pull up the covers; and let the little girl snuggle thankfully into her arms.

"You're almost — almost like my dear muvver," murmured Louise sleepily, nosing into her neck and settling down on her sister's arm with a sigh of content; and Cornelia thought how sweet it was to have a little sister to love and be loved by, and wondered how it was that she had dreaded having her for a roommate.

Then, too weary to think any longer, she fell asleep.

Hours afterward, it seemed, she was awakened by a stumbling footstep up the stairs, halting and fumbling about in the hall, and then going on, stumbling again, up to the third story. She heard a low muttering, too, and it frightened her. Had Carey been drinking? A strange, rank smell of cigarette smoke — and more — drifted into the door which had been left ajar; and a cold frenzy took hold of her heart. Carey had been drinking! She felt sure. A moment more, and she heard light footsteps from the little hall bedroom above, and Harry's indignant young voice remonstrating, the sounds of a brief struggle, the thud of a heavy body on the bedsprings above, and then Harry's voice coming clearly down the stairs in disgust as he pattered back to his hard little cot.

"Ow! You great big fish, you! You oughtta be ashamed of yourself!"

It was hours after that that Cornelia finally fell asleep again, and during those hours she found herself praying involuntarily, praying and pleading: "O God, help me to help Carey. Don't let Carey be a drunkard. Don't let him be wild and bad! Help him to want to be good and right. Help him to be a man. O God, help me to do something about it!"

The first thing of which Cornelia was conscious in the morning was a scuffle overhead. Louise was sitting up, rubbing her eyes and looking apprehensively toward the ceiling; and the sounds grew louder and more vigorous, with now and then a heavy thud, like a booted foot dropping inertly to the floor.

Cornelia sat up also, and listened.

"It's Harry, trying to wake Carey up!" whispered Louise knowingly. "Harry's mad. I guess Carey came in late again, and didn't undress. He does that way sometimes when he's tired."

"Yes?" said Cornelia with a shiver of understanding. "Yes, I heard him come in."

"Oh, did you?" Louise turned a searching glance on her sister, and then looked away with a sober little sigh. "Something ought to be done about that kid before mother gets home," she said maturely. "It'll kill mother."

"Something shall be done. There! don't look so sorrowful, dear. Carey is young, and I'm sure we can do something if we all try with all our souls. I'm so glad I came home. Mother ought not to have been bearing that alone. Come, let's get up." She snatched her blue kimono, and dashed to the foot of the stairs.

"Harry! Harry!" she called softly. "Never mind. Let him sleep."

Harry appeared angrily at the head of the stairs, his own costume only half completed, his hair sticking all ways.

"Great, lazy boob!" he was saying. "He never undressed at all!"

"Hush, dear! Don't wake him. It will be better in every way if he gets his sleep out."

"But he hasn't seen the poetry at all," wailed the disappointed boy. "I held it in front of his face, and he wouldn't open his eyes. I washed his face for him, too; and he wouldn't get up."

"Well, never mind, dear; let him alone. I'll save him some cakes after you are gone."

"Yes, pet him up, the great, lazy baby! That's what's the matter with him; he's too big a baby, selfish, *selfish!* That's what he is."

"Sh-sh, dear! Never mind! You can't do anything when a person is as sleepy as that, and it's no use trying. Come. Let's have breakfast. I'll be down as soon as you will"; and Cornelia smiled brightly above her aching heart, and hurried into her own clothes.

"Cakes! Cakes!" said Louise happily.

"Won't it be great? Oh, I just can hardly wait for them. I'm sorry Carey isn't awake."

"Never mind, dear; it will all come out straight pretty soon, and we mustn't expect to succeed right away."

So she cheered them on their way, and made the morning meal a success, steadily keeping her father's thoughts from the absent boy upstairs until he had to run to catch his car. She put up a delightful lunch for Harry and Louise, with dates and cheese in some of the sandwiches and nuts and lettuce in others, and a big piece of gingerbread and an orange apiece.

"It's just like having mother again," said Louise fervently as she kissed her sister good-bye and ran to catch Harry, who was already half-way to the corner.

Cornelia held the thought of those words in her heart, and cherished them over against the words she had heard from her young brother and sister the day before; and it comforted her. She watched them until they were out of sight, and then with a sigh climbed the stairs to Carey's room. But Carey was locked in heavy slumber, with a flushed face and heavy breathing. She pinned up a paper to keep out the light, threw the eider-down quilt over him, and opened the window wide. Then she tiptoed

110

away and left him. There was no use doing anything now. The fumes of liquor were still about him, and the heavy breath of cigarettes. She felt a deep horror and disgust in her soul as she thought about her brother, and tried to work out a plan for saving him as she went about clearing off the breakfast table and washing the dishes.

There was plenty of meat for dinner that night, and lots of gravy left. She would need to think only about vegetables and a dessert. Chocolate blanc-mange would be good. She would make it at once and set it on the ice. Then, when the milkman came, she must remember to get a small bottle of cream to eat with it. By and by she would run down to the store and get a few carrots and a stalk of celery, and stew them together. That made a good combination. No, that wouldn't do, either, too much sweetness, carrots and blanc-mange. A can of tomatoes cooked with two onions and a little celery would be better. That she could put on in the middle of the afternoon. There was plenty of pancake batter left for Carey and herself for lunch. She fixed the griddle far back on the range, and set the batter in the refrigerator. Then she went with swift steps to the disordered front room.

She went to work unpacking the boxes

and setting things in order in the hall and the dining-room. She discovered many needed kitchen utensils and some more dishes, and these she washed and put away. It was discouraging work, and somehow she did not seem to have accomplished much when at eleven o'clock she straightened up from a deep packing-box from which she had removed the last article, and looked about her. Piles of things everywhere, and not a spot to walk anywhere! When would she ever get done? A great weariness from her overwork of the day before was upon her, and she wanted to sit down in the midst of the heaps and cry. It was just then in her weakness that the thought of college came upon her, college with its clean orderliness, its regular places for things, its delightful circle of companions, its interesting work, never any burden or hurry or worry.

Just at this hour the classes were filing into the halls and going to new work. If she were back there, she would be entering her psychology class, and looking at the blackboard for the announcement of the day's work assigned to each member of the class. Instead of that here she was in the midst of an unending task, hopeless and weary and frightfully discouraged. A tear of self-pity began to steal out, and she might have been weeping in a minute more if she had not been suddenly arrested in her thoughts by sounds overhead, far away and slight, but nevertheless unmistakable.

She wiped her eyes, and went out into the hall, softly listening. Yes, undoubtedly Carey had waked up at last. She could hear the bedsprings rattle, and hear his feet moving lightly on the bare floor, as if he might be sitting up with his elbows on his knees and his face in his hands. Her instinct told her that he would not be very happy when he awoke. She could fancy how disgusted he must be with himself; for Carey had a conscience, and he could not but know that what he was doing was wrong. She could remember how good and helpful a boy he used to be, always thoughtful for his mother. It did not seem possible that he had completely changed.

She could hear him moving slowly about now, a few steps and stopping a long time. Perhaps he had found the poetry on the bureau, although she reflected that it was altogether likely that Harry in his wrath might have cast it under the bed or anywhere it happened. Well, she would better be getting the griddle hot.

She hurried into the kitchen, and pulled the griddle forward over the fire, opened the draughts, and began to get the table in order for an early lunch. She glanced at the clock. It was half past eleven. She would have everything ready the minute he came down. She could still hear him stirring around. He had come down to the bathroom, and the sound of his razor-strop whirred faintly. Well, that was a good sign. He was going to fix up a little before coming down. She put the last touches to her table, set the plates to warm, put on the syrup, and made the coffee. Then she took a broom, and went back to the front room to wait until he came down.

Oh, that front room! It seemed more dreary than ever as she attempted to make a little path in the wilderness.

She was trying to drag a big packing-box out into the hall when Carey finally came down, looking wholly a gentleman except for a deep scowl on his brow. He came at once to her assistance, somewhat gruffly, it must be owned, but quite efficiently.

"What on earth are you trying to do, Nell?" he asked. "Don't you know that's too heavy for a girl to move? I told you I'd help. Why didn't you wait for me?"

Cornelia, feeling a strange excitement upon her, looked up brightly, and tried to ignore the fact that he ought to have come down several hours before.

"Well, there's so much to be done," she said. "I certainly am glad to see you, though. But suppose we have lunch first. I'm hungry as a bear, and see, it's five minutes to twelve. Can you eat now?"

"Oh, any time!" he said indifferently. "What is it you want done, anyway? This room's a mess. Some dump, the whole house! It makes me disgusted."

He stood with his hands in his pockets, surveying the desolate scene, and voicing Cornelia's own thoughts of a few moments before. But it was Cornelia's forte to rise to an occasion when every one else was disheartened. She put on a cheery smile.

"Just you wait, brother, till I get through. I've plans for that room, and it won't be so bad when it gets cleaned and fixed a little. Suppose you take those boxes down cellar, and those pictures and tubs, and the old trunk and chest out to the shed room beyond the kitchen, while I scramble some eggs and settle the coffee. Everything else is ready. Then after lunch we'll get to work. I shall need your help to turn the piano around and open those boxes of books. Why do you suppose they put the bookcase face against the wall, with the piano in front of it? Seems to me that was dumb."

115

"All movers are dumb!" declared Carey with a sweep of his arm, as if he would include the whole world. But he went to work vigorously, and carried out the things with a whirl, and Cornelia perceived she must rush to have a plate of cakes before he was done with his assigned task.

"Aw, gee! You saved me some cakes!" he said with a grin of delight when they sat down at the table. "I oughtta 've got up for breakfast. But I was all in. We took a joy ride last night down to Baltimore. I saw your poetry. It was great. Who wrote it? You, of course."

"We wanted you to be sure to get up, but of course you must have been sleepy riding all that way in the wind. It must have been great, though. It was full moon last night, wasn't it?" said his sister, ignoring the horror that the thought of the "joy ride" gave her.

"It sure was," said the boy, kindling at the memory. "The fellas put ether in the gas, and she certainly did hum. We just went whizzing. It was a jim-dandy car, twelve-cylinder, some chariot! B'longs to a fella named Brand Barlock. He's a prince, that boy is! Has thousands of dollars to spend as he pleases; and you'd never know he had a cent, he's so big-hearted. Love him like a brother. Why, he'd let me take that car anywhere, and never turn a hair; and it cost some money, that car did, this year's racing model! Gee, but she's a winner. Goes like a streak of greased lightning."

Cornelia suppressed her apprehension over the possibilities of accident both physical and financial, and bloomed with interest. Of what use would it be to reprove her brother for taking such chances? It would only make him angry, and turn him against her. She would see whether she could win him back to the old comradeship, and then there might come a time when her advice would reach him. At present it would be useless.

"It must be great to have a fine car," she said eagerly. "I love to ride. There were two or three girls at college who had cars, and used to take us out sometimes; but of course that didn't happen very often."

"I'll borrow Brand's car and take you sometime," he said eagerly. "He wouldn't mind."

"O Carey! No, you mustn't do that!" she cried in alarm, "at least" — as she saw his frown of displeasure — "not till I know him, you know. I shouldn't at all like to ride in a car whose owner I didn't know. You must bring him here when we get all fixed up, and I'll meet him. Then perhaps he'll ask

117

me to go along too sometime, although I'm not sure I'd like to go like a streak of lightning. Still, I've never tried it, and you know I never used to be afraid of things."

"Sure, you're all right, Nell. But I'd never bring Brand to this dump! He's a rich man's son, I tell you, and lives in a swell neighborhood."

"Doesn't he know where you live?"

Carey shrugged his shoulders.

"Oh, yes; he drives around, and honks the horn for me, and brings me home again; but I wouldn't ask him in —"

"Wait, I say, till we get it fixed up. You know I'm an interior decorator! Oh, I wish there was just a fireplace! It makes such a cozy, cheerful place."

"I could build one if I had the stuff," declared Carey, interested. "What kind do you want? But then, everything costs so darned much. If I only had a job!"

"Oh, you'll get a job, of course," said his sister sympathetically, trying to reconcile his troubled look with what the children had said about his indifference toward work. "Where did you work last?"

The color rolled in a slow, dull wave over Carey's restless young face; and a look of sullen hopelessness came into his handsome eyes.

"Oh, I haven't had anything regular since I left school. I — you see — that is — oh, hang it all! I can't get anything worth while. I've been doing some tinkering down at the garage. I could work steady there, but Dad makes it so hot for me when I do that I have to do it on the sly. He says it's just a lazy job, hanging round with the fellas getting rides. He don't know anything about it. It's real man's work, I tell you, hard work at that; and I'm learning all about machinery. Why, Nell, there isn't a fella at the garage can tell as quick as I can what's the matter with a car. Bob sends for me to find out after he's worked half a day, and I can tell right off the bat when I hear the engine go what's wrong."

Cornelia watched his eyes sparkle as he talked, and perceived that when he spoke of machinery he was in his element. He loved it. He loved it as she loved the idea of her chosen profession.

That being the case, he ought to be encouraged.

"Why, I should think it was a good thing to stick at it while you are looking around for something better," she said slowly, wondering whether her father would blame her for going against his advice; "I should think maybe it will prepare you for something else in the line of machinery. What is there big and really worth while that you'd like to get into if you could? Of course, you wouldn't want to be just a mender of cars all your life."

His face took on a firm, manly look, and his eyes grew alert and earnest.

"Of course not!" he said crisply. "Father thinks I would, and I can't make him see it any other way. He's just plain disappointed in me, that's all" — the young man's tone took on a bitter tinge, — "but I know it will be a step to something. Why, there's all sorts of big concerns now that make and sell machines; and if you understand all about machinery, you stand a better chance for getting in to be business manager some day. There's tanks, and oilwells, and tractors, and a lot of things. Of course I couldn't jump into a thing like that at the start. Dad thinks I could. He thinks if I had any pep at all I could just walk up to the president of some big concern, and say, 'Here I am; take me,' and he'd do it, just like that. But — for one thing, look at me! Do I look like a business man?" He stood back, and lifted his arms with a dramatic gesture, pointing toward his shabby raiment.

"And then another thing, I've got to get

experience first. If I only had a pull some-where — but —"

"I'll talk to father," said Cornelia sooth-ingly. She looked at him thoughtfully. "You ought to earn enough for a new suit right away, of course, and have it ready — keep it nice, I mean, so that, when a good op-portunity offers, you will be suitably dressed to apply for it. Suppose I talk to father; I'll do it to-night. Meantime, you help me here a day or two, and then you go back to that garage, and work for a week or two, and earn money enough for your suit and what other things you need, and keep your eye open for something better all the while."

"That's the talk!" said Carey joyfully. "Now you're shouting! You put some heart in a fella. Gee, I'm glad you're home. It's been awful without mother. It was bad enough the last few months when she was sick, but it was some dump when she went away entirely."

"Yes, I know," said the sister sympatheti-cally, reflecting that it would be wiser not to suggest that he might have helped to make the mother sick by his careless life. "Well, we must get things fixed up nice and pleasant for her when she gets back, and try to keep her well and happy the rest of her life."

"That's right!" said Carey with a sudden deep note in his voice that came from the heart, and gave Cornelia a bit of encouragement.

"I think I could clean that suit up a little for you, and make it look better —"

Carey looked down at himself doubtfully.

"It's pretty bad," he said; "and it costs a lot to have it cleaned and pressed. I tried last week to do something, but we couldn't find the irons."

"I found them yesterday," said Cornelia brightly. "We'll see what we can do this evening if you can be at home."

"Oh, this evening!" said Carey doubtfully.

"Yes, we can't spare the time till then, because this house has got to be put in order." She gave him a swift anxious glance and a winning smile. "If you have another engagement, break it for once. There's so much to be done, dear, and we do need you terribly. Tell that Brand friend of yours that you're busy for a few days, and you'll make it up by inviting him to a fudge party when we get settled."

"Oh! Gee! Could we?" said Carey half doubtful, half pleased. "Well, all right! I'll do my best. Now, what do you want done with this old junk?"

"Those go in the back shed, over by the

tubs. Take that out in the yard and burn it, and this pile goes upstairs. Just put it in the upper hall, and I'll attend to it later. My! What a difference it makes to get a little space clear!"

They worked steadily all the afternoon, Carey proving himself as willing as herself.

They washed the windows and the floor, and swept down the walls of parlor and hall.

"Ugly old wall-paper!" said Cornelia, eyeing it spitefully. "That's got to come off if I have to do it myself and have bare walls."

"Why, that's easy!" said Carey. "Give me an old rag!" and he began to slop the water on and scrape with an old caseknife.

"Well, that's delightful!" said Cornelia with relief. "I didn't know it would be so easy; we'll do a little at a time until it is done, and then we'll either paper it ourselves or paint it. I do wish we could manage to get a fireplace."

"Well, maybe we can find some stone cheap where they're hauling it away. Harry'll know some place likely; he gets around with that grocery wagon. You know I helped a stone-mason last summer for a while. Mother hated it, though, so I quit; but I learned a lot about mixing cement and how to lay it on. I know about the draughts too. I bet I could make as good a fireplace as the next one. Gee! I wish I knew where to get some stone or brick."

"Stone would be best," said Cornelia; "it would make a lovely chimney mantel, but I suppose you couldn't be so elaborate as making a mantel!"

"Sure, I could! But it would take some stone to do all that."

"I know where there's a lot of stone!" They turned around surprised and there stood Harry in the doorway, with Louise just behind him, looking in with delighted faces at the newly cleaned room and the hard-working elder brother.

"Where?" Carey wheeled around eagerly.

"Down on the dump. It was brought there yesterday, a whole lot of it, several cartloads; came from a place where they have been taking down an old wall, and they had no place to put it, I guess. Anyhow, it's there."

"I'll go see if there's enough," said Carey, flashing out of the door and up the street.

He was back in a minute with a big stone in his hand.

"It's just cellar stone," he said deprecatingly; "but there's plenty."

"Humph!" said Louise maturely. "Well, I never thought I'd be glad I lived near that old dump! Do you mean we're going to have a real fireplace, Carey?"

"That's the contract, kid, and I guess I can make good. But how are we going to get that stone here?"

"There's the express-wagon," said Louise thoughtfully. "Harry has to work, but I could haul some."

"You!" said Carey contemptuously; "do you suppose I'd let a *girl* haul stone for me? No, I'll go borrow a truck. I know a fella has one, and it's almost quitting time. I know he'll lend it to me; and, if he docs, I'll work until I get those stones all landed, or like as not somebody else will get their eye on them. Stones like that cost a lot nowadays, even if they are only cellar stones."

"Cellar stones are lovely," said Cornelia delightedly. "They have a lot of iron in them, and make very artistic houses. I heard a big architect say that once in a lecture at college."

"Well, there's nothing like being satisfied with what you have to have," said Carey. "Here, Nell, you look out for the rest of that basc-board; I'm off to borrow a truck. Next time you see me I'll be riding a load of stone!"

"I'll come down at six o'clock and help you load!" shouted Harry from the third story, where he was rapidly changing into his working-clothes.

"All right, kid; that's the stuff. Nell will save us some supper, and we'll work till dark."

"It won't be dark," said Louise sagely. "It's moonlight tonight."

"That's right too," said Carey as he seized his hat and dashed out of the house.

 **8**

"You've got him to work!" said Louise joyously, looking at her sister with shining eyes.

"I didn't do it," said Cornelia, smiling. "He came of his own accord, and seems awfully interested."

"Well, it's because you're here, of course; that makes all the difference in the world."

"Thank you, Louie," said her sister, stooping to kiss the warm cheek lovingly.

"Now," said Louise pulling off her clean middy blouse, and starting upstairs, "what do you want me to do first?"

"Well, I thought maybe you'd like to dust these books and put them in the bookcase, dear; then they'll be out of our way."

Louise was rapidly buttoning herself into her old gingham work-dress when Cornelia came hurriedly from the kitchen and called up the stairs, a note of dismay in her voice:

"Louie, I don't suppose you happen to know who owns this house, do you? It's just occurred to me we'll have to ask permission to build a fireplace, and that may upset the whole thing. Maybe the owner won't want an amateur to build a fireplace in his house."

"Oh, that's all right," shouted Louise

127

happily, appearing at the stair-head. "Father owns it. It was the only thing he had left after he lost his money."

"Father owns it?" said Cornelia incredulously. "How strange! A house like this! When did he buy it?"

"He didn't buy it. He signed a note for a poor man; and then the man died, and never paid the money, and father had to take the house."

"Oh!" said Cornelia thoughtfully, seeing more tragedy in the family history, and feeling a sudden great tenderness for the father who had borne so many disappointments and yet kept sweet and strong. "Well, then, anyhow we can do as we please with it," she added happily. "I'm awfully glad. I guess we shan't have to ask permission. Father'll like it all right."

"Well, I rather guess he will, especially if it keeps Carey busy a little while," said Louise.

They worked rapidly and happily together, and soon the books were in orderly rows in the bookcase.

Cornelia had found a bundle of old curtains in one of the boxes; and now she brought them out, and began to measure the windows.

"The lace curtains all wore out, and

mother threw them away," volunteered Louise sadly.

"Never mind; I've found a lot of pretty good scrim ones here, and I'm going to wash them and stencil a pattern of wild birds across them," said Cornelia. "They'll do for the bedrooms, anyway. The windows are the same size all over the house, aren't they? I have some beautiful patterns for stencilling up in my trunk that I made for some of the girls' curtains at college."

"How perfectly dear!" said Louise. "Can't I go up and find them?"

"Yes, they are in the green box just under the tray. I wish we had a couple more windows in this room, it is so dark. If I were a carpenter for a little while I would knock out that partition into the hall, and saw out two windows, one each side of the fireplace over there," said Cornelia, motioning toward the blank sidewall where already her mind had reared a lovely stone fireplace.

"There's a carpenter lives next door," said Louise thoughtfully. "He goes to work every morning at seven o'clock, but I suppose he would charge a lot."

"I wonder," said Cornelia. "We'll have to think about that"; and she stood off in the hall, and began to look around with her eyelashes drawn down like curtains through

129

which she was sharply watching a thought that had appeared on her mental horizon.

On the whole it was a very exciting evening, and a happy one also. When Harry and his father came home, there were two loads of stone already neatly piled inside the little yard, and Carey was just flourishing up to the door with a loud honk of the horn on his borrowed truck, bringing a third load. Harry had of course told his father the new plans, and the father had been rather dubious about such a scheme.

"He'll just begin it, and then go off and leave a mess around," he had told Harry with a sigh.

But, when he saw the eager light on his eldest son's face, he took heart of hope. Carey was so lithe and alert, worked with so much precision, strength, and purpose, and seemed so intent on what he was doing. Perhaps, after all, something good would come of it, although he looked with an anxious eye at the borrowed car, and wondered what he would do if Carey should break it and be liable for its price.

Harry turned to, and helped with the unloading; and both were persuaded to come in barely for a five minuses' bite at the good dinner that was already on the table. They despatched it with eagerness and little ceremony, and were off for another load, asking to have their pudding saved until they returned, as every minute must count before dark, and they had no time for pudding just now.

When the boys were away again, Cornelia began to talk with her father about Carey. She told him a little of their talk that morning, and persuaded him not to say anything for a while to stop Carey from working at the garage until he had earned enough to buy some new clothes and get a little start. The father reluctantly consented, although he declared it would not do any good, for Carey would spend every cent he earned on his wild young friends; and, if he bought any clothes, they would be evening clothes. He had seen before how it worked. Nevertheless, although he spoke discouragedly, Cornelia knew that he would stand by her in her attempt to help Carey back to respectability; and she went about clearing off the supper table with a lighter heart.

After supper she saw to it that there was plenty of hot water for baths when the boys got through their work, and she got out an old flannel shirt and a pair of Carey's trousers, and set a patch, and mended a tear, and put them in order for work. Then she had the ironing-board and a basin and soap ready for cleaning his other clothes when he came in. For Carey-like he had gone to haul all that stone in the only suit he had to wear for good. She sighed as she thought what a task was before her. For something inside Carey needed taking out and adjusting before Carey would ever be a dependable, practical member of the family. Nevertheless, she was proud of him as she listened to the thud of each load and glanced out of the front window at the ever-increasing pile of stones that now ran over the tiny front yard and was encroaching on the path that led to the back door.

"Gotta get 'em all, or somebody else'll get onto it, and take 'em," declared Harry when he came in for a drink, his face and hands black and a happy, manly look around his mouth and eyes.

It was ten o'clock when the last load was dumped, by the light of all the lamps in the house brought out into the yard, and it was more than an hour later before the boys got back from returning the truck to its owner. They were tired and dirty almost beyond recognition, but happier than they had been for many a day, and glad of the bit of a feast which their sister had set out for them, and of the hot baths.

"Well, if we don't have a fireplace now,

it won't be my fault!" declared Harry, mopping a warm red face with a handkerchief that had seen better days. "Gee! We certainly did work. Carey can work, too, when he tries, I'll say"; and there was a note of admiration in his voice for his elder brother, which was not missed by either the brother or the watching sisters. Everybody slept well that night, and they were all so weary that they came near to oversleeping next morning.

It was after the children had gone to school and Carey was off getting lime and sand and cement for his work that Cornelia went out into the back yard to hang up the curtains which she had just washed, and, turning away from the line, she encountered a pair of curious eyes under the ruffle of a gay calico boudoir-cap whose owner was standing on the neighboring back porch, the one to the left, where Louise had said the carpenter lived.

"Good morning!" said the other woman briskly, as if she had a perfect right to be intimate. "You all ain't agoing to build, are you? I see all them stones come last night, and I couldn't make out what in life you all was going to do with 'em, lessen you was goin' to pull down and build out."

Cornelia had a foolish little hesitancy in

133

responding to this lively overture, for her instinct was to look down upon people who lived in so mean a neighborhood; but she reflected quickly that she was living there herself, and perhaps these people didn't like it any better than she did. Why should she look down upon them? So she looked up with a pleasant smile, if a trifle belated.

"Oh, good morning. No, we're only going to have a fireplace. I wish we were going to build; the house isn't arranged at all the way I should like it, and it's such fun to have things made the way you want them, don't you think?"

"Yes," said the neighbor, eying her curiously. "I s'pose it is. I never have tried it. My husband's a carpenter, and of course he don't have time to make things for me. It's like the shoemaker's children goin' barefoot, as the sayin' is. I was going to say that, if you all was buildin', my husband, being a carpenter, might be handy for you. He takes contracts sometimes."

"Oh, does he?" Cornelia's color rose brightly. "I certainly wish we could afford to have some work done. There are two windows I need badly, and a partition I want down; but I can't do it now. Perhaps later, when mother gets home from the hospital, and we're not under such heavy expense, we can manage it."

The neighbor eyed her thoughtfully.

"Be nice if you could have 'em done when she got back," she suggested. "Your mother looked to be an awful sweet woman. I saw her when she come here first, and I said to my husband, I said: 'Jim, them's nice people. It does one good to have a woman like that livin' next door, she's so lady-like and pretty, don't you know, and so kinda sweet.' I was awful sorry when I heard she had to go to the hospital. Say, she certainly did look white when they took her away. My! but ain't she fortunate she's got a daughter old enough to fill her place? You been to college, ain't you? My! but that's fine! Well, say, I'll tell Jim about it. Mebbe he could do your work for you nights if you wasn't in a hurry, and then it wouldn't come so high, you know. It would be nice if you could get it all fixed up for your ma when she comes back, Jim wouldn't mind when you paid him, you know. I'll tell him to come in and look it over when he gets in this afternoon, anyhow."

"Oh!" said Cornelia, taking a quick breath of astonishment. "Oh, really I don't believe you better. Of course, I might manage part of what I want if it didn't cost too much, but I've heard all building is very high now."

She was making a lightning calculation, and thinking of the money she had brought back from college. Would it — could she? Ought she? It would be so nice if she dared!

"That's all right. You're a neighbor and Jim wouldn't mind doing a good turn. He'd make it as cheap as he could. It won't cost nothing for him to look it over, anyhow. I'll tell him when he comes back. My goodness! I smell that bread burning. Excuse me, I must go in"; and the neighbor vanished, leaving Cornelia bewildered and a trifle upset, and immediately certain that she ought not to allow the woman to send in her husband. Well, she would think it over, and run in later to tell her it was impossible. That was clearly the only thing to do.

So she hurried back to put on the irons, for her curtains would soon be dry enough to iron, and she wanted to get them stencilled and up as soon as possible, the windows looked so bare and staring, especially up in Carey's room.

 Carey came back, and worked all the morning in the cellar at the foundation for his fireplace, occasionally coming up to measure and talk learnedly about draughts, and the like. Cornelia was very happy seeing him at it, whether a fireplace ever resulted or not. It was enough that he was interested and eager over it; and, while she was waiting for her irons to heat, she sat down and wrote a bright little letter to her mother, telling how Carey was helping her put the house to rights, although she carefully refrained from mentioning a fireplace; for she was still dubious about whether it would be a success. But late in the afternoon, after the lunch was cleared away, the dinner well started, and the beautifully laundered curtains spread out on the dining-room couch ready for decoration, Carey called her down cellar, and proudly showed her a large, neat, square section of masonry arising from the cellar floor beneath the parlor, to the height of almost her shoulders, and having its foundation down at proper depth for safety so he told her.

"My! How you've worked, Carey! I think it's wonderful you've accomplished so much in such a short time."

"Aw! That's nothing!" said Carey, exuding delight at her praise. "I coulda done more if I hadn't had to go after the stuff. But say, Nell, I promised Pat I'd come around and help him with a big truck this afternoon; and I guess I better go now, or I won't get home in time for supper. Pat owes me five dollars anyhow, and I need it to pay for the stuff I bought this morning. I told the fella I'd bring it round this afternoon."

Cornelia thought of her hoarded money, and opened her lips to offer some of it, then thought better of it. It would be good for Carey to take some of the responsibility and earn the money to beautify the house. He would be more interested in getting a job. So she smiled assent, and told him to hurry and be sure to be back in time for supper, for she was going to have veal potpie, and it had to be eaten as soon as it was done, or it would fall.

Carey went away whistling, and Cornelia sat down to her stencilling.

She had done a great deal of this work at college, often making quite a bit of money at it; so it was swift work, and soon she had a pair of curtains finished, and pinned one up to the window to get the effect. She was just getting down from the step-ladder when she heard a knock at the door; and, wondering, she hurried to open it.

There stood a tall, bronzed man with a red face, very blue eyes, and a pleasant smile; and it suddenly came over her that this must be "Jim," and she had forgotten to tell his wife not to send him over.

"My wife said you wanted me to come over and see about some work you wanted done," he said, pulling off his cap and stepping in. "I thought I'd just run right in before dark, if you didn't mind work-clothes."

"Oh, no," said Cornelia, looking worried, "of course not; but really I'm afraid I didn't make it plain to your wife I haven't any idea of doing anything now — that is, I don't suppose it would be possible — I haven't any money, and won't have for a while."

"That's all right," said the man, looking around the house alertly; "it don't cost nothing to estimate. I just love to estimate. What was it you was calculating to do when you do build over?"

"Oh!" said Cornelia, abashed. "I don't know that I had really thought it all out, but this house is so cramped and ugly I was just wishing I could take down this partition and throw the parlor and hall all into one. Do you think the ceiling would stand that?

I suppose it's a foolish idea, for I don't know a thing about building; but this would really make a very pretty room if the hall wasn't cut off this way."

The man stepped into the doorway, and looked up, eying the ceiling speculatively, with his mouth open.

"Why, yes, you *could* do that," he drawled. "It's a pretty long span, but you could do it. You'd have to use a couple colyooms to brace her up, but that's done — without you used a I beam. That you could do."

"An eye beam! What's an eye beam?" asked Cornelia, interested.

"Why, it's an iron beam running along underneath. You might be able to get her under out of sight, but most likely you'd have to have her below the ceiling. You could box her in, and you could make some more of 'em, and have a beamed ceiling if you want."

"Oh, a beamed ceiling! But that would be expensive. How much does an eye beam cost?"

"Oh, I should say a matter of fifteen or eighteen dollars fer one that long," said the man, letting his eye rove back and forth over the ceiling as if in search of a possible foot or two more of length concealed somewhere.

"Oh!" said Cornelia again wistfully. "And would it cost much to put it in?" She was trying to think just how much of that money was lying in her drawer upstairs.

"Well, not so much if I did it evenings. That would make a mighty nice room out of it, as you say. I'd be willing to let you have the stuff it took at cost, and I might be able to get a second-handed I beam. Come to think, there is one down to the shop a man ordered, and then done 'ithout. I might get it for you as low as five dollars if it would be long enough."

He took out his foot rule and began to measure, and Cornelia drew her breath quickly. It seemed too good to be true! If she only could make over that room before her mother got home!

"What else was it you was calculatin' to do?" the man asked, looking up suddenly from the paper on which he had set down the measurement. "I'll look at that there I beam in the morning when I go down to the shop. I believe she's long enough. Was there anything else?"

"Well, my brother is trying to build a stone fireplace over on that blank wall opposite, and I was wishing I had a window on each side, the room is so dark. But I guess we would have to wait for that, even if we did this. Windows are expensive, aren't they?"

"Well, some; and then again they ain't, if you get a second-handed one. Sometimes people change their minds, and have a different kind of winder after one's made, and then it's left on the boss's hands, and he's glad to get rid of it at cost. Got a lot of winders all sizes layin' round over there. Get 'em cheap I guess. Say, you'd oughtta have a couple them di'mon'-pane winders, just smallish ones, over there each side your chimney."

He cast his eye around back to the hall, and pointed uncertainly toward the long blank space of dull-brown faded wall-paper.

"Then you need a bay there," he said interestedly. "Say, them bays now do make a pretty spot in a room. Got one where I was workin' yesterday, just sets right outa the room 'bout the height of a table, like a little room; has three winders to it, and the woman has cute little curtains to 'em, and ferns and a bird-cage. Say, that would make your room real pleasant like."

"It certainly would," said Cornelia, her eyes shining and a wistful sigh creeping to her lips; "but I guess it won't be pos—"

"Say! You got some real nice curtains to your winders. I like them birds flying."

Then he caught a glimpse of the table over which Cornelia had spread the curtain on which she was working. He saw the three birds already finished, and the brush and paints and patterns lying there; and then he glanced back at her in astonishment.

"Say, you don't mean to say you're *makin'* them birds on them curtains! My! Ain't that interesting? How do you do it? Make one, and le'me see."

Cornelia obligingly sat down, and made two birds in flight while the carpenter watched every movement, and exclaimed admiringly. It would not have been Cornelia if she had not visioned at that instant how her college-mates would laugh if they could see her now; but she smiled to herself as she pleasantly showed him all the tricks of her small craft.

"Well," he said as she finished the second bird, "now ain't that great? I never supposed any one could do a thing like that. I supposed it was done by machinery somehow. Say, I hope you won't take no offence, but would you be willing to do something like that fer pay? Your saying you couldn't afford them winders made me think of it. I'd like mighty well to get some curtains for my wife for all over the house; and if you could do some kind of a fancy pattern on 'em, — you and she could talk it over, and fix that, — I'd be willin' to trade off your work fer mine. She'd tell her friends, too, and you could get other orders. I think it would pay."

Cornelia's cheeks grew rosy, but she held up her spirited little head, and tried to be sensible about it. This wasn't exactly what she had expected, of course, to get her first order from a common working man, but then, what difference? It was a real order and would bring her and the family what they needed, more windows, more light, more room; why not? And, if her dream of uplifting and beautifying homes had been a true ideal, why, here was her opportunity. Everybody began in a small way, and it really was wonderful to have opportunity, even so humble as this, open up right at the beginning. She caught her breath, and tried to think. Of course everybody began everything in a small way at first.

"Well," she said, hesitating, "I think perhaps I could. That is really my business, you know, interior decorating. I mean to do it on a large scale some day."

"You don't say!" said the man, looking at her admiringly. "I know women is getting into business a lot these days. But I ain't never heard of that — what do you call it

— interior decorating? You don't mean wall-paper and painting? 'Cause I could introduce you to my boss. He builds a lot of houses."

"Well, yes," said Cornelia, trying not to laugh. "My business is after the house is all built. I select wall-papers and curtains, and tell them what furniture to get, or how to arrange what furniture they have so it will look well in a room. I've been studying along those lines in college; it's artistic work, you know."

"I see!" said the man, looking at her with narrowing, speculative eyes; "good idea, real good idea! Like to have some one arrange my house. Tell us what to buy. We're laying out to get some new furnitoor, either a parlor soot or a dining-room, though my wife's got her heart set on a new bedroom outfit, and I don't know which'll come off first. Guess I'll send her in to talk it over with you. I like them little birds real well. Where you goin' to put 'em? Here?" He looked at the two long front windows.

"No, these are going up on the third floor in my brother's room, the front room. I'm going to make that all blue and white, and these blue birds will make it look cheerful."

"H'm! I guess when Nannie sees 'em she'll be strong fer the bedroom set, and let

145

the other rooms go a spell till we can afford it."

"Why not paint your old bedroom set, and have it decorated like your curtains, and save the money for some good furniture downstairs? They are using painted furniture a lot now for bedrooms."

He stared at her eagerly.

"There, now, see? I told you you were going to be real useful to me. You've saved me the price of a bedroom set already. It's a bargain. You do the decorating, and I'll do the carpentering. I'll see about them winders, and let you know tomorrow afternoon."

When he had gone, Cornelia stood in the middle of her dreary little parlor, and looked around with startled eyes. Here she had contracted to have windows put in and the partition taken down, and promised to go into business herself right away at once. What would her father say to it all?

But she could see Harry and Louise coming down the street, and she hurried into the kitchen to prepare the dessert for dinner; for it was getting late for what she had planned.

She must put the new ideas out of her mind and get back to her work, or dinner would be late.

The children came bursting into the kitchen, eager to see how much Carey had accomplished, and clattered down cellar and up again, their hands full of cookies their sister had baked, their eyes happy, and somehow home and life looked good to Cornelia. This was the great day at college when the play on which she had spent so much time and thought was to come off, and she had expected to have a hard time bearing the thought that all that was going on and she not in it; but she never once thought of it all day until just as her head was touching the pillow that night, and then she was so sleepy that it only came as a floating thought of some far-off period of her existence in which she now had no part. She was wholly and entirely interested just now in her home and what she was going to do for the neighborhood. She had not told her father yet about the carpenter and his propositions. She wanted to have something more definite to tell, perhaps to surprise her family with, if possible; so she had merely asked him casually if he objected to her making little inexpensive changes in the house, things that she could manage herself; and he had joyously told her to do what she liked, pull the walls down if she wanted to, only so she got things fixed to please her.

10

Cornelia awoke with a great zeal for work upon her. She had dreamed a living room that would lift the whole house out of the sordid neighborhood and make it a place of delight. She had thought out some built-in seats with lockers where many of the odds and ends could be stowed; she had planned to paint the old, cheap dining-room furniture a wonderful deep-cream enamel and decorate it like some of the expensive sets in the stores; so would she treat the old bedroom sets that were not of real wood. The set in Carey's room was old walnut and valuable. A little oil would bring it back to its rich brown beauty. The set in her mother's room was a cheap one; and that she would paint gray with decorations of little pink buds and trailing vines. The set in her own room should be ivory-white with sepia shadows. She would go somewhere and learn how to put on wall-paper, or find a man who would do it very cheaply; and little by little the old house should be made over. Cheap felt-paper of pale gray or pearl or cream for the bedrooms, and corn-color for the living room. She wasn't sure what she would do with the dining-room yet till she had the furniture painted, perhaps paint the walls white, and tack little moldings in patterns around for panels outlined in green. Green! That was the color for the dining-room furniture. A green and white dining-room, with a fern-dish for the centre of the table and a grass rug under the table. White curtains with green stencilling! That was it! And Carcy's room should be painted white, walls and ceiling and all. She would set him at it as soon as he finished the fireplace, and then she would stencil little birds, or a more conventional pattern around the top of the walls for a border, in the same blue as the curtains. That would be a room to which he could bring home his friends. A picture or two well chosen, — she had the Lone Wolf in her trunk done in steel-blues, the very thing for one, — and an unbleached muslin bedspread and pillow roll also stencilled in blue. That would make a beautiful room. Then the bathroom, of course, must be all white, heavy white enamel. She saw where her money would go now, in pots of paint and brushes, and the work would take days, weeks; but it would be beautiful. She could see her dream before her, and was happy.

She went downstairs, and found the fire out. That made delay. It was her own fault, of course; she had forgotten to look after it the last thing at night, and also everybody else had forgotten. Her father had gone to bed early with a neuralgic headache. He usually looked after the fire. Carey ought to have thought of it, but Carey never thought of anything but himself and his own immediate plans unless his interest was held. Cornelia found on looking for it in her haste that her stock of patience had run low; and added to this she had a stiff shoulder from washing windows, and Harry had a bad toothache, and had to hurry away to the dentist's. Carey didn't get up at all when he was called, and Louise and Cornelia had a rough time of it making some coffee for their father over the gas-flame. There was no time to wait for the fire, for father must catch his car at the regular time, whether he had breakfast or not. When Louise had gone off to school, and Harry, returning redolent of cloves and creosote, had also been fed and comforted and sent off with an excuse to his teacher, Cornelia wanted to sit down and cry. Suddenly the whole thing seemed a house of cards. The sordid neighborhood became more sordid than ever, the house too dingy and hopeless for words, all her plans tawdry and cheap and useless. Why try, when the result to be attained at best would be but a makeshift of poverty?

To add to her misery, the morning mail brought letters of condolence from her classmates because she could not be with them at the play, and bits of news about how this and that were going wrong because she wasn't there, and who was trying to take her place and bungling things.

Suddenly Cornelia put her head down on the dining-room table in the midst of the breakfast clutter, and cried. She felt sorrier and sorrier for herself. Carey upstairs, great, big, lazy fellow, sleeping and letting her make the fire and do the work and carry the burden. He ought to be out hunting a job and helping to fill the family purse. He ought to be up and at his fireplace. She felt like going up and shaking him and telling him just how despicable he was; and she wished she could shut up the house and go off all day somewhere, and have a good time. She was tired, and she loathed the thought of washing windows and scouring the floor and getting meals. Even stencilling curtains had lost its charm.

She became ashamed of herself presently, remembering her mother and how many years she had done all these things and more. She dried her eyes and began to clear off the table. She had barely finished when she had a visitation from the woman next door, who came beaming in to see the curtains her husband had told her about, and to ask whether Cornelia minded her having blue birds on some of her curtains if she put them on the other side of the house. Somehow the woman's eagerness to have her home made over into an artistic one melted away some of Cornelia's gloom, and she was able to rise to the occasion and talk with her neighbor almost as enthusiastically as if she had been really interested. Perhaps she was interested; she wasn't sure. Anyway, it was going to be fun to get rid of ugly things in that woman's house and substitute simple, pretty ones. When Mrs. Barkley got up to go Cornelia thought she heard faint movements up in the third story, and took heart. When she opened the door to let her neighbor out, promising to run in sometime within a day or two and look over the rooms, the sun shot out from behind a grim cloud, and flooded the damp street with glory; and Cornelia began to feel better.

Carey came down whistling, and twinkling with good humor; and she hadn't the heart to give him the reprimand he richly deserved. She smiled a good morning, and he went at the kitchen range with a good will.

They had an early lunch and breakfast together, and Carey went to work at his stonework once more.

It was a trifle after two o'clock when Brand Barlock arrived on the scene.

Carey was down cellar picking up the last stones and poking them through the opening he had cut in the parlor floor. He was making such a racket that he did not hear the insistent honk! honk! of the horn. But Cornelia polishing off the front window where some of the wet paper of the day before had stuck, did hear; and she looked out at the expensive car with a sinking heart. That must be Brand Barlock! But surely, *surely*, Carey wouldn't go off now in the midst of his work, when he was so anxious to finish!

After several almost insolent honks of the horn, and imperious looks houseward, a boy in the back seat got out, received some brief instruction from the handsome youth who was the driver, and came and knocked at the door. Cornelia stepped into the hall, and opened the door.

"Kay here?" asked the boy. "Oh!" Seeing Cornelia, he dragged off his cap perfunctorily.

The boy had a pleasant face, though weak; and Cornelia smiled. If this was one

153

of Carey's friends, she would know him sometime, and she must make a good impression upon him. She wanted the boys to come and see Carey rather than to always be carrying him off.

"Why, yes, he's here," said Cornelia. "But he's awfully busy. We're getting settled, you know. Could I give him a message?"

"Why, oh, yes! Tell him Brand Barlock wants him. Tell him he wants him right away quick, please. Brand's in an awful hurry."

If he had said, "The President of the United States is here, and wants to see Carey," he could not have given the order more loftily.

Cornelia turned doubtfully. She wanted to resent this imperious tone; but perhaps Carey wouldn't like it, and, after all, boys were — well, just boys. When they were at that age, they likely thought they were it.

"I'll tell him," she said pleasantly. "Won't you step in? We don't look very nice here yet, but we hope to be ready to offer more hospitality to our friends soon."

The boy looked at her as if he was surprised to find her human. "Naw, thanks. I'll stay here," he replied, and tapped his foot impatiently. She gathered that Carey's family meant nothing at all and less than nothing to this uninteresting youth; but she turned and went swiftly through the hall and the dining-room and down the cellar stairs rather than to call Carey through the opening in the floor. Carey might not care to see these friends of his in his present attire.

"Gosh!" said Carey, looking down at his dishevelled self when she had told him. "Well, I s'pose I've got to go up. Can't keep Brand waiting. Oh, gee! I thought I'd get this up through the floor today."

"But Carey," cried his sister, putting out a detaining hand, "can't I explain to him what you're doing? Surely he will understand that you are busy and can't come. Can't I ask him to come down to you if he must see you now? If he sees what you are doing, you won't look so bad."

He stopped short in the cellar, and looked at her witheringly.

"Ask Brand Barlock to come down *here?* Well, I should say *not!*"

"Why not?" she asked with unconscious scorn. "Is he as grand as all that? Who on earth is he, anyway?"

But Carey was gone, taking the stairs three steps at a time. He was out at the car when his sister got back to her window, staying only a minute, and then tearing back and up the two flights of stairs to his room, while the car waited in front in grave importance. The sounds above stairs indicated that Carey was performing a hasty and tempestuous toilet. The water gushed in the bathroom in full force; and splashing, slamming doors, dropping shoes, hurrying footsteps, succeeded one another. The jamming of a bureau drawer, the dropping of a hairbrush, told his worried sister that Carey was "dressing up" and going somewhere.

Cornelia climbed the stairs to remonstrate, but was prevented with a snort before she spoke.

"Oh, doggone that collar button! That's always the way when I'm in a hurry."

"Carey, are you — you're not —" She stopped to gather breath, and began again, "Carey, is there anything I can do to help you?"

"Only just get out of my way — *please!*" he roared as he tore past her down the stairs to the bathroom again and began to strop his razor furiously.

She came downstairs slowly, trying to think what to do. Calamity of unnamed proportions loomed ahead, and she felt she must prevent it somehow. She paused in the hall.

"Carey, is anything the matter?" she asked anxiously.

"There you are again, doggone it! Now you've made me cut myself, and I haven't another collar. No, of course there isn't anything the matter. I'm just in a hurry, can't you *see?* They're waiting for me!"

"Well, but why are you so cross?"

"Aw! I'm not cross. I'm just nervous. Now, just look at that collar! It's just like all my luck."

"I think your laundry came this morning," volunteered his sister.

"Well! Why didn't you say so? Where is it?"

"Look here, Carey," she said with fire in her eye, "you have no need to be a bear; and, if you want me to get your collar, you'll have to speak decently, or I won't have anything more to do with you."

There was silence in the bathroom for the space of half a second; then an obviously controlled voice said:

"Pardon me, Nell. I'm almost cr-r-azy. Can't you see?"

"Why, yes!" said his sister significantly, and went swiftly downstairs for the package of laundry.

Carey was elaborately polite when she presented it, but he refrained, boy-like, from

157

telling her that he was going after a job he had heard about, which would have made the whole affair perfectly reasonable to her. "What business is it of hers?" he reasoned. "And then suppose I didn't get it?"

So he stormed from the house like a whirlwind, leaving no word of when he would return; and Cornelia was too much on her dignity to ask him. She stood at the window, watching him out of sight, the quick tears springing into her eyes. What a boisterous, gay bunch they were, all of them, piling into the car, which started even before they were in. What a noise the car made, as if it too had partaken of the spirit of its owner and went roaring through the world with a daredevil blare and throb of a converted fire-engine just to attract attention and show the world they didn't care! Her cheeks grew hot with shame over it, and for some strange reason her imagination conjured up a possible day in the future when that fair lady, her fellow traveller of the other day, with her handsome son should perhaps come to call upon her. How terrible to have it happen when her brother would go roaring away from the house in this wild fashion! Oh, how had Carey ever grown into such a person? So impossible a combination!

She came and stood beside the yawning hole in the parlor floor. How hard he had worked. How much in earnest he had been! And then at a snap of the finger from this young lord of creation he had dropped it all and fled on some fool whim or other, who knew?

She felt sick and utterly tired, and as if she could not go on with her own work. She had just dropped into a chair and covered her face with her hands when there came a knock at the door. For an instant she meditated not noticing it, but, thinking better of it, hastily brushed her hand across her wet eyes and hurried to answer the knock.

It was her carpenter, tall and smiling, with a kit of tools and a big window-frame on a wheelbarrow just behind him.

"Well, I brought one along fer you to see," he said, stooping to lift the frame and bring it in. "They said you could have 'em fer two and a half apiece, and I thought that was reasonable. Now, where was it you wanted 'em? There's four or five available. You can take as many as you want and leave the rest, and there's a bay like I was telling you. He says he'll make it five, 'cause he wants to get it out of the way. It has these here di'mon panes. It's real pretty like."

Cornelia had stood back aghast at sight of the window-frame; but, when she heard the price, she opened the door wide, and forgot all her troubles for the moment.

"Oh, how wonderful!" she said, her eyes shining. "Come in. Could you — you couldn't — put it in *now?*"

"Why, yes, that's what I come fer, if you want it done. Course I don't want to force it on you, but I thought you could tell if it would do. We quit early today, 'count of being all done at one place and not wanting to begin another till Monday cause the stuff ain't come yet; so I just thought to me I'd bring my tools and work all day tomorrow and Saturday, — course that's a half, but then — And, if you wanted, I'd go at this job right off. I oughtta be able to get this winder in by dark. Of course that's working after union hours, but this here don't count, being right next door home, you know; it's kind of a favor to a neighbor, see? I brought the sash and all; it's standing just outside, against the house. Now, you want these one each side the fireplace, don't you?"

Cornelia drew a deep breath of daring and said, "Yes!" and then suddenly was glad — just a little — that Carey had been called away. Now she could surprise the whole family.

With her heart in her mouth she stood by the open parlor door, and watched a great hole arrive in the blank wall, and then with a breath of relief turned and sped quickly upstairs to make up for lost time and to put the rooms there in order. It would soon be time for the children to come home from school. How surprised they would be! She knew she could count on both of them to be delighted; but she wished it had been possible for that window to be in before they arrived it would be such fun to surprise them with it. Then she glanced out the window, and saw a little girl coming in the gate; and she hurried down to the door to see what was wanted.

"Why," began the small maiden, "your sister Lou said to tell you she ner Harry wouldn't be home till late. She said they had to practice that play for the entertainment. She said you needn't to worry. She said to tell you Harry had telephoned to the store, and it's all right."

"Oh, thank you!" said Cornelia with a pleased smile. Now there would be something done to show them when the children got home. How nice that the rehearsal should happen today! She had almost forgotten her disappointment about Carey in her desire to surprise the family.

The man went right at the work, and she could see in five minutes that he was interested and was no laggard. In half an hour they had located the window, and he had half of the opening sawed out. Cornelia went back to the kitchen to get some neglected cooking under way; and, when she returned, he was fitting the window-frame. She looked around the little room with delight. What a difference it was going to make to have light and air from that side! She slipped happily back to her work again, and the sound of the saw and hammer was like music to her soul. There was no longer any doubt whether she ought to have waited. Now and then the thought of Carey hurt through her brain like a sting of something sharp, but she soothed herself by making custard pies for supper. Carey liked custard pies, and while she was making them it seemed easier to believe he would return in time for the evening meal.

At a quarter to six the carpenter went home. He had finished putting in the window, and he had marked out the place for the other one. He had also ripped off the base boards on the parlor side of the wall that was to come down, and had taken off the trim of the door-frame. It began to look like business. He promised to come in the morning and bring the I beam and the other window. As he had to go to his boss's shop for them, she had no fear he would arrive before her family were away. So with a gleeful glance at the new window Cornelia carefully closed the parlor door, and turned the key in the lock, putting it into her pocket. If the family questioned, she would say that she thought it safer to keep it locked lest some one might forget in the dark and fall into that open fireplace hole. Then, hugging her secret to her heart, she hurried back to get her dinner ready to serve.

The children came tumbling joyously into the side door both talking at once about the play and demanding to know how much Carcy had got done on the fireplace, and their father smiling behind, interested in all — but Carey had not come yet!

11

The children found out at once that Carey had gone with Brand, and a gloom settled over the little household. Cornelia had no trouble in keeping them out of the parlor; they did not want to go in. Even Harry seemed oppressed, and broke out every few minutes while he ate his supper with, "Aw, gee! If I was a fella!"

Cornelia suddenly roused to break the gloom that had fallen upon them. She looked at her younger brother with a cheery smile.

"Well you will be some day. You are already, you know, really."

Harry looked up proudly, and met her appreciation with a glow.

"I think," said Cornelia thoughtfully, "that this would be a nice night to clean the kitchen, if you all could help."

"Clean the kitchen!" They looked up unenthusiastically. "Why, I thought you cleaned that the first day. It looked awfully nice," said Louise. Somehow kitchens seemed uninteresting places.

"Oh, but not really clean," said Cornelia, taking a deep breath and trying to get courage for the evening, for she was already weary enough to rest; but she must do something to take the family mind off Carey and that locked parlor door if she wanted her plans to succeed.

"I want to paint it all white, walls and ceiling and woodwork; and then I want to paint the floor gray, and put that waterproof varnish on it so it will wash up easily. Those boards are very hard to keep clean the way they are, and show every grease-spot. Did you ever paint, Harry?"

"Oh sure. I painted the porch down to the grocery, and the hen-house, and all around the window-sills for Mrs. Brannon. I can paint. Got any brushes?"

"Yes, I got one for each of us the other day, and a can of paint to be ready when there was time. Then, father, I wonder if you couldn't put up some brackets, and fix those old marbles for me."

"Marbles?"

"Yes, those old marbles that came off the wash-stand and bureau that fell to pieces. They are out in the back shed, and I want one of them out on the dresser, screwed on, you know, so I can use it for a molding-board, and the other two, the back and top of the old wash-stand put up on brackets for shelves in the kitchen, near the sink. They'll save buying oil-cloth, and be lovely to work on, and simply delightful to clean."

"Why, I guess I can fix them. There's an old marble-topped table around somewhere, too."

"I know; I'm going to paint the woodwork white, and get some ball-bearing casters for it, and use it in the kitchen to work on. Then I can wheel it around where I need it, over by the sink when I'm washing dishes, over by the stove to hold the bowl of batter when I'm baking cakes."

"Say, that'll be great!" cried Louise. "Oh! I never realized a kitchen could be pretty. Why, I'd like to wash dishes in a place like that — all white! Say, Nellie, is that a part of interior decorating? Kitchens?"

"Surely!" smiled the sister. "We want to make it pleasant where we have to work the most. Now let's get these dishes out of the way first, and then you children put on your oldest clothes, something that won't be hurt with the paint; and we'll go to work."

"You ought to have one of those 'lectric dish-washers, Nell," said Harry energetically, getting up with a pile of dishes and starting toward the kitchen. "They got one down to the store on exhibition. Say, it's great! You just stick 'em in, and they come out all washed and dried. I'll buy you one some day when I get ahead a little."

"Do," said Cornelia warmly, smiling. "That would be wonderful!"

And so in the bustle and eagerness the disappointment over Carey was somewhat forgotten. They all worked away happily together until ten o'clock, painting and pounding and scrubbing; and, when they finally put up the brushes and went to bed, the kitchen was in a fair way toward reconstruction. The window-frames had lost their grimy, years-old green paint under a first coat of white; the doors had been sandpapered and primed; the side walls had been patched with plaster-of-Paris and received a coat of shellac. Everything began to look clean and hopeful.

"Aw, gee! Carey don't know what he's missin'," mourned Harry as he climbed reluctantly up the stairs, loath to leave till he had finished all the first coat, and persuaded to bed by his sister only on the ground that he wouldn't want to get up in the morning.

For three days Carey stayed away without a sign, and for two evenings Cornelia kept her family interested in the kitchen so that they did not notice the locked parlor door.

It was a bit hard on Cornelia. She worked steadily all day, then worked again all the evening, and lay awake most of the night worrying about her brother. She was beginning to get dark circles under her eyes, and her father looked at her anxiously and asked her whether she didn't think she was doing too much. But she managed to smile cheerfully and keep a brave front. She knew by the weary little wrinkles around his eyes that he too was lying awake nights, worrying about Carey. But the kitchen was beginning to take on the look of a lily and was rapidly becoming a spot where the family loved to go and gaze around, so transforming is a little white paint.

Later on the second afternoon Cornelia went to a telephone pay-station, and looked among the B's for Barlock. When she had found it, she called up the one with the initials R. B., taking a chance between that and Peter, Mary Silas, and J. J., tremblingly put in her nickel, and waited. It was a young girl's voice, fresh and snappy, that answered her; for she had called the residence and not the business office; and she tried to control her voice and answer calmly as she asked whether Mr. Brand Barlock was at home. The girl's voice at the other end was a trifle haughty as she answered: "No, he's motored down to Baltimore. I don't know when he'll be home. Maybe two or three days. Who is this?"

"Oh," said Cornelia a trifle relieved,

"then I'll call again," and hung up the receiver in the face of the repeated question, "Who is this?" Her cheeks were glowing as she emerged from the telephone-booth and hastened out to the street as if she were afraid some one would chase her. That was likely Brand Barlock's sister on the telephone, and Cornelia had appeared to her like a bold girl calling up her brother and then retreating without giving her name, but it had been the only way. At least, she knew this much, that Brand also was still away. Carey was likely safe; that is, probably nothing had happened to his body, though there was no telling what had happened to his soul on such a wild trip with such companions.

But the third day the carpenter took down the parlor partition, and threw the hall and parlor into one; and Cornelia could no longer conceal the interesting changes that had been going on within the old front room.

There was a fine big window each side of the big fireplace hole, with a box window-seat under it, and the little "bay" had been put into the long, dark wall of the hallway, with a row of three diamond-paned windows opening just over the staircase. Cornelia had managed to conceal the first bay window, which had been put in the second day, by means of an old curtain tacked across the wall. But, when the third night came, there stood the big new room with all its windows, a place of great possibilities.

"Now," said the carpenter as he stood back and surveyed his finished task, "there's just two more things I'd like to see you do to this room. You need to break that there staircase with a landin' about four steps up. You got plenty-a room this side yer dining-room door, an' 'twould jest strike them three winders fer the landin'. They got a half-circle an' two long, narrer side winders down to the shop would jest fit around that there front door. Ef you say the word, I'll put 'em in tomorra. I jest about could do it in a day. But I'd like to turn them stairs around. I certainly would."

So with fear and trembling Cornelia told him to go ahead. He assured her she needn't worry about the pay, that his mother-in-law and his two cousins' wives all wanted curtains; and it began to look as if she would be stencilling birds the rest of her natural life; so she had no fear but she would be able to pay him sometime. She was getting five dollars a set for her curtains, and felt quite independent. Perhaps, after all, she would be an interior decorator some day,

170

even if this was a day of small things, scrim curtains instead of rich fabrics and rare hangings.

That night, when the children came home, they discovered the changes in the front part of the house, of course; and their sister found them standing in awe on the stairs looking about them as if they had suddenly stepped into a place of enchantment.

"O Nellie, Nellie, how did you do it?" they cried when they saw her. "Isn't this great? Isn't it wonderful;" And then, with a look at the yawning cavity in the floor where the fireplace was to be: "Oh what will Carey say? Why doesn't he come home?"

And that night after they were all in bed Carey came.

Even the children heard the car drive up to the door, and the whole shabby house seemed to be straining every alert nerve to listen.

Carey came whistling a jazzy little tune up the path, with a careless happy-go-lucky swag, not at all like the prodigal son that he was, with the whole family in a long three days' agony over him. It was almost virtuous, that whistle and the way he subdued it as he unlocked the dining-room door and groped his way through the dark to where the foot of the stairs used to be.

They heard him strike a match; and then, as if they had all been down there to watch him, they could visualize his amazed face as he stood in the little halo of the match, and looked around him at the strange room, and the strange staircase with a turn in the stairs and only one rail up yet, and a platform. They heard him strike another match, and then they heard his footsteps and more matches as he walked around looking. Cornelia knew when he sighted the bay window and the seats under the two windows by the fireplace. She heard the gentle thud of the top as he opened it and closed it again. She heard the soft whistle of approval, and drew a long breath of relief. At least he was interested.

She knew that the little sister heard too and was following Carey's every movement; for she felt the quick grip of the little hand on her shoulder, and the soft, tense breath against her cheek; and somehow it gave her courage and strength. With all the family united in loving anxiety for him, surely, *surely* Carey would be saved and made a good man. She found herself praying again: "O God, reach him, save him, show him! Help us to know what to do for him."

Afterwards she thought about it, and wondered at herself, and resolved to pray regularly again, even if just to pray for Carey. It was so necessary that Carey be saved and made a good man. It was necessary just for their mother's sake, and it must be done before she came home, or she would be likely to get sick again worrying about him.

Carey came slowly up the stairs, and went to his room. The family listened to his movements overhead, listened for his shoes to fall, and then to the creak of the springs as he at last got into bed. Listened longer as the springs continued to creak while Carey rolled around, settling himself — thinking, perhaps? — and then at last when all was still they slept.

It was well for Carey that a night intervened between his home-coming and the meeting with his family. The sharp words that swelled in the heart of each of them, and would surely have arisen to the lips of them, would not have been pleasant for him to hear. They might have been salutary; they undoubtedly would have been true; but it is exceedingly doubtful whether in his present state of mind he would have endured them graciously. He had had a good time, and he had come home. He was in no mood for fault-finding. The sight of the unfinished fireplace in the wide desolation of the renovated and enlarged room had given him a good-sized pang of remorse which was in a fair way to stay with him for a day or so. Sharp words would most certainly have dispelled it instantly and put him on the defensive. To blame as he undoubtedly was, he preferred to blame himself rather than to have his family do so; and the fact that he arose before light, before any of the others were even awake, and descended to the cellar quietly to pursue his interrupted work proved that he had begun to apprehend the likelihood of blame and wished to forestall it.

It was Harry who awoke first, feeling rather than hearing the dull thuds of the silent worker in the cellar. Hastily dressing, he stole down in wonder and delight, and was so well pleased with what he saw and with the most unusually cordial greeting from his older brother that he remained to help and not to blame. When Louise came down, followed almost immediately by Cornelia, and found the two brothers working so affably, with a whole row of stones reared in the parlor, they gave one another a swift, understanding glance, and greeted their brothers collectively and joyously as if nothing had happened for the last four days.

Carey rattled off jokes, and worked away

like a beaver, keeping them all in roars of laughter; and the father, waking late from his troubled sleep, heard the festive sound, and hurried down, relieved that the cloud of gloom had lifted from his home. He had had it in mind to give Carey a regular dressing down when he returned. Words fitly framed for such a proceeding had been forming redhot in his worried mind all night. But the sight of his four children in gales of laughter over some silly little story Carey had told, and the sight of the clock hastening on to the moment of his car, restrained him; and perhaps it was just as well. Cornelia hurried him into his place, and gave him his breakfast, chattering all the time about the rooms and the changes, and so kept his mind busy. At last they all got away without a word of reproof to Carey, and Cornelia was left to wonder whether she ought to open the subject.

All the morning they worked eagerly together, finding personal conversation impossible because of the presence of the carpenter. At lunch time, however, Carey, having been most courteous and apologetic, seemed to feel his time had come. Or perhaps he appreciated his sister's silence. At any rate, he remarked quite casually that he had been out for a job in Baltimore, and hadn't got it, worse luck! Missed the man he went to see by half an hour, but had a dandy time.

Cornelia took the news quietly, thoughtfully, and presently raised her eyes.

"Carey, dear, next time you go wouldn't you be good enough to tell us where you are going and how long you expect to be gone? You've given us all an extremely anxious time, you know."

She managed to make her voice quiet and matter-of-fact, without the least bit of fault-finding; for a black cloud hovered almost imperceptibly over the handsome young brows across the table, and she had no mind to spoil the pleasant atmosphere that had surrounded them all the morning.

"The idea!" said Carey, excited at once. "Why should I do that? I'm not a baby, am I? I'm a *man*, ain't I? Disabuse yourself at once of the notion that I'm in leading-strings. I guess I can go as far as I like, and stay as long as I like, can't I?"

"Yes, you can, of course," soothed his sister. "But, if you really are a man, you've noticed how gray and worn father looks. How sick he looks! He's been through a lot, you know; and he can't help thinking that maybe something else dreadful is coming. He has to worry for himself and mother too, you know. Because just now everything is very critical on mother's account. I know you wouldn't want to worry mother, and you wouldn't want to worry father, either, if you just stopped to think."

"Well, but how absurd! A trip down to Baltimore that any fella would take. You aren't such a goose as to worry over that, are you?"

"Of course it is a bit silly," admitted the sister; "but I must confess I lay awake several hours every night myself. You remember you had just got done telling me what a wild driver that Brand Barlock is, and how he put ether in the mixture. And one can't help knowing there are hundreds of terrible automobile accidents every day. They might happen even to a *man*, you know; and then — well we *love* you, Carey, you know."

"Oh, gosh! Well, I didn't know you were that sort of a goose. I know of course mother — but then she isn't here."

"Well, when it comes down to it, Carey, I guess we all care about as much as mother." She smiled at him through a sudden mist of tears that all unexpectedly welled into her eyes. "And you know it was quite sudden, and well, if you had just thought to telephone, you know, to say you would be gone several days."

"Aw, gee! Well, I suppose I might have done that. I will next time. Sure, Nell, I'll try to remember. It was kind of rank in me not to say anything, but I figured that, if I didn't get it, no one would be the wiser."

"Well, I guess you can't cheat your family." She smiled again, ignoring the mist in her eyes. "We're a kind of gang together; isn't that what you call it? And what affects one affects all. Why, even little Louie cried herself to sleep in my arms last night because she thought maybe you had been killed."

"Aw! Gee!"

Carey got up swiftly, and went over to the window, where he gazed out past the neighbor's blank wall until he had control of himself; then he turned with one of his lightning smiles.

"All right, Nell, I'll give you the tip next time. I'm sorry I had to stay so long, but I waited for the man. See?"

"Well, Carey, I suppose you thought that was the right thing to do, but I've been wondering since you've been talking whether there isn't something good for you in all this big city where we live without going away to Baltimore."

"I'd like to see it," gloomily answered the boy, with a sudden grim look in his eyes.

"I've tried everything I heard of."

"Well, it will come," said his sister brightly. "Come, let's get this house finished first, and then we'll be ready for the big position you're going to have. Next week, you know, you've got to go back to the garage and earn that suit. You need it badly."

Carey caught her suddenly, and gave her a bear-hug, and then spun her around the room till she was dizzy; and so, happily, they went back to their work, Cornelia wondering whether she had done right to pass the matter off so lightly. But brother, as he worked away at his stones silently, was thinking more seriously on the error of his ways than he had thought for four years past.

 **12** It was several weeks before the Copley house was finished. Even then there were cushions to make out of old pieces brightened up by the stitches of embroidery or applique work of leaves cut from bits of old velvet. There were rugs to braid out of all the old rags the house afforded and there were endless curtains to wash and hem and hemstitch and stencil and put up. All the family united to make the work as perfect a thing of the kind as could be accomplished. Every evening was spent in painting or papering, or rubbing down some bit of old furniture to make it more presentable, and gradually the house began to assume form and loveliness.

Paint, white paint, had done a great deal toward making another place of the dreary little house. The kitchen was spotless white enamel everywhere, and enough old marble slabs had been discovered to cover the kitchen table and the top of the kitchen dresser, and to put up shelves around the sink and under the windows. Mr. Copley brought home some ball-bearing casters for the kitchen table, and spent an evening putting them on, so it would move easily to any part of the kitchen needed. Cornelia and Louise rejoiced in scrubbing the smooth white surfaces that were going to be so convenient and so easily kept clean. Even the old kitchen chairs had been painted white and enamelled, and Cornelia discovered by chance one day that a wet sponge was a wonderful thing to keep the white paint clean; so thereafter Louise spent five minutes after dinner every evening going about with her wet sponge, rubbing off any chance fingermarks of the day before and putting the gleaming kitchen in battle-array for the next day.

The dining-room had gradually become a place of rest and refreshment for the eyes as well as for the palate. Soft green was the prevailing color of furniture and floor, with an old grass rug scrubbed back to almost its original color. The old couch was tinkered up and covered with gay cretonne in greens and grays, with plenty of pillows covered with the same material. The curtains were white with a green border of stencilling. The dingy old paper had been scraped from the walls, which had been painted with many coats of white; and a gay green border had been stencilled at the ceiling. The carpenter had found an old plate-rail down in the shop, which, painted white, made a different place of the whole thing, with a few bits of mother's rare old china rightly placed, two Wedgwood plates in dull yellow, another of bright green, a big old blue willow ware plate, some quaint cups hung on brass hooks under a little white shelf. One couldn't ask for a pleasanter dining-room than that. It dawned upon the family anew and joyously every time any one of them entered the room, and made them a little better and a little brighter because it spoke "home" so softly and sweetly and comfortingly.

"Mother won't know the place!" said Louise, standing back to survey it happily after putting the sideboard in perfect order with clean linen cover. "She won't know her own things, will she? Won't it be great when she comes?"

But the living room was the crown of all, wide and pleasant and many-windowed, with its stone fireplace, wide mantel, adorned with a quaint old pair of brass candlesticks that had belonged to the grandmother; the walls covered with pale-yellow felt-paper like soft sunshine; the floor planed down to the natural wood, oiled and treated with shellac; and the old woolen rugs in two tones of gray, which used to be bedroom rugs when Cornelia was a baby, washed and spread about in comfortable places; it no more resembled the stuffy, dark little place they used to call a "parlor" than day resembles night. Soft white sheer curtains veiled the windows everywhere, with overcurtains of yellow cotton crêpe; and the sunshine seemed to have taken up its abode in that room even on dark days when there was no sun to be seen. It was as if it had stayed behind from the last sunshiny day, so bright and cheerful was the glow.

The little "bay" was simply overflowing with ferns the children had brought from the woods, set in superfluous yellow and gray bowls from the kitchen accumulation. Harry ran extra errands after hours, and saved enough to buy the yellowest, throatiest canary the city afforded, in a big wicker cage to hang in the window.

Cretonne covers in soft gray tones covered the shabby old chairs and couch, and Carey and his father spent hours with pumice-stone and oil, polishing away at the piano, the bookcase, and the one small mahogany table that was left, while Cornelia did wonderful things in the way of artistic shades for little electric lamps that Carey rigged up in odd, unexpected corners, made out of all sorts of queer things: an old pewter sugar-bowl, this with a shade of silver lace lined with yellow, a relic of some college costume; a tall gray jug with queer blue Chinese figures on it that had been among the kitchen junk for years, this with a dull blue shade; a bright yellow vase with a butterfly-yellow shade; and a fat green jar with willow basket-work around it on which Cornelia put a shade of soft green, with some old brown lace over it.

The room was really wonderful when it was done, with two or three pictures hung in just the right spot, and some photographs and magazines thrown comfortably about. Really one could not imagine a pleasanter or more artistic room, not if one had thousands to spend. The first evening it was all complete the family just sat down and enjoyed themselves in it, talking over each achievement of cushion or curtain or wall as a great connoisseur might have looked over his newly acquired collection and gloated over each specimen with delight.

Carey's delight in it all was especially noticeable. He hovered around, getting new points of view, and changing the arrangement of a chair or a table, whistling wildly and gleefully, a new Carey to them all. For the whole evening he did not offer to go out, just hung around, talking, singing snatches of popular songs, breaking into a clumsy two-finger "rag" on the piano now and then, and finally ending up with a good sing with Cornelia at the piano. It was curious, but it was a fact that this was the first time Cornelia had had time since her homecoming to sit down and play for them; and it seemed like a revelation to all. They had not realized how well she could play, for she had been studying music part of the time in college. Also no one had realized how well Carey could sing. Perhaps he had never had half a chance with a good accompaniment before. At any rate, it was very plain that he liked it, and would sing as long as any one would play for him.

And the father liked it, too. Oh, *how* he liked it! He took off his glasses, put his head back on the new cretonne cushion, closed his eyes, and just enjoyed it. Now and then he would open his eyes and watch the flicker of the fire in the new fireplace, look from the one to the other of his children, sigh, and say, "I wish your mother were here now," and again; "We must write mother about all this. How she will enjoy it!"

Then right into the midst of this domestic scene there entered callers.

Carey was singing when the knock came, and did not hear them; or else he would most surely have disappeared. It was a way Carey had. But the knock came twice before Louise heard it and slipped to the door, letting in the strangers, who stood listening at the door, motioning to her to wait until the song was finished.

Then Mr. Copley saw them, and arose to come forward. Carey, feeling some commotion, turned; and the song stopped like a shot, a frown of defiance beginning to grow between his brows.

The strangers were a man and a woman, and a young girl a little older than Louise and younger than Cornelia; and one could see at a glance that they were cultured, refined people, though they were quietly, simply dressed. Carey, in his gray flannel shirt open at the neck and the old trousers in which he had assisted in the last rites of putting the room in perfect order, looked down at himself in dismay, and backed precipitately around the end of the piano as far out of sight as possible, meeting the intruders with a glare of disapproval. Cornelia was the last to stop playing and look around, but by that time the lady had spoken.

"Oh, please don't stop! We want to hear the rest of the song. What a beautiful tenor voice!"

Cornelia arose to her duties as hostess, and came forward; but the man by this time was introducing himself.

"I hope we haven't intruded, brother." He grasped Mr. Copley's welcoming hand. "I'm just the minister at the little church around your corner here, and we thought we'd like to get acquainted with our new neighbors. My name is Kendall, and this is my wife and my daughter Grace. I brought the whole family along because I understood you had some daughters."

"You're very welcome," said Mr. Copley with dignity that marked him a gentleman everywhere. "This is my daughter Cornelia; this is Louise, and Harry; and" — with an almost frightened glance toward the end of the piano, lest he might already have vanished — "this is my son Carey."

There was something almost proud in the way he spoke Carey's name, and Cornelia had a sudden revelation of what Carey, the eldest son, must mean to his father in spite of all his sharpness to the boy. Of course Carey must have been a big disappointment the last few months.

Carey, thus cornered, instead of bolting, as his family half expected of him, came forward with an unexpected grace of manner, and acknowledged the introduction, his eyes resting interestedly on the face of Grace Kendall.

"I'm not very presentable," he said. "But, as I can't seem to get out without being seen, I guess you'll have to make the best of me."

Grace Kendall's eyes were merry and pleasant.

"Please don't mind us," she said. "You look very nice. You look as if you had been playing tennis."

"Nothing so interesting as that," said Carey. "Just plain work. We're still tinkering around this house, getting settled, you know."

"There's always such a lot to do when you move, isn't there? But what a lovely spot you've made of it!" She turned, and looked about her. "Why, I shouldn't know it was the same house. What a lot you have done to it! This room looks so big! How did you get the space? You've changed the partitions, haven't you? I used to come here to visit a little lame boy, and it was such a tiny little front room; and now this is spacious! And that wonderful fireplace! Isn't it beautiful?"

"Yes," put in Mr. Copley, as the whole group seemed absorbed in gazing about them at the lovely room. "My son did that.

He built it all himself."

Carey looked up in surprise, with a flush of pleasure at his father's tone of pride; and then his eyes came back to the girl's face all sparkling with eager admiration.

"You don't mean you did it yourself? How perfectly wonderful! That darling mantel! and the way the chimney curves up to the ceiling! It has charming lines! O father, can't you coax him to come over and build one for us?"

"Sure! I'll build you one!" said Carey graciously, as though he kept stone fireplaces in his vest pocket. "Start tomorrow if you can get the stone."

"Oh, great! Just hear that, father! We're going to have a fireplace! Now, don't you let him off. Did you design it, Mr. Copley?"

Carey lifted embarrassed eyes to his elder sister's face, and met her look of loving pride, and flushed happily.

"Why, no, I guess my sister Nell's to blame for that. She suggested it first, and worked it out mostly," he said.

"Indeed, you did it all yourself, Carey," said Cornelia. "I only wanted it, and Carey did the rest."

"Yes, Gracie, that's where you're lacking," said the minister, laughingly; "you haven't any brother to carry out your every wish. Only a busy old father, who doesn't know how."

"My father's all right!" said the daughter loyally; and Carey with a swift, appraising glance decided that he certainly looked it and that for a minister it certainly was surprising. He had a faint passing wonder what this man's church might be like. Then they settled down in groups to talk, Carey beside the minister's daughter, Cornelia beside the minister's wife, and Mr. Copley with the minister, while Harry and Louise sat down together in the window-seat to watch them all.

"Doesn't Carey look handsome?" whispered the little girl, with her eyes on her elder brother. "My, but I guess he's mad he didn't put on his other shirt."

"I should say! Serves him right," said Harry caustically, yet with a light of pride in his eye. "Say, she's some bird, isn't she? Better'n that little chicken we saw him have out last Saturday!"

"O Harry! You mustn't call *any* girl a chicken. You know what mother would say."

"Well, she *was* a chicken, wasn't she?"

"I think I'd rather call her a — a fool!" said Louise expressively.

"Call her what you like, only don't call

her at all!" said the boy. "Say, doesn't our sister look great though?"

So they sat quietly whispering, picking up bits of the conversation and thinking their wise young thoughts.

Mr. Copley's face looked rested and happy.

"My! I wish my wife were at home," he said wistfully. "You know she's been very sick, and she's away getting a rest. But we hope she'll soon be back with us before many months now. How she would enjoy it to have you run in like this! She's a great church woman, and she felt it, coming away from the church we have always attended over on the other side of town —"

Then the talk drifted to the little church around the corner, and to its various organizations and activities.

"Father'll be after you for the choir," confided the daughter to Carey; "a good tenor is a great find."

"No chance!" said Carey, looking pleased in spite of himself. "I can't sing."

Then they all began to clamor for Carey to sing; and right in the midst of it there was another knock at the door, and in walked the carpenter and his wife.

Carey began to frown, of course; for, although he liked the carpenter, he felt that he was of another social class from the delicate young girl who sat by his side; but when he saw her rise and greet the carpenter's wife as cordially as if she were some fine lady, his frown began to disappear again. This certainly was a peach of a girl, and no mistake. In fact, the whole family were all right. The minister was a prince. Just look at the way he took that carpenter by the hand, and made him feel at home.

The carpenter, however, didn't seem to be troubled by embarrassment. He entered right into the conversation comfortably, and began to praise Cornelia Copley and her ability as an interior decorator; and before any one knew how it happened the company had started to see the dining-room and kitchen.

Nobody realized it, but they were all talking and laughing as if they had known one another for years, and everybody was having a happy time. When they came back to the living room, they insisted that Carey should sing and Cornelia should play for them. Harry and Louise whispered together for a moment, then slipped silently back to the kitchen while the music was going on, and returned in a few minutes with a tall pitcher of lemonade and a plate of Cornelia's delicious gingerbread. Carey went for plates, and acted the host beautifully. It all passed off delightfully, even with the presence of the carpenter, who proved to be a good mixer in spite of his lack of grammar.

Before they went away the minister had asked the brother and sister to join the choir and come to the Sunday school and young people's society and all the various other functions of the church, and had given a special urgent invitation to the whole family, including the callers, to come to a church reception to be held the coming week. Carey acted as if church receptions and young people's prayer meetings were the joy of his life, and acquiesced in everything that was suggested, declaring, when the door closed behind them, that that girl was "some peach." And the household retired to their various pillows with happy dreams of a circumspect future in which Carey walked the happy way of a wise young man and had friends that one was not ashamed of. And then the very next afternoon, being Saturday, everything went to smash in one quick happening, and a cloud of gloom fell over the little household.

For it happened that Cornelia and Louise had taken an afternoon off, having arisen quite early and accomplished an incredible amount of Saturday baking and mending and ironing and the like, and had gone down to the stores to choose a much-needed pair of shoes for Louise. The shoes were purchased, also ten cents' worth of chocolates; and they were about to finish the joyful occasion by a visit to a moving-picture show when suddenly, walking up Chestnut Street, they came face to face with Carey and a girl! Carey, who was supposed to be off that whole afternoon hunting for a job! And *such* a girl!

The most noticeable thing about the girl was the whiteness of her nose and the rosiness of a certain circumscribed portion of her cheeks. As she drew nearer, one also noticed her cap-like arrangement of hair that was obviously stained henna, and bobbed quite furiously under a dashing hat of jade-green feathers. Her feet were fat, with fat, overhanging flesh-colored silken ankles, quite transparent as to the silk, and were strapped in with many little buckles to a very sharp toe and a tall little stilt of a heel. Her skirt was like one leg of a pantaloon so tight it was and very short, so that the fat, silken ankles became most prominent; and her mincing gait reminded one of a Bach fugue. She wore an objectionable and conspicuous tunic much beaded with short sleeves and very low neck, for the street.

A scrubby little fur flung across the back of her neck completed her costume unless one counted the string of big white beads that hung around her neck to her waist, and the many rings which adorned her otherwise bare hands. She was chewing gum rhythmically and industriously, and giggling up into Carey's face with a silly, sickening grin that made the heart of Cornelia turn sick with disgust.

As she drew nearer, a pair of delicately pencilled stationary eyebrows, higher than nature usually places them, emphasized the whole effect; and the startling red of the girl's lips seemed to fascinate the gaze. They were coming nearer; they were almost near enough to touch each other; and Carey — Carey was looking down at the girl — he had drawn her arm within his own, and he had not seen his sisters.

Suddenly, without any warning Cornelia felt the angry tears starting to her eyes, and with a quick movement she drew Louise to a milliner's window they were passing, and stood, trembling in every nerve, while Carey and the girl passed by.

 **13** Louise had given her sister one swift, comprehending look, and stood quietly enough looking into the window; but her real glance was sideways, watching Carey and the girl.

"That's the one! That's the chicken, Nellie!" she whispered. "Now, isn't she a chicken? Don't you think Harry is right? Turn around and watch her. They've gone ahead so far they'll never see us now. Look! Just see her waddle! see her toddle! Aren't those shoes the limit? And her fat legs inching along like that! I think she's *disgusting!* How can my brother not be ashamed to be seen with her? And down here on Chestnut Street, too, where he might meet *anybody!* Think if that Grace Kendall should come along and see him! She'd never speak to him again. Oh, Nellie, isn't she *dreadful?*"

"Hush, dear! Somebody will hear you. Yes she's pretty awful."

"But, Nellie, can't we do something about it? Can't Carey be ordered not to go with a thing like that anymore? Why, even the girls in my school are talking about them. They call her my brother's *girl!* Nellie, aren't you going to *do* anything about it? Aren't you going to tell father, and have it stopped?"

"Hush, darling! Yes, I'm going to do something — but I don't know what yet. I don't know what there is to do."

She tried to smile with her lips in a tremble; and, looking down, she saw that tears were rolling down the little sister's cheeks.

"Darling! Don't do that!" she cried, roused out of her own distress. "Here, take my handkerchief, and brighten up a little. You mustn't cry here; people will think something dreadful has happened to you."

"They can't think any worse than it is," murmured Louise, snubbing off a sob with the proffered handkerchief. "To have my nice, handsome big brother be a big *fool* like that! Oh, I'd like to *kill* that girl! I would! I'd like to choke her!"

"Louie! Stop! This is awful!" cried Cornelia, horrified. "You mustn't talk that way about anybody, no matter how much of a fool she is. Perhaps there's another side to it. Perhaps Carey is just as much to blame. Perhaps the girl doesn't know any better. Maybe she has no mother to teach her. Maybe Carey is sorry for her."

"He — didn't look sorry; he looked glad!" murmured the little girl, trying to bring her emotions into control; "and anyhow I can't help hating her. Even if she hasn't got a mother, she doesn't need to dip her face in a flour-barrel like that, and make eyes at my brother."

"Listen, Louie." Cornelia's voice was very quiet, and she felt a sudden strength come to her from the need to help the little girl. "Dear, it won't do any good to hate her; it will only do you harm, and mix us up so we can't think straight. Besides, it's wicked to hate anybody. Suppose you stop being so excited and let us put some good common sense into this thing. There must be a way to work it out. If it's wrong for Carey to go with her, there will be a way somehow to make him see it. Until Carey sees it himself there isn't a bit of use in our trying to stop his going with her. He probably has got to the place where rouge and powder are attractive to him, or else perhaps there is more to the girl than just the outside. At any rate, we've got to find out what it is about her that attracts our brother. And, Louie, do you know I've a notion that there's nobody but God can help us in this thing? Mother used to say that, you know, when any big trouble came; and several times lately when I've been worried about things I've said, 'O God, help me,' and things have seemed to straighten out right away. Suppose you and I try that tonight."

Louise looked up through her tears, and smiled.

"You're an awfully dear sister, Nellie. I'm glad you came home"; and she squeezed her sister's hand tenderly.

"Thank you, lovey; I'm glad I came too, and you're rather dear yourself, you know, Lou. I think we'll come through somehow. Now shall we go into this picture-show?"

"I don't believe I feel much like it, do you, Nellie?" said the little girl, hesitatingly and studying a picture on the billboard outside the theatre. "Look! That's one of those pictures with cabaret stuff in that daddy doesn't like us to see. I don't want to go in. Those girls in that picture make me think of her."

"I'll tell you what; let's go home and get a good dinner for Carey and the rest, and perhaps we can think of a way to keep him home tonight and have a good time."

So home they went, and got the dinner, and waited half an hour after the usual time; but no Carey appeared that night until long after the midnight hour had struck. When at last he came tiptoeing up the creaking stairs, trying not to arouse anybody in the house, his two sisters lay hand in hand listening and both praying, "O God, show us how to keep Carey away from that girl, and make him a good man."

Carey slept late on Sunday morning, and came down cross, declining utterly to go to church. Cornelia and Louise went off alone sorrowfully. Carey had lounged off in the direction of the drug store, and the father had a nervous headache, and decided to nurse it up lest it keep him away from work on the morrow. Harry volunteered to stay home and get dinner.

The sermon was about prayer, very simple and interesting. Cornelia did not remember having listened to many sermons in her life. Somehow this one seemed unique, and struck right home to her need and experience. The preacher said that many people prayed and did not receive because they had failed to meet the conditions of answered prayer. Even Louise sat up and listened with earnest eyes and flushed cheeks. Here was something she felt would help the Copley family if they could only get hold of the secret of it. Mother prayed, and mother had great faith in prayer; but none of the rest of them had ever specialized along those lines. Unless perhaps father did, quiet father with all his burdens and disappointments.

These thoughts flitted through the minds of the two daughters as they sat listening intently, reaching out for the help they needed. The preacher said that there were many promises in the Bible concerning prayer, but always with a condition. The first was faith. One must believe that God hears and will answer. The second was will-surrender. One must be ready to let God answer the prayer in *His* way, and to leave that way to Him, believing that He will do what is best. Then one must pray with a free heart, out of which hate and sin have been cast; and he quoted the verse: "If thou bring thy gift to the altar, and there remem- berest that thy brother hath aught against thee, leave there thy gift before the altar, and go thy way; first be reconciled to thy brother, and then come and offer thy gift."

Louise cast a fleeting, questioning glance toward her sister. Did that mean that she must forgive that hateful, bold Dodd girl? But the speaker went on.

There were gifts for which one may ask with a definite assurance of receiving if one comes asking with all the heart, namely, the forgiveness of sin, the strength to resist temptation, the gift of the Holy Spirit. And one may always be sure that it is God's will that other souls should be saved, and so we can pray always for others' salvation, knowing that we are not asking amiss.

But there is a condition in which it is the privilege of every child of God to live, in which one may be sure of receiving what one asks, "If ye abide in me, and my words abide in you, ye shall ask what ye will, and it shall be done unto you."

The two sisters listened most carefully to the simple, clear description of the life that is hid with Christ in God, the life that lets Christ live instead of trying to please self, and that studies daily the Word of God and keeps the word constantly in mind. And the preacher spoke with confidence about answers to prayer for daily needs, as if he had known great experience in receiving.

On their way home Louise, walking along with her eyes on the sidewalk, asked shyly, "Nellie, do you s'pose that's all true, what he preached about?"

"Why, yes — of course," said the elder sister, hesitating, scarcely knowing whither her words were leading her; "why, certainly," she added with belated conviction and a sense that, if it were so, she had placed herself in a very foolish position; for she had never lived as if she had believed it, and the little sister must know that.

"Well, then," with the quick conclusion

of childhood, "why do we worry? why don't we do it?"

"We — could," said her sister thoughtfully; "I don't know why we never did. I guess we never thought about it. Shall we try it?"

"It won't do to *try* it," said the matter-of-fact little girl, "because he said we had to believe it, you know; and trying is holding on with one hand and watching to see. We've got to walk out with both feet and trust. I'm going to!"

"Well, so will I," said Cornelia slowly, her voice low and almost embarrassed. It seemed a strange topic to be talking about so familiarly with a little girl, her little stranger-sister; but she could not let the child get ahead of her. She could not dash the bright spirit of faith.

"That's nice," said Louise with satisfaction. "I'll tell Harry too. I guess he will; boys are so funny. I wish he'd been in church. But say, Nellie, we can be happy now, can't we? We don't need to worry about Carey any more; we can just pray about it and it will all come right."

Cornelia smiled, and squeezed the little hand nestling in hers.

"I guess that's what we're expected to do," she said thoughtfully.

"Yes, and I think God'll show you what to do about that — that — chicken girl, too, don't you, if you ask Him?"

"I guess He will."

The whole family, of course excepting Carey, who telephoned that he wouldn't be home till late, went to church that night, and lingered to be introduced to some of the church people by the cordial minister who had come down to the door to detain them. They finally went home cheered in heart both by the earnest spiritual service and by the warm Christian fellowship that had been offered them.

That night as Louise nestled into her pillow, she whispered:

"Nellie, have you been shown yet? I mean anything about Carey and that girl."

Cornelia drew the little girl into her arms, and laid her lips against the warm, soft cheek.

"I'm not quite sure, dear," she answered. "I've been thinking. Perhaps it will seem queer to you, but I've almost come to think perhaps we ought to get to know her."

"Oh-h-h!" doubtfully. "Do you really think so? But she's — why, she's just *awful,* sister!"

"I know, dear, and I'm not sure yet. But you see we can't do a thing till we really get acquainted with her. She may be simply silly, and not know any better. She may not have any mother, or something; and perhaps we could help her, and then, if we get acquainted with her, we would perhaps be able to make Carey see somehow. Or else we might help her to be — different."

"Oh-h! But how could we get acquainted with her?"

"Well, I don't know. We'd have to think that up. Do you know her name?"

"Yes, it's Clytie Amabel Dodd. They call her Clytie, and it makes me sick the way they say it. She — she smokes cigarettes, Nellie!"

"She does!" exclaimed Cornelia. "Are you sure, dear? How do you know?"

"Well, Hazel Applegate says she saw her on the street smoking with a lot of boys."

There was a long pause, and the little girl almost thought her sister was asleep; then Cornelia asked, "Do you know where she lives?"

"No, but I guess Harry does. He gets around a lot delivering groceries, you know. Anyway, if he doesn't, he can find out."

"Well, I'll have to think about it some more — and — pray, too."

"Nellie."

"Well, dear?"

"Nellie, you know that verse the minister said this morning about if two of you agree to pray for anything you know; why couldn't you and I do that?"

Cornelia pressed the little fingers close. Then it was all very still, and presently the two slept.

The next afternoon, while they were getting dinner and working about in the kitchen, the older sister suddenly asked:

"When is Carey's birthday? Isn't it this week? The twenty-fifth, isn't it?"

"Yes," said Louise gravely. "It's Thursday. Are you going to do anything? O Nellie!" in consternation. "You're *not* going to invite that girl *then?*"

"I don't know," said Cornelia. "I know it wouldn't be very pleasant for us, but I thought perhaps it would be a good excuse. There isn't really any other that I know of."

The little girl was silent for a moment.

"Wouldn't it make her think we thought — I mean wouldn't she get a notion we liked — That is, wouldn't she be awfully set up — and think we wanted her to go with Carey?"

"I'm sure I don't know, dear, and I don't suppose that part of it really matters if we just get this thing sifted down and find out what we've got to do. We simply can't say anything about her to Carey till we've somehow come in contact with her in his presence, or he will think we've been snooping about watching him; and he will just be angry and go with her all the more."

"I know," sighed the little girl.

"If we have her here," went on the older sister thoughtfully, "we'll at least know what they both are doing; and, if she doesn't act nicely, we'll have some ground to influence Carey."

"Yes," answered the little girl with another sigh. "Have you thought, Nellie, perhaps he won't like it?"

"Yes, I've thought that too, but I guess it won't really matter much. It may do good, you know."

"But he might not come home to supper that night. Or he might get real mad, and get up and leave while she's here."

"Well, I don't see that that would really do any harm. I guess we've got to try something, and this seems kind of a plain way to do. If mother were here, it would be better. Mother would know how to give dignity to the occasion. But I guess for mother's sake I've got to do something to either improve her or get rid of her before mother comes home. It would kill mother."

"Yes, I know. What do you suppose father'll say?"

"Well, I don't believe I'll tell father, either, only that I'm going to have a girl here to supper. It would only worry him if he knew she went with Carey; and you can always depend on father to be polite, you know, to anybody."

"Yes," said Louise soberly. "He'll be polite, but — he won't like her, and she can't help knowing it, no matter how thick-skinned she is; but maybe it'll do her good. Only I'm afraid Carey'll be mad, and say something to father or something."

"No, I don't think he will, not before a girl. Not before any girl. Not if I know Carey. He may say things afterwards, but we'll have to be willing to stand that. And, besides, what can he say? Aren't we polite to one of his friends? We're not supposed to know anything about her. When it comes down to facts, little sister, we don't really *know* anything about her except that she dresses in a loud way, chews gum, and talks too loud on the street. The other things you have only heard, and you can't be sure they are true unless you see them yourself, or some one you trust perfectly has seen them. I know she may get a notion in her head that Carey is crazy about her if we single her out and invite her alone, but I've about decided it's the only way. Anyhow, she's let herself in for things of that sort by getting herself talked about. I believe we've got to do something quite radical, and either kill or cure this trouble. I've thought about asking that Brand fellow too, and maybe some one else, some other girl. But who would it be?"

Louise thought a moment, then she clutched her sister's hand eagerly.

"Nellie! The very thing! Invite Grace Kendall! She would make them all fit in beautifully. I'd hate awfully to have her know our Carey went with that Clytie thing; but I guess there isn't any other way, and somehow I think a minister's daughter ought to understand, don't you? And help?"

Cornelia was still struggling with her pride.

"Yes," she said thoughtfully. "I guess you're right, little sister. Grace Kendall would understand — and help. I think God must have given you that idea. We'll invite Clytie and Brand and Grace Kendall, and then trust God to show us how to make them all have a good time without suspecting what it's all about. We'll just tell Carey that he must come home early because we have a birthday cake and a surprise for him

— make him promise to be there; you know; and then we'll take him into the living room, and they'll be there waiting. If he thinks it strange and says anything about it afterwards, we'll tell him we invited all the people we knew were his friends, and we couldn't ask him about it beforehand because it had to be a surprise party. Now, little sister, I think you've solved the problem with your bright idea; and we can decide on that."

14

They had the hardest time with Harry when they confided to him their plans and asked for his assistance. It took a great deal of argument and much tact to make him believe that anything good might come out of inviting "that chicken," as he persisted in calling Carey's latest admiration. He had little less scorn for Brand Barlock; but, when he heard that Grace Kendall was to be included in the list of guests, he succumbed.

"Aw, gee! It's a rotten shame to mix her up with that gang, but if she'll come, it'll be some party. Gee! Yes, I'll take your invites round, but you better find out if the minister's girl will come before you get any of the others."

The sisters decided that Harry's advice was wise, and after the children had gone to school and the morning work was done up Cornelia took her walk to market around by the way of the minister's house and proffered her request.

"I'm not at all sure you'll like the company," she said with a deprecatory smile; "they are some young people Carey got to know last winter, and I want to get acquainted with them and see if they are the right kind. I thought maybe you'd be willing to help make it a success."

That was all the explanation she gave; but the other girl's face kindled sympathetically, and she seemed to understand everything.

"Oh, I'd love to come. Shall I bring some games? We have a table-tennis that is a lot of fun; you use it on the dining-room table, you know; and there are several other games that we enjoy playing here when we have a jolly crowd. Suppose I bring my violin over, and we have some music, too. I'll bring some popular songs; we have a bunch for when the boys come in from the church."

When Cornelia started home, she felt quite cheerful about her party. Grace Kendall seemed to be a hostess in herself. She had offered to come around and help get ready, and the two girls had grown quite chummy. Cornelia hummed a little song, and quite forgot that across the miles of distance her classmates were this day preparing for the elaborate program that had long been anticipated for their class-day exercises. Somehow college days and their doings had come to seem almost childish beside the real things of every day. This party, for instance. How crude and home-made it was all to be! Yet it stood for so much, and it seemed as if momentous decisions depended upon its results.

She stopped in an art shop on her way back, and studied little menu cards and favors, purchasing a roll of pink crêpe paper, some green and yellow tissue paper, wire, and cardboard. As soon as she had finished the dessert for dinner she hurried to get out scissors, paste, pencils, and went eagerly to her dainty work. Before Louise and Harry came home from school she had fashioned eight dainty little candy baskets covered with ruffled pink paper, and on each slender thread-like pink handle there nodded a lovely curly pink rose with a leaf and a bud, all made of the paper, with their little green wire stems twining about the pink basket. Eight little blue birds, with their claws and tails so balanced that they would hover on the rim of a water glass, and bearing in their bills a tiny place card, also lay on the table beside the baskets, the product of Cornelia's skillful brush and colors. The children went into ecstasies over them and even Harry began to warm to the affair.

"I guess *she'll* see we're fashionable all right," he swaggered scornfully. "I guess she'll see she's got to go some to be good enough to speak to our Carey. Say, what did the Kendall girl say? Is she coming? Say,

213

she's a peach, isn't she? I knew she'd be game all right Did you tell her 'bout the other one? You oughtta. She might not like it."

"I told her as much as was necessary. You needn't worry about her, she's pure gold."

"You're talking!" said the boy gruffly, and went whistling upstairs to change his clothes. But Louise stood still, enraptured before the little paper baskets and birds. Suddenly she turned a radiant face to her sister, and in a voice that was almost expressive of awe she said softly:

"But it's going to be real; isn't it, Nellie? I never knew we could be real. I never knew you could do things like that. It's like the pictures in the magazines, and it's like Mrs. Van Kirk's luncheon. Hazel and I went there on an errand to get some aprons for the Red Cross for our teacher at school, and we had to wait in the dining-room for ten minutes while she hunted them up. The table was all set for a luncheon she was going to give that day, and afterwards we saw about it in the paper; and she had baskets and things just like that."

Cornelia stooped and kissed the eager young face tenderly, and wondered how she could have borne to be separated all these years from her little sister and brother, and not have known how satisfactorily they were growing up.

"What are you going to put into them?" asked the little girl.

"Well I haven't decided yet," said Cornelia. "Probably salted almonds, don't you think?"

"Oh, but they're awful expensive!"

"Not if you make them, dear. You and I will make them. I've done tons of them at college for feasts. It's easy; just blanch them and brown them in a pan with butter and salt or oil and salt."

"Oh, can you?" More awe in the voice. "And what will we have to eat?"

"Well, I'm not sure yet. We'll have to count the dishes and let that settle some questions. We must have enough to go around, you know, and all alike. I wonder if there are enough bouillon cups. It takes eight, you know — Father, Carey, you, and Harry, three guests and myself. Yes, that's eight. Climb up to the top shelf there, dear, and see if there are enough of mother's rosebud bouillon cups."

"There are nine and an extra saucer," announced Louise.

"Well, then we'll have some kind of soup, just a little; I think maybe spinach, cream of spinach soup, it's such a pretty color for spring, you know, that pale-green, and matches the dining-room. It's easy to make, and doesn't cost much; and then we can have the spinach for a vegetable with the meat course. Now, let's see, those little clear sherbet glasses, are there enough of those?"

"A whole dozen and seven," announced Louise.

"Then we'll use those at the beginning for a fruit cocktail — orange, grapefruit, banana, and I'll color it pink with a little red raspberry juice. I found a can among the preserves mother had left over from last winter. It makes a lovely pink, and that will match the baskets."

"Oh, lovely!" exclaimed the little girl ecstatically; "but won't that cost a lot?"

"No, dear, I think not. I'll figure it down pretty close tonight and find out; but it doesn't take much fruit to fill those tiny glasses, and it's mostly show, you know — one grapefruit, a couple of oranges, and bananas, and the rest raspberry juice. Spinach is cheap now, you know; and we can make the body of the soup with a can of condensed milk. We can eat corn-meal mush and beans and things for a few days beforehand to make up."

"I just love fried mush and bean soup."

"You're a ducky! And, besides, I'm going

to save on the dessert."

"Aren't we going to have ice-cream?" Louise's voice showed anxiety.

"Yes, but we'll make it ourselves. I found the freezer out in the back shed under all those carpets yesterday. And we'll have pale-green peppermint water-ice. It's beautiful, and costs hardly anything. You just make lemonade and put in a few drops of peppermint and a drop or two of confectioner's green coloring; and it is the prettiest thing you ever laid eyes on, looks like a dream and tastes — wonderful!"

"Oh!" said Louise, her eyes shining.

"We'll have angel cake for the birthday cake, I think," went on the sister, "with white icing and little pink candles. Eggs are not expensive now, and anyway I found a recipe that says measure the whites, and such big eggs as we get take only nine to a cup. How will that be, angel cake and green water-ice for dessert?"

Louise sat down, and folded her hands, her big, expressive eyes growing wide and serious.

"It's going to be a success!" she said solemnly with a grown-up air. "I was afraid she wouldn't be — well — impressed but she will. It's regular! You wanted her to be impressed, too; didn't you, Nellie?"

Cornelia couldn't help laughing at the solemn question, but she sobered instantly.

"Yes, dear, I guess I did. I wanted her to have respect for Carey's family and to know that, however foolish he may be, there is something, as you say, 'regular' behind him. Because there is, you know, Louie. Father and mother are 'regular'."

"They are!" said the little girl.

"It sounds rather queer to try to impress people with fuss and show and food fixed up in fancy styles; but, if I can judge anything about that girl, she hasn't reached the stage yet where she can appreciate anything but fuss and fancy and fashion. So we've got to use the things that will appeal to her if we want to reach her at all. If it were just Grace Kendall coming, or even the young man Brand, I would have things very plain and simple. It would be in better taste and more to my liking. But I have a notion, kitten, that, if we had everything very simple, that young lady with the fancy name would rather despise us, and set out to ride right over us. They talk a great deal nowadays about people's reaction to things; and, if I know anything at all about that girl, I feel pretty sure that her reaction to simple, quiet things would be far from what we want. So for this once we'll blossom out and have things as stylish and fancy and formal as possible. I've heard it said that there is nothing so good to take the pride out of an ignorant person as an impressive array of forks and spoons; so we'll try it on Miss Clytie, and see if we can bring her near enough to our class to get acquainted with her real self. Now get a pencil, and write down the menu, and see how it reads."

"But what are you going to have in the middle, Nellie, after the soup? Any meat?"

"Why, surely, round steak, simmered all day with an onion, and browned down with thick gravy the way you love it so well; only we'll cut it into small servings like cutlets before we cook it, and nobody will ever dream what it is. Then we'll have new potatoes creamed, with parsley sprinkled over them, and spinach minced, with a hard-boiled egg on top; and for salad we'll make some gelatin molds in the custard cups with shredded cabbage and parsley in it, that on a lettuce leaf will look very pretty; and I'll make the mayonnaise out of the yolks of the eggs from the angel cake. There'll be enough left over to make a gold cake or some custard for the next day besides. Now write the menu. Raspberry fruit cocktail, cream of spinach soup, round-steak cutlets with brown gravy, creamed new potatoes with parsley, spinach, aspic-jelly salad, angel cake, mint sherbet, and coffee. Doesn't that sound good?"

"I should say," answered the little girl with a happy sigh. "We'll have everything all ready beforehand, so that the serving will be easy," went on the elder sister. "The butter and water and fruit cocktail will be on the table. We can fill the soup cups and keep them in the warming oven; and you and Harry can get up quietly; remove the fruit glasses, and bring on the soup cups. You see I've been thinking it all out. I've planned to buy two more wire shelves to fit into the oven. You know there are grooves to move them higher or lower; and I find that, if we use the lowest groove for the first, there will be room to set the eight plates in there; and we'll just have everything all served on the plate ready, the little cutlet with gravy, the creamed potatoes, and the spinach. Then, if we light only one burner and turn it low, and perhaps leave the door open a little, — I'll have to experiment, — I think they will keep hot without getting dry or crusty on the top, just for that little while. The only thing is, you'll have to be tremendously careful not to drop one getting them out; they'll be hot, you know, and you'll have to use a cloth to take them out. Just think, if you dropped one, there wouldn't be enough to go around."

Louise giggled, and squeezed her sister's hand.

"O Nellie, isn't it going to be just packs of fun? I won't drop one; indeed I won't; but if I should I just know I'd laugh out loud, it would be so funny, all that grand dinner-party in there acting stylish, and those potatoes and spinach and meat sitting there on the floor! But don't you worry; if I did drop 'em, I'd pick 'em up again, and take that plate for myself. Our kitchen floor's clean, anyway. When do we bring in the salad?"

"Oh, we'll just have that on the kitchen table by the door, ready. And then, while the people are finishing, you and Harry can slip out and get the sherbet dished out. Do you think you two can manage it?"

"Oh, sure! Harry does it at school every time we have an entertainment. The teacher always gets him to do it 'cause he gets it out so nice, and not messy, she says. Shall we cut the cake beforehand, or what?"

"Oh, no; the cake will be on the table with the candles lit when we come into the dining-room; and when the time comes, Carey will have to blow out the candles and cut his own cake."

And so they planned the pretty festival, and almost forgot the unloved cause of it all, poor, silly little Clytie Amabel Dodd.

Cornelia's hardest task was writing the letter of invitation to the guest she dreaded most of all. After tearing up several attempts and struggling with the sentences for half an hour, it was finally finished, and read:

My dear Miss Dodd,

We are having a little surprise for my brother Carey on his birthday next Thursday, the twenty-fifth, and would be very glad if you will come to dinner at six o'clock to meet a few friends. Kindly say nothing to Carey about it, and please let us know if we may expect you.

Looking forward to meeting you, I am,

Very sincerely,
Carey's sister,
Cornelia Copley

After a solemn conclave it was decided to mail this missive, and then the three conspirators waited anxiously for two whole days for a reply. When Harry and Louise arrived from school the third day and found no answer yet, anxiety was strong.

"Yes, Harry, you oughtta have taken that note yourself, the way Nellie said," declared Louise.

"Not me!" asserted Harry loftily. "Not if that chicken never comes! We don't want her anyway. I guess we can have a party without her!"

But a few minutes later a clattering knock arose on the front door, and a small boy with an all-day sucker in his cheek appeared.

"My sister, she says sure she'll come to your s'prise party," he announced indifferently; "she didn't have no time to write; so I come."

He waited expectantly for a possible reward for his labors. Cornelia smiled, thanked him, said she was glad; and he departed disappointedly. He was always on the lookout for rewards.

"That's Dick Dodd," Louise explained. "He's an awful bad little kid. He put gum in the teacher's hat and hid a bee in her desk; and once she found three caterpillars in her lunch basket, and everybody knew who put them there. He never washes his hands nor has a handkerchief."

The little girl's voice was full of scorn. She was returning to her former dislike of their expected guest with all that pertained to her.

"Well, there's that," said Cornelia smiling. "She's coming, and we know what to expect. Now I think I'll call up the Barlock house, and find out when they expect that Brand fellow to be at home. I think I can do that more informally over the phone."

It just happened that Brand Barlock was passing through the house where he was supposed to reside, probably for a change of garments, or something to eat, or to get his pocketbook replenished; and he answered the phone himself. Cornelia was amused at the haughty condescension of his tone. One would think she had presumed to invite royalty to her humble abode by the lofty way in which he answered: "Why, yes, — I might come, if nothing else turns up. Yes, I'm sure I can make it. Very nice, I'm sure. Anything you'd like to have me bring?"

"Oh, no, indeed!" said Cornelia emphatically, her cheeks very red indeed. "It's just a simple home affair, and we thought Carey would enjoy having his friends. You won't mention it to him, of course."

"Aw'right! I'll keep mum. So-long!" and the young lord hung up.

Cornelia emerged from the drug-store telephone-booth much upset in spirit and wishing she hadn't invited the young upstart. By the time she reached the outer door she wished she had never tried to have a party for Carey. But, when she got back to Louise and her shining interest, her common sense had returned; and she set herself to bear the unpleasantness and make those two queer, incongruous guests of hers enjoy themselves in spite of everything, or else make them feel so uncomfortable that they would take themselves forever out of Carey's life.

Steadily forward went the preparations for the party, and at last the birthday morning arrived.

 **15**

Arthur Maxwell over his morning grape-fruit, buttered toast and coffee, which he usually had served in his apartment, began in a leisurely way to open his mail.

There was a thick enticing letter from his mother which he laid aside till the last. He and his mother were great pals and her letters were like a bit of herself, almost as good as talking with her face to face. He always enjoyed every word of them.

There were the usual number of business communications which he tore open and read hurriedly as he came to them, frowning over one, putting another in his pocket to be answered in his office, and then at the very bottom, under a long envelope which carried a plea for money for his Alma Mater to help build a new observatory, he came suddenly upon a square, foreign-looking envelope addressed in a dashing illegible hand and emitting a subtle fragrance of rare flowers, a fragrance that had hovered exquisitely about his senses from the moment the mail had been laid by his plate, reminding him dimly of something sweet and forbidden and half forgotten.

He looked at the letter, half startled, a trifle displeased and yet greatly stirred. It represented a matter that he was striving to put out of his life, that he thought he had succeeded in overcoming, even almost forgetting. A grim speculative look came into his face. He hesitated before he reached out his hand to pick up the letter, and questioned whether he should even open it. Then with a look that showed that he had taken himself well in hand he picked it up, ran his knife crisply under the flap of the envelope and read:

Dear Arthur,

I am passing through Philadelphia tomorrow on my way to Washington and am stopping over for a few hours especially to see you about a matter of grave importance. I feel that you will not be angry at my breaking this absurd silence that you have imposed between us when I tell you that I am in great trouble and need your advice. I remember your promise always to be my friend, and I know you will not refuse to see me now for at least a few minutes.

I am coming down on the two o'clock train from New York and shall go directly to Hotel —— and await your coming anxiously. I know you will not fail me.

Yours eternally,
Evadne

The subtle fragrance, the dashing script, the old familiar turn of sentence, reached into his consciousness and gripped him for a second in spite of his being on his guard. Something thrilling and tragic seemed to emanate from the very paper in his hand, from the royal purple of the lining of the expensive envelope. For an instant he felt the old lure, the charm, the tragedy of his life which he was seeking to outlive, which he had supposed was already outlived.

In his senior year in college Arthur Maxwell had become acquainted with Evadne Chantry at a house party where both had been guests. They had been thrown together during the two days of their stay, whether by the hostess's planning or at the lady's request is not known, but Arthur, at first not much attracted by her type, found himself growing more and more interested.

Evadne was a slender, dark, sophisticated little thing with dreamy eyes and a naïve appeal. His chivalry was challenged and when it further appeared that she was just from England, and was of the old family of

Chantrys whom his mother knew and visited, he got down from his distance and capitulated. They became close friends, in spite of the fact that Evadne's ways were not the ways in which he had been brought up, and in which his young manhood had chosen to walk. But he had found himself excusing her. She had not been taught as he had. She had lived abroad where standards were different. She had been in boarding schools and convents, and then travelled. He felt she could be brought to change her ways.

It appeared that she was going to be for sometime in the city where his college was located, and the friendship ripened rapidly, taking Arthur Maxwell into a social group as utterly foreign to his own as one could imagine, in fact one which he did not really enjoy, yet he went for Evadne's sake.

When he came to the point of telling his mother of the friendship, about which it had been strangely hard to write, he found that it was no easy matter. In the light of her clear eyes there were matters which could not be so easily set aside as his own conscience had been soothed to do. He suddenly realized what a shock it would be to his conservative mother to see Evadne smoking, to watch her in her sinuous attitudes, to know that her son was deeply interested in a young woman who had plucked eyebrows and used a lip stick freely. When he came to think of it some of her costumes might be exceedingly startling to his mother. Yet he believed in his mother so thoroughly that he felt she could be made to understand how much this girl had suffered from lack of a mother, and how much she was in need of just such a friend as his mother could be.

When the time arrived that Mrs. Maxwell had to learn these things her son was even more startled than herself to find out how much she really was shocked at his choice of a girl. The stricken look that came into her eyes the first time they met told him without further words from her lips. In that moment he might be said to have grown up as he suddenly looked upon the girl whom he thought he loved beyond all women, through the eyes of his mother.

His mother had been wonderful even though she carried the stricken look through the entire interview. She had perhaps not exactly taken Evadne into her arms quite as he had hoped, but she had been gently sweet and polite. His mother would always be that. She had been quiet, so quiet, and watchful, as if she were gravely considering some threatened catastrophe and meeting it bravely.

Afterwards, she had met his eyes with a brave, sad smile, without a hint of rebuke, not a suggestion that he should have told her sooner, only an acceptance of the fact that the girl was here in their lives and must be dealt with fairly. She listened to his story of Evadne's life, considered his suggestion that she might help the girl, heard how they had met and his reasons for feeling that she was the one and only girl. As he told it all he was conscious of something searching in her sweet, grave eyes that turned a knife in his heart, yet he was full of hope that she would eventually understand and come under Evadne's spell with himself.

Only once she questioned about the girl. How did he know she belonged to the Chantrys she knew? What relationship did she bear to them? Was she Paul Chantry's sister? Cousin? She did not remember that there had been a daughter.

Evadne had not taken kindly to his mother. She wept when Arthur talked with her alone after their meeting, and said she was sure his mother did not love her. But the days passed on and Mrs. Maxwell kept her own counsel, and invited the girl to her home, doing all the little gracious social things that might be expected of her, yet with a heavy heart, till one day when it seemed that an announcement of the engagement should be the next thing in order, there came a letter from England in answer to one Mrs. Maxwell had written, disclaiming any relationship between Evadne and the distinguished old family who were her friends.

This was a matter that Arthur could not ignore when his mother brought it to his notice, and Evadne was asked for an explanation.

Evadne met his questions with haughty contempt and then with angry tears and retired into an offended silence that seemed as impenetrable as a winter fog, from which she presently emerged like a martyr with vague explanations of a distant cousinship that seemed full and sufficient to his gallant, young spirit, till he tried to repeat them to his clear-eyed mother and then they did not seem so convincing.

The matter was finally smoothed over, however, and it seemed as if the mother was about to be called upon to set the seal of her approval upon a speedy marriage between the two, when there came a revelation through the medium of an old friend who had met Evadne abroad, and asked her quite casually, in the presence of the Maxwells, where her husband was. Explanations followed, of course, and it appeared that Evadne was married already and had left her husband in South Africa without even the formality of a divorce.

Gradually, however, the girl's clever story broke down his indignation at her deception, as she told him sobbingly how lonely she was and how she longed for friendship and something real in life; and it took many days and nights of agonizing thought before the plummet of his soul was able to swing clear and tell him that no matter how lonely she was or who was to blame, or how much or when or why, there was one thing true, if Evadne was married, she was not for him, no, not even if she got a divorce. So much inheritance had he from long lines of Puritan ancestors, and from the high, fine teachings of his mother. It was a law of God, and it was right. He was not altogether sure just then that he believed in the God who had let all this tragedy come into his life, but he believed in the law and he must keep it. He had felt himself grow old in those days while he was coming to that inevitable conclusion that if it was not right for them to love one another, then they must not see one another.

For days he could not talk about it to his mother, and she spent the hours upon her knees, while he went about stern and white, and Evadne did all in her power to make him see that time had changed and modern ways did not accept those puritan lives any more which he was holding forth as final and inexorable. Sin! What was *sin?* There *was* no such thing! *Law!* She laughed. Why keep a law that everyone else was breaking? It was all of a piece with his old-fogy notions about drinking wine and having a good time. He was the dearest in all the world of course, but he was narrow. She held out her lily arms from the sheath-like black velvet gown she had assumed and pleaded with him to come with her, come out into the broad, free air of a big life! She was clever. She had caught most of the modern phrases. She knew how to appeal to the finer things in him, and *almost* she won her point. Almost he wavered for just the fraction of a second, and thought, perhaps she is right — perhaps I am narrow. Then he lifted his eyes and saw his mother standing in the doorway, being shown in by a blundering servant, his fine patrician mother with her true eyes, and pure, sorrowful face, and he knew. He knew that Evadne was wrong and his mother — yes his mother and he were right. There could be nothing but sin in a love that was stolen — a love that transgressed.

He had gone away then and left his mother to talk to the other woman, and something, somewhere in his manhood had kept him away after that. He had written her fully his final word, with so stern a renunciation that even Evadne knew it was unalterable. He had laid down the law that they must not meet again; and had then gone away to another part of the country and established himself in business and tried to forget.

That had been two years ago. Long years, he called it when he thought of them by himself. The haggard look of the gray young face had past away gradually, and the stern lines had softened as his fine mind and strong body and naturally cheerful spirit came back to normal, but there had been a reserve about him that made people think him a year or two older than he really was, and made some women when they met him call him "distinguished." He had passed in the struggles of his soul, slowly away from the place where he regarded Evadne as a martyr, and had come at last to the time when he could look his experience squarely in the face and realize that she had been utterly untrue to all that was fine and womanly, and that he was probably saved from a life of sorrow and disappointment. Nevertheless, back in his soul there lingered his pity for her slender beauty, her pretty helplessness. A natural conclusion had come to him that all girls were deceitful, all beautiful women were naturally selfish and untrue. There were no more good, sweet, true girls nowadays as there were when his mother was a girl.

Away from home he drifted out of church-going. He immersed himself in business and began to be a brilliant success. He wrote long letters to his mother and enjoyed hers in return, but his epistles were not revealing. She sensed his reserves, and when they met she felt his playful gentleness with her was a screen for a bitterness of soul which she hoped and prayed might pass. And it did pass, gradually, until she had almost come to feel that his soul was healed, and the tragedy forgotten. More and more she prayed now that some day, when he was ready, he might meet a different kind of girl, one who would make him forget utterly the poor little vampire who had almost ruined his life's happiness. In fact, the last time she had seen him on her recent trip to Philadelphia he had laughingly told her that she needn't worry about him any more. He was utterly heart whole and happy.

But it is a question, whether if she had been permitted to look in on him this morning as he read Evadne's letter, she would have felt that his words had been quite true.

He had promised his mother, in those first days after the break with Evadne, that he would not see her nor communicate with her for at least two years. The time was more than past, yet he felt the righteous obligation of his promise still upon him. He knew that he ought not to see Evadne again. He knew that the very sight of her would stir in him the old interest, which he now felt to be of a lower order than the highest of which he was capable. He could see her sitting now flung back in some bewildering costume that revealed the delicate, slim lines of her figure, some costly bauble smouldering on the whiteness of her neck that might have graced an Egyptian queen, her hair moulded in satin-like folds about her small head, and her slanted eyes half closed, studying him tauntingly as she held her cigarette in her jewelled fingers and considered with what clever personality to bind him next.

The distance of time had shown him that he had been bound, that he had been a fool, and had brought him disillusionment; yet he knew that if he gave it half a chance the enchantment would work again upon him, and he felt contempt for himself that it was so. Yet strangely he found a law within himself that longed again to be enchanted, even while he sneered at the emptiness of it all.

Suppose he should go tonight to meet her — it was tonight. He glanced at the date of the letter to make sure. He could tell almost to a flicker of an eyelash what would happen.

She would meet him as if they had parted but yesterday, and she would ignore all that was passed except that they loved each other. His soul rebelled at the thought of that for he did not now feel that he loved her any longer. The cleanness of his spirit had put that away. She was not his, she was another's. She was not fit for a real love, even if there had been no barrier. That had been his maturer thought, especially at times when he remembered her deceit. Yet human nature is a subtle thing. Though he resented her thinking that he had continued to care for her, he feared for himself lest when he saw her he would allow her to think that it was so. And yet he longed to go and see how it would be. He felt curious to try his dearly-bought contentment and see if it would hold. Should he go?

His mother would advise against it, of course. But he was a man now. This was his personal responsibility. Whether he should see her or not. All that about her needing advice in trouble was rot, of course. There were plenty of people who could advise her. He could send the old family lawyer to her if necessary. Her plea had been well planned to make him come because she wished to see if he still cared, or if he had forgotten her. But yet it might be salutary for them both for him to go for a few minutes and show her that there was nothing to all the tragedy that they had thought they were living through.

Well, — there was plenty of time to decide what to do. She wasn't coming till afternoon — he could go, of course, and take her to the Roof Garden for dinner — or perhaps she would better enjoy one of the quieter places — he knew a little Chinese Restaurant that was more her style. However, he would thrash it out during the day. It was getting late and he must hurry to the office. But he must read his mother's letter first, of course. There might be something she wanted done at once. She was staying in the mountains for a little while with her sister who was recovering from a severe illness, and there often was some shopping she wanted him to attend to at once.

He opened the letter, his mind preoccupied with thoughts of Evadne.

The letter was filled with wonderful descriptions of views and people his mother had met, mingled with wise and witty comments on politics and current events. He skimmed it hastily through to the last paragraph which read:

I came on a lovely clump of maidenhair ferns yesterday in my walk, and I had the gardener at the hotel take them up and box them carefully for me. I want to send them to my little friend, the interior decorator whom I met on the train a few weeks ago. You remember? But after they were all ready to go and I came to look for the address I remembered that I left it in the little drawer of the desk in your apartment. I have tried my best to rack my brains for a clue to the street and number, and can't remember a thing except that her name was Cornelia Copley. I remembered that because of the Copley prints of which we are both so fond. So rather than give up the idea or trust to the ferns finding her in that big city with just her

name and no street address I am sending them to you. I want you to slip the
box into your car and take a run out
that way the very day they come and
deliver them for me, please. I like that
little girl, and I want her to have these
beautiful ferns. They will help her decorate her forlorn little house. I hope you
won't consider this a nuisance, son. But
you never do when I ask a favor. I know.
Be sure to do it *at once*, for the ferns
won't stand it long without water.

A knock came on the door just then, and
the young man looked up to see the wife of
the janitor, who looked after the apartment
and cooked his breakfast, standing in the
open door.

"The 'spressman done brung a box, Mr.
Maxwell," she said. "What you want did
with it?"

"Oh, it's come! Well, tell him to put it
into my car. It ought to be out at the door
waiting by this time, and just sign for it
please, Hannah. I'm in a hurry this morning. I have an appointment at half past
eight."

Five minutes later, when Maxwell hurried
down; he found the big box on the floor of
his car, with feathery fronds reaching out to

the light and blowing delicately in the breeze.

"Well, I should say she did send a few!" he grumbled to himself. "Trust mother to do a thing thoroughly! I don't see when I can possibly manage to deliver these today! I'll have to get away somehow at lunch time I suppose. I certainly wish mother hadn't chosen this special day to wish one of her pet enthusiasms on me! She's always hunting out some nice girl! I wish she wouldn't!"

With that he slammed shut the door, threw in the clutch, and was off, and never thought of those ferns all day long until late in the afternoon, later than his usual hour for going to his dinner, he climbed wearily into the car again. He had had a hard day, with perplexing problems to solve and a disagreeable visiting head to show all over the Philadelphia branch, and keep in good humor. There had not been a minute to get away, not even for a bit of a run in the car at noon; for the visitor had a cold, and didn't care to ride; so they lunched in the downstairs restaurant, and went back to work again all the afternoon. The visitor at last was whirled away in the car of another employee to whose home in the suburbs he had been invited to dinner, and Maxwell with a sigh of relief, and feeling somehow very lonesome and tired, was free at last, free to consider the problem of the evening.

He was just backing out of the garage, and turning to see that his wheels had cleared the doorway, his eye caught a gleam of green.

"Oh, doggone those fool ferns!" he said under his breath. "Now I'll simply *have* to get them off my hands tonight, or they'll 'die on me' as the elevator man said his first wife did. Mother didn't know what a nuisance this would be. I haven't a minute to waste on such fool nonsense tonight. I really ought to call up Evadne at once and let her know I'm coming — *if* I am. I wonder if I am. Well, here goes with the ferns first. It won't take long if I can find the dump, and it will give me a few minutes leisure to decide what I'll do. I haven't had a second all day long. I never saw such a day!"

He sent the car shooting forward on the smooth road climbing the long grade into the sunset.

16

The morning had opened most favorably in the Copley home, with everybody in good spirits. At the breakfast table Cornelia had informed the male portion of the family quite casually that there was to be a birthday supper and they must all come promptly home and dress up for it and Harry had given a grave wink at Louise which almost convulsed her.

Carey was in charming spirits. When he awoke, he had found two new shirts and two pairs of silk socks by his bedside "with love from Cornelia," and a handkerchief and necktie apiece from each of the children; and he came down with uproarious thanks to greet them. Mr. Copley, thus reminded of the occasion got up before he had finished his first cup of coffee, and went into the living room to the desk. When he came back, he carried a check in his hand made out to Carey.

"There, son, that's from mother and me for that new suit you need," he said in a voice warm with feeling. "I meant to get around to it last night, but somehow the date slipped me."

And Carey taken unaware, was almost

embarrassed, rising with the check in his hand and his color coming and going like a girl.

"Why Dad! Really, Dad! You ought not to do this now. I'm an old chump that I haven't earned one long ago. Take it back, Dad; you'll need it for mother. I'll take the thought just the same."

"No, that's all right, son; you earn the next one," said the father with a touch on his son's arm almost like a caress.

And so the little party separated with joy on every face, and went their separate ways. Carey was still working at the garage. He had been secretly saving up to buy a second-hand automobile that he knew was for sale, excusing the desire by saying it would be good for his mother to ride in when she came home; but now he suddenly saw that his ambition was selfish and that what he must first do was to get a job where he could help his father and pay his board at home. To that end he resolved to hand twenty-five dollars to Cornelia that very night if he could get it out of Pat, and start the new year aright, telling her it was board money.

He promised most solemnly to be at home in time to "fix up" before supper, and Cornelia went about the day's preparations with a light heart. There seemed a reasonable amount of hope that the young man himself would be likely to be on hand at his own birthday party. Having secured the two most likely sources of other engagements, Clytie and Brand, there didn't seem much else that could happen to upset her plans.

The birthday cake had been a regular angel the way it rose and stayed risen when it got there, and blushed a lovely biscuit brown, and took its icing smoothly. It was even now reposing in state in the bread-box ready for its candles, which Louise was to add when she returned from school at noon. Both children were coming home at noon, and Harry was not going to the grocery that day.

Cornelia had put the whole house in apple-pie order the day before, made the cake and the gelatin salad, and had done all the marketing. The day looked easy ahead of her. She set the biscuits, and tucked them up in a warm corner, washed the spinach in many waters, and left it in its last cold bath getting crisp, with the lettuce in a stone jar doing the same thing. Then she sat down with a silver spoon, a sharp knife, a big yellow bowl, and a basket of fruit to prepare the fruit cocktail.

While she was doing this, Grace Kendall

ran in with her arms full of lovely roses that had been sent to her mother that morning. She said her mother wished to share them with the Copleys. Grace put the flowers into water and sat down with another spoon to help. Before long the delicious pink and gold mixture was put away on the ice all ready for night. Grace helped scrape the potatoes and dust the living room, then went home promising to be on hand early and help entertain the strange guests. Somehow Grace seemed to understand all about both of them and to be tremendously interested in the whole affair. Cornelia went about her pretty living room putting the last touches everywhere, setting a blue bowl of roses at just the right angle on the table, putting an especially lovely half-open bud in a tall, slender glass on the bookcase, pushing a chair into place, turning a magazine and a book into inviting positions. She kept thinking how glad she was for this new girl friend, this girl who, though a little younger, yet seemed to understand so well. She sighed as she touched the roses lovingly, and recognized a fleeting impossible wish that her brother might have chosen to be interested in a girl like this one instead of the gum-chewing, ill-bred child with whom he seemed to be pairing off.

The children were so excited when they arrived at noon that she had difficulty in persuading them to eat any lunch. They ate the sandwiches and drank the milk she had set out for them, in one swallow, it seemed to her; and then they flew to the tasks that had been assigned to them. Harry brought in armfuls of wood and stowed them neatly away in the big locker by the fireside, and built up a beautifully scientific fire ready to light. It was a lovely warm spring day, but with all the windows open in the evening a good fire in the fireplace would be quite acceptable and altogether too charming to omit. He swept the hearth, and then went out and scrubbed the front steps, swept the front walk, and mowed the little patch of lawn, trimming the edges till it looked like a well-groomed park.

Meantime Louise and her sister set the table with the air of one who decks a bride. It was so nice to use the table full length, to spread the beautifully laundered cloth, mother's only "best" cloth that was left, treasured from the years of plenty; to set the best china and glass in place, and make the most of the small stock of nicely polished silver. And then the crystal bowl of roses in the centre of each end made such a difference in the glory of the whole thing!

"Wasn't it dear of her to send them?" exclaimed Louise, pulling a great luscious bud over to droop at just the right angle.

Of course the crowning glory of all was the big angel cake with its gleaming white frosting set in the midst of a wreath of roses, with the twenty-one candles in a little pink circle cunningly fastened to the cardboard circle concealed by the rose foliage. It certainly was a pretty thing. The little pink paper baskets filled with delicately browned and salted nuts were placed at each place by the exalted Louise, whose eyes shone as if she were doing the honors at some great festival; and the little birds with their name cards tilted on the rims of the glasses delightfully. The little girl stood back with clasped hands, and surveyed it all.

"It's *real!*" she said delightedly. "It truly is. And she'll be — she'll be impressed, won't she, sister?"

There was no question between the two which of their young lady guests they desired to impress. Their eyes met in sympathy. Then Cornelia with a fleeting fear of being misunderstood:

"Yes, dear, I hope she will. But you know it's not that I want to make a show before her. It's that — well, she is the kind of girl who lacks all the formalities and refinements of life, and we have to do a little extra to make her understand. You know formalities are good things sometimes. They are like fences to keep intruders out and hedges to keep in the sacred and beautiful things of life."

Louise went and threw her arms around Cornelia, exclaiming, "Nellie, you are just dear! You are like mother! You seem to find such pretty things to say to make me understand."

Cornelia stooped and kissed the warm pink cheek, realizing how very dear this little sister was growing, and how happy a time they had had getting ready for their party.

Meantime the cutlets were simmering away gently, getting themselves tender and brown, and every dish and platter and spoon and knife was in position for serving. Harry had come in, and was cracking ice and getting the freezer ready; and Cornelia mixed the materials for the water-ice. There was an excited half-hour while Harry ground away at the freezer and then the paddle was taken out, and everybody had a taste of the delectable green mixture that looked like a dream of spring, and tasted "wonderful," the children said.

"Now," said Cornelia, putting the biscuits into the oven and looking at the clock, "it's time to go upstairs and rest a bit and get dressed. There's plenty of hot water, and Harry had better take his bath first while you lie down, Louie. Yes, I want you to rest on the bed at least ten minutes with your eyes shut. It will make a big difference. You are so excited you don't even know you're tired, and you've got a long evening before you. You want to be rested enough to enjoy it. Oh, yes, I'm coming up to rest, too, just as soon as I get the water on for the potatoes, and spinach. Then we'll rest together; and, when Harry gets his bath, we'll get up and begin to dress. Harry, you must polish your shoes and make them look fine. I'm glad you had your hair cut yesterday. It looks very nice. Now let's go upstairs."

But a sudden gloom had fallen over the face of Louise. In all the planning, strange to say, it had never once occurred to her to think what she herself would wear. Now the old, perplexing problem of the ages swept down upon her darkly.

"But, Cornie, what shall I put on?"

She looked down at her blue checked gingham, and thought of the faded blue challis that had been her best all winter, washed and let down, and made to do because there was no money to buy anything else. It had a great three-cornered tear where it caught on the key of the door last Sunday night, forgotten until now.

Cornelia seemed not to notice her dismay.

"I laid your things out on a chair up in our room," she said pleasantly. "Everything is ready."

"But I — there's a — at least, don't you think I better wash out my collar? It's just awful dirty!"

"Everything's all right dear," said her sister, bending over to look at the oven flame and be sure it was just high enough to bake the biscuits the right shade of brown. "Run up, and you'll see."

Louise turned and walked slowly up the stairs revolving the possibility of her sister's having mended the tear and washed the collar, and resolving not to be disappointed if she had done neither.

"She had a lot to do this morning, and couldn't, of course; and I wouldn't want her to. I'll hurry and do it myself," said the loyal little soul. Then she entered the bedroom and stood entranced.

"O Harry, Harry! Come quick and see!" she cried to the boy, who was pattering downstairs barefoot in his bath robe with a bunch of clean garments under his arm. "She's made over her beautiful pink organdie with the lace on it for me! Isn't she *dear?* Isn't it a darling? And the little black velvet bows! And there's a white apron with lace ruffles for me to wait on the table in, and some of her own white silk stockings, and look at the ducky rosettes on my old pumps! They look like new! Oh! Isn't she the dar-lingest sister in the world?"

"She sure is!" fervently agreed Harry; and Cornelia, halfway up the stairs, stopped suddenly and brushed away two tears that plumped unannounced into her tired eyes. "Gee! That's some dress," went on Harry. "Put it all over Clytie, won't you? Glad you got it, kid! You deserve it"; and Harry bolted into the bathroom after this unusual display of affection, and slammed the door after him, while Louise came like a young whirlwind into Cornelia's arms to hug and kiss her.

"And what are you going to wear, Nel-lie?" the little girl asked anxiously when they were resting together on the bed. "You know you must look just right, because you're the centre of it all, the head, kind of, you know — the — the — well — *more* than mother, because you're young and have to look stylish. We've got to have that girl un-derstand you know; and clothes do make such a lot of difference — to a girl like that!

253

I'll tell you a secret if you won't feel bad. I was planning to stay mostly in the kitchen so she wouldn't see my old blue challis. I thought she wouldn't have much opinion of us if Carey's little sister dressed like that at a party. But now, *now* I can come out and have a good time."

"Darling!" Cornelia patted her tenderly on the shoulder. "I'm so sorry you've been troubled about your clothes. I ought to have got at them sooner, and not made you worry. I think I'll wear my white rajah silk with the burnt-orange trimmings. I made it after a French model, and I always liked it. It's right to have everything pretty and neat, of course, but I hope I haven't made you too conscious about such things. You know it really doesn't matter about clothes if we look clean and neat and behave well. I think we've been placing too high a value on looks anyway. Of course looks do count a little; but they are, after all, only a trifle beside real worth; and, if we can't impress that girl with our refinement by our actions, why, we can put on all the clothes in the universe, and we won't be able to do it any better."

"I know it," answered the little girl wisely: "only it is nice to have everything nice this time, because really and truly, Nellie, it's going to be just awful hard to have that girl here. I — I — just kind of *hate* her! It seems as if she's going to spoil this whole nice party."

Cornelia had been stifling some such sinking of heart herself as she stood looking at the pretty table and thought of the insignificant little flirt who had brought it all into being, but now she roused to the danger.

"Dearie! We mustn't feel that way! We just mustn't. You know we've been praying, and now we've got to trust. And after all, I don't suppose she is so very formidable. We'll just be polite and try to forget she is any different from Grace Kendall."

"Oh, but she is, Nellie; how can we forget it? Why do there have to be such girls made? And why do brothers have to have anything to do with them? I just feel so sore all over when the girls at school talk about her and then look at me. My face always burns."

"There, dear! Now you mustn't think such things. Just remember that for tonight at least she is our guest and we've got to treat her as well as any guest we ever expect to have. The rest is up to her."

"And to God," breathed the little girl softly and solemnly.

"Yes, dear. Think of that"; and she came close and kissed the pink cheek tenderly.

Then Harry came whistling from the

bathroom, and shot upstairs, leaving a pleasant odor of scented soap and steam behind him; and the two on the bed knew it was time to rise and get to work; for the last round was on in the game, and there was no time to idle.

17 Carey came in at a quarter to six, a most unwonted thing for him to do, even though he had been implored to do so by both sisters; and a great anxiety rolled from their minds as he went whistling merrily up the stairs and was heard splashing around in the bathroom. He had not been allowed to go into the dining-room. Louise had met him at the front door, showed him the glories of her new dress, and piloted him straight to the upper floor; but the general gala atmosphere of the house and the breath of the roses in the living room gave him the sense of festivity. He had not yet recovered from his boyish pleasure of the morning gifts and the unwonted tenderness of his father. He had the air of intending to do his part toward making this evening a pleasant one. As he went about an elaborate toilet, he resolved not to go out at all, but to stay at home the whole evening and try to make himself agreeable to his family, who were going to so much trouble for him. This virtuous resolve gave an exalted ring to the jazzy tune he whistled above the sound of the running water and also served to hide from his ears numerous sounds below stairs.

Grace Kendall arrived and slipped into the kitchen; donned a big apron, and did efficient service arranging the lettuce leaves on the salad plates and turning out the pretty quivering jelly on them. Louise was posted at the front window with wildly throbbing heart and earnest little face, awaiting the guest of anxiety, afraid she would come before Carey got out of the bathroom and safely up into his room, afraid and half hoping she wouldn't come at all, after all — and yet! Oh! There she was coming right in the gate! Suddenly Louise's feet grew heavy, and for one awful second she knew she couldn't walk to the front door and open it. And Carey — yes Carey was unlocking the bathroom door. He was going upstairs. Strength returned to her unwilling feet, and she sped to the door, and found herself opening it and bowing pleasantly to the overdressed and somewhat embarrassed young woman standing on the steps. Suddenly the sweetness and simplicity of the little pink organdie her sister had made for her enveloped all Louise's shyness and anxiety, and she felt quite able to carry off the situation.

"Come right in," she said sweetly with a tone of real welcome.

Clytie stepped in, and stared around curiously, almost furtively. It was evident she had not at all known to what sort of place she was coming and was startled, embarrassed. She was dressed in a vivid turquoise-blue taffeta evening frock composed of myriads of tiny ruffles, a bit of a girdle, and silver shoulder straps, the whole being much abbreviated at both ends and but partially concealed under a flimsy evening coat of light tan. Her face had that ghastly coloring of too much powder and paint. Her hat was a strange creation of henna ostrich-feathers hanging out in a cascade behind and looking like a bushy head of red hair. Rings and bracelets glittered and tinkled against a cheap bead hand-bag, and her gauzy hosiery and showy footgear were entirely in keeping with the *tout ensemble*. But when she stepped into the beautiful living room with its flickering fire, its softly shaded lights, its breath of roses and harmony of color, she seemed somehow as much out of place as a potato-bug in a lady's boudoir. Louise had a sudden feeling of compassion for her as the victim of a terrible joke, and she felt afraid of her no longer.

"Will you come upstairs and take off your hat?" she asked sweetly, and led the way up to her bedroom, where everything was in dainty order. A single rose in a tiny vase in front of the mirror under a pink-shaded candle-light set the key-note for the whole room.

Clytie stepped awesomely into the pretty room, and gazed about fearsomely, almost as if she suspected a trap somewhere, almost as if she felt herself an intruder, yet bold enough to see the experience through to the finish. It wasn't in the least what she had expected of Carey, but it was interesting. She decided they were "highbrows" whatever that was. She took off the elaborate hat, and puffed out her hair, bobbed in the latest way and apparently electrified to make every hair separate from every other, in a whirl around her head, much like a dandelion gone to seed.

Louise watched her as she prinked a moment before the mirror, rubbing her small tilted nose with a bit of a dab from her hand-bag, touching her eyebrows and lips, and ruffling out her hair a little wilder than before. The little girl was glad that the guest said nothing. Now if she could only get her down into the living room before Carey suspected! Somehow she felt that it would not be well for Carey to know before he came downstairs that that girl was in the house. There was no knowing what Carey might do. So she led the silent guest downstairs, and remarked as they reached the safety of the landing, "It's a pleasant evening."

The guest stepped down, took another survey of the astonishingly lovely room, and responded absently: "Yeah! It is!"

"Just sit down, and I will tell my sister you have come," said Louise airily, and vanished with relief, her awful duty done.

Cornelia came in at once, followed by Grace, and overwhelmed the young woman with their pleasant welcome. Astonishment and wary alertness were uppermost in the guest's face. She had begun to suspect something somewhere. She was sharp. She knew a girl of this kind would never have chosen her as a guest. Could it be that Carey had demanded it? She resented the presence of this other pretty, quiet girl in a blue organdie with no rouge on her face. Who was she, and what did they have to invite her for? Was she another of Carey's girls? She sat down uncomfortably on the edge of the chair offered her, and tried to pull down her inadequate little skirts. Somehow these graceful girls made her feel awkward and out of place.

Cornelia excused herself, and went back to the kitchen after a few pleasant words; and Grace Kendall took over the task of entertaining the silent guest, who eyed her sullenly and could not be made to vouchsafe more reply to any question than "Yes" or "No." But Grace had not been born a minister's daughter for nothing, and she was past mistress of all the graces of conversation and of making people feel at their ease. She was presently deep in the story of a certain set of photographs of strange lands that had been gathered by her father in a trip he had taken several years before, and the other girl in spite of herself was getting interested.

It is curious how many little things manage to get across into one's consciousness at a time like this. How, for instance, did Cornelia in the kitchen, taking up the cutlets and placing them on the hot plates, know just the precise instant when Brand Barlock's car drew up before the door, and Carey's clear whistle in the third story ceased? She felt it even before the door opened and Louise's excited whisper announced: "He's come, Nellie! Hurry!" and she was even then unbuttoning the big enveloping apron and hurrying forward.

So she met Brand Barlock at the front door with a welcoming hand outstretched to greet him, and a hearty low voiced "I'm so glad you could come! Carey doesn't know about it yet, but I expect he'll see your

car out of his window. He's upstairs dress-
ing. Come in. Let me take your hat. Mr.
Barlock, let me introduce Miss Kendall and
Miss Dodd."

Brand Barlock stared. First at Cornelia,
swiftly, approvingly, and with an answering
smile for her cordial one; then at the lovely
room which he entered, and gave a swift,
comprehensive survey; and then at the
lovely girl in blue who came forward to
greet him.

"Pleased to meet you, I'm sure!" he said
giving her a direct appraisement, a respect-
ful interest, and shaking her hand quite unnecessarily. He was entirely at his ease, and
altogether accustomed to rapid adjustments
to environment, one could see that at once;
yet it was also perceptible that he was surprised, and agreeably so. He held Grace
Kendall's slim young hand impressively, a
trifle longer than was in keeping with polite
usage, yet not long enough to be resented;
and his eyes made several sentences' progress in acquaintance with her before he took
them from her face and let them rest upon
Miss Dodd, who had at last risen with some
show of interest in life again and come a
step or two forward. Then he stared again.

"Oh! Hello, Clytie! You here?" he greeted
her carelessly, and went and sat down be-

side Miss Kendall. His tone said that Clytie Dodd was decidedly out of her element, and suddenly under the heavy veneer of white Clytie Dodd grew deeply red. Cornelia with a glance took in all these things, and a wave of sudden compassion swept over her, too, for the girl whom she had thus placed in a trying position. Had she done well? She could not tell. But it was too late now. She must go forward and make it a success. She tried to make it up by smiling at the girl pleasantly.

"Now, if you will just talk a minute or two, I think Carey will be down soon. It is time for father's car to come, and we'll have dinner at once." Cornelia disappeared through the dining-room door again.

Just at that precise moment Arthur Maxwell slowed up his car at the corner where Mr. Copley's trolley was about to stop, and looked perplexedly about him, studying the houses on either side.

"I beg your pardon," he said politely, as Mr. Copley got out of the trolley and crossed the street in front of him. "Could you tell me if there is a family by the name of Copley about here? I seem to have mislaid the address, but my memory of it is that they live somewhere along this block or the next."

"Copley's my name, sir," said Mr. Copley with his genial smile. "What can I do for you?"

"Glad to meet you, Mr. Copley," said Maxwell cordially. "I've had no end of a time finding your house. Thought I could go directly to it, but find my memory wasn't so good as I banked on. I must have left the address at home, after all. I've a box here to deliver to your daughter. You have a daughter, haven't you?"

"Why, yes, two of them," said the father, smiling. He liked this pleasant young man with the handsome smile and the expensive car, asking after his daughter. This was his idea of the kind of friends he would like his daughters to have if he had the choosing. "I guess you mean Cornelia. I suppose you're somebody she met at college."

"No, nothing so good as that. I can't really claim anything but a second-hand acquaintance. It was my mother who met her on a journey to Philadelphia some months ago. Mother quite fell in love with her, I believe; and she's sent her some ferns, which she asked me to deliver. Suppose you get in, and I'll take you the rest of the way. Is it in this block?"

Mr. Copley swung his long limbs into the seat beside the young man.

"No, the next block, middle of the block, just at the top of the hill, right-hand side," he said. "I remember Cornie speaking of your mother. She was very kind, and Cornie enjoyed her. It certainly is good of her to remember my little girl. Ferns!" He looked back at the box. "She certainly will like those. She's a great one for fixing up the house, and putting flowers about and growing things. She'll be pleased to see you. Here's the house, the one with the stone chimney. Yes, that's new, my son built it since Cornie came home. She wanted a fireplace. Now you'll come right in. Cornie'll want to thank you."

"Thank you," said the young man, lifting out the heavy box. "That won't be necessary. She can thank mother sometime when she sees her. I'll just put the box here on the porch, shall I? — and not detain your daughter. I really ought to be getting along. I haven't had my dinner yet."

"Oh, then you'll come right in and take dinner with us. The young people will be delighted to have you, I know. Cornie said they were going to have a company supper tonight because it's my son's birthday, twenty-one. I'd like you to meet my son; that is, I'd like him to know you, you know"; and the father smiled a confiding smile.

"Oh, but really," Arthur Maxwell began.

But Mr. Copley had a detaining hand upon the young man's arm.

"We couldn't really let you go this way, you know," said the father. "We couldn't think of it. We haven't any very grand hospitality to offer you, but we can't let you go away without being thanked. Cornie!"

Mr. Copley threw wide the door of the living room. "Cornie, here's Mr. Maxwell. He's brought you some ferns, and he's going to stay to dinner with us. Put on another plate."

It was just at this instant that Carey Copley, humming his jazzy tune and fumbling with a refractory cuff-link, started down the front stairs, and paused in wild dismay.

 **18** Cornelia, alert to make everything pass off smoothly, and aware that Carey was coming down the stairs, had slipped off her apron and entered the living room exactly as her father flung open the front door. Now she came forward easily, brightly, as if strange guests flung at her feast at the last moment were a common occurrence in her life, and greeted this tall, handsome stranger.

"The plate's all on," she answered gayly, putting out a welcoming hand and meeting a pair of very nice, very curious, wholly interested eyes that for the moment she wasn't aware of ever having seen before. She was aware only of the eight plates back in the oven keeping piping hot, and the eight places at the pretty table, and the awful thing that her father had done to her already incongruous party, and wondering what she should do. Then suddenly she recognized the young man; and a pretty color flew into her cheeks, and a brightness into her eyes. The room with its strange guests, Grace Kendall trying to interest Brand and Clytie in her lapful of photographs, Carey standing on the stair-landing, even her young brother and sister peeping curiously in at the dining-room door, fell away, and she put out her hand in real welcome to this stranger. An instant more, and her pulses swept wildly back into frightened array again, and her thoughts bustled around with troubles and fears. What should she do now? How should he ever mix? That awful girl with her face all flour? That slam-bang Brand with his slang and bold indifference! How could she ever make the party a success, the party over which she had so worked and prayed and hoped? And Carey! Would he vanish out the back door? The birthday candles around the cake were all lighted. Harry had lighted them as she came in. If Carey should bolt, how could they ever go out into that dining-room, into the flicker of those foolish pink candles, and have a birthday dinner without the chief guest?

"Oh, but, indeed, I couldn't think of intruding," the young man's words interrupted her anxious thoughts. "I merely dropped in on my way to dinner to leave this box of ferns that my mother sent with very explicit directions to be delivered to you at once before they died. As I'm not much of a florist myself, and as they have already had to wait all day without water, I'm ashamed to say, I wouldn't answer for the consequences if I hadn't got them here tonight. Mother is very particular about having her directions carried out. I hope the ferns will live and be worthy of this most beautiful setting"; his glance went appreciatively about the pretty room. "You certainly look cozy here, and I know you're going to have a beautiful time. I won't keep you a minute longer."

There was something wistful in his tone even as he lifted his hat to put it on and began backing out the door. Cornelia's resolve to let him go was fast weakening even before her father spoke up.

"Daughter, Mr. Maxwell has come four miles out of his way to bring those ferns, and it will be late before he gets any dinner. He ought to stay. I told him he was welcome."

Cornelia's cheeks flamed, but a smile came into her eyes.

"We shall be *very* glad to have you stay," she urged gently, "unless — some one else is waiting for you."

A quick flush mounted into the young man's face and he suddenly felt strangely loath to have this clear-eyed girl think that anyone was waiting for him. He would not like her to know what kind of girl was expecting his coming.

"Oh, it's not that" — he managed to say lamely, "but I simply couldn't think of butting into a family party like this." His eyes glanced about questioningly, hesitating at Brand and pausing with a reflective wonder at Clytie in the background.

"But it's not a family party," said Cornelia laughingly; "it's just a few friends called in to help us celebrate my brother's birthday, and — they don't even know one another very well yet; so won't you come in and be another? We really would be glad to have you, and we'll try to make you feel at home. We're not a bit formal or formidable. Let me introduce my brother Carey. Carey, come here and meet Mr. Maxwell. You remember my telling how nice his mother was to me on the way home from college."

She was talking fast, and the pretty color was in her cheeks. She was aware that the stranger was watching her admiringly. Her heart was thumping and the blood was surging through her ears so that it seemed as though she could not hear anything but her own high-pitched voice, and she wanted nothing so much as to break out crying and run and hide. Would Carey come, or would he —

Carey came, dazed, but polite. He was

271

well dressed and groomed, and he knew it. He had no objection to meeting a pleasant stranger who owned a car like the one he had seen drive up at the door before he had left his room. Carey had a habit of judging a man by his car. The two young men appraised each other pleasantly, and there seemed to be a mutual liking. Then suddenly Brand Barlock, never allowing himself long to be left out of consideration, came noisily over to the group, and slapped Carey on the back.

"Hello, old man! Got a birthday, have you?"

"Oh, hello, Brand! Forgot you were here. Saw your car out the window. Meet Mr. Maxwell, Mr. Barlock," and the two acknowledged the introduction.

"My father, Brand."

Mr. Copley spoke graciously to the young man, yet with a degree of dignity, looking him over speculatively. This was not the kind of young man he would choose for his son's intimate; yet he regarded him with leniency.

Suddenly Carey turned and saw Grace Kendall.

"Oh, I say, Miss Kendall! This is awfully good of you." He took a step, and shook hands with her. "Say, this is a real party, after all, isn't it? A surprise party. Upon my word I thought Cornelia was kidding me when she said we were going to have a birthday party."

Grace Kendall laughed, and clapped her hands, and all the rest followed her example. In the din of laughter and clapping Carey suddenly sighted Clytie glowering back by the fireplace, and a wave of panic swept over his face. He turned startled eyes on his sister and father, and stood back while Cornelia introduced their guests to Maxwell and her father. He wondered how she could say "Miss Dodd" so easily, and how she had got acquainted with Clytie. His cheeks began to burn. Then she must have seen him that day on Chestnut Street, after all. And Louise had talked too! And yet his sister's face was sweet and innocent!

Then he became aware that an appeal was being made to him to keep the young stranger to dinner and that the stranger was protesting that he could not thrust himself on a birthday party in this way. Carey roused to the occasion, and gave an eager invitation.

"Of course you're going to stay to my party!" But even as he said it he wondered what a man of Maxwell's evident type would think of a girl like Clytie. Oh, if only she weren't here! And Grace Kendall! What must she think? He stole a look at her, standing there so gracefully in that blue dress like a cloud, talking to Brand. What business did Brand have looking at her like that as if he had known her always? Now Brand would rush her. Carey could see that Brand liked her. He always rushed a girl he took a notion to. He would take her out riding in that car of his, and —

But everybody was talking now, and Cornelia had called upon him to bring in the box of ferns. She herself had suddenly disappeared into the kitchen, and was standing against the closed door, pressing her hand against her forehead and trying to think.

"What shall we do, Louie, dear? What *shall* we do? Father has invited that man." Cornelia found she was trembling; even her lips were trembling so she could hardly speak.

"Do?" said Louise maturely. "We'll go right ahead. We heard it all. Harry has fixed it up that he'll stay out and help. There's plenty of things left over for him to eat, and I'll fix him a plate between times."

"I can fix my own plate," growled Harry happily. "You know I didn't want to sit in there with all those folks any of the time."

"But Harry! It's Carey's party, and you not at it!"

"Sure! I'm at it! I'm *it!* Don't you see? I'm the chauffeur running this car. I'm the chef cooking this dinner! Get out there quick, Cornie, and file those folks into their seats. This soup is getting cold, and they ought to get to work. That's a good guy; and he's got some car, I'll tell the world!"

So Cornelia went back to marshall the party out to the table. Maxwell was turning to leave, saying once more that it was awfully kind of them to ask him but he could not possibly stay. And just then the dining-room door was flung open by Harry and the whole company stopped and breathed a soft "Ah!" as they saw the pretty candle-lit room. Then as one man they went forward and began to search for their places, all save Maxwell who went forward indeed to get a closer glimpse of the pretty table, but lingered in the doorway. There was something so wholesome and homelike about the place, something so interesting and free from self-consciousness about the girl, that he was held in spite of himself. He had not realized that there were such girls as this in his day. He was curious to watch her and see if she really was different.

So far Carey had not even spoken to his own special guest, Clytie. Since he had sighted her afar he had religiously kept his eyes turned away from her vicinity.

It was Grace Kendall who took her by the arm and led her to her seat at the right of the host, for Cornelia had known she could depend upon her father's kindliness to make all go smoothly during the supper; and, much as he might dislike the looks of the girl, she felt sure he would be polite and see that she was well taken care of: Brand Barlock was on Clytie's right with Louise next, and she had placed Carey opposite Clytie, not liking to seem to separate them too much, and yet not wishing to throw them together too conspicuously. Grace Kendall was on Carey's left, with Harry's place next her. This would have to be for the stranger, and would place him on Cornelia's right, the fitting place for the guest of honor; yet — her cheeks burned. What would he think? Still, he had come unannounced. He had stayed. Let him take the consequences! What did she care what he thought? She would likely never see him again.

Perhaps he was not going to stay, after all. He was lingering still in the doorway, but seemed just about to go.

Suddenly from behind her came a low whistle:

"Hiss! Whist!"

Harry from behind the kitchen door was signalling violently, forgetting that his white shirt-sleeve in his excited gestures was as visible to the rest of the company as to the astonished young man in the opposite doorway about to take a hasty leave.

"Oh, I say! Come 'ere!" came Harry's sepulchral whisper, as he beckoned wildly with a hand that unconsciously still grasped a muggy dish-towel.

"Are you — calling me?" young Maxwell signalled with his lifted eyebrows.

Harry's response was unmistakable, and the young man slipped past the group who were studying place cards and sliding into chairs and bent his head to the retreating head of the boy.

"I say, don't you *see* I don't want to come in there with all those folks? Be a good sport, and stay, 'r I'll have to. I'd ruther stay out here and dish ice-cream. You go take my chair. That's a good guy."

Maxwell smiled with sudden illumination, and lifted his eyes to find that Cornelia had heard the whole affair.

"All right, old man, I'll stay," said the young man. "You win. Perhaps you'll let me come into the kitchen afterwards and help clean up."

"Sure!" said Harry joyfully, with the tone of having found a pal. "We'll be glad to have you, won't we, Cornie?"

To himself Maxwell said: "It will be just as well to go later to see Evadne. Better in fact. I don't want her to think I'm too keen. I can have more time to decide what to say to her. This is a good atmosphere in which to decide. Besides, I'm hungry and the dinner smells good. It would be ages before we got settled to eating at the roof garden or some cabaret. I'd have to go home and dress."

Then he became aware that Cornelia was speaking to him.

Cornelia's cheeks were red as roses, and there was a look in her laughing eyes as if tears were not far off; but she carried the thing off bravely, and declared that those things could be settled later; they really must sit down now, or the dinner would be spoiled. So they all sat down, and there was a moment's awkward silence till Mr. Copley bowed his head and asked a blessing, Clytie and Brand openly staring the while. When it was over, Maxwell discovered the place card with "Harry" on it, and gravely deposited it in his vest-pocket, saying in a low tone to Cornelia: "I shall make this up to him later."

"You mustn't think you're depriving him," said Cornelia, smiling and lifting her spoon to the luscious cup of iced fruit. "He really has tried in every way he knew short of running away to get out of coming to the table. He knows he has me in a corner now, and he's tremendously pleased; so don't think another thing about it. Suppose you play you're one of our old friends, and then it won't worry you any more. It's really awfully nice of you to come in this way."

But all the time in her heart she was wondering why, oh, why, did this have to happen just this night when she wanted to devote all her energies to making the other people feel at home, and now she was so distracted she didn't know what she was saying?

However, the other people seemed to be getting along famously. When she glanced up, she saw that her father was talking pleasantly to Clytie, keeping her at least employed with questions to answer, about where she lived, and how her father was employed, and whether she had brothers and sisters. He had just asked: "And what school do you attend? High school, I suppose?" and Cornelia caught a fleeting glance of annoyance on Carey's face as she replied with a giggle:

"Oh, my goodness, no! I quit school when I was thirteen. I couldn't stand the place. Too dull for me!"

**19** Carey turned to Grace eagerly, and began to ask about Christian Endeavor. Cornelia wondered at his sudden interest in matters religious, and perceived that Brand had been carrying on a lively conversation with Grace across the table, and Carey had cut in. She felt like a person who has jumped into an aeroplane, somehow started it, and knows nothing of running or stopping it. She had started this thing, and this was what had developed and now she would have to watch the consequences.

Yet it appeared there was no opportunity to watch the consequences, much as she so desired. The young man on her right was determined to talk to her. He had drawn Louise into the little circle also, and Louise was smiling shyly, and evidently pleased. Cornelia could not help noticing how sweet the little girl looked with the wild-rose color in her cheeks and the little soft tendrils of curls about her face. The organdie dress certainly was becoming, and she must get at it right away and make some more pretty clothes for the dear child.

Then her eyes travelled down the table once more. Brand was laughing uproariously; Clytie was endeavoring to get in on his conversation and divert it to herself, and Carey was looking like a thunder-cloud and talking very rapidly and eagerly to Grace Kendall. How handsome he looked in his new necktie! How the blue brought out the blue of his eyes! And how dear and good and kindly polite her father looked! Then she noticed with a panic that the fruit-cups were nearly empty, and it was time for the soup. Would Harry and Louise be able to make the transfer of dishes without any mishaps? She had not felt nervous about it before till this elegant stranger had appeared on the scene. She knew by his looks that he was used to having everything just so. She remembered his mother's immaculate attire, the wonderful glimpse she had caught of the fittings of her travelling-bag, everything silver-mounted and monogrammed. This man would know if the soup was not seasoned just right and the dishes were served at the wrong side.

Perhaps she was a little distraught as Louise slipped silently from her seat, and took the empty dishes on her little tray that had stood unseen by the side of her chair.

"What a charming little sister!" said Maxwell.

Cornelia's heart glowed, and she looked

up with an appreciative smile.

"She is a darling!" she said earnestly. "I'm just getting to know her again since I came home from college. She was only a baby when I went away."

He looked interestedly at the sweet older sister. "I should imagine that might be a very delightful occupation. I think I should like an opportunity myself to get acquainted with her. And say, suppose you tell me about these other people. Now I'm here, I'd like to know them a little better. I haven't quite got them all placed. Your father I know. We came up together, and it doesn't take long to see he's a real man. I shall enjoy pursuing the acquaintance farther if he is willing. But about these others. Are they — relatives? This girl at my right, is she another sister, or only a friend?"

"Oh, she is our minister's daughter," answered Cornelia brightly. "She's rather a new friend, because we've only been living in this part of the city a short time; but we like her a lot."

"She looks it," he said heartily. "And the next one is your brother. I like his face. He is — a college boy, perhaps?"

"No, he's only finished high school," Cornelia said with a bit of a sigh. "Mother wanted him to go to college, but he didn't seem to want to, and — well — I suppose the real truth about it was I was in college and the family couldn't afford to send another. I was blind enough not to know I ought to come home and give the next one a chance. However, Carey —"

She looked at him wistfully; and the young man, keenly alert to her expression perhaps read a bit of her thoughts.

"College isn't always the only thing," he said quickly. "You, being a college woman, have naturally thought so, I suppose; but upon my word I think sometimes it's more harm than good to a boy to go to college."

Cornelia gave him a grateful smile, and he saw that this had been one of her pains and mortifications. He liked her more, the more he talked with her. She seemed to have her family so much at heart. He lifted keen eyes to the young man across the table.

"That's one of his friends, I suppose?"

Cornelia nodded half dubiously.

"He owns the car at the door?"

"Yes." There was a whole volume expressed in her tone.

The keen eyes looked Brand over a second. "Interesting face," he commented. "Does he belong to the automobile Barlocks?"

"Why, I don't know," said Cornelia. "I've

only just come home, you know. He's Carey's friend; that's all I know. I didn't even remember he had the same name as the automobile people."

"And who is the other young women? She is not — a minister's daughter, too?" he asked with an amused twinkle in his eyes.

Cornelia gave him a quick deprecatory glance, "No," she said, half ashamed. "She is just — an experiment."

"I see," he said gravely, giving Clytie Dodd another keen look.

"You must be like your mother," she said, smiling. "She seemed to me so interested in just people. And she read me like a book. Or perhaps you are a psychologist?"

"You couldn't give me a greater compliment than to tell me I'm like mother. She's always like that, interested in everybody about her, and wondering what circumstances helped to form them as they are."

"It was your mother that gave me the idea of fixing up this old house on nothing." She gave a laughing deprecatory glance about. "I was just awfully unhappy and discouraged at having to leave college and go to a poor little house in a new neighborhood, and she managed to leave with me the suggestion of making it all over in such a way that I could not get away from it."

"You certainly have done wonders," he said with an admiring look about. "That was one reason I was so anxious to stay and look around me, the rooms opened up so charmingly and were such a surprise. You really have made a wonderful place out of it. This room, now, looks as if it might have come out of the hands of some big city decorator, and yet there is a charm and simplicity about it that is wholly in keeping with a quiet home life. I like it awfully. I wish mother could see it. Were those panels on the walls when you began?"

"Oh, no. There was some horrible old faded red wallpaper, and in some places the plaster was coming off. Carey and I had a lot to do to this wall before we could even paint it. And there were so many layers of paper we thought we never would get it all scraped off."

"You had to do all that?" said the young man appreciatively. "It was good you had a brother to help in such rough, heavy work."

"Yes, Carey has been very much interested. Of course he hasn't had so much time lately, as he could give only his evenings. He has been working all day. He built the fireplace in the living room too. I want you to look at that after dinner. I think it is very pretty for an amateur workman."

"He built that fireplace!" exclaimed Maxwell. "Well, he certainly did a great thing! I noticed it at once. It is the charm of the whole room, and so artistic in its lines. I love a beautiful fireplace, and I thought that was most unusual. I must look at it again. Your brother must be a genius."

"No, not a genius," said Cornelia. "But he always could make anything he wanted to. He is very clever with tools and machinery, and seems to know by instinct how everything is made. When he was a little boy, I remember, he used to take everything in the house apart and put it together again. I shall never forget the day mother got her new carpet-sweeper and was about to sweep the parlor, and was called away to answer a knock at the back door. When she came back Carey had the whole thing apart, strewn all around the room; and mother sat down in dismay, and began to scold him. Then she told him sadly that he must go upstairs to bed for punishment; and he looked up and said, 'Why, muvver, don't you want me to put it together again first?' And he did. He put it all together so it worked all right, and managed to get out of his punishment that time."

Maxwell glanced down the table at the bright, clever face of the young man who was eagerly describing to Grace Kendall an automobile race he had witnessed not long ago.

"That's a great gift!" he commented. "Your brother ought to make a business success in life. What did you say he is doing?"

Cornelia flushed painfully.

"That's the sore point," she said. "Carey hasn't anything very good just now, though he has one or two hopeful possibilities in the near future. He is just working in a garage now, getting together all the money he can save to be ready for the right job when it comes along. Father is rather distressed to have him doing such work; he says he is wasting his time. But it is good pay, and I think it is better than doing nothing and just hanging around waiting. Besides, he is crazy about machinery, seems to have a natural instinct for finding out what's the matter with a thing; and of course automobiles — he would rather fuss with one than eat."

"It's not a bad training for some big thing in the future, you know," said Maxwell. "There are lots of jobs today where a practical knowledge of machinery and especially of cars is worth a lot of money. I wouldn't be discouraged about it. He looks like an awfully clever fellow. He'll land the right thing pretty soon. I like his personality. That's another thing that will count in his favor. I want to get acquainted with him after dinner. Say, do you know you have let me in for an awfully interesting evening?"

"Why, that's very nice," said Cornelia, suddenly realizing that she had forgotten to worry about Louise's getting the next course on the table safely; and here it was, hot and inviting, and she sitting back and talking like a guest. What a dear little capable sister she was, and how quietly Harry was keeping the machinery in the kitchen going!

Everybody seemed to be having a nice time; even Clytie Dodd was listening to something her father was telling, something about a young man where he worked who had risked his life to save a comrade in danger. Clytie was subdued, that was certain. Something, either the formality of the meal, or the impressiveness of the guests, had quieted her voice and suppressed her bold manner. She was not talking much herself, and she was not feeling quite so self-sufficient as when she came. It was most plain that she was quite out of her element in such an atmosphere, but she was a girl who was quick to observe and adjust herself to her environment. This might not be her native atmosphere, but she knew enough to keep still and keep her eyes open. Cornelia noticed that she was being left very much to herself so far as the two young men were concerned, and perhaps this had something to do with the subduing influence. Clytie was not a girl who cared for the background very long. She was one who forced herself into the limelight. Was it possible that just a little formality and a few strangers had changed her so completely? Perhaps she was not so bad, after all, as the children had led her to suppose. Just a poor little ignorant child who was trying her untaught hand at vamping. There might even be a way to help her, though Cornelia felt opposed to trying it when Carey was about. She could not yet consider Carey in the light of a companion of this girl without mortification. In all that little circle about the table her common little painted face shone up as being out of place, unrefined, uncultured, utterly untaught.

More and more as the courses came on the table Clytie grew silent and impressed; and, as the meal drew to its close, Cornelia gained confidence. The dainty salad had been eaten with avidity; the delectable ice in its pale-green dreamy beauty had come on in due time and brought an exclamation of wonder from the whole company, who demanded to know what it was, and tasted it as one might sample a dish of ambrosia, and praised and tasted again.

There was much laughter and fun over the blowing out of the candles by Carey and the cutting of the angel cake, which also brought a round of applause. Cornelia poured the amber coffee into the little pink cups that looked like seashells, and finally the meal was concluded and the company arose to go into the living room.

Then Clytie came into her own again. It seemed that rising from the formalities of the table had given her back her confidence once more. Seizing hold of Carey's arm as he stood near her, she exclaimed:

"Come on, Kay, let's go have a dance and shake some of this down. I'm full clear up to my eyes. Haven't you got a victrola? Turn it on, do. I'm dying for a dance!"

 **20** By this time they were in the living room and in full view of the whole company. Cornelia was standing in the doorway, with Maxwell just behind.

It seemed that Clytie had chosen the moment when her remark would be best heard by every one, and a horrible silence followed it, as if some deadly explosive had suddenly been flung down in their midst. Maxwell heard a sudden little breathless exclamation from Cornelia. He flung a swift glance around the company. Grace Kendall stood quietly apart. Brand Barlock looked amused with a keen appraisement of the effect of Clytie's words on every one present. Carey, caught by the unexpected momentum of the girl's action, was whirled about in spite of himself, and recovered his balance angrily, flinging her off.

"What's the matter with you?" he said in a low, muttering tone; then, trying to recover his politeness in the face of everybody, he added haughtily, "No, we haven't got a victrola, I'm thankful to say!" and he cast a swift furtive glance at the minister's daughter. What must she think of him for having a girl like that make free with him.

His face was crimson, and for the first time since he had known Clytie Dodd he put the question to himself whether she was exactly the kind of girl he wanted for an intimate friend.

The silence in the room was intense. There seemed to be a kind of spell over the onlookers that no one was able to break. Clytie looked defiantly about upon them, and felt she had the floor.

"Oh, well, be a boob if you want. You ain't the only pebble on the beach. Come on, Brand. Let's do the shimmy. You can whistle if no one knows how to play." It was plain that she was angry, and did not care what she said or did. Carey had turned white and miserable, Cornelia looked ready to drop. Young Maxwell noticed the worn hands of the father clinch and his face grow gray and drawn. Mr. Copley gave the impression that he would like above all things to take Clytie in thumb and finger and, holding her at arm's length, eject her from the room as one would get rid of some vulgar little animal that was making an unpleasant scene.

The young man gave one more swift look at the annoyed face of the girl beside him, and then stepped forward, noticing as he did so that even Brand was a bit annoyed at the turn affairs had taken. Even he saw that Clytie's suggestion was out of place.

"Miss Dodd," said Maxwell in a clear, commanding voice, with a pleasant smile that at once held Clytie Dodd's attention. She turned to him eagerly, all too evidently expecting he was going to offer to dance with her; and the rest of the little audience stood in breathless waiting. "I'm sure you won't mind if we interrupt you. Miss Copley was just going to play for some singing. You'll join us, of course. I'm sure you have a good voice, and we want everybody. Let's all gather around the piano."

He turned with a swift appeal to Cornelia to bear him out. He had taken a chance, of course. What if Miss Copley did not play? But there was the piano, and there was music scattered about. Somebody must play.

A little breathless gasp went from one to another in visible relief as Cornelia came forward quickly, summoning a wan smile to her lips, trying to steady her fingers to select something from the mass of music on the piano that would meet the present need. Her music did not include many popular favorites, a few that Carey had brought home, that was all. But this if ever was the time to bring it forth. Ah! Here was "Tim Rooney's at the Fightin'." It would do as well as anything, and she placed it on the piano, and forced her fingers into the opening chords, not daring to look around the room, wondering what Clytie Dodd was doing now, and how she was taking her interruption.

But Maxwell was not idle. She felt his protective presence behind her. He was summoning every one into the chorus, even the father; and he asked Clytie Dodd whether she didn't sing alto, a challenge which won a giggling acknowledgment from her.

"I thought so," he said. "I can almost always tell when people sing alto. Then come over on this side of the piano with me. I sing bass; and Mr. Copley, are you bass, too? I thought so. Now, you two fellows," — turning to Brand and Carey, who were standing abashed in the background, uncomfortable and half ready to bolt, but much impressed by the tactics of the stranger, — "it's up to you to sing tenor. You've got to, whether you can or not, you know, because we can't do it, and it's obvious that we have to have four parts. Miss Kendall sings soprano, doesn't she? And Miss Copley. Now, we're off! Give us those chords again, please."

He started off himself with a splendid

voice, and even a lame singer found it easy to follow. They all had good voices, and, while no one felt exactly like singing after a big dinner, they nevertheless stumbled along bravely, and before the second verse was reached were making quite a gallant chorus.

Before they had sung three songs they were quite in the spirit of the thing; and Harry and Louise, emerging from a last delicious dish of water-ice, joined in heartily, lending their young voices vigorously. Clytie proved to have a tolerable voice. It was a bit louder than was necessary, with a nasal twang now and then; but it blended well with the other voices, and was not too obvious. Even Mr. Copley seemed to have forgotten the unpleasant happening of a few moments before, and was singing as lustily as when he was a young man.

Only Cornelia felt the tense strain of it all. They could not sing always. Sometime it would have to stop, and what would happen then? The wonderful stranger could not always be expected to step in and pilot the little ship of the evening safely past all rocks. He had done wonders, and she would never cease to be grateful to him, but, oh, if he would go home at once as soon as they stopped singing, and not be there to witness further vulgarities! Grace Kendall, too. But then Grace understood somewhat. Grace was a minister's daughter. What, oh, *what* could they do next to suppress that awful girl?

Cornelia's head throbbed, and her face grew white and anxious. She cast an occasional glance at Carey who was singing away vigorously out of the same book with Grace Kendall, and wished she might weave a spell and waft all the rest of the guests away, leaving her brother to the influence of this sweet, natural girl. How could she manage to obviate another embarrassing situation? But it seemed as if the brain that had brought out so many lovely changes in a dismal old house, that had planned so carefully every detail of this evening and looked far ahead to results in the lives of her dear ones, had utterly refused to act any longer. Her nerve was shaken, and she could scarcely keep the tears back. Oh if there were some one to help her! Then her heart took up its newly acquired habit, and cried out to God: "O God, send me help. What shall I do next?"

As if young Maxwell read her thoughts, he turned at the close of the song, and, addressing them all promiscuously, said: "I guess we're about sung out for a while, aren't we? I'm hoarse as a fog-horn. Miss Dodd, why don't you teach me how to play this game? I've been looking at it for quite a while, and it fascinates me. I believe I could beat you at it. Suppose we try."

Clytie giggled, quite flattered. It was a feather in her cap to have this handsome stranger paying her marked attention. His car was even finer than Brand Barlock's. Not so sporty, perhaps, but much sweller. And the man was older, besides. It was something wonderful to have made a hit with him. She preened herself, still giggling, and sat down at the table, eying with indulgent curiosity the little board with its colored squares and bright carved men.

"I d'no'z I know m'self," she vouchsafed, glinting her beringed fingers among the bits of colored wood. "Whaddaya do, anyhow?"

Cornelia, with a flush of gratitude in her face, gave a brief clew to the object of the game; and they were soon deep in the attempt to get their men each into the other's territory first.

Clytie was clever and soon got the idea of the game. She might have grown restive under it and petulant if she had been playing with some people, but Maxwell could be interesting when he chose to exert himself; and he was choosing just now, studying the calibre of the girl before him and leading her in spite of herself to take a real interest in what she was doing. To tell the truth, Clytie was interested in a man of almost any kind, especially if he was good-looking, but this particular man was a specimen different from any that had ever come into her path in a friendly way before. She had met such men as this only in a business way when she was ordered curtly to write a business letter over again or told she could not hold her position in an office unless she stopped chewing gum and talking so much to the other stenographers. Never had a man of this sort stepped down from his height to be really nice to her; and she was not only astonished, but pleased at it. There was nothing of the personal about his manner, just a nice, pleasant, friendly way of taking it for granted that she liked being talked to, and was as good as anybody; and it gave her a new feeling of self-respect that she would never forget, even if she never met the man again.

Cornelia, watching furtively and thankfully from her corner where she was showing Brand Barlock a book of college photographs and explaining some of the college jokes inscribed beneath them, marvelled at his patience and skill. She had not known him long, only two hours; but he was so obviously of another world from this girl, and yet was making her feel so entirely comfortable and happy, that she felt humiliated and ashamed that she had not been able to do the same for the girl. She had invited her with a real feeling that she might be able to help her somehow; at least, that was what she thought she had for one of her objects; but now she began to suspect that perhaps she had in reality desired to humiliate the girl and put her into such a position that Carey would not want to go with her any longer. The girl had shown that she was unhappy and out of her element, and Cornelia had not helped her to find any possible basis for understanding with those about her. It was all wrong, and she ought to have gone further into things and planned to uplift that girl, even if she didn't want to lift her up to the social plane of her own brother. There might be senses in which Carey wasn't so very much higher than the girl, too. He needed uplifting a lot. Of course that girl wouldn't help lift him nor he her as things were; but Cornelia had had no right whatever to humble her for the sake of saving her brother.

Maxwell was tactful. He managed to draw Louise and Brand Barlock into the game after a while; and, when they had grown tired of that, he led them into the dining-room, where Carey and Grace had just finished a game of ping-pong on the dining-room table, and insisted that they four play a set. Brand soon gave up his racket to Harry, and drifted into the other room; but it was half past ten when the others came back into the living room, where Grace Kendall was singing some Scotch songs, and sat down to listen.

Cornelia looked at Clytie Dodd in surprise. All the boldness and impudence had melted out of her face, with much of the paint and powder that had been transferred to her handkerchief during the heated excitement of the game. Her hair had lost its tortured look, and her face was just that of an ordinary happy little girl who had been having a good, healthy time. She felt almost on an equality with the people around her because this nice man had been nice to her. She rather hated that yellow-haired girl in blue who had absorbed the attention of her own two special satellites, but what were they but kids beside this man of the world? She stole a look at his fine, strong face, and had perhaps a fleeting vision of what it might be to have a man friend such as he was; and who shall say but a fleeting revelation, too, of what a girl must be to have such a friend? She saw him look across the room to where his young hostess sat, and smile, a smile with a kind of mysterious light to it like signal-lights at sea. She looked curiously to where Carey's sister sat, and saw with a startled new insight how young and really lovely this girl was; and she sat silent, a little wondering, in unwonted thoughtfulness.

Grace Kendall finished her song, and suddenly whirled around on the piano-stool, and looked at her watch.

"Oh, my dear!" she said, glancing up at Cornelia. "Do you see what time it is? And I have to be up at half past five tomorrow morning to get father's breakfast before he goes to New York. I must say, 'Good night,' and hurry right home."

Both Carey and Brand rose, and hurried up to her in a confidential way.

"I'll take you —" began Carey.

"My car is right at the door," put in Brand dictatorially. "I'll take you, of course."

Carey looked vexed, then met Brand's eyes sheepishly. "Well, I'll take her, and you can drive," he said; and then suddenly they both looked at Clytie, and their tongues clove to the roofs of their mouths, for Clytie had risen with black brows, her sullen, defiant glance returning.

Then Maxwell stepped forward as if he had heard nothing.

"Miss Dodd, my car is here. I'll be glad to see that you get safely home"; and Clytie's face cleared. She sped upstairs to get her wraps.

"Haven't we had a beautiful time?" said Grace Kendall, putting an intimate arm around her as they reached the top of the stairs. "I think they're just charming people. Do you know you have a lovely alto voice? Do you live near here? We'd love to have you in our young people's choir if you don't belong somewhere else."

"Where is't?" asked Clytie casually, half suspiciously. She was surprised that there was no look of rivalry in the face of the girl who had obviously carried off both the younger men from her following; but it seemed as if this strangely sweet girl did not realize that she had done such a thing, did not even seem to have wanted to do it. Clytie suddenly smiled, and showed the first glimpse of real simplicity and childlikeness that had been visible that evening. She was little more than a child, anyway, and perhaps would not have gone in her present ways if any other that promised a little pleasure had been opened to her.

"No, I don't b'long nowheres," she giggled, "not since I was a kid. I useta go ta two er three Sunday schools, but I cut 'em all out after I grew up. Took too much time. I like my Sundays fer fun. That's when you get the most auto rides, you know. But I wouldn't mind singing sometime, mebbe."

When they came downstairs, they were arm in arm and chatting quite pleasantly. Grace had promised to come and see her, and take her to Christian Endeavor the next Sunday night and introduce her to the leader of the young people's choir; and Cornelia, waiting to receive her guests' farewell, wondered and was thankful.

They all went out together, talking a bit loudly and hilariously, Clytie's voice now raised in her old shrill, uncultured clang. Maxwell lingering for a moment in the doorway, spoke to Cornelia.

"I want to thank you for letting me come."

She turned to him with a look of suffering in her eyes.

"I don't know what you must think of us," she said in a low tone, "having that impossible girl here! An invited guest!"

He looked down at her, smiling with a hint of tenderness in his look, for he saw that she was very tired.

"I think you are a brave girl," he said earnestly. "And I think your experiment was a success. May I come back a few minutes, and help wash dishes? I'm taking your young brother Harry with me, and shall have to bring him back, you know. We'll talk it all over then."

He touched his hat, and vanished into the starlit night.

Cornelia flushed, wondering, half dismayed, ready to drop with fatigue, yet strangely elated. She stood a moment in the doorway, looking after the two cars as they whirled away down the street, and letting the cool evening breeze blow on her hot forehead, then turned back to the bright, pretty room, somehow soothed and comforted. A thought had come to her. She had prayed for help, and God had sent it; right into the midst of her consternation He had sent that young man to help! And how he had helped! What a tower of strength he had been all the awful evening!

But then Louise fell upon her with joyful exclamations.

"It *was* a success, Nellie, wasn't it? A *great* success! Wasn't he great? Wasn't it wonderful that father should have found him and brought him in? Wasn't it just like an answer, Nellie, don't you think? He kept her away from Carey all the evening, and Carey had a lovely time with Miss Kendall. And Brand said he had a good time, too, and told me he wished you would ask him again. He talked to me a lot while you were talking to the others. He said he'd take us all out in his car sometime if you would go; and he said he thought you were a wonderful sister, and a beautiful girl! He did, Nellie, he said it just like that, 'Your sister is a *bee-yew*-ti-ful girl'! And he meant it! And it was true, Nellie; you did look just wonderful. Your cheeks were such a pretty pink, and you didn't have your nose all white like that Clytie. Say, I guess she saw it wasn't nice to be the way she is, don't you think she did? I don't think she liked it the way Carey acted. I guess maybe she'll let him alone some now, and I hope she does. My, I hope she does! I didn't think he liked her being here, either, did you, Nellie? And say didn't the water-ice look lovely? And the table was the prettiest thing! Miss Kendall said she never saw such a pretty table. She said you were an artist, Nellie. And Mr. Maxwell, he couldn't say enough things about the house. Even that Brand said he wished he had a nice cozy home like this. He said his sister didn't have time to get up birthday parties, or his mother, either; they had to have a whole townful when they had parties, and he just loved it tonight. He said twice he wished you'd ask him again. I guess he means to stick, Nellie; will you like that?"

"He's not so bad," said Cornelia, patting the little girl's cheek. "I think maybe we can find a way to help him a little if we try. And I think maybe we ought not to feel so hard toward that poor, foolish girl, either, dearie. Now, come, kitty dear, you ought to be in bed."

" 'Deed, no, Nellie dear. I'm going to see the whole thing through," she chatted, hopping around on the tips of her toes. "We've got to wash the dishes. Harry said that Mr. Maxwell was coming back to help, too. We better get some clean aprons ready."

"Where is father, Louie? Did he go up to bed?"

"Oh, no, he went with Brand and Carey and Miss Kendall. They asked him, and he seemed real pleased. I shouldn't wonder if Brand will come back too, and help. He asked me if he might. I said I guessed you wouldn't care. I thought if he didn't maybe he'd carry Carey off for all night or something."

Cornelia stooped, and kissed the sweet, anxious little face.

"It's all right, dearie, and I guess everything's all right. Somehow we came out of an awful place tonight, and I guess God means to see us through."

"I know," said the little girl wisely. "When Clytie danced, you mean. That was awful, wasn't it? Father looked — just — sick for a minute, didn't he? Poor daddy, he didn't understand. And he doesn't like dancing. And I thought for just a minute how awful mother would feel. She doesn't like it either. And that girl — she was so — awful! But my! I'm glad it's over, aren't you, Nellie? And say! There they come! There's enough water-ice for everybody to have some more. Shall we have it? My isn't this fun?"

They all came in, and frolicked through the dishes, Brand and Maxwell entering into it with spirit. Brand didn't do much helping; but he made a show at it, and he certainly enjoyed the angel cake and water-ice, which was most thoroughly "finished" that night. Even the father came out into the kitchen, and watched the fun, and talked with Maxwell, who was flourishing a dish-towel and polishing glasses as if he had always done it.

Harry and Maxwell grew very chummy, and Maxwell declared that he was under deep obligation to the boy for his supper.

"How about it, Mr. Copley? Will you let this boy take a trip with me sometime pretty soon? I'm to go after mother in a week or so now, and I'd like mighty well to have his company. I shall probably start next Friday, sometime in the afternoon, and expect to get back Monday sometime. That wouldn't take him out of school many hours, and I think we'd have a first-rate time. Would you like it, son?"

Harry's eager face needed no words to express his joy. His eyes fairly sparkled.

The young man took a business card from his pocket, and handed it to Mr. Copley.

"I'm really an utter stranger to you, you know," he said with a smile; "and I can understand how you wouldn't want to trust your boy to a stranger. I shall consider it a favor if you will look me up; ask any of the men in my firm about me. I want you to be sure about me, because I intend to come again if you will let me. I'm not running any risk of losing such perfectly good new friends as you all are, and I want Harry for the trip."

Mr. Copley looked the young man over admiringly.

"Don't you think I can tell a *man* when I see one?" he asked amusedly. "It's generally written on his face, and no one can mistake."

"Thank you," said Maxwell. "That *is* a compliment!"

After the dishes were done there were the ferns to be unboxed and admired, and it was after midnight when at last the two young men said, "Good night," and drove away, each with the hearty assurance that he had had a wonderful time and wanted to come again soon.

When Cornelia went up to her room and took off her apron, out of its pocket fell a letter which she had received that morning and had been too busy to read. She opened it now. It was a brief, rattling epistle from one of her classmates in college, begging her to put off everything else for a few days and come to a house-party with them all. It was to be down at Atlantic City, near enough to home not to make the trip expensive; and they all were crazy to see her again and tell her all about commencement. She smiled reminiscently as she laid it away in her desk-drawer, and found to her surprise that she had no great desire to go. She knew what the party would be, full of rollicking fun, and care-free every minute of it; but somehow her heart and soul were now in her home and the new life that was opening before her. She wanted to finish the house; to make the white kitchen as charming in its way as the other rooms were getting to be; to help Carey plan a front porch he had said he would build with stone pillars; to set out some plants in the yard, finish the bedrooms, and make out a list of new furniture for the carpenter next door to buy. The minister had said he knew of some people who were refurnishing their house and wanted her professional advice. She wanted to stay and work. Mr. Maxwell was coming to take them all motoring some evening, too; and Brand had declared he would bring his sister around to call, and they would go out to ride. Life was opening up full and beautiful. College and its days seemed far away and almost childish. Tomorrow morning she and Grace Kendall were going to make curtains for one of the Sunday-school classrooms. Carey had promised to help put them up. Oh, life wasn't half bad! Even Clytie Amabel Dodd did not loom so formidable as earlier in the evening. She knelt and thanked God.

 **21** When Maxwell finally turned his car cityward it was with the feeling of a naughty boy who had run away from duty and was suddenly confronted by retribution.

He glanced at the clock in the car and noted that the hour was getting very late, and compunction seized upon him. Now that he had done the thing it suddenly seemed atrocious. He had ignored a lady in trouble and gone on a tangent. It wasn't even the excuse of a previous engagement, or the plea of old friends. It was utterly unnecessary. He had followed an impulse and accepted an utter stranger's invitation to dinner, and then had stayed all the evening, and gone back to wash dishes afterward. As he thought it over he felt that either he was crazy or a coward. Was it actually true that he, a man full grown, with a will of his own, was afraid to trust himself for an hour in the company of the woman who had once been supreme in his life? What was he afraid of? Not that he would yield to her wiles after two years' absence; not that he would break his promise to himself and marry her in spite of husbands and laws either moral or judicial. It must be that he was afraid to have his own calm disturbed. He had been through seas of agony and reached a haven of peace where he could endure and even enjoy life, and he was so selfish that he wished to remain within that haven even though it meant a breach of courtesy, and an outraging of all his finer instincts.

He forgot that his struggle earlier in the evening had been in an exactly opposite line, and that the finer feelings had urged him to remain away from the woman who had once been almost his undoing. However, now that it was almost too late to mend the matter he felt that he ought to have gone. Even if her plea of asking his advice had merely been a trumped-up excuse to bring him to her side, yet was it not the part of a gentleman to go? A true gentleman should never let a lady ask for help in vain. And he had promised always to be her friend. It might be that it had been an ill-advised promise, but a promise was a promise, etc.

By that time he had arrived at his apartment and was hastening through a rapid evening toilet. The evening and its simple experiences seemed like a pleasant dream that waking obliterates. It might return later, but now the present was upon him, and he knew Evadne when she was kept waiting. If she had not changed there was no pleasant interview in store for him. However, he need not tell her that he had been enjoying himself all the evening and had forgotten how fast time was flying.

Arrived at the hotel he went at once to the desk and asked for the lady. The clerk asked his name and called a bell-boy. "Go page Miss Chantry," he said. "She's in the ballroom." Then turning to Maxwell, he said: "She left word you were to wait for her in the reception room over there."

"No, don't page her," said Maxwell sharply, "I'll go and find her myself."

"Oh, all right! Just as you please! Those were her orders."

Maxwell turned toward the elevators, half inclined after all not to see her. She had not been in such distress but that she could amuse herself after all. But that was Evadne, of course. He must expect that. Besides, she was doubtless angry at his delay.

Maxwell got off at the gallery floor expecting to find the lady seated in one of the little quiet nooks overlooking the gay throng, but he made the rounds without finding her, and paused at the last door to look down on the moving, throbbing, colorful life below.

The orchestra was beating out a popular bit of elevated jazz and the floor below was like a kaleidoscope as the couples wove their many colored patterns in and out among each other.

Maxwell watched the dancers idly for a moment. He was not a dancer himself and not particularly interested in it. As he looked he was suddenly struck with the contrast between this scene and the quiet little home where he had spent the evening. How hard these people were trying to enjoy themselves, and how excited and restless and almost unhappy many of them looked.

A group of ladies scated near the railing quite close to where he stood were discussing one of the couples on the floor.

"She is disgusting," said one, "I wonder who she is? How dare she come to a respectable place and dance in that way?"

His eyes followed their glances and he easily singled out the two who were under their criticism. The man, a tall, dark, bizarre looking fellow he knew by sight, with money enough and family irreproachable enough to get away with anything in these days.

But the woman! Why did there seem to be something familiar about her? Sleek, black hair wound closely about a small, languid head, lizard-like body inadequately sheathed in gold brocade, sparkle of jewels from lazy graceful feet.

A break in the throng as some one went off the floor, and the two swept around facing him. The woman looked up and met his eyes. *It was Evadne!*

Something clicked and locked in his soul as if the machinery could not go on any longer without readjustment. He stood staring down at her, a growing wonder in his face, aware that she was looking at him and waving, aware that he was expected to smile. Instead he felt as if he were glaring. Was this the woman for whom he had spent two years of agony and struggle? This little empty faced creature with a smile upon her painted selfish mask? As he stood looking at her he was struck with a fleeting fancy that she resembled Clytie, poor feather-brained Clytie trying to exploit her own little self in the best way she knew, to play the game of life to her own best advantage. What was the difference between them?

Was it for a woman like this that he had wasted two of the best years out of his young manhood? He used to call her beautiful, but now her face seemed so vapid. Was it just the years that had come between or had she changed, grown coarser, less ethereal? A vision of Cornelia Copley floated in his mind. Why hadn't he known sooner that there was a girl like that some where in the world? What a fool he had been!

Evadne had signalled to him and led her partner off the floor. Now they were coming to him. He wished he might vanish somewhere. Why had he come? This girl had no real need of him. She was merely enjoying herself.

"What made you so late?" she challenged gaily, "We've been waiting supper for an age. I met an old friend tonight. Bob, meet Artie Maxwell. Come on, I've had the food served in my suite, and I've ordered lobster Newburg and all the things you used to like."

"I'll answer for the drinks," broke in the one called Bob, "I've sampled them already."

"Sh! Naughty! Naughty! Bob!" hushed Evadne with her finger on her lips. "Artie is a good little boy. He doesn't break the law —" she laughed. "Come on, Artie, I'm nearly starved. I thought you never would get here. Ring for the elevator, Bob, please."

Maxwell's whole being simply froze.

He didn't want to remain, and he didn't like the other man, but he could not ask her point blank what she wanted of him in

317

the presence of this stranger. He was gravely silent as the elevator carried them to the right floor and Evadne did the talking. But when the door opened into the apartment and showed a table set for three with flowers and lights and preparations for a feast he made a stand.

"I can't possibly stay for supper," he declared, "I've dined only a little while ago, and I must leave for New York on business very early in the morning. I only dropped in to explain —"

"Indeed, you are not going to leave in that way!" she flashed upon him angrily, "I told you in my note that I had something very important to tell you."

Maxwell looked at the other man politely:

"If we could have just a word together now," he said, turning back to the girl. "I really must get back to my apartment at once. I have important papers to prepare for tomorrow."

The other man turned away toward the table haughtily, with a scornful: "Why certainly," and poured himself a glass from the flask that stood there.

Maxwell turned to the angry girl:

"Now, what can I do for you? I shall be very glad to do anything in my power of course." He spoke stiffly as to a stranger.

The girl perceived that her power over him was waning. Yet she was too subtle to let him see it.

"I am in deep trouble," she sighed with a quiver of the lips, "But I can't tell it in a moment. It is a long story." Her eyelids fluttered down on her lovely painted cheeks. She knew the line that would touch him most.

"What sort of trouble?" he asked almost gently. He never could bear to see a woman suffer.

She clasped her little jewelled hands together fiercely and bent her head dejectedly.

"I cannot tell you all now," she answered desperately, "you would have to hear the whole before you could understand. Wait until we are alone."

"Is it financial trouble?" he urged after a pause with a gentle persistence in his voice.

"Yes, that — and — *other things!*" Evadne forced a tear to the fringes of her almond lids.

He studied her gravely.

"I'll tell you what I want you to do," he said at last, "I will not be here tomorrow nor possibly for several days, but I would like you to talk with our old family lawyer. He was a friend of my father's, and is very wise and kind. Anything you could tell to me you can tell to him. He knows you and will fully understand. I can call him tonight when I get back and explain, and he will be glad to come here and see you I am sure; or if you prefer you can go to his office."

But Evadne lifted her sleek, black head wrathfully, flicked off the tear, flung out her chin, and looked him down with her almond eyes as if from a great height:

"Thank you!" she said crisply, "When I want a family lawyer I can get one! And YOU — can — GO!"

She pointed to the door with her jewelled hand imperiously and Maxwell arose with dignity, his eyes upon her as if he would force himself to see the worst, and went.

"Bob!" said Evadne to the bibulous man at the table when the elevator door had clanged shut after her one-time lover, "I'm not sure but I shall come back to Philadelphia after a few days and stay awhile. I wonder if you could keep track of that man for me and tell me just where he goes and what he does. I'll make it worth your while you know."

"Surely, old dear, I'll be delighted. No trouble at all. I know a private detective who would be tickled to death for the job. What did you say the poor fish's name is? Seemed a harmless sort of chump. Not quite your kind is he? Come, Vaddie, let's have another drink."

But Evadne's eyes narrowed thoughtfully as she took the glass and drank slowly. She was not one to take lightly any loss.

Out in the night the young man drew a deep breath of the clean air thankfully. It seemed as though he had escaped from something unwholesome and tainted. He was glad that he had the sense to know it, and he thought back again with relief to the happy evening in the simple, natural home.

22

Carey had been working quite steadily at the garage and giving money to his father and Cornelia every week. It really made things much easier in the home. Word had come that the mother was steadily progressing toward health, and everybody was much happier. It seemed that Carey was happier, too. He was not away so much at night, which relieved his sister and his father tremendously.

Nothing had been said about Clytie Dodd. Carey had thanked his sister for the party and for taking so much trouble to make a pleasant evening, but he utterly ignored the presence of the girl who had been the cause of the whole affair. It was as if she had not been there. Mr. Copley had asked as he sat down to dinner the next evening after the birthday: "Where did you pick up that queer Dodd girl you had here?" and Cornelia had answered quite casually, as if it didn't matter at all, "Oh, she was just a girl I thought perhaps we ought to know," and slipped back into the kitchen to get the potatoes just as Carey entered the dining-room. He must have heard the conversation, and heard his father's reply:

322

"Well, I guess she's not quite our sort, is she? I guess we can get along without her, can't we?" — he made no comment, and began to talk at once eagerly about the new stone porch he was going to build. It appeared that he had discovered a lot of stone that was being dug from the street where they were putting down new paving, and it was to be had for little more than the carting away. Pat would let him have his truck at night, and he was going to bring the first load that very evening. Brand was coming around to help. Brand wanted to have a hand in the building.

Brand appeared soon after, coming breezily out to the dining-room without an invitation and sitting down for a piece of lemon pie as if he were a privileged friend of long standing. There was nothing backward about Brand. Yet somehow they all liked him, and Cornelia could see that Carey was pleased that they did. She felt a glow of thankfulness in her heart that it was possible to like one of Carey's friends when the other one was so unspeakably impossible.

Brand took off his coat, and put on an old sweater of Carey's; and they went off together after the truck. In a little while they were back with the first load of cobblestones, and worked till long after dark, load after load, piling them neatly between the sidewalk and the curb, till they had a goodly lot. Brand seemed as interested in that porch as if it were his own. After they took the truck back Brand came in again, and wanted to sing. They sang for nearly an hour; and, when he left, Cornelia felt as if they had fully taken over Brand as a part of their little circle. She couldn't help wondering what his society mother and elegant sister would say if they knew where he had spent the last two evenings. Then she reflected that there were much worse places where he might spend them, and probably often did; and she began to take Brand into her thoughts and plans for the future with almost the same anxious care as she gave to Carey. Brand was a nice boy, and needed helping. He was too young to spend his time running around with girls like Clytie Dodd and taking joy rides with a gay crowd. She would make their little home a haven where Carey and his friends would at least be safe and happy. She could not give them anything elaborate in the way of entertainment; but there should always be a welcome, plenty of music, and something to eat.

Cornelia could see her father visibly brighten day by day as the week went by, and Carey seemed to stick to his task and spend his evenings at home. Brand had bought a pair of overalls and made blisters on his hands digging for the foundation of the stone porch; and every afternoon Carey came home from the garage at five o'clock and worked away with a will.

At this rate it did not take long for the wall to rise. It was level with the front door-step now, and Carey had put a plank across and a few stones for steps to go up and down.

It was late on Thursday afternoon, and Carey was hard at work trying to finish the front wall before dark. Brand's racing-car was standing by the curb with the engine throbbing, and Brand himself was standing with one foot on the wall talking to Carey.

Cornelia had just come out with a plate of hot gingerbread for them, and was standing a moment watching them enjoy it when another car suddenly came down the hill and stopped in the road just in front of Brand's car. A wriggling child in the front seat peered out curiously from beside the driver, and Cornelia had a glimpse of a fretful elderly woman's face in the back seat. Then the door on the driver's side of the car was opened and some one got out and came around. She hadn't thought of its being Maxwell until he was in full view, and a soft flush came into her cheeks with the welcome light in her eyes.

"Come in and have a piece of hot gingerbread!" she called, holding out the plate.

He came springing up the plank, and stood beside her.

"Oh, thank you! Isn't this wonderful?" he said, taking a piece eagerly. "But I'm afraid I must eat and run. I'm taking my chief's aunt and her grandchild down to the train, and mustn't delay. I just stopped to say that I'm leaving for the mountains tomorrow afternoon about three o'clock, and will stop here for Harry. Do you think that will be too early for him?"

"Oh, no, indeed. He can come home from school at noon and be all ready for you. It is wonderful of you to take him. He has talked of nothing else since you were here, and father and I appreciate your kindness, I'm sure."

"No kindness about it. It will be great to have a kid along. I hate to go anywhere alone. Say, this gingerbread is luscious! No, really I mustn't take another bite. I must go this minute. I've left my engine going, and the lady is inclined to be easily annoyed. I —"

He happened to look up at that moment

and saw to his horror that his car had begun to move slowly on down the hill. The child on the front seat had been doing things to the brakes and clutch. She had no idea what she was doing, but she always did things to everything in sight. If it was an electric bulb, she unscrewed it; if it was openable, she opened it; if it was possible to throw anything out of gear, she always could be depended upon to throw it. She was that kind of a child. She once threw a pair of heavy sliding doors off the track and almost down upon her, and was saved from a timely death only by the presence of some elderly rescuer. Had Maxwell known the child, he never would have left her alone in that front seat. She had wriggled herself into the driver's seat, and her fat hands were manipulating the wheel. As the car began to move she gave a shout of horrid glee. A scream from the woman on the back seat, and Maxwell turned sick with the thought of the possibilities, and sprang down the wall toward the street.

But, quick as he was, Brand and Carey were ahead of him. At the very first sound, even before the car had been really in motion, Carey looked up over the wall he was building, gave a low whistle, and cried: "Hey there! Brand! Your car! Get a hustle!"

Brand turned, and needed not an explanation. He dashed across the intervening space to his own car, sprang to the driver's seat, and was off. Carey, though handicapped by the wall he had to leap over, was scarcely a hair's breadth behind, and alighted on the running-board after the car had started.

"We've got to catch her before she reaches the corner," he shouted above the noise of the racing engine. "There's a trolley coming around the curve at the foot of the hill, and you can't tell what that kid'll do. It's a cinch she never ran a car before; look at her wabble. She's getting scared now. Look! The fool in the back seat has dragged her away from the wheel! Hey there! Give her plenty of room! Now curve her around, and give me space to jump her!"

Maxwell was running frantically and vainly down the street after his car, which was now going at a wild pace. From either direction on the cross street at the foot of the hill he could see cars speeding along. Who would know that the oncoming car was managed by a child who had never run a car in her life, a child who knew nothing whatever about cars, was too young to know, had never even been accustomed to ride in one, but lived in a little country village where cars were scarce articles? All this he knew because the grandmother had talked much to the youngster on the way down, and the child had said she had never been in a car but once before, but she wished she had one; she knew she could run it.

Horror froze in his veins as he remembered all these little details. He had made running a specialty when he was in college athletics, but now, although his way was downhill, his feet were like lead and his knees weak as water. He saw himself a murderer. Every possible detail of disaster rose and menaced his way as he sped onward, determined to do all in his power for rescue. The blood was pounding through his head so that he could scarcely see or hear. His breath came painfully, and he wondered blindly how long this would last. Then suddenly he saw the long, clean body of the racing-car slide down the hill like a glance of light, glide close to the run-away car, then curve away and cross the street just in front of the oncoming trolley. He looked to see his own car smash into the trolley-car; but instead it swept around in a steady, clean curve that just cleared the trolley-car and veered away to the right. It crossed the car track behind the trolley-car, and circled around and back up the hill again, a steady hand at the wheel. An instant more, and the car stopped before him where he stood in the middle of the road, his face white, his eyes staring, unable to believe that the catastrophe had really been averted. He looked up and there sat Carey in the driver's seat as coolly as if he had been taking a pleasure trip.

"Shall I turn her around?" asked Carey nonchalantly, "or do you want to go back to the house?"

"How did you do it?" asked Arthur Maxwell, grasping Carey's grimy hand eagerly. "I didn't see you catch her."

"Oh, just jumped her from Brand's running-board. Dead easy. Guess she gave you a little start though. That kid ought to be spanked. I guess the lady's pretty badly scared."

The lady and the "kid" were bathed in tears and wrapped in each other's arms in the back seat. The child was experiencing a late repentance, and the grandmother was alternately scolding and petting and in a fair way to make the little criminal feel she had done a smart thing. Maxwell gave them a withering glance, and turned to Carey, who had swung out over the door and was standing in the road, looking at the car like a lion tamer who has just subdued a wild creature.

"I shall never forget this, Copley," said Maxwell, grasping his hand once more in the kind of a grip a real man gives to another. "I'll talk about it later when I've taken these people to the train. Meantime accept my thanks for yourself and your friend. You're both princes, and I'll see that everybody knows it."

"Forget it!" chanted Carey, and swung himself like a thistledown to the running-board of Brand's car as he swept slowly, scrutinizingly up.

"Got her all right, didn't you, old man?" said Brand admiringly. "Any scratches? You had a mighty close shave!"

"Yep! She's all right. Well, so-long Maxwell; we gotta beat it back to work," and with a great whizzing and banging of joyful celebration the racer shot its way back up-hill, and the two jumped out quite casually as if they had been off to get a soda and come back to work again.

Cornelia, white, and trembling from the horror of the thing, tried to praise, to question, to exclaim; but, failing to make an impression on the two indifferent workers, went upstairs, fell on her knees, and cried. Somewhere in the midst of her tears her crying turned into a prayer of thanksgiving, and she came down with an uplifted look on her face. Now and then as she went about her duties she stole to the front window, and looked out on the two sturdy workers. She could have hugged them both she was so proud of them — they were so cool, so capable, and so indifferent! Just regular boys!

Maxwell came back that evening. She had somehow known he would. He was filled with gratitude to the two who had so gallantly saved him from a catastrophe which would have shadowed his whole life. He still shuddered over the thought of what might have happened.

"I will never again leave a child alone in an automobile," he declared. "That girl was a little terror. I never saw one so spoiled and disagreeable in my life. She was determined to be allowed to run the car from the minute she got in, and she annoyed me constantly by playing with the electric buttons and getting her hands constantly on the wheel. I never dreamed she would have the strength to start the car, although she is large and strong for her age. But she has all kinds of nerve and impudence, and I might have known better than to stop here at all when I had such a passenger. Her grandmother is a nervous wreck; but she doesn't blame me, fortunately, although I blame myself decidedly. It is my business to know men, and I should have known that child well enough to realize it was a risk to leave her."

"Kid ought to be spanked!" declared Carey gruffly. "Know what she did? When she saw she was going to run into that car, she lost every bit of nerve, and began climbing over the back of the seat. Some kid that! Just bad all through. Any nervy kid I know would have stuck it out and tried to steer her somehow, but that kid had a yellow streak."

"You're right there," declared Maxwell with watchful eyes upon the young man. "But you had your nerve with you all right, I noticed. When you swung off that running-board, it was an even chance you took. If you had missed your calculation by so much as a hair's breadth, you would have been smashed up pretty badly, crushed between the cars, probably."

Carey gave his shoulders a slight shrug.

"It's all in a lifetime," he said lightly. "But, say, that's a peach of a car you've got. Had it long?" and they launched into a lengthy discussion of cars in general and Maxwell's in particular. Cornelia noticed that all the time Maxwell was watching her brother keenly, intently. As he got up to leave, he asked casually:

"Are you still working with the garage people?"

Carey colored, and lifted his chin a trifle haughtily.

"Yes. I — *yes!*" he answered defiantly.

"Stick to it till something better comes along," advised Maxwell. "It isn't a bad line, and you get a lot of good dope about machines that won't do you any harm in the future. You're a good man, and there's a good job waiting for you somewhere"; and with that he said, "Good night."

Mr. Copley came in presently with a late edition of the evening paper. He had been called to the home of his manager, who was ill, on a business consultation. He looked tired but exalted. He spread the paper out on the table under the lamp, and called the children.

"See!" he said. "Do you know who that is?"

They all gathered around, and behold there was Carey looking at them from the pages of the *Evening Bulletin.* Carey! Their brother! They stared and stared again.

The picture had him in football garb, with one eye squinting at the sun, and a broad grin on his lips. It was Carey two years ago, on the high school football team; but it looked like him still. Beneath from a border looked forth the bold, handsome features of Brand Barlock, and to one side another border held the round fat, impertinent face of the child who had started the car that afternoon. The article below was headed in large letters:

FOOTBALL HERO SAVES TWO LIVES
Carey Copley Jumps From Moving Car and Saves Child and Grandmother!

"Now, isn't that the limit? How did that thing get in *there?*" demanded the young hero angrily. "And say! How'd they get my picture? Some little fool reporter went around to school, I suppose. Wouldn't that make you mad? How'd they find that out I'd like to know? Brand never told; that's one thing sure. Brand knows how to keep his mouth shut. You don't suppose that guy Maxwell would give it to them, do you?"

"He said he was going to see that everybody knew about it," chuckled Louise happily. "I think it oughtta be known, don't you, Daddy? When a boy — that is a *man* — does a big thing like saving two lives, I think everybody oughtta know how brave he is."

"Nonsense!" said Carey. "You don't know what you're talking about, kid. That wasn't anything to do." But his tone showed that he was pleased at the general attitude of his family. Nevertheless, he slammed around noisily in the dining-room, pretending not to hear when his father read aloud the account of the accident in the paper, and went whistling upstairs immediately after. At the top he called down:

"Say, I'm mighty glad they were fair to Brand in that ad. Brand's a great fellow. I couldn't have done a thing without him and his car. He knew just what to do without being told, and he can drive, I'll say. Brand deserves all they can say of him. He's a good fellow."

Altogether, the household slept joyously that night, and Harry dreamed of going to the mountains in an airship, and flying back tied to the tail of a kite.

When Maxwell came to get Harry the next afternoon, he asked Cornelia one question that made her wonder a little. It seemed almost irrelevant.

"Did your brother ever have anything to do with handling men?" he said looking thoughtfully at the neat masonry that was growing steadily longer and wider and higher.

"Why — I — hardly know," she replied, laughing. "I've been away so much from home."

"Captain of the basketball team in high school," announced Harry shrewdly, "and captain of a local baseball team they had out the other side of the city last summer. Some team it was, too; licked everything in sight and then some. Carey had 'em all right where he wanted 'em; and when a team treated 'em mean once, Kay just called the fellows off, and they wouldn't play one of 'em till he got a square deal with the ump!"

Harry's eyes sparkled. He made an earnest young advocate.

"Fine! I must hear more about that. I foresee I'm going to have a thrilling trip. There'll be lots to talk about. Well, Miss Copley, we'll bid you good-bye and get on our way. I want to get on well this afternoon in case we have bad weather tomorrow. But it looks clear now. We'll travel late tonight. There ought to be a wonderful moon. I wish you were going along." He gave her a wistful glance, and she flushed with pleasure.

"Thank you," she said appreciatively. "If I were only a little boy with nothing to do!"

"Sister!" protested Harry. "I've lots to do. I guess I work every day after school."

"You're not a little boy, Harry; you're almost a man," answered his sister lovingly. "I wasn't meaning you at all; I said, if *I* were a little boy with nothing to do, then I could go along. I meant you could take care of me, see?" She gave a dear little smile at him, and he grinned.

"Aw! Quit yer kiddin'. So-long, Cornie! Be back Monday. Take ker o' yerself!"

Maxwell's eyes met hers; they laughed together at the boyishness of it, and Maxwell said good-bye, and departed. Cornelia, as she went into the house, wondered why the brief conversation had seemed to lighten the monotony of the day so much, and then fell to wondering why Maxwell had asked that question about Carey.

Five minutes later the door-bell rang; and, when she opened the door, there stood Clytie Dodd, a brilliant red feather surrounding a speck of a hat, and her face painted and powdered more wickedly than ever. She was wearing a yellow organdie dress with scallops on the bottom and adornments of colored spheres of cloth attached with black stitches at intervals over the frock. She carried a green parasol airily, and there was a "man" with an incipient and tenderly nursed mustache waiting for her at the gate. She greeted Cornelia profusely, and talked very loudly and very fast.

"Is Kay here? I'm just dying to see him and kid him about having his picture in the paper. He always said he'd never get his there. But isn't it great, though? Some hero, I'll tell the world! Who was the kid? Anybody belonging to the family? The paper didn't state. Oh, darn! I'm sorry Kay isn't here. I wanted him to meet my friend," nodding toward the man at the gate. "We've got a date on for tonight, and we want him and his friend Mr. Barlock. Some girl friends of mine are coming, and we're going to have a dance and a big feed. It's just the kind of thing Kay likes. When'll he be back? Where is he? At the garage? We stopped there, but Pat said he'd went off with a car for some high muckymuck. I thought p'raps he'd stopped off here to take you a ride er something. Well, I s'pose I'll have to leave a message. Say, Ed, what time we going to start? Eight? Oh, rats! we oughtta start at half past seven. It's a good piece out to that Horseheads Inn I was tellin' you 'bout. We'll start at half past seven. Say, you tell your brother to call me up soon's he gets here. He often phones from the drugstore. Tell him I'll give the details. But in case he don't get me tell him we'll stop by here for him at half past seven. Tell him not to keep us waiting. I gotta go on now 'cause we gotta tell two other people, a girl and a man. It's awful annoying not having telephones everywhere. I don't know what we'd ever do without ours. S'-long! Don't forget to tell Kay!" and she flitted down the steps and out the gate to her "man."

That awful girl!

Cornelia shut the door, and dropped weakly into a chair. Her punishment was come upon her. She might have known she ought not to meddle with a girl like that, inviting her to the house and making her feel free there, setting the seal of family friendship on an intimacy that never ought to have been between her and the son of the house.

And now what should she do? Should she conceal the message and try to get Carey to go somewhere else with her? Or should she tell him the truth, and let him choose his own way? She knew beforehand that any kind of remonstrance from her would be vain. Carey was at the age when he liked to feel that he owned himself and took no advice from anybody unless he asked for it. She was enough of a stranger to him yet to realize that she must go slowly and carefully. It is a pity that we cannot more of us keep the polite relation of comparative strangers with our own family; it might tend to better things. It is strange that we do not realize this. The fact is, the best-meaning of us often antagonize the ones we love, and send them swiftly toward the very thing we

341

are trying to keep them from doing. The wisdom of serpents and the harmlessness of doves are often forgotten in our scheme of living, and loving consideration of one another is a thing far too rare in even Christian homes today.

Cornelia's honest nature always inclined to telling the truth, the whole truth, and nothing but the truth. She would have liked to go to her brother and give the message straight, knowing that he would decline it; but the fact was, she was not at all sure of him. Clytie's manner implied that this sort of thing had been habitual amusement with him. And Cornelia was not at all sure that Clytie's behavior on the night of the party had made any deep impression against her. Carey was young, and liked fun. These young people were ready to show him a good time, and what boy of his age could resist that? If she only knew of some way of getting up a counter-attraction! But what would a mild little fudge party or a walk to the park be beside the hilarity offered by Clytie's program?

Moreover, even if she succeeded in getting Carey away from the house before the wild crowd arrived, Clytie would be sure to tell him afterwards, and he would blame the sister for not giving the message. She was sure he would do that even if he did not intend to go. And there was Brand! He was invited, too. Of course Carey would go if Brand did. She wildly reviewed the idea of taking Brand into her confidence, and rejected it as not only useless, but a thing that would be regarded by Carey as a disloyalty to himself. Her perplexity deepened. Then she suddenly remembered her new source of help and, slipping to her knees beside the big chair in which she had been sitting, she prayed about it.

An outsider would think it a strange coincidence, perhaps. It did not seem so to the weary, perplexed sister that even while she knelt and poured out her worries to her heavenly Father the answer to her prayer should be on the very doorstep. She rose as the bell pealed through the house once more, and, opening the door, found Grace Kendall standing there. She seemed like an angel from heaven, and Cornelia almost wondered whether she shouldn't tell her troubles to this new friend.

"I've come to ask a favor," Grace said eagerly. "And you're to promise first that you will tell me truly if there is any reason why it isn't convenient to grant it. Now do you promise?"

Cornelia laughingly promised, but before

the request was made she heard Carey's step at the side door, and a shadow of anxiety came into her eyes. Carey, not knowing of their visitor, came straight into the living room in search of his sister.

"I couldn't get any more cement tonight. Isn't that a shame?" he said before he saw their guest, and then came forward, half abashed to greet her, apologizing for his rough working garb.

"Please don't apologize," said Grace eagerly. "You look fine. You couldn't work in evening clothes, could you? And wait till you hear what I've come to beg you to do. Are you awfully busy this evening, both of you?"

"Not a thing in the world to do," said Carey eagerly. "I'm at your service. What can I do for you? Anything but sing. I really can't sing well enough to go into a choir."

"Well, I don't want you to sing tonight," said Grace, laughing. "Guess again. Now you're *sure* you haven't any engagement?"

"No, indeed, honor bright," he declared, smiling.

"Well, then I'm going to beg you to do a big favor. You see father is asked to speak over at Glen Avon tonight and he has just discovered that they only have two trains a day, and the evening train will get him there too late for the meeting; so he had to hurry around and try to get some one to take him in a car. We have found the car. It belongs to Mr. Williams, and he is just eager to lend it; but he can't drive it himself, because he has to go to New York at five o'clock. He's rather particular about who drives it, and he said, if we could get a good, reliable driver, we were welcome to it. Father knew that you were used to cars; he's watched you driving Mr. Barlock's car sometimes, and he wondered if you would be willing to go and drive us. The car is a great big, roomy one, and we can take as many along as want to go; and I thought perhaps you and the children would like to go too." She turned to Cornelia and then back to Carey. "You're quite sure there isn't any reason at all why it isn't convenient for you?"

"Perfectly," said Carey with shining eyes; "I'd rather drive than eat any day in the week. And it will be a dandy trip. The roads over there are like velvet. There's going to be a moon tonight, too! Gee! I'm glad you asked me. When do we start?"

"Why, father has to be there by eight. How long do you think it will take? We must not run any risk of being late. It is some kind of a convention and father has charge of the hour from eight to nine. We won't have to stay late, you know, and we can ride a while afterward if we like."

"Great!" said Carey. "I'll bring you home by the way of the river. It'll be peachy that way tonight. Say! This is wonderful! I think we ought to start by half past six or quarter to seven. Cornie, can you get through dinner by six thirty? That would be safer."

"Oh, surely," said Cornelia eagerly. "We'll have the dinner on the table the minute father gets in, five minutes to six; and we'll just stack the dishes and run. Won't it be delightful?"

Then suddenly the thought of Clytie Dodd and her party came back with a twinge of horror. Ought she to tell Carey at once?

Grace Kendall was hurrying away with many thanks and happy exclamations of how glad she was she had made up her mind to come. She could not tell it before Grace, anyway, although perhaps Carey would have thought she ought.

"What's the matter, Nell?" asked her brother as he came in and shut the door. "Don't you want to go? I should think it would be a good rest for you."

"Oh, yes, indeed! I want to go, of course; but I just remembered. Perhaps I should have told you before you promised. Clytie

Dodd was here —"

"What?" he looked angry and disgusted.

"She wanted you to go to some ride and dance tonight and get Brand to go too. She wants you to call her up at once."

"Aw! Forget it! She's always got something on the brain. Call her up. I shan't call her up. She's a little fool, anyway."

He looked half ashamed as he said it. He was perfectly aware that his sister must have seen him all dressed up taking her to a moving-picture show several weeks ago.

"But — they're going to stop here for you at half past seven."

"Well, let 'em stop! We'll be gone, won't we? She'll have her trouble for her pains, won't she?" He really was speaking in a very rude tone to his sister; but she could see that he was annoyed and mortified to have to talk with her at all on this subject, and the things he said filled her with a triumphant elation.

"But, Carey, oughtn't you to call her up and tell her you have another engagement? Isn't that the right thing, the manly thing, to do?"

"Oh, bother! You don't understand! Let *me* manage this, please. I guess I know my own business. I tell you she's a — fool!"

Carey slammed upstairs to his room, and

she could hear him presently in the bathroom stropping his razor, and whistling a merry tune. He had forgotten all about Clytie. Cornelia's hand trembled as she slipped the hot apple pie out of the oven, and dusted it with powdered sugar. Then she suddenly straightened up, and said out loud, "He answered!"

For a moment the little white kitchen seemed a holy place, as if a presence unseen were there; and her whole being was thrilled with the wonder of it. God, the great God, had listened to her troubled cry and sent His angel in the form of the minister's daughter, who had averted the danger. Other people might doubt and sneer at supposed answers to prayer if they knew the circumstances, perhaps call it a coincidence, or a "chance," or a "happening"; but she *knew!* There was something more than just the fact that the trouble had been averted. There was that strange spiritual consciousness of God answering her, God coming near and communicating with her, as if their eyes had met across the universe, and He had made her certain of His existence, certain of His interest in her and care for her and her affairs.

It was a little thing, an intangible thing; but it glorified her whole life, the day, the moment, and her work. It was real, and something she could never forget. She went swiftly about the last details of the evening meal, had everything on the table absolutely on time, even found a moment to run up to her room, smooth her hair, and put on a fresh blouse. Yet through it all, and on through the beautiful evening, it kept ringing back sweetly in her heart. She had a refuge when things grew too hard for her, a God who cared, and would help in time of need. She had not thought that faith was given like that, but it had come and made a different thing entirely of living.

They had a wonderful drive, Grace sitting in the front seat with Carey, and carrying on a merry conversation, his father and the minister in the back seat, with Louise and Cornelia in the two little middle seats. For the minister had insisted on the whole family going. So for the first time since Cornelia's return from college the little house was shut up and dark through the whole evening, and now and again Cornelia's thoughts would turn back and wonder what Clytie thought when she arrived with her gang of pleasure-seekers.

But the evening was so wonderful, the moonlight so perfect, the company so congenial, that Cornelia found it hard to harbor unpleasant thoughts, and for one evening was carefree and happy. Now and then she thought of her little brother riding afar with young Maxwell, and wondered what they were talking about, and whether they would all know him any better when he got back with Harry. It was always so revealing to have a member of one's family get really close to every-day living with a person. Then her thoughts would come back to the drifting talk from Grace and Carey in front, and she thought how handsome her brother looked, and how at ease driving the car and talking to this sweet, cultured girl. She remembered his accents when he called Clytie Dodd a fool so vehemently, and compared them with his face as he walked on Chestnut Street, chewing gum, and looking down attentively to his over-dressed, ill-behaved companion. Which was the real Carey? And do we all have two people shut up inside ourselves? Or is one the real self and the other a mask?

The service which they attended for an hour was intensely interesting, and quite new to Cornelia. She had never seen anything like it before. It was a "conference." Nobody said for what, and she did not happen to get hold of a program until they were leaving. Mr. Kendall at the desk seemed like a father among his children, or a close friend of them all; and he led their thoughts to the heavenly Father in a most wonderful way, speaking of Him as if He were present always with each one, ready to help in any need, ready to conquer for them; and the thought he left with them at the close of his ten-minute talk was drawn from the verse, "My grace is sufficient for thee, for My strength is made perfect in weakness."

Cornelia listened in wonder, and instantly to her mind sprang once more her own experience of the afternoon and a conviction that she was being watched and guarded and led and *loved* by an unseen Power. This sense of God had never come to her before. Religion had been a dreamy, mysterious necessity, the wholly respectable and conventional thing to believe in, of course, and a kind of comfortable assurance for the darkness of the beyond. She had never had any particular tendency to the modern doubts. Her mother's faith and her father's living had been too real for that; and always, when a teacher had voiced some sceptical flippancy, she had turned away with an inner conviction that the teacher did not know, because there was her mother; and a feeling that she preferred to stick to the faith of her fathers. But as far as concerned any particular reason for doing so, or any particular conviction on her own part, she was absolutely without them.

But now suddenly she saw and felt something that had never come to her realization before. She felt as firmly assured of all the vital truths she had been taught as if some mystic curtain had suddenly been rolled back and revealed to her things hidden from mortal eye. She remembered somewhere in the Bible there was a verse, one of her mother's favorites, "He that believeth hath the witness in himself." Was this possibly what it meant? Was "the witness" coming to her because she had put her childhood belief to the test?

She came out of the church with a firm resolve to begin to study her Bible and find out more about this wonderful spirit world that was all about her, and by which perhaps she was guided through her life much more than she had ever dreamed. Her feeling that God was somewhere close and taking personal notice of her and her interests was so strong that she could not ignore it, and yet she regarded it almost shyly, like a bird that has quietly alighted on one's hand and might be frightened away. She did not dare to touch it and lay hold on its wonder firmly lest it should prove to be a figment of her imagination; but it gave her a deep, new joy for which she found no name. Could it be that she had found Christ? She had heard her mother speak of "finding Christ," and had never had much idea of what it could be. Now a deep conviction grew in her that she was experiencing it herself.

The ride home was one of wondrous beauty, and there was a serene happiness in each heart that made it seem a most unusual occasion, one to look back upon with a thrill of pleasure for many a day. Even Louise seemed to feel it. She nestled close to her sister, and watched with wide, happy eyes the fleeting starry darkness, and drew long breaths of spring and ferny sweetness as they passed through some wooded road, and every little while would whisper: "Aren't we having just a wonderful time, Nellie, dear? I wonder if it's as pretty where Harry is now. I wonder if they've stopped for the night yet."

The minister and Mr. Copley were on the two middle seats now, having a deep discussion about whether the world was growing better or worse, and Cornelia was on the back seat with her little sister. The evening seemed like an oasis in the great desert of hard work and worry through which she had been passing for the last few weeks. Just to see Carey there in the front seat talking and smiling to Grace was enough to rest her heart. If she could have heard the earnest little talk about real Christian living they were having, she would have been filled with wonder and awe. Carey talking religion with a young girl! How unbelievable it would have seemed to her! But the purr of the engine sheltered the quiet sentences; and Grace and Carey talked on deep into the heart of life and the simplicity of the gospel, and Carey expressed shy thoughts that he never would have dreamed before of letting even the angels of heaven guess. His living hadn't always been in accordance with such thoughts or beliefs; but they were there all the time, and this girl, who was a real Christian herself, had called them forth. Perhaps the spirit of the remarkable meeting which they had just attended had helped to make it a fitting time and prepare their minds so that it came about quite naturally. Grace was no insistent evangelist, flinging her message out and demanding an answer. She breathed the fragrance of Christianity in her smile, and her words came involuntarily from a heart that thought much "on these things."

The immediate result of the talk became

apparent as they were getting out of the car at the minister's house. Carey was to drive his own people on to their home, and then put the car in its garage, two blocks farther up the hill.

As Grace turned to say, "Good night," Carey leaned out and asked, "What time did you say that Christian Endeavor met?"

"Oh, yes, seven o'clock!" said the girl eagerly, not at all as if it were a doubtful question whether the young man would come or not. "And don't forget the choir rehearsal. That is Friday evening at our house, you know."

"I'll be there!" said Carey graciously.

Cornelia, too astonished for words that Carey was arranging for all these church functions, easily yielded to the request; and they parted for the night, the sister with a singing in her heart that her brother was getting to be friends with a girl like the minister's daughter. Now surely, surely he would stop going with girls like Clytie Dodd. Probably that girl would be offended at the way she had been left without even an apology, and would drop Carey now. She sat back with a sigh of relief, and dismissed this one burden from her young heart. Could she have known what plots were at that very moment revolving in the vengeful girl's mind, and being suggested to her hilarious and willing group of companions amid shouts of laughter, she would not have rested her soul so easily, nor enjoyed the wonderful moonlight that glorified even the mean little street where she lived. The devil is not idle when angels throng most around, and Cornelia had yet to learn that a single victory is not a whole battle won. But perhaps, if she had known she would not have had the courage and faith to go forward; and it is well that the step ahead is always just out of sight.

24 For three long, beautiful weeks Cornelia enjoyed her calm and hope climbed high.

The stone columns of the pretty front porch grew rapidly, and began to take on comeliness. Brand endeared himself to them all by his cheerful, steady, patient aid, coming every afternoon attired in overalls, and working hard till dark, getting his white hands callous and dirty, cut with the stones, and hard as nails. Once Cornelia had to tie an ugly cut he got when a stone fell on his hand; and he looked at her lovingly, and thanked her just like a child. From that time forth she gathered him into her heart with her brothers and sister, and began genuinely to like him and be anxious for his welfare. It seemed that his mother and sister were society people, and made little over him at home. He had his own companions and went his own way without consulting them; and, although he must have had a wonderful mansion of a home, he seemed much to prefer the little cozy house of the Copley's, and spent many evenings there as well as days. He seemed to be as much interested in getting the stone porch done as Carey himself, and he often worked away alone when Carey felt he must stay at the garage awhile to get money enough for more stone or more cement and sand. Once or twice Cornelia suspected from a few words she gathered, as the boys were arguing outside the window, that Brand had offered to supply the needed funds rather than have Carey leave to earn them; but she recognized proudly that Carey always declined emphatically such financial assistance.

Now and then Brand would order Carey to "doll up," and would whirl him away in his car to see a man somewhere with the hope of a position; but as yet nothing had come of these various expeditions, although Carey was always hopeful and kept telling about a new "lead," as he called it, with the same joyous assurance of youth.

Brand, too, had been drawn into the young people's choir, and took a sudden interest in Sunday-night church. Once he went with Cornelia, and found the place in the hymn book for her, and sang lustily at her side. The next Sunday he was sitting up in the choir loft beside Carey and acting as if he were one of the chief pillars in that church. It was wonderful how eagerly he grasped a thing that caught his interest. He had a wild, care-free, loving nature, and bubbled over with life and recklessness; but he was easily led if anybody chose to give him a little friendship. It seemed that he led a starved life so far as loving care was concerned, and he accepted eagerly any little favor done for him. Cornelia soon found that he grew pleasantly into the little family group; and even the children accepted and loved him, and often depended upon him.

Arthur Maxwell, too, had become an intimate friend of the family circle, and since Harry had come back from his trip to the mountains he could talk of nothing else but "Mr. Maxwell says this and Mr. Maxwell does that," till the family began gently to poke fun at him about it. Nevertheless, they were well pleased that they had such a friend. He came down one day, and took Cornelia off for the whole afternoon on a wonderful drive in the country. They brought back a great basket of fruit and armfuls of wild flowers and vines. Another day he took her to a nursery where they selected some vines for the front porch, some climbing roses and young hedge-plants, which he proceeded to set out for her on their return. Then next day a big box of chocolates was delivered at the door with his card. But his mother had not been out for her promised visit yet; for she had been called away on a business trip to California the day after she reached home, and had decided to remain with her relatives there for a month or six weeks. Cornelia as she daily beautified her pretty home kept wondering what Mrs. Maxwell would say to it when she did come. But most of all she wondered about her own dear mother, and what she would say to the glorified old house when she got back to it again.

Great news had been coming from the sanitarium where the mother was taking the rest-cure. The nurse said that she grew decidedly better from the day the letter arrived telling how Carey was singing in the church choir and going to Christian Endeavor, and building a front porch. The nurse's letter did not show that she laid any greater stress on any one of these occupations than on the others, but Cornelia knew that her mother's heart was rejoicing that the boy had found a place in the church of God where he was interested enough to go to work. In her very next letter she told about the minister's people, and described Grace Kendall, telling of Carey's friendship for her. Again the nurse wrote how much good that letter had done the mother, so that she sat up for quite a little while that day without feeling any ill effects from it. Cornelia began to wonder whether Clytie had been at the bottom of some of her mother's trouble, and to congratulate herself on the fact that Clytie had suffered eclipse at last.

About this time Maxwell arrived one evening while Carey was putting the finishing-touches to the front porch, and instead of coming in as was his custom, he sat down on a pile of floor-boards and talked with Carey.

Cornelia, hearing low, earnest voices, stepped quietly to the window and looked out, wondering to see Maxwell talking so earnestly with her brother. She felt proud that the older young man was interested enough in him to linger and talk, and wondered whether it might be politics or the last baseball score that was absorbing them. Then she heard Maxwell say: "You'll be there at eight tomorrow morning, will you? He wants to talk with you in his private office before the rush of the day begins."

In a moment more Maxwell came into the house, bringing with him a great box of gorgeous roses, and in her joy over the roses, arranging them in vases, she forgot to wonder what Maxwell and her brother had been talking about. He might have told her, perhaps, but they were interrupted almost immediately, much to her disappointment, by callers. First, the carpenter next door ran in to say he was building a bungalow in a new suburb for a bride and groom, and the man wanted to furnish the house throughout before he brought his wife home, to surprise her. The bride didn't know he was building, but thought they would have to board for a while; and he wanted everything pretty and shipshape for her before she came, so they could go right in and begin to live. He didn't have a lot of money for furnishing, and the carpenter had found out about it, and told him about Cornelia. Would she undertake the job on a percentage basis, taking for selecting the things ten per cent, say, on what they cost, and charging her usual prices for any work she had to do?

Cornelia at the door facing out into the starlight, flushed with pleasure over the new business opportunity, and made arrangements in a happy tone to meet the new householder the next morning, talk plans over with him, and find out what he wanted. The young man in the living room, waiting for her, pretending to turn over the pages of a magazine that lay on the table was furtively watching her the while and thinking how fine she was, how enterprising and successful, and yet how sweet withal! How right his mother had been! He smiled to himself to think how nearly always right his mother was, anyhow, and wondered again, as he had done before, whether his mother had a hidden reason for sending him out with those ferns that first night.

Cornelia returned in a flutter of pleasure, and was scarcely seated when there came another summons to the door; and there stood the minister's wife. She came in and met Maxwell, and they had a pleasant little chat. Then Mrs. Kendall revealed her errand. She wanted Cornelia to give a series of talks on what she called "The House Beautiful and Convenient" to the Ladies' Aid Society in the church. She had the course all outlined suggestively, with a place for all the questions that come up in making a house comfortable and attractive; and she wanted Cornelia to keep in mind the thought that many of her auditors would be people in very limited circumstances, with very little money or time or material at hand to use in making their homes lovely. She said there were many people in their church neighborhood who would be attracted by such a course to come to the church gatherings, and she wanted Cornelia to help. The Ladies' Aid had voted to pay five dollars a lesson for such a course of talks as this, and had instructed her to secure some one for it at once, and she knew of no one so well fitted as Cornelia. Would Cornelia consider it for the trifle they could afford to pay? They were going to charge the women twenty-five cents a lesson, and hoped to make a little money on the enterprise for their Ladies' Aid. Of course the remuneration was small; but with her experience the work ought not to take much time, and she could have the added reward of knowing she was doing a lot of good and probably brightening a lot of homes. Also it would bring her opportunities for other openings of the sort.

"I just wish they could all see this lovely house from top to bottom," she said as she looked around. "It would do them a world of good."

"Why, they could," said Cornelia, smiling. "I suppose I could clear it all up and let them go over it, if you think that would help any. I'd love to do the work if you think I'm able. I never talked in public in my life. I'm not sure I can."

"Oh, this isn't talking in public," said the minister's wife eagerly. "This is just telling people that don't know how, how to do things that you have done yourself. I'm sure you have that gift. I've listened to you talking, and you're wonderfully interesting. But would you consider giving them a reception and letting them see how you have made your house lovely? That would be a wonderful addition, and I'm sure the ladies would be delighted to pay extra for that; and we'd all come over and help you clear up afterwards; and before, too, if you would let us, although I'm sure you always look in immaculate order for a reception or anything else every time I've ever been here."

When the matter was finally arranged and Mrs. Kendall had left, Carey came in, scrubbed, shaved, neatly attired, and proposed that they have a sing. Maxwell, nothing loath, joined in eagerly, and sang with all his splendid voice. Then after a time he asked Cornelia to play, and before they realized it the evening was over. Not until Carey said in his casual way, "Call me at quarter to seven, will you, Nell? — and turn on the hot water when you get down; that's a dear," did Cornelia remember her curiosity concerning the conversation between her brother and Maxwell. Carey said nothing about it, and Cornelia was enough of a wise woman not to ask.

But Carey told her the next morning. He was so excited he couldn't keep it to himself.

"Didn't know I was going to be a salesman up at Braithwaite's, did you?" he said quite casually between mouthfuls of breakfast.

Harry paused in his chewing a second, and eyed him sceptically.

"Yes, you are *not!*" he remarked scornfully, and went on chewing again.

But Cornelia, eager-eyed, leaned forward. "What do you mean, Carey? Is that a fact?"

"Well, just about," said Carey, enjoying their bewilderment. "Maxwell told me the manager wants to see me this morning. Says he's had his eye on me for three months, been looking up everything about me, and, when that picture came out in the paper, he told Maxwell he guessed I'd do. Said they wanted a man that could jump into a situation like that and handle it, a man with nerve, you know, that had his wits about him. It's up to me now to make good. If I do, I get the job all right. It isn't great pay to start, only thirty bucks a week; but it's all kinds of prospects ahead if I make good. Well, so-long; wish me luck." And Carey flung out of the house amid the delighted exclamations of his astonished family.

"O God, you have been good to us!" breathed Cornelia's happy soul as she stood by the window, watching Carey's broad shoulders and upright carriage as he hurried down the street to the car. Carey was happy. It fairly radiated even from his back, and he walked as if he trod the air. Cornelia was so glad she could have shouted, "Hallelujah!" Now, if he really got this position, — and it looked reasonably sure, — he was established in a good and promising way, and the family could stop worrying about him.

What a wonderful young man Maxwell was to take all that trouble for a comparative stranger! Her eyes grew dreamy and her lips softened into a smile as she went over every detail of the evening before, remembering the snatches of talk she had caught and piecing them out with new meaning. She leaned over, and laid her face softly among the roses he had brought, and drew in a long, sweet breath of their fragrance. And he had been doing this for them all the time, and not said a word, lest nothing would come of it. As she thought about it now, she believed he had had the thought about doing something for Carey that first night when he came so unexpectedly to dinner, that dreadful dinner party! How far away and impossible it all seemed now! That terrible girl! What a fool she had been to think it necessary to invite any one like that to the house! If she had just let things go on and take their natural course, Maxwell would have dropped in that night, and they would have had a pleasant time, and all would have been as it was at present, without the mortification of that memory. Carey with his new ambitions and hopes would surely never now disgrace himself by going again with a girl like that. It had been an unnecessary crucifixion for the whole family.

Yet they never would have known how splendid Maxwell could be in a trying time without her, perhaps. There was always something comforting somewhere. Still, she would like to be rid of the memory of that evening. It brought shame to her cheek even yet to remember the loud, nasal twang of the cheap voice, the floury face, the low-cut tight little gown, the air of abandon! Oh! It was awful!

Then her mind went back to the day she returned from college, and to the sweet-faced, low-voiced woman who was the mother of this new friend. It hardly seemed as if the two belonged to the same world. What would she think if she ever heard of Clytie? Would the young man ever quite forget her, and wipe the memory from his mind so completely that it would never return to shadow those first days of their acquaintance?

Carey returned early in the afternoon with an elastic step and a light of triumph in his face. He had been engaged as a salesman in one of the largest firms in the country, a business dealing with tools and machinery and requiring a wide grasp of various engineering branches. He was just in his element. He had been born with the instinct for machinery and mechanics. He loved everything connected with them. Also he was a leader and natural mixer among men. All these things Maxwell later told Cornelia had counted in his favor. The fact that he was not a college man had been the only drawback; but after the accident, and after the manager had had a long, searching talk with him, it had been decided that Carey had natural adaptability and hereditary culture enough to overcome that lack; and they voted to try him. The manager felt that there was good material in him. Maxwell did not tell Cornelia that what he had told the manager concerning her ability and initiative had had much to do with influencing the decision. The manager was a keen man. He knew a live family when he saw it; and, when he heard what Cornelia had accomplished in her little home, he was keen to see the brother. He felt that he also might be a genius! Now if Carey could only make good!

It was a wonderful day of June skies and roses. Maxwell had sent a note by special messenger to Cornelia to say that two world tennis champions were to play at the Cricket Grounds that afternoon and would she like to go? If so he would call for her at two o'clock.

So Cornelia had baked macaroni and cheese, roasted some apples and made a chocolate cornstarch pudding. There was cold meat in the refrigerator, and she wrote a note to Louise in case she should be late.

She looked very pretty and slim in her dark blue crêpe de chine made over with an odd little idea in pockets to cover where it had to be pieced. She resurrected an old dark blue hat with a becoming brim, redyed it and wreathed it with a row of little pale pink velvet roses. Nobody would ever have guessed that the roses were old ones that had been cleaned and retouched with the paint brush till they glowed like new ones. She added a string of queer Chinese beads that one of the girls at college had given her, and looked as chic and pretty as any girl could desire when Maxwell called for her. His eyes showed their admiration as he came up the steps and found her ready, waiting for him, her cheeks flushed a pretty pink, her eyes starry, little rings of brown hair blowing out here and there about her face.

"That's a nice hat," he said contentedly, his eyes taking in her whole harmonious costume, "New one isn't it? At least I never saw it before." He noted with pleasure that her complexion was not applied.

"A real girl!" he was saying to himself in a kind of inner triumph! "A *real* girl! What a fool I used to be!"

The day was wonderful, and there was a big box of chocolates in the car. Cornelia listening to her happy heart found it singing.

They made long strides in friendship as they drove through the city and out to the Cricket Club grounds, and Cornelia's cheeks grew pinker with joy. It seemed as though life were very good indeed to her today.

They drove the car into the grounds, found a good place to park it and were just about to go to their seats on the grand stand when a young, gimlet-eyed flapper with bobbed hair rushed up crying:

"Oh, Arthur Maxwell, won't you please go over to the gym dressing rooms and find Tommy Fergus for me. He promised to meet me here half an hour ago, and I'm nearly dead standing in this sun. I'd go in and sit down but he has the tickets and he promised on his honor not to be late. I knew it would be just like this if he tried to play a set before the tournament."

There was nothing for Maxwell to do but introduce the curious-eyed maiden to Cornelia and go on the mission, and the young woman climbed up beside Cornelia and began to chatter.

It appeared that her name was Dotty Chapman, that she was a sort of cousin of Maxwell's, and that she knew everybody and everything that had to do with the Cricket Club. She chattered on like a magpie, telling Cornelia who all the people were that by this time were coming in a stream through the arched gateway. Cornelia found it rather interesting.

"That's Senator Brown's daughter. She won the blue ribbon at the Horse Show last winter. That's her brother — no, not the fat one, the man on the right. He's the famous polo player. And that's Harry Harlow, yes, the tall one. He's a *nut!* You'd die laughing to hear him. There, that girl's the woman champion in tennis this year, and the man with her is Mrs. Carter Rounds' first husband, you remember. They say he's

gone on another woman now. There goes
Jason Casper's fiancée. Isn't she ugly? I
don't see what he sees in her, but she's got
stacks of money, so I suppose he doesn't
care. Say, do you know Arthur Maxwell's
fiancée? I'm dying to meet her. They say
she is *simply stunning*. I saw her in the distance dancing at the Roof Garden the other
night, but it was only for a second. Somebody pointed her out, I'm not sure I'd know
her. They say she is very foreign in her appearance. Have you met her yet? Isn't that
she now, just getting out of that big blue
car with Bob Channing? I believe it is.
Look! Did you ever see such a slim figure?
And that frock is the darlingest. They say
all her clothes come from abroad and are
designed especially for her. The engagement
isn't announced yet you know, but it will
be I suppose as soon as Mrs. Maxwell gets
home again. Miss Chantry doesn't wish it
spoken of even among her most intimate
friends until then, she doesn't think it is
courteous to her future mother-in-law,
that's why she goes around with other men
so much. She told my cousin Lucia so. But
everybody knows it of course. You, I suppose you know all about it too? There he
comes! They're going to meet! I wonder
how they'll act. Isn't it thrilling. My good-

373

ness! Don't they carry it off well, he's hardly stopping to speak. I don't believe she likes it, I wouldn't, would you? Isn't that white crêpe with the scarlet trimmings just entrancing? But where on earth is Tommy! He didn't bring him. Oh — why *Tommy!* Is that you? Where on earth have you been? Didn't Mr. Maxwell find you? He's been after you, there he is coming now! What made you keep me waiting so long? I've stood here an hour and simply cooked! What? You meant the *other* gate? Well, what's the difference? Why didn't you say so? Oh, well, don't fuss so, let's go find our seats. What? Oh, yes, this is Miss — *Cope* did you say? Copley? Oh yes! Miss Copley, Mr. Fergus. Thank you so much, Cousin Arthur. Good-bye."

She was gone, vanishing behind the neighboring grand stand, but so was the glory of the day.

Cornelia's face looked strangely white and tired as Maxwell helped her down, and she found her feet unsteady as she walked beside him silently to their seats. There was something queer the matter with her heart. It kept stopping suddenly and then turning over with a jerk. The sun seemed to have darkened about her and her feet seemed weighted.

"That girl is a perfect pest," he said

frowning as he helped Cornelia to her seat. "I was just afraid she was going to wish herself on us for the afternoon. She has a habit of doing that and I didn't mean to have it this time. I was prepared to hire a substitute for the lost Tommy if he didn't materialize. Her mother is a second or third cousin of my grandmother's aunt or something like that and she is always asking favors."

Cornelia tried to smile and murmur something pleasant, but her lips seemed stiff, and when she looked up she noticed that he was hurriedly scanning the benches on the other side of the rectangle. Following his glance her eyes caught a glimpse of white set off by vivid scarlet. Ah! Then it was true! Her sinking heart put her to sudden shame and revealed herself to herself.

This then had been the secret of her great happiness and of the brightness of the day. She had been presuming on the kindness of this stranger and actually jumping to the conclusion that he was paying her special attention. What folly had been hers! How she had always despised girls who gave their hearts before they were asked, who took too much for granted from a few pleasant little attentions.

Mr. Maxwell had done nothing that any gentleman might not have done for a casual friend of his mother's. When she began to sift the past few weeks in her thoughts, his attentions had mainly been spent on her brothers. A few roses and this invitation this afternoon. Nothing that any sensible girl would think a thing of. She was a fool, that was all there was of it, an everlasting fool, and now she must rouse herself somehow from this ghastly sinking feeling that had come over her and keep him from reading her very thoughts. He must never suspect her unwomanliness. He must never know how she had misconstrued his kindness. Oh, if she could only get away into the cool and dark for a minute and lie down and close her eyes, she could get hold of herself. But that was out of the question. She must sit here and smile in the sun with the gleam of scarlet across the courts and never, never let him suspect. He was all right, of course he was, all right and fine, and he doubtless thought that she too knew all about his fiancée, only he could not speak about it now because the lady had placed her commands upon him for his mother's sake. How nice to honor his mother!

A breath of a sigh escaped her and she straightened up and tried to look bright and interesting.

"You *are* tired!" he said turning to look

into her eyes. "I don't believe this is going to be a restful thing for you at all. Wouldn't you rather get out of here and just take a ride or something — in the Park perhaps?"

"Oh, no *indeed!*" said Cornelia quickly sitting up very straight and trying to shake off the effects of the shock she had suffered, "I've always wanted to see a great tournament, and I've never had the opportunity. Now tell me all the things I need to know please to be an intelligent witness."

He began telling her about the two world famous men who were to play, about their good points and their weak ones, and to give a scientific treatise on certain kinds of services and returns, and she gave strict attention and asked intelligent questions, and was getting on very well, keeping her own private thoughts utterly in the background, when suddenly he said:

"Do you see that lady in white just directly opposite us? White with scarlet trimmings. I wish you would look at her a moment. Here, take the field glasses. Sometime I am going to tell you about her."

Cornelia tried to steady her hand as she adjusted the glasses to her eyes, and to steady her lips for a question:

"Is she — a — *friend?*"

"I hardly think you'd call it that — *any*

more!" he answered in a curiously hard tone. But Cornelia was too preoccupied to notice.

"Shall we — meet her?" she asked after studying the exquisite doll face across the distance, and wondering if it really were as wonderfully perfect close at hand. Wondering too why she seemed to suddenly feel disappointed in the man beside her if this was his choice of a wife.

"I think *not,*" he said decidedly, and then as a sudden clapping arose, growing, like a swift moving shower, "There, there they are! The players. That's the Englishman, that big chap, and this man, this is our man. See how supple he is. He has a great reach. Watch him now."

After that there was no more opportunity to talk personalities and Cornelia was glad that she could just sit still and watch, although with her preoccupied mind she might as well have been at home cooking dinner for all she knew about that tournament. The players came and went like little puppets in a show, the ball flew back and forth, and games and sets were played, but she knew no more about it than if she had not been there. Now and then her eyes furtively stole a glance across the way at the scarlet line on the white.

Maxwell had glanced at her curiously several times. Her attitude was one of deep attention. She smiled just as pleasantly when he spoke, but somehow her voice had lost the spring out of it and he could not help thinking she was weary.

"Let's get out of here before the crowd begins to push," he whispered, as the last set was finished and the antagonists shook hands under fire of the heavy rounds of applause.

He guided her out to the car so quickly that they almost escaped the rush, but just within a few paces of the car they came suddenly upon the voluble Dotty and her escort.

"Oh, Cousin Artie!" cried Dotty eagerly, "I've just been telling Tommy that I knew you would take us over to Overbrook if we could catch you in time. You see we both have a dinner engagement out to Aunt Myra's and we've missed the only train that would get us there in time. You won't mind will you, Miss Cope, Copley, I mean. It isn't far and you know how cross Aunt Myra gets when any of us are late to an engagement with her, don't you, Artie?"

"Not at all!" answered Cornelia coolly as soon as there was opportunity to speak, "my home is right on the way."

Maxwell accepted the situation with what

grace he could. Dotty climbed into the front seat when he opened the door for Cornelia.

"You can sit back there with Miss Copley, Tommy," she laughed back at the other two. "I choose front seat. I just *love* to watch Cousin Arthur drive."

Arthur Maxwell scarcely spoke a word during the whole drive and Cousin Dotty chattered on in an uninterrupted flow of nothings. Cornelia found herself discussing the game and various plays with a technique newly acquired, and being thankful that she did not have to ride alone with Maxwell — not now — not until she had got herself in hand. It was all right of course, and he was perfectly splendid but she had been a silly little fool and she had to get things set straight again before she cared to meet him as a friend. Oh, it would be all right, she assured herself minute by minute, only she must just get used to it. She hadn't at all realized how she had been thinking of him and she was glad that the romance of this afternoon had been destroyed, so that she would not find herself in future weakness lingering over any pleasant phrases or little nothings that would link her soul to disappointment. She wanted to be just plain, matter of fact. A respectable girl going out for an afternoon with a respectable man

380

who was soon to be married to another woman who understood all about it. There was nothing whatever the matter with that situation and that was the way she must look at it of course. She must get used to it and gradually make her family understand too. Not that they had thought anything else yet — of course, but it would be well for them to understand from the start that there was no nonsense about her friendship with Maxwell, and that they need not appropriate him in such wholesome manner as they had begun to do. She was a business woman, meant to be a business woman all her life, and she would probably have lots of nice friendships like this one.

Thus she reasoned in undertone with herself, the while she discussed tennis with the bored Tommy, and came finally to her own door realizing suddenly that Arthur Maxwell would perhaps not care to have his elegant cousin know from what lowly neighborhoods he selected his friends. But she held her head high as she stood on the pavement to bid them good-bye, and not by the quiver of an eyelash on her flushed cheek did she let them see that she did not like her surroundings.

Arthur Maxwell stepped up to the door with her in spite of his cousin's petulant protest, "Artie, we'll be *late* to Aunt Myra's" and said in a low tone:

"This whole afternoon has been spoiled by that poor little idiot, but I'm going to make up for it soon, see if I don't. I'm sorry I have a director's meeting this evening or I'd ask if I might return to dinner, but I'm going to be late as it is when I get those two poor fools to their destination, so I'll have to forego, but suppose I come over Sunday evening and go to church with you? May I? Then afterwards perhaps we'll have a little chance to talk."

Cornelia smiled and assented, and hurried up to dash cold water over her hot cheeks and burning eyes, and then down to the kitchen where Louise was bustling happily about putting the final touches to the evening meal.

"Oh, Nellie!" she greeted her sister, "Have you got back already? I thought perhaps he'd take you somewhere to dinner. They do, you know. I've read about it. But wasn't he *lovely* to take you to that game. All the boys at school were talking about it and one of the girls had a ticket to go with her brother. I think it was just *wonderful*. I'm so *glad* you had that nice time! You are so *dear!* Now tell me about it."

And Cornelia told, all she could remember about the day and the ride and the wonderful game, told things she had not known she noticed by the wayside, told about Dotty and Tommy, and even gave a hint of a wonderful friend of Mr. Maxwell's who wore a white, soft, silk dress lined with scarlet and carried a gold mesh bag, till Louise's eyes grew large with wonder, though she looked a little grave when she heard about the lady. Cornelia hid her heavy heart under smiles and words and was gayer than usual, and very very tired when she crept at last to bed, where she might not even weep lest the little sister should know the secret of her foolish heart.

Saturday morning dawned with all its burden and responsibility, a new day full of new cares, and the gladness of yesterday gone into graver tints. But Cornelia would not own to herself that she was unhappy. There was work to do and she would immerse herself in it and forget. There was no need being a fool always when once one had found out one was. And anyway she meant to live for her family — Her dear family!

26

Cornelia had had a brief space of anxiety lest her brother should begin to feel his own importance and perhaps offend his chief in being entirely too smart in his own conceit. But it soon became apparent that the chief was a big enough man to have impressed Carey and made him a devoted servant. He kept quoting what he said with awe and reverence and showing great delight at being admitted to the inner sanctum and intrusted with important affairs.

Carey was to begin his new work on Monday morning, and all Saturday as he went about doing various little things, pressing his trousers, picking up his laundry, getting his affairs in order to leave all day as other business men had to do every day, he kept dropping into the room where his sister was at work on some pretty dresses for Louise, and telling with a light in his eyes and a ring of pleasure in his voice what "the boss" had said or done, or how the office was furnished and how many salesmen and stenographers there were. And he could not say enough about Maxwell.

"That fellow's a prince!" he exclaimed. "D'ye know it? A perfect prince of a man.

He might have run in any number of friends, old friends, you know, instead of mentioning me. I can't make out what made him. The boss took me out to lunch with him today at a swell restaurant. Gee! It was great! Lobster salad, café parfait, and all that! Some lunch! Took the best part of a ten-dollar bill to pay for it, too. Oh, boy! It was great! Think of *me!* And he told me how much Maxwell thought of me, and how he believed I'd bear it out, and all that dope. He talked a lot about personal appearance, and a pleasant manner, and keeping my temper, and that line, you know. Gee! It's going to be hard, but it's going to be great. He told me that it was up to me how high I climbed. There wasn't any limit practically if I stuck it out and made good. And believe me, I'm going to stick. I like that guy, and I like the business. Say, Nell, do you think this necktie would clean? I always liked this necktie. And whaddaya think? I've got to wear hard collars. Fierce, isn't it? but I guess I can get used to 'em. Say where's that old silk shirt of mine? I wonder if you could mend a tear in the sleeve. I'll have to keep dolled up in glad rags a lot now, and I have to get everything in shape. Imagine it. I've got to take big guys out to lunch myself sometimes, and show them the ropes, and all that. Gee! Isn't it wonderful?"

So Cornelia laid aside the rose-colored gingham and the blue-flowered muslin she was making for Louise, and mended shirts, ironed neckties, and helped press coats, until Carey expressed himself as altogether pleased with his outfit, and joy bubbled over in the house. That night and all the next day their hearts seemed so light that they were in danger of having their feet lifted off the ground with the joy of it.

Brand came over after lunch as usual, and heard the news. He looked a bit sober over it, although he congratulated his friend warmly; but once or twice Cornelia caught him looking wistfully at Carey, as if somehow he had suddenly grown away from him; and she realized that it was the first break in their boyhood life. For Carey was a new Carey since the morning, walking with a spring in his step, giving a command in the tone of one who had authority, making a decision as one who had long been accustomed to being recognized as having a right. He had in a single morning become a man, and seemed for the time to have put away childish things. He even declined to take a ride with Brand after dinner, to which Brand had stayed, saying that he had promised to run over to the Kendalls after dinner and try over the music for tomorrow. Ordinarily Brand would have gone along without even being asked, but there was about Carey such a manner of masterfulness, and of being aloof and having grave matters to attend to, that the boy hesitated with a wistful, puzzled look; and, when Cornelia, half sensing his feeling, said, "Well, Brand, you stay here with me, and we'll go over that music too," he laughed happily, and sat down again, letting Carey go out by himself.

It was altogether plain that Carey didn't even see it. Carey was exalted. His head was in the clouds, and a happy smile played over his face continually.

Brand stayed all the evening till Carey came back at half past ten, still with that happy, exalted smile on his face; and then Brand, with an amused, almost hopeless expression, laughingly bade good night to Cornelia, telling her he'd had "a peach of a time." Just as he was going out the door he looked back, and said soberly: "I might have a job myself next week. Dad wants me to come in the office with him this summer, and I believe I will." Then he went away without any of the usual racket and showing off of his noisy car.

Carey's new dignity carried him to

church the next morning, and to a special Children's Day service in the afternoon, where he had been asked to usher; and joy still sat on his face when he returned at four o'clock and lolled around the living room, restless and talking of the morrow, now and then telling some trifling incident of the afternoon, humming over a tune that had been sung, and finally asking Cornelia to play and sing with him the music for the evening. It was altogether so unusual to have Carey at home like this all day Sunday, and seeming to be happy in it, that Cornelia was excitedly happy herself, and every little while Louise would look at him joyously and say, "O Carey, you look so nice in that new suit!"

It was like a regular love-feast, and Cornelia began to tell her anxious heart that Carey really was started on the right way. There was no further need to worry about him at all. Perhaps there hadn't ever been. Perhaps it was all only because he hadn't had the right kind of job.

It was just six o'clock. The Copleys had elected to have their Sunday-night supper after the evening service, and to that end Cornelia had prepared delectable lettuce, cheese, and date sandwiches, and had wrapped them in a damp cloth in the icebox to be ready. There was a fruit salad all ready also, and a maple cake. It would take but a few minutes to make a pot of chocolate, and they would eat around the fire in the living room. Maxwell had promised to come early and go to church with them. Cornelia rather dreaded the ordeal for she felt sure that Maxwell meant to tell her about the crimson lady. Well, she might as well get it over at once and have him understand that she knew exactly where she stood.

She had gone upstairs to dress and left Carey lying on the couch, looking into the fire, dreamily listening to Louise and Harry playing hymn tunes as duets. She planned to write a letter to her mother early the next morning giving her a picture of their beautiful Sunday and telling the news about Carey. She was flying around getting dressed for the evening when she heard a car come up to the front and stop. It came quietly, almost stealthily; so it could not be Brand. Could it be that Arthur Maxwell had arrived so soon? She tiptoed into her father's room to look out of the window. If it was Maxwell, she must hurry and go downstairs.

The car was a shabby old affair with a rakish air, and she could not see the face of the man who sat in the driver's seat. A small boy was coming in the gate with a letter in his hand, which he pulled from his pocket, looking up at the house apprehensively. There was something familiar about the slouch of the boy, and about the limpness of his unkempt hair as he dragged his cap off and knocked at the door, but she could not place it.

A vague unnamed apprehension seized her, and her fingers flew fast among the long strands of soft hair, putting them quickly into shape so that she might go down and see what was the matter. Two or three hairpins which had been in her hand as she hurried to the window she stuck in anywhere to hold the coils. She hurried to her room, seized her dress, began to slip it on, and flew back to the post of observation at the window. She heard Carey get up and open the door, and she strained to hear what the boy said, but could not make out anything but a low mutter. Carey was reading the note. What could it be? Clytie? Oh!

Her heart gave a great leap of terror. It was almost time for Christian Endeavor! But surely, *surely* Carey would not pay any heed to that girl now. With all the new ambitions and opportunities opening before him!

Carey had made an exclamation, and was following the boy rapidly out to the car. Oh! What could he be going to do?

Cornelia fastened the last snap of her dress, and fairly flew downstairs; but, when she reached the door the car was driving madly off up the hill, and Carey was nowhere in sight. The children were still playing duets, and had not noticed.

Cornelia turned back to look into the room again and make sure he was not there, and she saw Carey's new Panama hat hanging on the hook back by the staircase where he had put it when he came in from afternoon service. She drew a breath of relief, and called, in a lull of the music, "Louie, where is Carey?"

The little girl turned and looked wonderingly at her sister's anxious face.

"Why, he was here just a minute ago, Nellie; what's the matter? I think he went out the front door."

He was gone! Cornelia knew it, and her heart sank with a horrible sickening thud. She went back to the door, and looked down the street and then up the hill, where the car was a mere black speck in the distance. Her heart was beating so that it seemed the children must hear it. She tried to think, but all that came was a wild jumble of ideas. The meeting that night! Carey had a short solo in the anthem! Suppose he shouldn't get back! What should she say to Grace? How could his absence possibly be explained? He couldn't — he *wouldn't* do a thing like that, would he? He had gone without his hat; perhaps he expected to return immediately. She was foolish to get so frightened. Carey had been doing so wonderfully all day. He certainly had sense enough not to make a fool of himself now.

But her heart would not be quieted, and she trembled in every fibre. She hurried down the steps and to the sidewalk looking up the hill where the car had just disappeared, and her hand pressed against her heart to steady its fluttering. She did not see Maxwell's car drive up until it stopped; and, when she looked at him, a new fear seized her. Maxwell must not know that she was afraid about that girl. He had gone to a lot of trouble for Carey, and he would not like it. It might lose Carey the position. She tried to command a smile, but the white face she turned toward him belied it.

"Is anything the matter?" he asked, stopping his car and jumping out beside her. Then he stooped, and picked up something from the pavement at her feet.

"Is this yours? Did you drop it?"

She looked down, took the bit of paper, and her face grew whiter still as she caught the words, "Dear Carey." It must be the note the boy had brought, and suddenly she knew who that boy had been. It was Clytie Dodd's brother!

27

For a second everything swam before her eyes, and it seemed as though she could not stand up. Maxwell put out his hand in alarm to steady her.

"Hadn't you better go into the house?" he asked anxiously. "You look ill. Do you feel faint?"

"Oh, I'm all right," she said almost impatiently. "I'm just worried. Maybe there isn't anything the matter, but — it looks very — queer. This must be the note the boy brought."

She began to read the note, which was written in a clear feminine hand on fine note paper:

Dear Carey, I came out here to see a Sunday-school scholar who is sick, and I am in great trouble. Come to me quick! I'm out at Lamb's Tavern.
Grace

"I don't understand it," faltered Cornelia, looking up at Maxwell helplessly. "She — this! It is signed 'Grace,' and looks as if Grace Kendall wrote it. I am sure Carey thought so when he went. But — Grace

394

Kendall was at home only a few minutes ago. She called me up to ask me to bring some music she had left here when I come to church. How could she have got out there so soon?"

Maxwell took the note, and read it with a glance, then turned the paper over, and felt its thickness.

"Curious they should have such stationery at Lamb's Tavern. Who brought it?"

"A boy. I'm not sure. He looked as if I had seen him before. He might have been —" she hesitated, and the color stole into her cheeks. The trouble was deep in her eyes. "He might have been a boy who came here on an errand once; I wasn't certain. I only saw him from the window."

"You knew him?"

"Why — I had just a suspicion that he might have been that Dodd girl's brother." She lifted pained eyes to meet his.

"I see," he said, his tone kindling with sympathy. "Has she any — ah — *further* reason for revenge than what I know?"

"Yes," owned Cornelia. "She sent word to Carcy to call her up, and he didn't do it. She had invited him to go on an automobile ride. He didn't go, and we were all away when they must have stopped for him."

"I see. Will you call up Miss Kendall on some pretext or other, and find out if she is at her home? Quickly, please." His tone was grave and kindly, but wholly business-like and Cornelia, feeling that she had found a strong helper, sped into the house on her trembling feet, giving thanks that the telephone had just been put in last week.

Maxwell stood beside her as she called the number, silently waiting.

"Hello. Is that you, Grace? Was it 'Oh, eyes that are weary' that you wanted me to bring? Thank you, yes; I thought so, but I wanted to make sure; good-bye."

Maxwell had not waited to hear more than that Miss Kendall was at home. He strode out to his car; and, when Cornelia reached the door, he had his hand on the starter.

"Oh, you mustn't go alone!" she called. "Let me go with you."

"Not this time," he answered grimly. "You go on to church if I'm not back." He had not waited to finish; the car was moving; but a sturdy flying figure shot out of the door behind Cornelia, over the hedge, and caught on behind. Harry, with little to go by, had sensed what was in the air, and meant to be in at the finish. No, of course not; his adored Maxwell should not go alone to any place where Cornelia said "No" in that tone. He would go along.

Louise, white-faced and quiet, with little hands clasped at her throat, stood just behind her sister, watching the car shoot up the hill and out of sight.

"Sister, you think — it's *that girl* again — don't you?" she asked softly, looking with awe at the white-faced girl.

"I'm afraid, Louie; I don't know!" said Cornelia, turning with a deep, anxious sigh and dropping into a chair.

"Yes, it must be," said Louise. "And — that was that boy, wasn't it? — the same one she sent to say she was coming to the party. My! That was poor! She wasn't very bright to do that, Nellie."

Cornelia did not answer. She had dropped her lace into her hands, and was trembling.

"Nellie, dear!" cried the little sister, kneeling before her and gathering her sister's head into her young arms. "You mustn't feel that way. God is taking care of us. He helped us before, you know. And He's sent Mr. Maxwell. He's just like an angel, isn't he? Don't you know that verse, 'My God hath sent his angel, and hath shut the lions' mouths'? Mother used to read us that story so often when Harry and

I were going to sleep. Let's just kneel down and pray; and pretty soon Carey'll come back all right, I shouldn't wonder. I know he didn't mean to be away. He promised Grace; and I kind of don't think he likes that other girl so awfully any more now, do you?"

"No, I think not; but, dear, I'm afraid this is a trick. I'm afraid they mean to keep him away to pay him back."

"Yes, I know," said the wise little sister. "I read that note. You dropped it out of your pocket. Grace Kendall never wrote that. It isn't her writing. She put her name in my birthday book, and she doesn't make her Gs like that. She makes 'em with a long curl to the handle. They thought they were pretty smart; but Carey and Mr. Maxwell'll beat them to it, I'm sure, for they've got our God on their side. I'm glad Harry went too. Harry's got a lot of sense; and, if anything happens, Harry can run back and tell."

"O darling!" Cornelia clung to the little girl.

"Well, it might —" said the child. "I'm glad father isn't here. I hope it's all over before he gets back. Was he coming back before church?" Cornelia shook her head.

"He's going to stay with Mr. Baker while

his wife goes to church."

"Then let's pray now, Nellie."

They knelt together beside the big gray chair in the silence of the twilight, hand in hand, and put up silent petitions; and then they got up and went to the window.

The city had that gentle, haloed look of a chastened child in the afterglow of the sunset; and soft violets and purples were twisting in misty wreaths about the edges of the night. Bells were calling in the distance. A far-away chime could just be heard in tender waves that almost obliterated the melody. The Sabbath hush was in the sky, broken now and again by harsh, rasping voices and laughter as a car sped by on the way home from some pleasure trip. Something hallowed seemed to linger above the little house, and all about was a sweet quiet. The neighbors had for the moment hushed their chatter. Now and again a far-distant twang of a cheap victrola broke out and died away, and then the silence would close around them again. The two sat waiting breathlessly on the pretty front porch that Carey had made, for Carey to come home. But Carey did not come.

By and by the sound of singing young voices came distinctly to their ears. It seemed to beat against their hearts and hurt them.

"Nellie, you'll have to go pretty soon. It'll be so hard to explain, you know. And, besides, he might somehow be there. Carey wouldn't stop for a hat. I almost think he's there myself." Louise sounded quite grown up.

"Of course, he might," said Cornelia thoughtfully. "There's always a possibility that we have made a great deal more out of this than the facts merited." She shuddered. She had just drawn her mind back from a fearful abyss of possibilities, and it was hard to get into everyday untragic thought.

"I think we better go, Nellie," said the little girl rising. "Christian 'deavor'll be most out before we can get there now, and she'll think it queer if we don't come, after she gave us both those verses to read. You won't like to tell her you were just sitting here on the front porch, doing nothing, because you thought Carey had gone to Lamb's Tavern after her! I think we'd better go. We prayed, and we better trust God and go."

"Perhaps you're right, dearie," said Cornelia, rising reluctantly and giving a wistful glance up the hill into the darkness.

They got ready hurriedly, put the key into its hiding-place, and went. Cornelia wrote a little note, and as soon as they got there sent it up with the music to Grace, who was at the piano. It said:

"Dear Grace, Carey was called away for a few minutes, and he must have been detained longer than he expected. Don't worry; I'm sure he will do everything in his power to get back in time."

Grace read the note, nodded brightly to the Copleys at the back of the room, and seemed not at all concerned. Cornelia, glad of the shelter of a secluded seat under the gallery, bent her head, and prayed continually. Little Louise, bright-eyed, with glowing cheeks, sat alertly up, and watched the door; but no Carey came.

They slipped out into the darkness after the meeting was out, and walked around the corner where they could see their own house; but it seemed silent and dark as they had left it, and they turned sadly back and went into the church.

The choir had gathered when Cornelia got back, and she slipped into the last vacant seat by the stairs, and was glad that it was almost hidden from the view of the congregation. It seemed to her that the anxiety of her heart must be written large across her face.

Louise, still as a mouse all by herself down in a back seat by the door, watched — and prayed. No one came in at the two big doors that she did not see. Maxwell and Harry had not come back yet. The cool evening air came in at the open window, and blew the little feather in the pretty hat Cornelia had made for her. She felt a strand of her own hair moving against her cheek. There was honeysuckle outside somewhere on somebody's front porch across the street or in the little park near by. The breath of it was very sweet, but Louise thought she never as long as she lived, even if that were a great many years, would smell the breath of honeysuckle without thinking of this night. And yet the sounds outside were just like the sounds on any other Sunday night; the music and the lights in the church were the same; the people looked just as if nothing were the matter, and Carey had not come! What a queer world it was, everything going on just the same, even when one family was crushed to earth with fear!

Automobiles flew by the church; now and then one stopped. Louise wished she were tall so she could look out and see whether they had come. Her little heart was beating wildly; but there was a serene, peaceful expression on her face. She had resolved to trust God, and she knew He was going to do something about it somehow. But people kept coming in at the door, and hope would dim again.

The service had begun, and in the silence of the opening prayer the two sisters lifted their hearts in tragic petition. Their spirits seemed to cling to each word and make it linger; their souls entered into the song that followed, and sang as if their earnest singing would hold off the moment for a little longer.

Cornelia was glad that her seat was so placed that she could not see all the choir. She had given a swift survey as she sat down; and she knew her brother was not there. Now she sat in heaviness of heart, and tried to fathom it all! — tried to think what to do next, what to tell her father, whether to tell her father at all, tried not to think of the letter she would not write the next day to her mother; tried just to hold her spirit steady, steady, trusting, not hoping, but trusting, right through the prayer, the song, the Bible reading. Now and again a frightful thought of danger shot through her heart, and a wonder about Maxwell. Lamb's Tavern — what kind of a place was it? The very name "Tavern" sounded questionable. And Harry! He ought not to have gone, of course, but she had not seen him in time to stop him. Brave, dear Harry! A man already. And yet he knew he ought not to go! But the man in him had to. She understood.

Suddenly she found a tear stealing slowly down her cheek, and she sat up very straight, and casually slid a finger up to its source, and stopped it. This must not happen again. No one must know her trouble. How wonderful it was that she should have been able to get this little sheltered spot, the only spot in the whole choir loft that was absolutely out of sight, by the winding stairs down into the choir room behind! She would not be seen until she had to stand up with the rest of the choir to sing; and then she would step in behind the rest, and be out of sight again. She wondered what Grace would do about Carey's solo, and decided that she had probably asked some one else to take it. She cast a quick glance over the group of tenors, but she did not know any of them well enough to be sure whether there was a soloist present. She had been at only two rehearsals so far, and was not acquainted with them all yet. She was not afraid that the music would go wrong, for she had great faith that Grace at the organ would easily be able to fill the vacancy in some way; she only felt the deep mortification that Carey the first time he had been asked to sing in this notably conspicuous way had failed her, and for such a reason! It was terrible, and it was perplexing. It was not like Carey to be fooled by a note. And didn't Carey know that little Dodd boy? If he had been going to the Dodd house at all, wouldn't he know the brother? Why didn't he see through the trick? He was quick as a flash. He was not dumb and slow like some people.

The contralto solo had begun. It was a sweet and tender thing, with low, deep tones like a 'cello; but they beat upon the tired girl's heart, and threatened to break down her studied composure. A hymn followed, and the reading of another Bible selection. "All we like sheep have gone astray; we have turned every one to his way; and the Lord hath laid on him the iniquity of us all." She felt as if all the iniquity of her brother Carey were laid upon her heart, and a dim wonder came to her whether the Lord was bearing a like burden for her. She had never felt much sense of personal sin herself before. The thought lingered through the pain, and wound in and out through her tired brain during the offertory and prayer that followed; and at last came the anthem.

The opening chords were sounding. The choir was rising. She stumbled to her feet, and for the first time saw the audience before her, this congregation that was to have heard Carey sing his tenor solo. It was a goodly audience, for Mr. Kendall touched the popular heart, and drew people out at night as well as in the morning; and she felt anew the pang of disappointment. She glanced swiftly over the lifted faces and saw little Louise, white and shrinking, sitting by herself, and saw beyond her, at the open door, two figures just entering, Maxwell and Harry, looking a trifle white and hurried, and glancing anxiously around the audience. Then she opened her mouth and tried to sing, to do her little part among the sopranos in the chorus; but no sound seemed to come. All she could think of now was, "Carey is not here!" beating over and over like a refrain in her brain: "Carey has not come! Carey has not come!"

28

Carey had lost no time when he read that note of appeal signed "Grace." It was not his way to wait for a hat in any emergency, but he did not leave sagacity behind him when he swung himself into the already moving car that had come for him. He could think on the way, and he was taking no chances.

It was quite natural that Grace Kendall should have gone to see a sick pupil after Sunday school. It was not natural that any pupil would have lived out as far as Lamb's Tavern; yet there were a hundred and one ways she might have gone there against her plans. He could question the messenger on the way and lose no time about it, nor excite the curiosity of his family. That had perhaps been one of Carey's greatest cares all his life, amounting sometimes almost to a vice, to keep his family from finding out anything little or great connected with himself or anybody else. He had a code, and by that code all things not immediately concerning people were "none of their business." His natural caution now caused him to get away from his house at once and excite no suspicion of danger. Grace had written to him

407

rather than to her father with evident intention, — if she had written at all, a question he had at once recognized, but not as yet settled, — and it was easy to guess that she did not wish to worry her parents unnecessarily. He was inclined to be greatly elated that she had chosen him for her helper rather than some older acquaintance, and this was probably the moving factor in prompting him to act at once.

He would not have been the boy he was if he had not seen all these points at the first flash. The only thing he did not see and would not recognize was any danger to himself. He had always felt he could ably take care of himself, and he intended to do so now. Moreover, he expected and intended to return in time to go to that Christian Endeavor meeting.

He glanced at his watch as he dropped into the seat, and immediately sat forward, and prepared to investigate the situation. But the boy who had brought the note, and who had seemingly scuttled around to get into the front seat from the other side of the car, had disappeared, and a glance backward at the rapidly disappearing landscape gave no hint of his whereabouts. That was strange. He had evidently intended to go along. He had said, "Come on!" and hurried toward the car. Who *was* that kid, anyway? Where had he seen him?

For what had been a revealing fact to Cornelia, and would have greatly changed the view of things, was entirely unknown to Carey. Clytie Dodd kept her family in the background as much as possible, and to that end met her "gentlemen friends" in parks, or at soda-fountains, or by the wayside casually. She had a regular arrangement with a certain corner drug-store whereby telephone messages would reach her and bring her to the 'phone whenever she was at home; but her friends seldom came to her house, and never met her family. She had a hard-working, sensible father, an over-worked, fretful, tempestuous mother, and a swarm of little wild, outrageous brothers and sisters, none of whom approved of her high social aspirations. She found it healthier in every way to keep her domestic and social lives utterly apart; consequently Carey had never seen Sam Dodd, or his eyes might have instantly been opened. Sam was very useful to his sister on occasion when well primed with one of her hard-earned quarters, and could, if there were special inducement, even exercise a bit of detective ability. Sam knew how to disappear off the face of the earth, and he had done it thoroughly this time.

Carey leaned forward, and questioned the driver.

"What's the matter? Anything serious?"

But the driver sat unmoved, staring ahead and making his car go slamming along, regardless of ruts or bumps, at a tremendous rate of speed. Carey did not object to the speed. He wanted to get back. He tried again, touching the man on the shoulder and shouting his question. The man turned after a second nudge, and stared resentfully, but appeared to be deaf.

Carey shouted a third time, and then the man gave evidence of being also dumb; but after a fourth attempt he gave forth the brief word: "I dunno. Lady jes' hired me."

The man did not look so stupid as he sounded, and Carey made several attempts to get further information, even to ask for a description of the lady who had sent him; but he answered either, "I dunno," or, "Yep, I gezzo"; and Carey finally gave up. He dived into his pocket for the note once more, having a desire to study the handwriting of the young woman for whom he had newly acquired an admiration. It didn't seem real that expedition. As he thought of it, it didn't seem like that quiet, modest girl to send for a comparative stranger to help her in distress. It seemed more like Clytie. But that note had not been Clytie's writing. Clytie affected a large, round, vertical hand like a young school-child, crude and unfinished. This letter had been delicately written by a finished hand on thick cream stationery. Where was that note? He was sure he had put it in his pocket.

But a search of every pocket revealed nothing, and he sat back and tried to think the thing out, tried to imagine what possible situation had brought Grace Kendall where she would send for him to help her. Stay! Was it Grace Kendall? Grace, Grace, was there any other Grace among his circle of friends? No, no one that claimed sufficient acquaintance to write a note like that. It certainly was queer. But they were out in the open country now, and speeding. The farmhouses were few and far apart. It was growing dusky; Carey could just see the hands of his watch, and he was getting nervous. Once he almost thought of shaking the driver and insisting on his turning around, for it had come over him that he should have left word with Miss Kendall's people or called up before he left home. It wasn't his way at all to do such a thing; but, still, with a girl like that — and, if anything serious was the matter, her father might not

411

like it that he had taken it upon himself. As the car sped on through the radiant dusk, it seemed more and more strange that Grace Kendall after the afternoon service should have come away out here to visit a sick Sunday-school scholar, and his misgivings grew. Then suddenly at a cross-road just ahead an automobile appeared, standing by the roadside just at the crossings with no lights on. It seemed strange, no lights at that time of night. If it was an accident, they would have the lights on. It was still three-quarters of a mile to the Tavern. Perhaps some one had broken down and gone on for help. No, there was a man standing in the road, looking toward them. He was holding up his hand, and the driver was slowing down. Carey frowned. He had no time to waste. "We can't stop to help them now," he shouted. "Tell them we'll come back in a few minutes, and bring some one to fix them up. I've got to get back right away. I've gotta date."

But the man paid no more heed to him than if he had been a June bug, and the car stopped at the cross-roads.

Carey leaned out, and shouted: "What's the matter? I haven't time to stop now. We'll send help back to you"; but the driver turned and motioned him to get out.

"She's in there. The lady's in that car," he said. "Better get out here. I ain't goin' no further, anyhow. I'm going home by the cross-roads. They'll get you back," motioning to the other car.

Carey, astonished, hardly knowing what to think, sprang out to investigate; and the driver threw in his clutch, and was off down the cross-road at once. Carey took a step toward the darkened car, calling, "Miss Kendall"; and a man with a cap drawn down over his eyes stepped out of the shadow, and threw open the car door.

"Just step inside. You'll find the lady in the back seat," he said in a gruff voice that yet sounded vaguely familiar. Carey could dimly see a white face leaning against the curtain. He came near anxiously, and peered in, with one foot on the running-board.

"Is that you, Grace?" he said gently, not knowing he was using that intimate name unbidden. She must have been hurt. And who was this man?

"Get in; get in; we've got to get her back," said the man gruffly, giving Carey an unexpected shove that precipitated him to the car floor beside the lady. Before he recovered his balance the car door was slammed shut, and suddenly from all sides came peals of raucous laughter. Surrounding the car, swarming into it, came the laughers. In the midst of his bewilderment the car started.

"Well, I guess anyhow we put one over on you this time, Kay Copley!"

It was the clarion voice of Clytie Amabel Dodd that sounded high and mocking above the chug of the motor as the struggling, laughing company untangled themselves from one another and settled into their seats precipitately with the jerk of starting. Carey found himself drawn suddenly and forcibly to the back seat between two girls, one of them being the amiable Clytie.

In sudden rage he drew himself up again, and faced the girl in the dim light.

"Let me out of here!" he demanded. "I'm on my way to help some one who's in trouble, and I'm in a hurry to get back."

He reached out to the door, and unfastened it, attempting to climb over Clytie's feet, which were an intentional barricade.

"Aw, set down, you big simp, you," yelled Clytie, giving him a shove back with a muscular young arm. "This ain't no Sunday-school crowd, you bet yer life; an' the girl that wrote that note is setting right 'longside of you over there. My sister Grace!

414

Grace *Dodd.* Make you acquainted. Now set down, and see if you can ac' like a little man. We're off for the best feed ever and a big night. Comb your hair, and keep your shirt on, and get a hustle on that grouch. We're going to have the time of our life, and you're going along."

Carey was still, stern and still. The coarse words of the girl tore their way through his newly awakened soul, and made him sick. The thought that he had ever deliberately, of his own accord, gone anywhere in the company of this girl was like gall and wormwood. Shame passed over him, and bathed him in a cleansing flood for a moment; and, as he felt its waters at their height over his head, he seemed to see the face of Grace Kendall, fine and sweet and far away, lost to him forever. Then a flash of memory brought her look as she had thanked him for taking the solo that night, and said she knew he would make a success of it; and his soul rose in rebellion. He would keep faith with her. In spite of all of them he would get back.

He lifted his head, and called commandingly: "Stop this car! I've got to get back to the city. I've got an engagement."

The answer was a loud jeer of laughter.

"Aw! Yeah! We know whatcher engage-

415

ment is, and you ain't going to no Chris-shun 'deavor t'night. Pretty little Gracie'll have to keep on lookin' fer you, but she won't see you t'night."

Carey was very angry. He thought he knew now how men felt that wanted to kill some one. Clytie was a girl, and he couldn't strike her; but she had exceeded all a woman's privileges. He gripped her arm roughly, and pushed her back into the seat, threw himself between the two unidentified ones in the middle seat, and projected his body upon the man who was driving, seizing the wheel and attempting to turn the car around. The driver was taken unexpectedly, and the car almost ran into the fence, one wheel lurching down into the ditch. The girls set up a horrible screaming. The car was stopped just in time, and a terrific fight began in the front seat.

"Now, just for this, Carey Copley, we'll get you dead drunk and take you back to your old Chrisshun 'deavor. That's what we were going to do, anyway; only we weren't going to tell you beforehand — get you dead drunk and take you back to your little baby-faced, yella-haired Gracie-girl. *Then* I guess she'd have anything more to do with you? I guess anyhow *not!*"

Clytie's voice rang out loud and clear

above the din, followed by the crash of glass as somebody smashed against the windshield. This was what Maxwell heard as he stole noiselessly upon the dark car, running down a slight grade with his engine shut off. He stopped his car a rod away, and dropped silently to the ground while Harry, like a smaller shadow, dropped from the back, stole around the other side of the car, and hid in the shadows next the fence.

"What was that?" warned Clytie suddenly. "Grace, didn't you hear something? Say, boys, we oughtta be gettin' on. Somebody'll be onto our taking this car, and come after us; then it'll be good-night for us. Don't fool with that kid any longer. Give him a knockout, and stow him down in the bottom of the car. We can bring him to when we get to a safe place. Cheese it, there! Cheese it!"

Harry, watching alertly, saw Maxwell spring suddenly on the other side; and, stealing close with the velvet tread of a cat, he sprang to the running-board on his side, and, jumping, flung his arms tightly about the neck of the front-seat man next him, hanging back with his fingers locked around the fellow's throat, and dragging his whole lusty young weight to the ground. There was nothing for his man to do but follow, struggling, spluttering, and trying to grasp something, till he sprawled at length upon the grass, unable, for the moment, in his bewilderment to determine just what had hold of him.

Maxwell on his side had gripped the driver, and pulled him out, not altogether sure but it might be Carey, but knowing that the best he could do was to get some one before the car started again. The unexpectedness of the attack from the outside wrought confusion and panic in the car, and gave Maxwell a moment's vantage.

Carey was meanwhile fighting blindly like a wild man, his special antagonist being the man in the middle seat; and when he found himself suddenly relieved of the two in the front seat, he seemed to gain an almost superhuman power for the instant. Dragging and pushing, he succeeded in throwing his man out of the car upon the ground. Then before anyone knew what was happening, and amid the frightened screams of the three girls, Carey climbed over into the front seat, and, not knowing that a friend was at hand, threw in the clutch and started the car, whirling it recklessly round in the road, almost upsetting it, and shot away up the road toward the city at a terrible rate of speed, leaving Maxwell with three men on his hands and no knowledge of Harry's presence.

The man that Carey had thrown out of the car lay crumpled in a heap, unconscious. He had broken his ankle, and would make no trouble for a while. Maxwell was not even conscious of his presence as he grappled with the driver, and finally succeeded in getting him down with hands pinioned and his knee on the man's chest. Maxwell was an expert wrestler, and knew all the tricks, which was more than could be said of the boy who had been driving the car; but Maxwell was by no means in training, and he found himself badly winded and bruised. Lifting his head there in the darkness and wondering what he was to do with his man now he had him down, he discovered the silent form in the road but a step away. Startled, he looked about; and suddenly a gruff young voice came pluckily to him from across the ditch:

"All right, Max; I can hold this man awhile now. I've got the muzzle on the back of his neck."

The form on the bank beside Harry suddenly ceased to struggle, and lay grimly still. Maxwell, astonished, but quick to take Harry's lead, called back: "All right, sir. You haven't got an extra rope about you, have you, man?"

"Use yer necktie, Max," called back the boy nonchalantly. "That's what I'm doing. There's good strong straps under the seat in the car to make it sure. Saw 'em last week when you and I were fixing the car."

And actually Harry, with the cold butt of his old jack-knife realistically placed at the base of his captive's brain, was tying his man's hands behind him with his best blue silk necktie that Cornelia had given him the day before. It seemed a terrible waste to him; but his handkerchief was in the other side-pocket, and he didn't dare risk taking that knife in the other hand to get at it.

It happened that the boy that Harry had attacked in the dark was a visitor to the city, very young and very green indeed; and the others had promised to show him a good time and teach him what life in the city meant. He was horribly frightened, and already shaking like a leaf with a vision of jail and the confusion of his honorable family back in the country. The cold steel on the back of his neck subdued him instantly and fully. He had no idea that his captor was but a slip of a boy. The darkness had come down completely there in the shadow of a grove of maples, and a cricket rasping out a sudden note in the ditch below made him jump in terror. Harry, with immense scorn for the "big boob" who allowed himself to be tied so easily, drew the knots fast and hard, wondering meanwhile whether Cornie could iron out the necktie again. Then, feeling a little easier about moving, he changed hands, and got possession of his Sunday handkerchief, and proceeded to tie the young fellow's ankles together. After which he slid casually down the bank, hustled over to the car, got the straps, and brought them to Maxwell, who was having his hands full trying to tie the driver's wrists with his big white handkerchief.

Gravely they made the fellow fast, searched him for any possible weapons and put him into the back seat of the car.

Next they picked up the quiet fellow on the ground, made his hands fast, and put him on the floor of the car.

"It's no use trying to bring him to here," advised Harry gruffly. "No water; and, besides, we can't waste the time. He's just knocked out, I guess, anyhow, like they do in football."

But, when they went for Harry's man, they found no trace of him. Somehow he had managed to roll down the bank into the ditch and hid himself, or perhaps he had worked off his fetters and run away.

"Aw, gee!" said Harry, reluctantly turning toward the car. "I s'pose we gotta let him go; but that was my best new necktie."

"Oh, that's all right," said Maxwell almost relieved. "There's more neckties where that came from, and I think we better get this man back to a doctor."

Back they drove like lightning to the city, with Harry keeping watch over the prisoners, one sullen and one silent, and took them straight to the station-house with a promise to return with more details in a short time. Then they drove rapidly to the church, Maxwell anxious to be sure that Carey was all right, and bent on relieving Cornelia's mind.

They entered the church just as the choir stood up for the anthem, and Cornelia's white, anxious face looked out at the end of the top row of sopranos. Maxwell's eyes sought hers a second, then searched rapidly through the lines of tenor and bass, but Carey had not come yet. Where was Carey?

 **29** It was very still in the church as the opening chords of the anthem were struck. The anthems were always appreciated by the congregation. Since Grace Kendall had been organist and choir master there was always something new and pleasing, and no one knew beforehand just who might be going to sing a solo that day. Sometimes Grace Kendall herself sang, although but rarely. People loved to hear her sing. Her voice was sweet and well cultivated, and she seemed to have the power of getting her words across to one's soul which few others possessed.

Cornelia, as her lips formed the words of the opening chorus, wondered idly, almost apathetically, whether Grace would take the tenor solo this time. She could, of course; but Cornelia dreaded it like a blow that was coming swiftly to her. It seemed the knell of her brother's self-respect. He had failed her right at the start, and of course no one would ever ask him to sing again; and equally of course he would be ashamed, and never want to go to that church again. Her heart was so heavy that she had no sense of the triumph and beauty of the chorus as it burst forth in the fresh young voices about her, voices that were not heavy like her own with a sense of agony and defeat.

"I am Alpha and Omega, the beginning and the ending, saith the Lord."

It was, of course, a big thing for an amateur volunteer choir to attempt, but in its way it was well done. Grace Kendall seemed to have a natural feeling for expression, and she had developed a wonderful talent for bringing out some voices and suppressing others. Moreover, she trained for weeks on a composition before she was willing to produce it. This particular one had been in waiting some time until a tenor soloist fit for the part should be available. Carey had seemed to fit right in. Grace had told Cornelia this the night before, which made the humiliation all the harder now. Cornelia's voice stopped entirely on "the beginning," and never got to "the ending" at all. Something seemed to shut right up in her throat and make sound impossible. She wished she could sink down through the floor, and hide away out of sight somewhere. Of course the audience did not know that her brother was to have sung in this particular anthem; but all the choir knew it, and they must be wondering. Surely they had noticed his absence. She was thankful that her seat kept her a trifle apart from the rest, and that she was a comparative stranger, so that no one would be likely to ask where he was. If she could only get through this anthem somehow, making her lips move till the end, and sit down! The church seemed stifling. The breath of the roses about the pulpit came sickeningly sweet.

It was almost time for the solo. Another page, another line! At least she would not look around. If anybody noticed her, he should think she knew all about what was going to happen next. They would perhaps think that Carey had been called away — as, indeed, he had; she caught at the words "called away"; that was what she would have to say when they asked her after service, called away suddenly. Oh! And such a calling! Would Grace ever speak to him again? Would they be able to keep it from her that that detestable Clytie had been at the bottom of it all? It wouldn't be so bad if Grace had never met her. Oh, why had Cornelia been so crazy as to invite them together? Now! *Now! Another note!*

Into the silence of the climax of the chorus there came a clear, sweet tenor voice, just behind Cornelia, so close it startled her, and almost made her lose her self-control, so sweet and resonant and full of feeling

425

that at first she hardly recognized that she had ever heard it before.

"Holy, holy, holy, Lord God of Hosts!"

"Carey!"

Her trembling senses took it in with thrill after thrill of wonder and delight. It was really Carey, her brother, singing like that! Carey, standing on the top step of the little stairway winding up from the choir room, close beside the organ. Carey with his hair rumpled wildly, his coat-sleeve half ripped out, a tear in the knee of his trousers, a white face with long black streaks across it, a cut on his chin, and his eyes blue-black with the intensity of the moment, but a smile like a cherub's on his lips. He was singing as he had never sung before, as no one knew he could sing, as he had not thought he could sing himself, singing as one who had come "out of great tribulation," as the choir had just sung a moment before, a triumphant, tender, marvellous strain.

"Gee!" breathed Harry back by the door, in awe, under his breath, and the soul of Maxwell was lifted and thrilled by the song. Little Louise in her seat all alone gripped her small hands in ecstasy, and smiled till the tears came; and the father, who had found his friend too ill for his wife to leave him, and had stolen into church late by the side door and sat down under the gallery, bowed his head and prayed, his heart filled with one longing, that the boy's mother could have heard him.

Into Cornelia's heart there flooded a tide of strength and joy surpassing anything she had ever known in pride of herself. Her brother, *her brother* was singing like that! He had overcome all obstacles, whatever they might have been, and got there in time! He was there! He had not failed! He was singing like a great singer.

Out at the curbstone beside the church sat huddled in a "borrowed" car, with a broken wind-shield, borrowed without the knowledge of the owner, three girls, frightened, furious, and overwhelmed with wonder. All during that stormy drive to the city they had screamed and reasoned and pommelled their captor in vain. He had paid no more heed to their furor than if they had been three gadflies sitting behind him. When one of them tried to climb into the front seat beside him, he swept her back with one blind motion and a threat to throw them all out into the road if they didn't stop. They had never seen him like this. They subsided, and he had sat silent, immovable, driving like Jehu, until with a jerk he suddenly brought up at the church, and sprang out, vanishing into the darkness. And now this voice, this wonderful voice, piercing out into the night like the searching of God.

"Holy, holy, holy!" They listened awesomely. This was not the young man they knew, with whom they had rollicked and feasted and revelled. This was a new man. And this — this that he was voicing made them afraid. Holy, holy! It was a word that they hated. It seemed to search into their ways from the beginning. It made them aware of their coarseness and their vulgarity. It brought to their minds things that made their cheeks burn; and made them think of their mothers and retribution. It reminded them of the borrowed car, and the fact that they were alone in it, and that even now some one might be out in search of it.

"Holy, holy!" sang the voice, "Lord God of Hosts!" and, as if a searchlight from heaven had been turned upon their silly, weak young faces, they trembled, and one by one clambered out into the shadow silently, and slunk away on their little clinking high heels, hurriedly, almost stumbling. They were running away from that voice and from that word, "Holy, holy, holy!" They were gone, and the borrowed car stood there alone. Stood there when the people filed out from the church, still talking about the wonderful new tenor that "Miss Grace" had found; stood there when the janitor locked the door and turned out the lights and went home. Stood there all night silently, with a hovering watchman in the shadows waiting for some one to come; stood there till morning, when it was reported and taken back to its owner with a handkerchief and a cigarette and a package of chewing gum on its floor to help along the evidence against the two young prisoners who had been brought to the station-house the night before.

But the young man who had driven the car from the crossroads, and who had held on to his glorious tenor through the closing chorus, rising like a touch of glory over the whole body of singers until the final note had died away exquisitely, had suddenly crumpled into a limp heap and slid down upon the stairs.

Some one slipped around from among the basses, and lifted him up; two tenors came to his assistance, and bore him to the choir room; and Grace with anxious face slipped from the organ-bench and followed as the sermon text was announced; and no one was the wiser. Cornelia in her secluded seat with her singing heart knew nothing of the commotion.

A doctor was summoned from the congregation and discovered a dislocated shoulder, a broken finger, and a bad cut on the leg which had been bleeding profusely. Carey's shoe was soaked with blood. Carey, coming to, was much mortified over his collapse, looked up nervily, and explained that he had had a slight accident, but would be all right in a minute. He didn't know what made him go off like that. Then he promptly went off again.

Maxwell and Harry from their vantage of the doorway had seen the sudden disappearance, and hurried round to the choir room. Now Maxwell explained briefly that Carey had "had a little trouble with a couple of roughs who were trying to get away with somebody's car," and must have been rather shaken up by the time he got to the church.

"He sang wonderfully," said Grace in a low tone full of feeling; "I don't believe I ever heard that solo done better even by a professional."

"It certainly was great!" said Maxwell, and Harry slid to the outer door, and stood in the darkness, blinking with pride and muttering happily. "Aw, gee!"

Carey came to again presently, and insisted on going back for the last hymn and the response after the closing prayer. Carey was a plucky one; and, though he was in pain, and looked white around his mouth, he slid into his seat up by the organ, and did his part with the rest. His hair had been combed and his face washed in the meantime, and Grace had found a thread and needle and put a few stitches in the torn garments, so that the damage was not apparent. Carey received the eager congratulations of the entire choir as they filed past him at the close of service. It was a proud moment for Cornelia, standing in her little niche at the head of the stairs, unable to get out till the crowd had passed. Every one stopped to tell her how proud she ought to be of her brother; and her cheeks were quite rosy and her eyes starry when she finally slipped away into the choir room to find Maxwell waiting for her, a tender solicitude in his face.

"He's all right," he hastened to explain. "Just a little faint from the loss of blood, but he certainly was plucky to sing that solo with his shoulder out of place. It must have taken a lot of nerve. We've got him fixed up, and he'll soon be all right."

Cornelia's face went white in surprise.

"Was he hurt?" she asked. "Oh, I didn't

think there would be danger — not of that kind! It was so kind of you to go after him! It is probably all due to you that he got here at all." She gave him a look which was worth a reward, but he shook his head, smiling wistfully.

"No, I can't claim anything like that," he said. "Carey didn't even know I was there, doesn't know it yet, in fact. He fought the whole thing out for himself, and took their car, and ran away. It's that nervy little youngest brother of yours that's the brave one. If it hadn't been for Harry, I should have been a mere onlooker."

"Well, I rather guess not!" drawled Harry, appearing suddenly from nobody knew where, with Louise standing excitedly behind him. "You just oughtta a seen Max fight! He certainly did give that driver guy his money's worth."

"Oh!" said Cornelia. "Let's get home quick, and hear all about it. Where is Carey?"

Carey and Grace were coming down the steps together, and his sister came toward him eagerly.

"O Carey, you're hurt!" she said tenderly. "I hadn't thought —" she stopped suddenly with a half look at Grace.

Carey grinned.

"You needn't mind her," he said sheeishly. "She knows all about it. I 'fessed up! and he gave Grace a look of understanding that was answered in full kind.

"Wasn't his singing wonderful?" said Grace in an earnest voice with a great light in her eyes. "I kept praying and feeling sure he would come. And just at the last minute, when I'd almost made up my mind I must sing it myself, he came. I just had time to hand him the music before it was time for him to begin. It was simply great of him to sing it like that when he was suffering, and with only that second to prepare himself."

Carey smiled, but a twinge of pain made the smile a ghastly grin, and they hurried him into the car and home, taking Grace Kendall with them for just a few minutes' talk, Maxwell promising to take her home soon. They established Carey on the big couch with cushions under his shoulder; and then Harry could stand it no longer, and came out with the story, which he had already told in full detail to Louise outside the choir-room door, giving a full account of Maxwell's part in the fight. It was the first that Carey knew of their presence at the cross-roads, and there was much to tell, and many questions to answer on all sides.

arry had the floor with entire attention, much to his delight, while he told every detail of the capture of the two and his own tying of the man who got away. Maxwell had his share of honor and praise, and in turn told how brave Harry had been, fooling his man with his jack-knife for a revolver. Everybody was excited and everybody was talking at once. Nobody noticed that twice Carey called Grace by her first name; and once Maxwell said "Cornelia," and then talked fast to hide his embarrassment. The father came in, and sat quietly listening in the corner, his face filled with pride, gathering the story bit by bit from the broken sentences of the different witnesses, until finally Harry said,

"Say, Kay, whaddidya do with that stolen car?"

Carey grinned from his pillows.

"Left her on the road somewhere in front of the church, with the three girls in the back seat."

"Good night!" Harry jumped up importantly. "Kay, do you know that car was stolen? I heard 'em say so. They called it 'borrowed,' but that means they stole it. You might get arrested."

"I should worry!" shrugged Carey, making a wry face at the pain his move had cost him. "I'm not in it any more, am I?"

"But the girls!" said Harry again. "D ,
s'pose they're in it yet?"

"Don't you worry about those girls,
Harry," growled Carey, frowning. "They
weren't born yesterday. They'll look out for
themselves. And I might as well finish this
thing up right here and now, and own up
that I've been a big fool to ever have anything to do with girls like that; and I'm glad
my sister went to work and invited one of
'em here to show me what a fool I had been.
I don't mind telling you that I'm going to
try to have more sense in future; and say,
Nell, haven't you got anything round to eat.
I certainly am hungry, and I've got to work
tomorrow, remember."

Everybody laughed, and Cornelia and
Louise hurried out for the sandwiches and
chocolate that had been forgotten in the excitement; but the father got up and went
over to his son with a beaming face. Laying
his hand on the well shoulder, he said in a
proud tone: "I always knew you'd come out
right, Carey. I always felt you had a lot of
sense. And then your mother was praying
for you. I knew you couldn't miss that. I'm
proud of you, son!"

"Thanks dad! Guess I don't deserve that,
but I'll try to in the future."

just here Harry created a diversion saying importantly: "Max, don't you ink you oughtta call up the police station nd tell 'em 'bout that car? Somebody else might steal it you know."

While Maxwell and Harry were busy at the telephone and Cornelia and Louise were in the kitchen getting the tray ready, Carey and his father and Grace Kendall had a little low-toned talk together around the couch. When Cornelia entered, and saw their three heads together in pleasant converse, her heart gave thanks, and Louise close behind her whispered, "Nellie, He *did* answer, didn't He?"

A minute later, as they stood in the living room, Cornelia with the big tray in her hands, Harry whirled around from the telephone, and shouted.

"Hurrah for our interior decorator!" They all laughed and clapped their hands; and Maxwell hurried to take the tray from her, giving her a look that said so much that she had to drop her lashes to cover the sudden joy which leaped into her face. Just for the instant she forgot the crimson and white lady and was completely happy.

Maxwell deposited the tray on the sideboard, and took her hand.

"Come," he said gently, "I have something to say to you that won't wait another minute."

He drew her out on the new porch, behind the madeira vines that Carey had trained for a shelter while more permanent vines were growing, and there in the shadow they stood, he holding both her hands in a close grasp and looking down into her eyes which were just beginning to remember.

"Listen," he said tenderly. "They have been saying all sorts of nice things about you, and now I have one more word to add, 'I love you!' Do you mind — dearest!"

He dropped her hands and put his arms softly about her, drawing her gently to him as if he almost feared to touch one so exquisitely precious. Then Cornelia came to life.

"But *the lady!*" she cried in distress, putting out her hands at arm's length and holding herself aloof. "Oh, it is not like you to do a thing like this!"

But he continued to draw her close to himself.

"The lady!" he laughed, "But there is no other lady! The lady is really a vampire that tried to suck my blood. But she is nothing to me now. Didn't I tell you yesterday that she wasn't even a friend?"

"Oh," trembled Cornelia, "I didn't understand," and she surrendered herself joyously to his arms.

"Well, I want you to understand. It's a miserable tale to have to tell and I'm ashamed of it, but I want you to know it all. I meant to tell it yesterday but everything seemed to be against me. How about riding in the park tomorrow afternoon and we'll thrash it all out and get it done with forever. And meantime, can you take me on trust? For I love you with all the love a man can give to a woman, and nobody, not even in imagination, ever had the place in my heart that you have taken. Can you love me, dear heart?"

The company in the house missed them after a time and trooped out to find them, even Carey getting up from his cushions against the protest of Grace, and coming to the door.

"You know I've got to go to work tomorrow," he explained smiling, "I can't afford to baby myself any longer."

And Cornelia came rosily out from behind the vines and went in for the goodnights, her eyes starry with joy.

As they went up the stairs for the night Louise slipped an arm around her sister and whispered happily:

"Cornie, I don't believe that red lady is

anything at all to Mr. Maxwell, do you?"

Cornelia bent and kissed her sister tenderly and whispered back in a voice that had a ring in it:

"No, darling, I *know* she isn't!"

Louise falling cosily to sleep while her sister arranged her hair for the night said to herself sleepily:

"I wonder now, *how* she knows! She didn't seem so sure yesterday. He must have told her about her out on the porch."

 **30** Mr. Copley came up the hill with a spring in his step one evening in late September. Cornelia, glancing out of the window to see whether it was time to put the dishes on the table, caught a glimpse of his tall figure, and noticed how erectly he walked and how his shoulders had squared with the old independent lines she remembered in her childhood. It suddenly came over her that father did not look so tired and worn as he had when she first came home. The lines of worry were not so deeply graven, and his figure did not slump any longer. She was conscious of a glad little thrill of pride in him. Her father was not old. How young he seemed as he sprinted up the hill, almost as Carey might have done!

Cornelia hurried the dinner to the table, pulled the chain of the dining-room light, for the darkness was beginning to creep into the edges of the room, adjusted a spray of salvia that had fallen over the side of the glass bowl in the centre of the table, and then turned to greet her father. She was reaching her hand to strike the three silver notes of the dinner-gong that hung on the wall by the sideboard; but her hand stopped midway, and her eyes were held by the look of utter joy on the face of her father. For the first time it struck her that her father had once been a young man like Carey. He looked young now, and very happy. The spring was still in his step, a great light was in his eyes, and a smile that seemed to warm and kindle everything in the room. When he spoke just to say the commonplace "Good evening" as usual, there was something almost hilarious in his voice. The children turned to look at him curiously, but he seemed not to be aware of it. He sat down quietly enough, and began to carve the meat.

"Beefsteak!" he said with satisfaction. "That looks good! I'm hungry tonight."

Cornelia reflected that this was the first time she had heard him speak of being hungry since she came home. She looked curiously at him again, and once more that feeling of wonder at the young look in his eyes touched her. All through the meal, as their parent talked and smiled and told happy little incidents of the day, the children wondered; and finally, when the dessert was almost finished, Carey looked keenly at him and ventured, "Dad, you look as if you'd had a raise in your salary."

"Why, I have!" said Mr. Copley, looking at his son smilingly. "I'd almost forgotten, meant to tell you the first thing. By the way Cornelia, I'd like it if you'd get up some kind of a fancy supper tomorrow night. I'd like to bring — ah — an old friend home with me. Have chicken and ice-cream and things, and some flowers. You'll know what. You might ask the minister's daughter over, too, and Arthur Maxwell. I'd like them to be here. Can you fix it up for me, daughter?"

Cornelia, bewildered, said, "Yes," of course, and immediately plunged into questions concerning the increase of salary.

When did it happen? Was it much? Was his position higher, and did he have to work any harder?

"Yes, and no," he answered calmly, as if a raised salary were an every-day happening, and he were quite apart from it in his thoughts. "I shall have practically the same work, but more responsibility. It's a kind of responsibility I like, however, because I know what ought to be done, and they've given me helpers enough to have it done right. The salary will be a thousand dollars a year more; and I suppose, if you should want to go back to college by and by and get your diploma, we could manage it."

"Indeed, no!" interrupted Cornelia with a rising color in her cheeks and an unexplained light in her eyes. "I'm quite well enough off without a diploma, and I'm too deep in business now to go back and get ready for it. What's a diploma, anyway, but a piece of paper? I never realized how trivial, after all, the preparations for a thing are compared to the work itself. Of course it's all right to get ready for things, but I had practically done most of my preparation at college, anyway. The rest of the year would have been mostly plays and social affairs. The real work was finished. And, when I came home, I was no more ready to go out into the world and do the big things I had dreamed than I was when I entered college. It took life to show me what real work meant, and how to develop a life-ideal. I truly have got more real good from you dear folks here at home than in all my four years' course together. Though I'm not saying anything against that, either, for of course that was great. But, father, I'm not sorry I had to come home. These months here in this dear little house with my family have been wonderful, and I wouldn't lose them out of my life for all the college courses in existence."

She was suddenly interrupted by resounding applause from her brothers and sister, and smothered with kisses from Louise, who sprang from her seat to throw her arms around her neck.

"We all appreciate what you have done for us and your home," said the father with a light in his eyes. "Your mother will tell you how much when she has an opportunity to see what you have done here."

"But, dad," interrupted Carey, as he save his father rise and glance at his watch, "aren't you going to tell us about your raise? Gee! That's something that oughtn't to be passed over lightly like a summer rain. How did it happen?"

The father smiled dreamily.

"Another time. I must hurry now. I have an appointment I must keep, and I may not be home till late tonight. Don't wait up for me. It was just a promotion; that's all. You won't forget about the supper tomorrow night, Cornelia; and be sure to get plenty of flowers."

He hurried out, still with that preoccupied air, leaving his children sitting bewildered at the table.

"Well, I'll be hanged! What's dad got up his sleeve, I'd like to know? I never saw him act like that, did you, Cornie? Just a promotion! That's all! A mere little matter of a thousand more a year! Mere trifle, of course. Tell us the details another time! I say, Cornie, what's up?"

But Cornelia was as puzzled as her brother.

"Perhaps he's going to bring home one of the firm," she said. "We must make the house as fine as possible. Father doesn't have many parties, and we'll make this a really great occasion if we can. Strange he wanted to have others present, though. I wonder if he really ought. Hadn't I better talk it over with him again, Carey? If it's one of the firm, he would think it very queer to have outsiders."

"Grace Kendall isn't an outsider!" blustered up Carey. "No, don't bother dad about it any further. He told you what he wanted; ask them, of course. Max didn't cut his eye-teeth last year, either; they both know how to keep in the background when it's necessary. Anything I can do tonight before I go to choir rehearsal to help get ready for tomorrow?"

They bustled about happily, getting the house in matchless order. It was something they had learned to do together beautifully, each taking a task and rushing it through, meanwhile all singing at the top of their lungs some of the hymns that had been sung at the last Sunday's service, or a bit of a melody they had sung the last time Grace and Maxwell had been over. One voice would boom out from the top of the stairs, where Harry was wiping the dust from the stair railing and steps; another from the living room where Carey was adjusting a curtain-pole that had fallen; Cornelia's voice from the kitchen and pantry in a clear, sweet soprano; with Louise's bird-like alto in the dining-room, where she was setting the table for breakfast. They were all especially happy that evening somehow. A raise! A thousand more a year! Now mother could be given more comforts and get well sooner! Now father would not have to work so late at night going over miserable account-books for people, to earn a little extra money.

There was a song in Cornelia's heart as well as on her lips. She was remembering the words of her little brother and sister in that despairing conference she had overheard the first morning after her arrival and comparing them with what had been said to her tonight; and she was thinking how thankful she was for her home-coming just when it had been, and how she would not have lost the last five months out of her life just as it had been for worlds.

With tender thoughts and skilful hands

Cornelia prepared the festive dinner the next evening, and arranged a profusion of flowers everywhere. A few great luscious chrysanthemums, golden and white, lifting their tall globes in stately beauty from the gray jar in the living room; wild, riotous crimson and yellow and tawny brown, of the outdoor smaller variety, overflowing vases and bowls in the window-seats and on the stair-landing; a magnificent spray of brilliant maple leaves that Harry brought in from the woods before he went to school gracing the stone-chimney above the mantel; and on the dining table, glowing and sweet, a bowl of deep red roses, with a few exquisite white buds among them, the kind she knew her father liked because her mother loved them. There was nothing ostentatious or showy about the simple arrangement, nothing to make the member of the firm feel that the extra thousand dollars would be wasted in show. It was all simple, sweet, homelike, and in good taste.

There was stewed chicken, with little biscuits and currant jelly, mashed potatoes, and succotash, and for desert ice-cream and angel cake. A simple, old-fashioned dinner without olives or salads. She knew that would please her father best, because it was her mother's company dinner. It was the dinner he and mother had on their wedding-trip, and would always continue to be the best of eating to his old-fashioned mind. Doubtless the old-fashioned member of the firm would enjoy it for the same reason. So Cornelia hummed a little carol as she went about stirring up the thickening for the gravy, stopping to fasten Louise's pretty sprigged challis dress with the crimson velvet ribbon trimming, and smiling to herself that all was going well. She could hear Carey upstairs getting dressed, and Harry was already stumping downstairs. Everything was all ready. There were five minutes to spare before father had said he would arrive with his company. Grace had gone up to smooth her hair after being out all the afternoon in the wind, and Maxwell had telephoned that he was on the way and would not delay them.

Then, just as she finished taking up the chicken and went into the living room to be sure Carey hadn't left his coat and hat lying around on the piano or table, as he sometimes did, a taxi drew up at the door.

At first she thought it was Maxwell's car, and her cheeks grew a shade pinker as she drew back to glance out of the window. Then she saw it was her father getting out, and in a panic flew back to shut the kitchen door.

"They're coming!" she called softly to the brothers and sister chattering at the head of the stairs.

Pulling down her sleeves and giving a dab to her hair as she went, she hurried back to open the door; but before she could reach it, it was flung open, and there on the threshold of the pretty room stood mother! A new, well, strong mother, with great happiness in her sweet eyes and the flush of health on her cheeks; and close behind her, looking like a roguish boy, was father, his eyes fairly dancing with delight.

"Dinner ready?" he called. "Here's our guest, children, and we're both as hungry as bears! There, children, what do you think of your mother? Doesn't she look *great?*"

He pulled clumsily at the veil over Mrs. Copley's hat, helped her off with her travelling-coat, and set her forth in the midst of the room. The children after a gasp of astonished delight swarmed about her and fairly took her breath away; and, when any one of them became momentarily detached from her, he took up the time in whooping with joy and talking at the top of his lungs.

At last the greeting subsided, and mother became an object of tender solicitation and care again. They placed her in the biggest chair, and brought her a glass of water, looking at her as at something precious that had been unwittingly too roughly handled, and might have been harmed. In vain did she assure them that she was well again. They looked at their father for reassurance.

"That's right!" he said. "The doctor says she's as good as new. She might have come home sooner, but I told him to keep her till she was thoroughly well; and he did. Now, children, it's up to you to keep her so."

They swarmed about her again, and threatened to have the greetings all over once more, till Cornelia suddenly remembered her place as hostess, and straightened up.

"But, father, the company! When is he coming? And our other guests." She looked cautiously up the stairs to where Grace was discreetly prolonging her hair-dressing, and lowered her voice.

"It's too bad to have anyone here this first night. Mother will not like to have strangers."

But mother smiled royally.

"No, dear, I'm anxious to meet your friends. Father has told me all about them. It's one of the things that has helped to make me well, knowing that everything was going well with my dear children."

"O mother!" said Cornelia with a sudden succumbing to the joy of having mother home once more. "O mother!" and she knelt beside her mother's chair, and threw her arms again about the little mother whom she had been without so long, and never knew till now how she had missed.

It was the sound of Maxwell's car at the door and Grace Kendall's lingering step upon the stair that roused her once more into action.

Springing to her feet and glancing from the window, her face growing rosy with the sight of Maxwell coming up the walk; she exclaimed:

"But father, where is your guest, your friend? I thought you were going to bring him with you."

Father stepped smiling over to mother's chair, and stood with his hand resting softly on her ripply brown hair.

"This is my guest — my friend," he said, tenderly looking down at his partner of the years with a wonderful smile, which she answered in kind. "This is the one I asked you to prepare for, and I wanted her to meet our young friends. I wanted her to get an immediate taste of the atmosphere of our home as it now is, as it has been during her absence, thanks to you, Cornelia, our blessed eldest child."

The look he and her mother gave her would have been reward enough for any girl for giving up a dozen college graduations. But, as if that had not been enough for the full and free way in which she had given herself, she lifted her eyes; and there beyond them, standing in the doorway, stood Maxwell with such a look of worshipfulness in his face, as he witnessed this girl receiving her due from her family, as would have repaid a girl for almost any sacrifice.

Grace Kendall, coming slowly down the stairs into the pretty room, watched it all contentedly. Everything was as it should be. The mother was the kind of mother she had hoped she would be, and she liked the way Carey sat on the arm of her chair with his arm around the back protectingly. But suddenly Carey lifted his eyes, and saw Grace; and the light of love swept into them. He sprang up. and came to meet her eagerly. Taking her hand as if he were about to present a princess to an audience, he led her to his mother, and said, "Mother, meet the most wonderful girl in the world," and laid Grace Kendall's hand in his mother's. Mrs. Copley took Grace's rosy face between her two soft white hands, and, reaching up, kissed the sweet girl tenderly amid a little hush of silence that none of the family realized they were perpetrating, until suddenly father awoke to the young girl's sweet embarrassment, and reaching out a boyish hand to Maxwell, drew him to his wife's chair, and said roguishly, "Mother, and now meet the most wonderful man in the world!" and the little silence broke into a joyous tumult while they all went out to the waiting dinner, and did full justice to it with a feeling that that evening was just the real beginning of things.

Late that night, as they were going up to bed, Cornelia, lingering for some small preparation for the morning, heard Harry say to his younger sister: "Gee! Lou, it's good to have mother home again, isn't it? But somehow even she can't take Cornie's place, can she? Didn't Cornie look pretty tonight?"

"She certainly did," responded the little sister eagerly; "and she certainly is great. We can't ever spare her again can we, Harry?"

"Well, I guess you mighty well better get ready to," said Harry knowingly. "It looks mighty like to me that Max intends us to spare her pretty soon all right, all right."

"Yes, I suppose so," sighed Louise, "But

then that's nice. It isn't like somebody you don't know and love already. She'll always be ours, and he'll be ours, too. Won't it be nice? Don't you hope it's so, Harry?"

And Cornelia's cheeks grew pinker in the kitchen as she remembered words and looks that had passed that evening, and turned to her task with a happy smile on her lips.

31 It was just one year from the day when she had taken that first journey from West to East and met the pretty college girl on her tearful way home to her soul's trying that Mrs. Maxwell came back from her sojourn in California. The business that had taken her there had prolonged itself, and then unexpectedly the sick sister had telegraphed that she was coming out to spend the winter, and wanted her to remain; and because the sister had seemed to be in very great need of her she had remained.

But now the sister was gaining rapidly, was fully able to be left in the care of a nurse and the many friends with whom she was surrounded, and Mrs. Maxwell had been summoned home for a great event.

As the train halted, at the college station, and a bevy of girls came chattering round, bidding some comrade good-bye, she thought of the day one year ago when she had been so interested in one girl, and wondered whether her instincts concerning her had been true. She was going home to attend that girl's wedding now! That girl so soon to be married to her dear and only son, and since that one brief afternoon together she had never seen that little girl again.

Oh, there had been letters, of course, earnest, loving, welcoming letters on the part of the mother, glad letters expressing joy at her son's choice and picturing the future in glowing colors; shy, sweet, almost apologetic letters on the part of the girl, as if she had presumed in accepting a love so great as that of this son; and the mother had been glad, joyously glad, for was she not the first girl she had ever laid eyes upon whose face looked as if she were sweet, strong, and wise enough for her beloved son's wife?

But now as she neared the place, and the meeting again was close at hand, her heart began to misgive her. What if she had made a mistake? What if this girl was not all those things that she had thought at that first sight? What if Arthur, too, had been deceived, and the girl would turn out to be frivolous, superficial, unlovely in her daily life, unfine in soul and thought? For was she, the mother, not responsible in a large way for this union of the two? Had she not fairly thrown her son into the way of knowing the girl, and furthered their first acquaintance in her letters in little subtle ways that she hardly realized at the time, but that had come from the longing of her soul to have a daughter just like what she fancied this girl must be?

All the long miles she tortured her soul with these thoughts; and then would come the memory of the sweet, sad, girlish face she had watched a year ago, the strength, the character in the lovely profile of firm little chin and well-set head, the idealism in the clear eyes; and her heart would grow more sure. Then she would pray that all might be well, and again take out her son's last letter, and read it over, especially the last few paragraphs.

"You will love her, mother of mine, for she is just your ideal. I used to wonder how you were ever going to stand it when I did fall in love, to find out the girl was not what you had dreamed I should marry. For I honestly thought there were no such girls as you had brought me up to look for. When I went to college and found what modern girls were, I used to pity you sometimes when you found out, too. But Cornelia is all and more than you would want. She goes the whole limit of your desire, I believe, for she is notably a Christian. I speak it very reverently, mother, because I have found few that are, at least, that are recognizable as such; and generally those have managed to make the fact unpleasant by the belligerent way in which they flaunt it, and because of their utter crudeness in every other way. Perhaps that isn't fair, either. I have met a few who seemed genuine and good, but they were mortally shy, and never seemed to dare open their mouths. But this girl of mine is rare and fine. She can talk, and she can work, and she can live. She can be bright and gay, and she can suffer and strive; but she is a regular girl, and yet she is a Christian. You should hear her lead a Christian Endeavor meeting, striking right home to where everybody lives, and acts, and makes mistakes, and is sorry or forgetful as the case may be. You should hear her pray, leading everybody to the feet of Christ to be forgiven and learn.

"Yes, mother, dear, she has led me there, too; and you have your great wish. I have given myself to your Christ and hers. I feel that He is my Christ now, and I am going to try to live and work for His cause all the rest of my life. For, to tell the truth, mother, the Christ you lived and the Christ she lived was better than the best thing on earth, and I had to give in. I was a fool that I didn't do it long ago, for I knew in my heart it was all true as you taught me, even though I did get a lot of rot against it when I was in college; but, when I saw a young girl with all of life before her giving herself to Christian living this way, it finished me.

"So I guess you won't feel badly about the way things turned out. And anyway you must remember you introduced us, and sort of wished her on me with those ferns; so you mustn't complain. But I hope you'll love her as much as you do me, and we are just waiting for you to get back for the ceremony, mother, dear; so don't let anything hinder you by the way, and haste the day! It cannot come too soon."

She had telegraphed in answer to that letter that she would start at once. The day had been set for the wedding, and all arrangements made. Then a slight illness of her sister that looked more serious than it really was had delayed her again; and here she was travelling post-haste Philadelphia-ward on the very day of the wedding, keeping everybody on the *qui vive* lest she would not get there in time and the ceremony would have to be delayed. All these twelve months had passed, and yet she had not seen the reconstructed little house on the hill.

As she drew nearer the city, and the sun went down in the western sky, her heart began to quiver with excitement, mature, calm mother even though she was. But she had been a long time away against her will from her only son, and her afternoon with Cornelia had been very brief. Somehow she could not make it seem real that she was really going to Arthur's wedding that night, and not going to have an opportunity to meet again the girl he was to marry until she was his wife, and never to have met her people until it was over, a final, a finished fact. She sighed a little wearily, and looked toward the evening bars of sunset red and gold, with a wish, as mothers do when hard pressed, that it were all over and she going home at last to rest, and a feeling that her time was out.

Then right in the midst of it the brakeman touched her on the shoulder and handed her a telegram, with that unerring instinct for identity that such officials seem to have inborn.

With trembling fingers and a vague presentiment she tore it open, and read:

460

"Cornelia and I will meet you at West Philadelphia with a car and take you to her home. Have arranged to have your trunk brought up immediately from Broad Street, so you will have plenty of time to dress. Take it easy, little mother; we love you. Arthur."

Such a telegram! She sat back relieved, steadied her trembling lips, and smiled. Smiled, and read it over again. What a boy to make his bride come to the station to meet her two hours before the ceremony! What a girl to be willing to come!

Suddenly the tears came rushing to her eyes, glad tears mingled with smiles, and she felt enveloped in the love of her children. Her boy and her girl! Think of it! She would have a daughter! And she was a part of them; she was to be in the close home part of the ceremony, the beforehand and the sweet excitement. They were waiting for her and wanting her, and she was not just a necessary part of it all because she was the groom's mother; she was to stay his mother, and be mother to the girl; and she would perhaps be a sister to the girl's mother, who was now also to be her boy's mother. Now for the first time the bitterness was taken out of that thought about

461

Arthur's having another mother, and she was able to see how they two mothers could love him together, if the other one should prove to be the right kind of mother. And it now began to seem as if she must be to have brought up a girl like Cornelia.

At that very moment in the little house on the hill four chattering college-girl bridesmaids attired in four becoming silk negligees were bunched together on Cornelia's bed, supposed to be resting before they dressed, while Cornelia, happy-eyed and calm, sat among them for a few minutes' reunion.

"Isn't it awfully queer that you should be the first of the bunch to get married?" burst forth Natalie, the most engaged and engaging of the group. "I thought I was to be the very first myself right after I graduated, and here we've had to put it off three times because Tom lost his position. And Pearl broke her engagement, and Ruth's gone into business, and Jane is up to her eyes in music. It seems queer to have things so different from what we planned, doesn't it? My, how we pitied you, Cornie, that day you had to leave. It seems an awful shame you had to go home then, when such a little time would have given you all that fun to remember. I don't see why such things have to happen anyway. I think it was just horrid you never graduated. I don't see why somebody couldn't have come in here and taken care of things till you got through. It meant so very much to you. You missed so much, you know, that you can never, never make up."

Cornelia from her improvised couch by the window smiled dreamily.

"Yes, but that was the day I met my new mother," she said, almost as if she had forgotten their existence and were speaking to herself; "and she introduced me to Arthur. Probably I would never have seen either of them if I hadn't come home just that day."

A galaxy of eyes turned upon her, searching for romance, and studied her sweet face greedily.

"Don't pity her any more, girls," cried Natalie. "She's dead in love with him, and hasn't missed us nor our commencement one little minute. She walked straight into the land of romance that day when she left us, and hasn't thought of us since. I wonder she ever remembered to invite us to the wedding. But I'm not surprised either. If he's half as stunning as his picture, he must be a pippin. I'm dying to meet him! What kind of a prune is his mother? I think she must be horrid to demand your presence at the station to meet her two hours before the ceremony. I must say I'd make a kick at that."

"Oh," said Cornelia, a haughty color coming into her cheeks. "You don't understand. She didn't demand! She doesn't even know. Arthur and I are surprising her. Arthur just sent a telegram to the train for her to get off at the West Philadelphia station. She expected to go on to Broad Street. Oh! she is the dearest mother; wait till you see her."

A tap at the door interrupted her, and Louise entered shyly. "Nellie, dear, I hate to interrupt you; but that man, that Mr. Ragan, has come; and he's so anxious to see you just a minute mother said I better tell you so you could send him down a message. It's something about the curtains for his house. I think he wants birds on them, or else he doesn't, I don't know which. He's so afraid you've already ordered the material, and he wants it the way you said first, he says."

"That's all right, darling; I think I'll just run down and see him a minute; he's so anxious about his little house, and it will reassure him if I explain about it. Tell him to wait just a minute till I slip on my dress."

A chorus of protests arose from the bed.

"For mercy's sake, Cornie, you're surely not going down to see a man on business *now!* What on earth? Did you really get to be an interior decorator, after all? You don't *mean* it! I thought you were just kidding when you wrote about it. What do you mean? They're only poor people. Well, what do you care? You're surely not going on with such things after you're married?"

Cornelia, flinging the masses of her hair into a lovely coil, and fastening the snaps of her little blue organdie, smiled again dreamily.

"Arthur likes it," she said. "He wants me to go on. You see we both regard it, not exactly altogether as a business, but as something that is going to help uplift the world. I've done two really big houses, and they've been successful; and I have had good opportunities opening, so that I could really get into a paying business if I chose, I think. But I don't choose. Oh, I may do a fine house now and then if I get the chance, just to keep my hand in, for I enjoy putting rich and beautiful things together in the right way; but what I want is to help poor people do little cheap houses, and make them look pretty and comfortable and really artistic. So many don't have pretty homes who would really like them if they only knew how! Now, this man I'm going down to now is just a poor laborer, but he has been saving up his money to make a nice home for his girl, and he heard about me, and came to me to help him. I've been having the best fun picking out his things for him. I won't get a great fee out of it; indeed, I hate to take anything; only he wouldn't like that, but it's been great! Arthur and I have been together out to see the little cottage twice, and arranged the new chairs for him; and I even made up the beds, and showed him how to set the table for their first meal. They are to be married next week, and he's so worried lest the stuff I ordered for curtains won't get here in time to finish his dining-room. But mother is going to finish them; and Harry and Carey will put them up; and I want to tell him, so he will not worry." With a bright smile Cornelia left them, and flew downstairs to her customer.

"Goodness, girls! did you ever see such a change in any one? I can't make her out, can you?" cried Jane, sitting up on the foot of the bed and looking after her.

"I should say not!" declared Pearl. "What do you suppose has come over her? I suppose it's being in love or something, although that doesn't generally make a girl do slum work at a busy time like this. But I guess we wasted our pity on her. She said she was coming home to a horrid, poor little house. Did you ever see such a pretty nest of a house in your life? That living room is a dream. I'm crazy to get back to it and look it over again."

"Well, I never thought Cornie Copley would turn out to be that kind of a nut. Think of her going to the station to meet her mother-in-law just before the ceremony! Love certainly is blind. Girls, you needn't ever worry lest I'll do anything of that kind, not me!" cried Natalie. "That man must be some kind of a nut himself, or else she's been all made over somehow."

Jane tiptoed, and shut the door; and then in a whisper she said: "Girls, I want to tell you. I believe it's religion. It's queer, but I believe it is. I heard her talking about praying for somebody down in the hall when I stood up here waiting for my trunk to be unlocked by her brother. She was talking to her little sister, and they seemed to be praying for something or somebody; and she mentioned the church every other breath since we came, and the minister, and — look at there! There's her Bible with her name in it. I opened it, and looked, and *he* gave it to her; 'Cornelia from Arthur'; that's what it says. And see that card framed over the table? It's a Christian Endeavor pledge-card. I know for I used to belong when I was a child. She's going to have the Christian Endeavor society all at the wedding, too. I heard her say the Christian Endeavor chorus was going to sing the wedding march before they came in, and she talks about the minister's daughter all the time. You may depend on it, it's religion that's the matter with Cornie, not being in love. Cornie's a level-headed girl, and she wouldn't go out of her head this way just for falling in love. When religion gets into the blood it's ten times worse than any falling in love ever. I wonder what her Arthur thinks of it. Maybe he means to take it out of her when he gets her good and tied."

"Don't!" said Ruth sharply. "You make me sick, Jane. I don't care what it is that has changed Cornie. She's sweet, I know; that's all that's necessary. And, if it's religion, I wish we all had some of it. I know she looks all the time as if she'd seen a vision, and that's what precious few other people do. Come, it's time to take a nap, or we'll look like withered leaves for this evening. Now stop talking! I'm going to sleep."

The passengers in the parlor-car glanced

at the distinguished-looking lady with the sweet smile and happy eyes, and glanced again, and liked to look, there was such joy, such content, such expectancy, in her face. More than one, as the train slowed down at West Philadelphia, and the porter gathered her baggage and escorted her out, sat up from his velvet chair and stretched his neck to see who was meeting this woman to make her so happy since that telegram had been brought to her. They watched until the train passed on and they could see no more — the tall, handsome young man who took her in his arms and kissed her, and the lovely girl in blue organdie with a little lace-edged organdie hat drooping about her sweet face, who greeted her as if she loved her. As far as the eye could reach Mrs. Maxwell's fellow passengers watched the little bit of human drama, and wondered, and tried to figure out who they were and what relation they bore to one another.

"You precious child, you shouldn't have done it!" said Mrs. Maxwell, nestling Cornelia's hand in her own as her son stowed them away in the back seat of the car together and whirled them away to the Copley house. "But it was dear of you, and I shall never forget it!" she said fervently with another squeeze of the hand.

A few moments more, and she entered the living room that had been wrought out with such care and anxiety, and gazed about her, delighted.

"I knew you would do it, dear. I knew it! I was sure you could," she whispered with her arm around the girl; and then she went forward with a sigh of relief to meet the sweet mother of the Copleys, who came to greet her. The two mothers looked long into each other's eyes, with hands clapsed and keen, loving, searching looks; and then a smile grew on both their faces. Mother Maxwell spoke first with a smile of content:

"I was almost sure you would be like that," she said; "and I'm going to love you a great deal"; and mother Copley, her face placid with a calm that had its source in deep springs of peace, smiled back an answering love.

Then came father Copley, and grasped the other mother's hand, and bade her welcome too; and after that mother Maxwell was satisfied, and went to dress for the wedding.

The four bridesmaids did not see much of Cornelia, after all; for, when she came back from her ride, they were all breathlessly manipulating curling-irons and powder-puffs, tying sashes, and putting on pretty slippers; and no one had time to talk of other things. It seemed to be only Cornelia who was calm at this last minute, who knew where the shoehorn had been put, could find a little gold pin to fasten a refractory ribbon, and had time to fix a drooping wave of hair or adjust a garland of flowers.

It had been Cornelia's wish that her wedding should be very simple and inexpensive; and, though the bridesmaids had written many letters persuading and suggesting rainbow hues and dahlia shades, and finally pleaded for jades and corals, all was to no effect. Cornelia merely smiled, and wrote back: "I want you all in white, if you please, just simple white organdie, made with a deep hem and little ruffles; and then I want you to have each a garland of daisies around your hair, and daisies in your arms."

"White for bridesmaids!" they cried as one maid. "Who ever heard of such a thing?"

But the answer came back: "This isn't going to be a conventional wedding. We're just going to get married, and we want our dearest friends about us. I love white, and the daisies will be lovely on it and do away with hats. I'm going to wear a veil. I like a veil; but my dress is white organdie, too, and I'll have white roses."

And so it was, all natural and sweet like an old-fashioned country affair, and not one convention out of a thousand observed in the order and form of things.

For the bride herself had decked the church with the aid of her bridegroom and her brother and Grace Kendall. The lace-like boughs of tall hemlocks drooped back of the altar, and smothered the pulpit; and against it rose a waving field of daisies with grasses softly blending. The little field-flowers were arranged in concealed glass jars of water so that they kept fresh and beautiful, and were so massed that they seemed to be growing there. All about the choir gallery the daisies were massed, a bit of nature transplanted to the quiet temple. Every one exclaimed softly on entering the church at the wonderful effect of the feathery, starry beauty. It was as if a bit of the out-of-door world had crept into the sanctuary to grace the occasion. God's world and God's flowers of the field.

There were not many mighty among the guests. A choice few of the Maxwell and Copley connection and friends; the rest were new acquaintances, of all stations in life, all trades and professions, many humble worshippers in the church whom Cornelia and Maxwell had come to respect and love.

The two mothers came in together, and sat down side by side, attended by Harry and his father. Harry had most strenuously objected to being of the wedding party when it was suggested. He said he "couldn't see making a monkey of himself, all dolled up, going up the church aisle to music."

Grace Kendall was at the organ, of course, and above the daisy-bordered gallery the Christian Endeavor choir girls all in white, with wreaths of green leaves in their hair, sang the bridal chorus; and from the doors at either side of the front of the church there filed forth the bridesmaids and the ushers. The bridesmaids were led by Louise as maid of honor, with a wreath of daisies among her curls and a garland of daisies trailing down from her left shoulder over the little white organdie that made her look like a young angel. Carey as best man led the ushers, who were four warm friends of Maxwell's; and on either side of the altar they waited, facing toward the front door as Cornelia and Maxwell came arm in arm up the middle aisle together.

It was all quite natural and simple, though the bridesmaids were disappointed at the lack of display and the utter disregard of convention and precedent.

The minister spoke the service impressively, and added a few words of his own that put the ceremony quite out of the ordinary; and his prayer seemed to bring God quite near among them, as if He had come especially to bless this union of His children. Mother Maxwell's heart suddenly overflowed with happy tears, and the four bridesmaids glanced furtively and knowingly at one another beneath their garlands of daisies, as if to say, "It is religion, after all; and this is where she got it"; and then they began to listen and to wonder for themselves.

After it was over the bride and the groom turned smilingly and walked back down the aisle, preceded by Louise and Carey, and followed by the bridesmaids and ushers; and everybody rose and smiled, and broke the little hush of breathless attention with a soft murmur of happy approval.

"Such a pretty wedding, so sweet! so dear!" Mother Maxwell could hear them breathing it on every hand as she walked out with mother Copley.

Then just a chosen few came home to the wedding supper, which had been planned and partly prepared by Cornelia herself; and everybody was talking about the lovely wedding and the quiet, easy way in which everything moved without fuss or hurry or excitement, right and natural and as it all should be when two persons joined hands and walked out together into the new life.

"It is something inside her that makes her different," hazarded a sleepy bridesmaid several hours later, after the others had been still a long time and were almost asleep. "But wasn't it lovely? Only field-daisies and the grass and old pine-trees; but it certainly was a dream even if we didn't get to do much marching. Well, Cornelia Copley always did know how to decorate."

The employees of Thorndike Press hope you have enjoyed this Large Print book. All our Large Print titles are designed for easy reading, and all our books are made to last. Other Thorndike Press Large Print books are available at your library, through selected bookstores, or directly from us.

For information about titles, please call:

(800) 257-5157

To share your comments, please write: